'A nostalgic tale told with v
a bookmark' **Daily Mail**

'If you haven't read Trigia
time to discover her with t
writing is warm, and this d
opportunities for women s
old-fashioned tale of misguided love and missed opportunities, full of bittersweet moments and regrets, but Trigiani balances the light and dark to create the perfect feel-good read' **Glamour**

'A romantic romp about a shopgirl who becomes the toast of 1950s Manhattan' **New York Post**

'The compelling new novel from the author of the bestselling *Big Stone Gap* . . . Trigiani conjures the period beautifully' **Good Housekeeping**

'The author of *Big Stone Gap* triumphs again' **Heat**

'Poignant and feeling . . . This old fashioned drama wears its heart on its sleeve . . . readers will laugh and weep for Lucia and her lost dreams' **Publishers Weekly**

'Read this . . . a novel about a beautiful seamstress unwilling to sacrifice her independence for a man' **She**

'For Trigiani fans everywhere, this novel will certainly not disappoint' **Waterstone's Books Quarterly**

'A tender tale of being torn between family, career and love' **Company**

'A girly book, but sensitive men (and aren't they the ones women adore?) can also enjoy' **USA Today**

'Trigiani has a gift for creating the atmosphere of the past . . . very entertaining and accomplished' **Good Book Guide**

Also by Adriana Trigiani

BIG STONE GAP

BIG CHERRY HOLLER

MILK GLASS MOON

Lucia, Lucia

Adriana Trigiani

POCKET BOOKS

LONDON • SYDNEY • NEW YORK • TORONTO

First published in Great Britain by Simon & Schuster UK Ltd, 2003
This paperback edition published by Pocket Books, 2004
An imprint of Simon & Schuster UK Ltd
A CBS COMPANY

1 3 5 7 9 10 8 6 4 2

Simon & Schuster UK Ltd
Africa House
64–78 Kingsway
London WC2B 6AH

www.simonsays.co.uk

Simon & Schuster Australia
Sydney

A CIP catalogue record for this book
is available from the British Library

ISBN 0 7434 8933 0

Typeset by M Rules
Printed and bound in Great Britain by
Cox & Wyman Ltd, Reading, Berks

ACKNOWLEDGMENTS

How lucky I am to have been born one of the seven Trigiani kids! I have learned so much from my sisters and brothers, each one a magnificent person, each of whom I would be proud to call my friend if we were not related. Each one has given me a particular gift by their example, and it is a wonderful thing to finally be able to thank them; so, my gratitude to Mary Yolanda for your elegance, Lucia Anna 'Pia' for your compassion, Antonia 'Toni' for your strength, Michael for your humour and artistry, Carlo for your tenacity, and Francesca for your joy. I will be grateful to you all forever for your loyalty and big hearts.

At Random House, I thank my editor, the brilliant Lee Boudreaux; Todd Doughty, whose professionalism and good nature inspires me; Laura Ford, Anna McDonald, Vicki Wong, Dan Rembert, Beth Thomas, Allison Saltzman, Libby McGuire, Janet Cook, Tom Nevins, Allyson Pearl, Carol Schneider, Tom Perry, Sherry Huber, Ed Brazos, Eileen Becker, Ivan Held, Steve Wallace, Stacy Rockwood-Chen, Maureen O'Neal, Allison Heilborn, Kim

Hovey, Allison Dickens, Candice Chaplin, Cindy Murray and Beth Pearson. Gina Centrello, thank you for your support, energy and Italian moxie.

To Suzanne Gluck, the best agent on earth and an even better friend, my love and gratitude. More of the same to WMA's brilliant beauties, Emily Nurkin, Karen Gerwin, Jennifer Rudolph Walsh, Tracy Fisher, Alicia Gordon and Cara Stein. At ICM, more still to my champion, the great Nancy Josephson, and the fabulous Jill Holwager. In movieland, thank you Lou Pitt, Jim Powers, Todd Steiner and Michael Pitt.

I don't know what I would do without the amazing Lorie Stoopack, who works hard and makes it fun; and the astute 'Manuscript book club', Mary Trigiani, Jean Morrissey and Mary Testa. I would be lost without you.

For their sparkling and vivid memories of Manhattan in 1950, thank you Helen McNeill, Ralph Stampone and June Lawton. To the librarians of the New York Public Library system, thank you for your guidance. The recipes are from the files of my late friend and beloved grandmother Viola Trigiani. My grandmother Lucia Bonicelli, a craftsman in sewing and design, inspired the fashions throughout the story. To B. Altman expert, David Manning, director of media relations for the Graduate Center, City University of New York, thank you for your excellent research. To the gorgeous Elena Nachmanoff and Dianne Festa, I am devoted to you and Saul and Stewart for life.

Thank you with heaps of love to: Nancy Bolmeier Fisher, Kate Crowley, Eydie Collins, Elaine Martinelli, Elizabeth Dawson, Tom Dyja, Ruth Pomerance, Pam McCarthy, Nigel Stoneman, Ian

Chapman, Suzanne Baboneau, Carmen Elena Carrion, Melissa Weatherill, Rosanne Cash, Charles Randolph Wright, Bill Persky, Joanna Patton, Larry Sanitsky, Debra McGuire, John Melfi, Father Tony Rodrigues, Grace Naughton, Dee Emmerson, Gina Casella, Sharon Hall, Constance Marks, James Miller, Wendy Luck, Sharon Watroba Burns, Nancy Ringham, John Searles, Helen and Bill Testa, Cynthia Rutledge Olson, Jasmine Guy, Jim Horvath, Craig Fissé, Kate Benton, Jim Doughan, Ann Godoff, Joanne Curley Kerner, Max Westler, Dana and Richard Kirshenbaum, Sister Jean Klene, Daphne and Tim Reid, Caroline Rhea, Kathleen Maccio Holman, Rosemary and Anthony Casciole, Susan and Sam Franzeskos, Jake Morrissey, Beáta and Steven Baker, Eleanor Jones, Brownie and Connie Polly, Aaron Hill and Susan Fales-Hill, Karol Jackowski, Christina Avis Krauss and Sonny Grosso, Susan Paolercio, Greg Cantrell, Rachel and Vito Desario, Mary Murphy, Matt Williams and Angelina Fiordellisi.

Michael Patrick King, I adore you. If there is an afterlife, I hope I live downstairs from you there too.

To the Trigiani and Stephenson families, our Italian relatives, the Spada, Maj, and Bonicellis, thank you. To Ida Trigiani, the best mother on earth, my love always. To the people of Big Stone Gap, Virginia, my everlasting gratitude. To the great Jim Burns, please keep an eye on us from heaven. To my dear papa, Anthony, I miss you as much as I loved you, which is immeasurable.

And to my husband, Tim Stephenson, who puts up with more agita than ten men, your character and goodness still thrill me. As you lead me by the hand through parenthood, I am glad it is you who chose me. Thank you for our baby girl, who is lucky to have such a splendid papa.

For my sisters, Mary Yolanda, Lucia Anna,
Antonia and Francesca,
and my brothers, Michael and Carlo

Chapter One

From her window Kit Zanetti can see absolutely everything that happens on Commerce Street. The name doesn't really suit the street; it should be called Winding Trail, or Lavender Lane, or Rue de Gem. Greenwich Village doesn't get any more enchanting than this at night, with puddles of blue light around the roots of old trees that grow a few feet apart on either side of the street, or any lovelier by day, when the sun bakes the connecting row houses, none more than four storeys high, some festooned in ivy, a few of white clapboard with black liquorice trim, and one storefront so old that the brick facade has faded from maroon to pale orange. The brownstone stoops are hemmed with old terracotta pots containing whatever flowers grow in the shade, usually pink and white impatiens. The sidewalks are uneven, the concrete squares like slabs of layer cake. The shutters that swing from the windows are painted mottled shades of cream and Mamie pink, a powdery peach tone not seen since the Eisenhower administration (it appears the shutters have not been painted since then either).

This is the ideal home for a playwright: clusters of buildings filled with stories and people whose quirks play out with small-town regularity. Every morning Kit sits by the window while her coffee brews and witnesses the same scene: a petite woman with shocking red hair walks a Great Dane as tall as she is, and as they turn the corner, she yanks the leash, and he leaps into the air, setting off the car alarm in the Chevy Nova. On the opposite corner, a bald accountant in a suit the colour of a Tootsie Roll emerges from his basement apartment, looks up at the sky, takes a deep breath, and hails a cab. Finally, the superintendent from the apartment building across the street comes out of the foyer, hops on his stripped-down bike (essentially two wheels connected by a coat hanger), throws a broom over his shoulder, and rides off, looking very World War Two Italy.

There is a loud knock at the door. Kit is expecting her landlord and super, Tony Sartori, to stop by and unclog her sink for the tenth time this year. The tenants have never seen a professional anybody (plumber, electrician, painter) with actual tools work in the building. Everything from the wiring to the gas to the pipes is fixed by Tony with duct tape. The tape thing became so funny that Kit cut out a magazine article about how Miss America contestants create cleavage under their evening gowns by hoisting their breasts with duct tape, and put it in her rent envelope. Mr Sartori never mentioned receiving the article, but he began addressing Kit as Miss Pennsylvania.

'I'm coming,' Kit calls out sweetly in the high-pitched, grateful tone of a renter who doesn't want to be any trouble. She opens the door. 'Oh, Aunt Lu.' Lu is not actually Kit's aunt but everyone in the building calls her 'Aunt', so Kit does too. Sometimes Lu leaves gifts for Kit outside the door – a small bag of expensive coffee beans, a bar of lilac soap, a sample box of tiny perfume bottles – with a note that says, 'Enjoy!' in big, cursive handwriting. The stationery, small ecru cards with a gold 'L' engraved on them, is uptown tasteful.

'How are you?' Lu smiles warmly. She lives upstairs in the back apartment and is the only other single woman in Kit's building. She's in her seventies, but has the chic look of New York's older ladies who stay in the moment. Her hair is done, her lipstick is applied in the latest shade of fiery fuchsia, and she wears a vintage Hermès scarf wrapped around her neck and anchored by a sparkly brooch. Aunt Lu is trim and small. Her perfume is spicy and youthful, not flowery like a grandmother's.

'I thought you were Mr Sartori,' Kit says.

'What happened?' Lu peers into the apartment, expecting to see water gushing from the ceiling or worse.

'The sink. It's clogged again. And it won't open up no matter what I do. I plunged. I prayed. I used enough Drano to blow up Brooklyn.'

'If I see Tony, I'll tell him to get up here and fix it immediately.'

'Thanks.' If anybody has an in with the landlord, it is Aunt Lu. After all, she is a blood relative.

Aunt Lu pulls on her gloves. 'I was wondering if you were busy this afternoon. I'd love to have you up for tea.'

She has never invited Kit up to her place. They both know and live by the unwritten rules of apartment dwelling. It's best to keep a distance from neighbours in a small building; cordial greetings by the mailbox are acceptable, but beyond that it gets dicey, since there is nothing worse than a fellow tenant who stops by too much, chats too long, and borrows things. Kit says, 'Thanks, but I'm writing. Maybe we can do it another time.'

'Sure, whenever you can, you let me know. I've been cleaning out my apartment and I have lots of things I think you might like –' Lu looks around the apartment – 'or could use.'

Kit reconsiders. Nothing is more alluring than a free indoor flea market without other customers to beat to the prizes. And Aunt Lu reminds Kit of her own grandmother. She also seems self-sufficient and has an air of discernment, something Kit would like to cultivate. How many women can wear an enormous enamel dragonfly brooch and pull it off? 'Maybe I can make it around four.'

'I would love that!' Lu smiles. 'See you then.'

'How ya doin', Aunt Lu?' Tony Sartori asks as he climbs the stairs to Kit's apartment.

'I'm fine, but Kit's drain has seen better days.' Aunt Lu winks at Kit as Mr Sartori enters the apartment.

'Yeah, yeah, it's always something round here,' he grouses.

Lu grabs the hand railing and makes her way down the narrow stairwell. It's early October and not too chilly outside, maybe 50 degrees, but Lu is already wearing her full-length mink coat, which drags down the stairs behind her like the cape of a duchess. No matter the temperature, from September to June, Aunt Lu wears that mink coat.

'Come on in.' Kit need not invite him, since he's already in the bathroom. 'Aunt Lu's a pretty lady,' she tells him, hoping to score some points.

'You kiddin' me? In her day, she was a looker. They say she was the most bee-yoo-tee-ful gal in the Village.'

'Really?'

'Yep. You said you had a leak?'

'A clog. In the bathroom sink,' Kit corrects him.

'Again?' he says in a tone that implies it's Kit's fault. Tony Sartori is a small man with white hair and black eyebrows that look like thick hedges. He looks enough like Gepetto, the gentle cobbler in *Pinocchio*, to make Kit feel safe, but his vocal tone is pure New York rasp, which scares her a little.

Kit laughs nervously. 'Sorry. You know I spend my nights stuffing the drain with olive pits so you have to spend your days fixing it.'

Tony Sartori looks as though he may yell, but he smiles instead. 'Remain calm, Miss Pennsylvania. I'll fix it.'

Kit grins weakly, but knows better. He'll plunge the sink and then wrap some crappy tape around the join in the pipe and return in two weeks when the sticky stuff comes undone and Kit has another flood.

'We might have to get a plumber this time,' he says from under the sink.

'Halleluyah!' Kit claps her hands together joyfully.

Sartori grips the sink and pulls himself to a standing position. Kit's bathroom is wallpapered floor to ceiling with rejection letters from every regional theatre in the nation, from Alaska Rep to the Wyoming Travelling Players. They are all variations of the same message: good characters, good dialogue, but 'You don't know how to tell a story, Ms Zanetti.' Tony Sartori reads one and shakes his head. 'Don't you ever want to give up? I mean, with letters like these, what's the point?'

'I'm getting better,' Kit tells him.

'Maybe you are. But evidently there aren't a lot of people out there in the theatre world who think you can write a play.' Sartori shrugs. 'Besides, what *is* the theatre any more? It's not like it was. It used to be cheap and wholesome – dancing girls and good music. Now, it's too damn expensive. They herd you in like cows, and then the seats are so small you get a blood clot in your leg before the first song is over. My wife loved that *Phantom of the Opera* show. I thought it was all right. To me, it's just a guy in a mask scaring a girl with a good figure and then singing about it.'

'The reviews are in!' Kit says cheerfully. She is used to the barbs, criticisms and comparisons that come with her chosen profession. Playwriting as a career is pathetic. A writer can't make a living, and in this culture, plays are about as relevant as glass blowing or whittling forks out of wood. Kit will keep these thoughts to herself, since the last thing she needs is an artistic standoff with Tony Sartori.

'That's just my opinion.' Mr Sartori spins the roll of duct tape on his index finger and goes to the door. 'Can you hold off using the sink for a while?'

'How long? You know I do an intense beauty treatment each night and it requires running water to make the thick paste that I trowel on to prevent premature wrinkles.'

'That must be quite a sight. Use the kitchen sink for now.'

'Yes, sir.' Kit smiles. 'Mr Sartori?'

'Yeah?'

'Do you ever think anything I say is funny? Even just a little?'

'Not really.'

Tony Sartori closes the door behind him, and Kit hears him chuckle from the other side.

The Pink Teacup on Grove Street has the best coconut cake in the city. Made from scratch, it's a yellow cake so moist, for a moment it seems like it may not have cooked through. The mixture is full of tiny pineapple chips, and the icing is butter cream whipped so light the coconut curls sink into it. Juanita, the cook, likes Kit because she raved about the cake in an online-magazine piece. Whenever Kit passes by, Juanita cuts her a slab for free. Today Kit takes two slices, one for herself and one for Aunt Lu. As she walks back towards home, she makes a mental note to add some dishes to the article she is writing for *Time Out,* 'Best Food in the Village'. The articles don't pay much, but the perks are fabulous: free food in her favourite restaurants. So far her list includes:

Best Breakfast: the weekender at Pastis, on Ninth Avenue – includes a basket of sticky buns, chocolate *pane*, cocoa bread and nut loaf followed by scrambled eggs with crispy home fries made with onions and butter.

Best Lunch: the hamburger at Grange Hall, on the corner of Commerce and Barrow, with a glass of robust red wine.

Best Sandwich: the tuna salad with a delicate paste of avocado and sliced tomato at Elephant and Castle on Greenwich Avenue.

Best Dinner: Stafano's spaghetti pomodoro at Valdino West on Hudson Street.

Best Comfort Food: garlic mashed potatoes at Nadine's on Bank Street.

Kit's neighbourhood is often host to small literary tour groups who wander around with their guide books, pointing out the brownstones where Bret Harte and e e cummings lived, and the bar where Dylan Thomas raised his last glass before passing out in a booth and meeting his Maker. Kit imagines creating an eating tour of the Village. Literature *v.* a good sandwich. She has a hunch her tour would draw larger crowds.

Back home, Kit places the slices of cake in a Tupperware container and settles down to work. It takes all of her willpower not to eat the coconut cake before her four o'clock tea with Aunt Lu. She knows she will spend most of the afternoon circling it like a lonely hawk hovering over a platter of steak tartare in the desert. Of course, this is what writers do when they're not writing: they walk in circles around food and decide whether or not to eat it, as if taking a bite will somehow make a bit of dialogue work or help create a missing scene (it never does). This is why the Weight Watchers meetings at Fourteenth Street and Ninth Avenue are packed with women writers, including Kit, who has reached her goal weight twice in the last year. Eating and writing are the husband and wife of creativity.

Promptly at four o'clock, Kit climbs the stairs to Aunt Lu's apartment, feeling triumphant about her two gorgeous uneaten slices of coconut cake. She hopes hot tea and something sweet will get them through the visit, since she can't imagine what she and Aunt Lu will talk about.

Like most New Yorkers who live in walkups, Kit has never gone above her own floor. Lu's fifth-floor landing has charm, and there's a small skylight over a metal ladder that leads to the roof, resembling a periscope on a submarine. Kit has always wanted to check out the view, but the lease forbids tenants to go on the roof. The more Kit thinks about it, the more she realizes that Tony Sartori is stricter than her parents ever were. But it is worth a little suffering to live on Commerce Street.

'Aunt Lu?' Kit calls out. The door is propped open with a black iron kitten.

'Come in, darling.'

Kit eases the door open slowly. 'I brought . . .' She looks at the chintz wonderland in awe. Every corner, nook, cranny and wall is filled with stuff.

'What, dear?' Lu says from the kitchen.

'Cake,' Kit blurts. 'From the Pink Teacup. It's really good. I wrote about it. It's fresh daily. I hope you like it.'

'I've been there many times. The food is excellent.'

Aunt Lu answers the whistling tea kettle in her tiny kitchen, while Kit does a full turn and takes in the expanse of the apartment. The walls are high and much of the ceiling is covered by a large skylight, which slants down, making an eave to a door that leads to the terrace. It has begun to rain, and as the drops hit the glass, they tinkle like music. Aunt Lu's canopy bed is covered by a chenille bedspread, white with shaggy violets on scalloped trim. The furniture is precious and frilly: a pale blue velvet loveseat and two chintz slipper chairs with a pattern of irises. The coffee table holds a collection of silver mint-julep cups filled with tiny silk flowers.

'I have a lot of stuff, don't I?' Aunt Lu says, from the kitchen, chuckling.

'Yes, but it's all . . .' Kit struggles to describe what she sees, 'interesting. Like you've lived, I mean, live an interesting life.'

'Look around. Enjoy.'

Kit skirts the furniture carefully. Every flat surface is covered with knick-knacks – two pink ceramic poodles with a gold chain connecting them, tiny vases of Venetian glass, a jewelled letter opener, years of collected clutter, bad gifts, inherited bric-à-brac and sale items too cheap to resist. Even the print on the wallpaper says, 'old lady lives here', with its fat cabbage roses on a criss-cross trellis. Kit feels overwhelmed, as though she is standing in the middle of someone's hope chest, among layers and layers of stuff that have meaning but no purpose.

Kit turns and faces the long wall of the apartment. It is lined with red-and-white department store gift boxes, each one with swirly letters that say 'B. Altman'. The boxes at the top of the piles have been faded by the sun, so the red is more brown than on the boxes stacked underneath.

In the corner, next to the wall of boxes, is a small end-table dressed with a lace doily. Several photographs are arranged on top in ornate silver frames. In the centre is an eight-by-ten colour photograph of a beautiful girl in a strapless gold lamé gown. The colour in the photo is intense and saturated, like that of an old movie still. The young woman in the picture is about twenty-five, her heart-shaped face is creamy pink, her full lips are in a light pink pout, her almond-shaped eyes are set off by long black eyelashes and perfectly sculpted eyebrows, making her seem Egyptian or Italian. Something exotic.

'Who's the knockout?' Kit asks.

'That's me,' Aunt Lu tells her. 'When I was about your age.'

'Really?' Kit says, then immediately apologizes for her tone. 'I didn't mean that like it sounded. Of course it's you. That's your face for sure.'

'No, no, I'm an old lady now and that's over. It took a while for me to accept that. It's not easy to let go of your youth, believe me.'

'You would be on magazine covers today with your face. And that body! I write for magazines sometimes and they look for models who have that.'

'Have what, dear?'

'That quality. That golden kind of beauty, where each feature is perfect and it adds up to something original. Your eyes are a shade of blue I've never seen before. And your lips, now that's a cupid's bow. And I don't mean to sound funny, but your nose is the best I've ever seen: it's straight and the tip goes up just a little. That's a feat for us Italian girls. Sometimes we end up with real honkers.'

Aunt Lu laughs. 'Well, thank you.'

'No, no, it's true.'

Lu takes the photograph from Kit and looks at it. 'What a night that was. New Year's Eve at the Waldorf in 1951. The McGuire Sisters sang, with me, my boss Delmarr and my mother and father at a front table at the foot of the stage. That was one of the best nights of my life.'

'You're breathtaking,' Kit says.

'I was just lucky,' she says, then adds, 'You're a pretty girl, too.'

'Thanks. But my grandmother always says, it doesn't matter what a woman does to look young, when we hit seventy we all wind up looking like Mrs Santa Claus.'

Aunt Lu laughs. 'It sounds like I'd get along fine with your grandmother. Come sit down.' She places a silver tray with the cake, the teacups, a small pot of tea, sugar and creamer on a side table.

Kit leans back into the chair, which is so soft, the cushions must be filled with down. She pours cream into her tea while she tries to think of what to say next. 'Is your real name Lucy?'

'No. Lucia.' Aunt Lu says her name softly with a perfect Italian accent.

'Loo-chee-uh,' Kit repeats. 'Like the opera?'

Aunt Lu smiles, and Kit notices a deep dimple in her right cheek. 'Papa called me Lucia di Lammermoor.'

'What did he do?'

'He owned the Groceria.'

'On Sixth Avenue?' Kit leans forwards in amazement. The Groceria is revered as an authentic Italian market and therefore one of the biggest tourist traps in the city. It features all the best staples imported from Italy, including Tuscan olive oil, fresh pastas and salamis from every region. It sells cheeses from all over the globe, and mozzarella cheese, made fresh daily, which float in tubs of clear water like golf balls. The store is known for its elaborate displays of breads, meats and fish.

'Do you still own it?'

Aunt Lu frowns. 'No, dear. It was sold about twenty years ago. The family business is now centred round managing apartment buildings.'

'Tony Sartori owns *other* buildings?' Kit can't believe that the king of duct tape would have other properties.

'He and his brothers. Tony is a real piece of work. So impatient. That temper. The boys are nothing like my father. Sometimes they remind me of my brothers, but my brothers had respect for the family. Today, I'm lucky if they remember I live up here. I know old people aren't terribly interesting to young people but I am, after all, their aunt and their only connection to their father's people.'

Kit nods, feeling a little guilty. She hadn't been too excited about spending any time up here either.

Aunt Lu continues, 'Tony is the eldest son of my eldest brother, Roberto. Of course, my brother has been dead for many years.'

'So, how many of you were there growing up?'

'I had four older brothers. I was the baby.'

'What happened to them?'

'They're all gone. I'm the last of the original Sartoris. I miss them too. Roberto, Angelo, Orlando and Exodus.'

'Great names. Exodus. Were you all named after opera characters?'

'Just two of us.' Aunt Lu smiles. 'Do you like the opera?'

'My grandmother does, and she passed it along to me. I've offered to burn CDs of her record albums but she won't let me. She likes to stack them on her record player and let them drop and play through, scratches and all. Gram thinks the scratches make the music better.'

Aunt Lu refills Kit's teacup. 'You know, Kit, when you're old, you like to hold on to all the little things that meant something to you. It just feels comfortable and right. Let her have her old ways. They're *her* ways. You understand?'

'Yes, I do. Is that why you live in your nephew's building? Or is the Sartori family holding out to make a big sale on the building and then you'll cash in and move uptown with a view of Central Park?'

'Sure, sure. I'm holding out for my view of the park.' Aunt Lu smiles.

'I don't blame you. You should get something out of living here.

The place isn't exactly maintained, but I don't like to complain. I'm afraid Mr Sartori would throw me out.'

'I know the feeling,' Aunt Lu says quietly.

'Of course, my place is in worse shape than yours. My bathroom wall is ready to cave in.'

'How should they know how to take care of these properties when everything they have was handed to them? I worked my whole life, so I know the value of things.'

'When did you stop working?'

'I retired in 1989 when B. Altman's department store closed. Of all the employees, I had been there the longest, since 1945. They even gave me an award.' Lucia picks up an engraved crystal paperweight from the coffee table and hands it to Kit.

'This is kind of like a perfect-attendance certificate in high school.'

'That's exactly right.'

Kit returns the award to its place on the table. 'You were there so long. You must have liked your job.'

'Oh, I loved it.' As Aunt Lu remembers, her face is transformed. Beneath the distinguished older woman she is now, Kit can see the young woman with moxie and beauty. She is ashamed she tried to come up with an excuse to avoid this cup of tea. After all, Lucia Sartori is no Greenwich Village kook like the guy on Fourteenth Street who dresses up like Shakespeare and walks through Washington Square Park broadcasting sonnets. Kit looks over into the alcove where Lucia's mink coat hangs on a dress mannequin. The sleek black fur looks almost new in what little light is coming through the windows. The rain has stopped and left behind a late-afternoon sky the colour of a grey pearl.

'Aunt Lu? May I call you Lucia?'

'Absolutely.'

'I've always wondered, since you wear it a lot, what's the deal with the mink coat?'

Lucia looks off into the alcove. 'The mink coat is the story of my life.'

'Well, Lucia, if it's not too much trouble, can you tell me the story?' Kit picks up her cup of tea and settles back in her chair as Lucia begins.

Chapter Two

'Loo-chee-uh! Loo . . .'

'Mama, I'm coming!' I shout from the top of the stairs.

'*Andiamo*! Papa needs the envelope!'

'I know, I know, I'm on my way!' Quickly, I grab my purse and throw in lipstick, keys, my small leather date book, a bottle of clear nail polish and my felt pincushion in the shape of a small red tomato with its elastic wristband. I'm wearing a simple navy-blue dress with a full skirt, deep tiered pockets, and a button-down bodice with a stand-up white collar, mist-blue stockings and blue high-heeled shoes with a single strap and beige button. I throw open my everyday hatbox and pull out a small turquoise velvet cloche, which swoops over one eye, keeping my side parting flat and neat. I grab my short white gloves, slam my bedroom door and click down the stairs so fast, I'm in the vestibule in less than a minute.

'Tell Papa I want him home at six.' When Mama issues an order, I obey. She pushes a loose curl back into place, tucking it into her chignon. The strands of white in her black hair are becoming more pronounced, but her skin is still smooth like a girl's. Her high cheekbones are flushed with pink and her jawline is strong.

'Remember,' my mother says as she tucks the envelope into my purse, 'we have our big dinner tonight.'

'What are you making?'

'*Bracciole*. Papa is cutting the tenderloin himself. The meat will be so *delicato*, it will fall off of Claudia DeMartino's fork.'

'Good. I really want to impress her.'

'And we will. Make sure you're on time.' Mama kisses my cheek and pushes me out the door. What a perfect autumn day. The sun is so bright on Commerce Street, I close my left eye to let the pupil in the right adjust, then open both.

'*Bellissima* Lucia!' our neighbour Mr McIntyre comments as I pass.

'Why can't I find a good Irish boy with that brand of blarney?' I ask him.

Mr McIntyre laughs heartily, chomping down on the end of his cigar. 'I'm too old. Anyhow, you're destined for a nice Italian boy.'

'So they say.' He knows and I know that from the moment we were born Mama had the same wish for me and my brothers: bring home an Italian. Mama's sermons about 'marrying our people' can be recreated by my brother Exodus down to the praying-hands gesture she makes when invoking God, begging Him that we use our heads. We may laugh when he imitates her, but we know Mama means business. Papa is no problem. He always says, '*Stai contento*.' If we're happy, he's happy.

The schoolboys on Seventh Avenue South whistle as I pass. 'Lucia!' one of the boys calls out. When I don't respond, he hollers again, 'Lucia! Lucia!' Sometimes I turn and wink; after all, they're just boys.

My brother Angelo hoses down the sidewalk in front of Sartori's Groceria, our family business and Greenwich Village's only Italian fresh market. My brother has opened the wall-size display windows and rolled back the awnings to let the sun dry the terracotta floor.

Angelo has a classic, angular face, wide-set brown eyes, full, even lips and a small nose. At five foot eight he's the shortest of my brothers, but many people believe he's the best-looking. Mama thinks he should have been a priest, because he's the peacemaker in the family. Angelo spritzes the Halloween pumpkins stacked neatly near the entrance and makes a motion as if to spray me with the hose.

'Don't you dare!'

Angelo laughs. He's twenty-nine, a full four years older than me, but he'll never be too old to tease me.

'Where's Papa?'

'Can't you hear him?'

I lean in the doorway and hear Roberto and Papa's voices raised in an argument. 'They're fighting again?'

'As usual. I serve two masters. One wants everything as it was in the old country and the other wants it like the A&P up the street. Nobody wins.'

'Not yet, anyway,' I tell him.

The door is propped open with a giant can of crushed tomatoes. Papa and Roberto are nose to nose in front of a stack of crates full of ruby-red apples.

'I buy the apples where I buy the apples!' Papa yells.

'You pay too much!' Roberto counters.

'I know the farmer for thirty-two years! He grows the apples just for me! I don't buy produce off a truck. Who knows where it comes from?'

'From an apple tree! An apple tree, Pop. They're all the same! And who cares where they come from when they're fifty cents less a bushel?'

'I care! I care a lot! Half the fruit on those trucks is rotten! I won't sell old and rotten in my shop!'

'I give up! You hear me? I give up, Pop!' Roberto grabs his clipboard.

'Don't yell at Papa!' I holler at my brother.

Roberto, at six foot one, is much taller than our father but he shrinks a bit at the sound of my voice. 'It's none of your business. Stick to your sewing,' he says petulantly, then turns and goes to the stockroom. Roberto looks like my mother's people, black hair and brown eyes, long, straight nose and thick, expressive eyebrows. He acts like them too; he has a terrible temper. When I was little, he always seemed to be shouting and his anger frightened me. Now, I yell back.

'Here's the envelope from Mama.' I give Papa the envelope filled with cash.

'Grazie.' Papa takes the money to the register and places the bills neatly under the metal catch. 'How's my girl?' he asks in a serious tone.

'Papa, why do you worry about me?' I ask, but I know the answer. He worries about everything: his family, his business and the world that is changing too fast for him. Since the war, business has doubled, his daughter has become a career girl and his sons have developed big mouths and lots of opinions.

'I can't help it.' Papa shrugs and dumps the coins into the register. 'I want you to be happy.'

'Papa, I *am* happy,' I promise him. Everything about my father exudes warmth and humour; the room fills when he enters. Papa has curly salt-and-pepper hair and blue eyes. I'm the only one of his children who inherited his blue eyes, and this is one of the many things that seem to bind us in a special way. When Papa laughs, which is often, his eyes crinkle shut. He has broad shoulders and a thick waist like a dock worker, but his hands are like a musician's, with long, tapered fingers.

'What's happiness, anyway, Pop?' I throw my arms around him and give him a big hug. On my way out I shout towards the stockroom at Roberto, 'Now I have to go to work. Lots of sewing to do! See you later, Pop.'

When I'm out on the sidewalk, I hear Papa holler, 'Lucia di Lammermoor!' I turn back. 'Be careful!' he calls after me.

I throw him a kiss and walk to the bus stop.

Every morning when I hop off the bus at Thirty-Fifth Street and Fifth Avenue I am still awed by the fact that I have a job at the best department store in New York City. I never take it for granted. My favourite moment is when the passengers exiting the Thirty-Fourth Street subway station merge with the crowd on the sidewalk and, like a great wave, we walk up a hilly portion of the street; suddenly it dips down and reveals B. Altman & Company, so grand it covers an entire city block.

When the store opened at this location in 1906 it was called the Palace of Trade, and the name still fits. On Fifth Avenue, where most of the buildings stand out as architectural wonders, this one is special. The style is Italian Renaissance, six sprawling floors with twenty-foot ceilings, immense and spectacular. The majestic storefront has a series of colonnades made of French limestone reaching up to the second floor. Over each giant window is a half-shell awning of smoky green glass; from the opposite corner they look like a series of elegant Tiffany lampshades.

The interior is filled with the highest-quality goods from every corner of the world, each item carefully selected and displayed to fill the customer with longing, just like Papa's store. Each time I walk through the main entrance – and it's been this way every day of my working life – I feel a rush of excitement, followed by a jolt of self-confidence. I look up at the twinkling chandeliers, inhale the fine perfumes, sweet notes of delicate freesia, woodsy musk and fresh roses, and feel that anything is possible.

I still can't believe this is where I work, that every second Friday I receive a cheque, printed on pale blue paper, with my name typed neatly in black: 'Pay to the Order of: Miss Lucia Sartori.' The bottom right-hand corner bears the official stamp of 'R. Prescott, Vice President', and in the bottom left-hand corner 'Custom Department' is printed neatly.

I never take the elevators to our offices on the third floor. I prefer the escalators because I don't want to miss a single one of the displays, which are changed monthly by the window dressers who are renowned for their realistic mannequin tableaux. Last winter they built an ice-skating pond with mirrors on the floor, surrounded by evergreen trees with clumps of artificial snow, and set out two mannequins skating *à deux* with glass stars swinging over their heads. The male mannequin wore a navy-blue-and-white Nordic wool sweater. The display was so popular that every daughter in New York City, including me, bought her father that sweater for Christmas.

As I pass the display cases, deep glass boxes lined in velvet and trimmed with polished cherry wood, I do a quick inventory of new arrivals: the latest Austrian crystal brooches, sleek leather gloves from Spain, and beaded evening bags twinkle under the soft white lights. Everywhere you look, a treasure. Thank heavens for layaway!

My route never changes. Each morning I walk across the Main Floor, through Men's Furnishings, past Custom Shirts, through the Silk Department, past the Camera Department, around Engraving and Stationery to the escalator, up to the second floor, through Infants' and Children's, to Misses' Wearing Apparel, and then up to the third floor through Furs, Stoles and Coats. By now, I've removed my gloves and I touch the sumptuous mink and fox-fur coats as I pass. The luxurious sable! Regal ermine! Chic leopard! A girl could get lost in here forever and never tire of the glamour.

By the time I push through the double doors marked Special Order Department for Dressmaking and Tailoring into the Hub, a large workroom with a long cutting table, drawing boards, sewing machines and steam presses, I'm ready to work. My boss and the Chief Designer Delmarr (no last name, how avant-garde!) pours himself a cup of coffee from a black-and-white-checked herringbone Thermos. He looks as though he posed for the 'Seen Around Town' article in the *Herald* in his grey tweed jacket with the black suede elbow patches and black cashmere slacks. 'Half the battle is looking the part,' Delmarr tells us. He is tall and lean, with feet so large, he has his tasselled suede loafers custom-made. 'Navy subs,' he calls them. 'A good cobbler is a genius. Making a stylish and comfortable pair of shoes takes artistry and architecture.'

Delmarr has an open face with wide cheekbones, deep dimples and a strong chin. It's a handsome face but there is substance in his intelligent eyes and wisdom in his greying temples. Delmarr is 'a sophisticate', my best friend Ruth would say. When he isn't working long hours, he's out on the town with one of a long line of society girls. Delmarr is the quintessential ladies' man, tall and handsome, with no intention of ever settling down. Now and then his name shows up in the society pages. Delmarr knows everybody, it seems. When a new client walks in for a consultation, Delmarr doesn't rest until he figures out some connection to her. And when it comes to design, he knows what will be fashionable before the pack. Delmarr has a talent for the moment.

'Hey, kid,' he says now with a big grin. 'What's the word from Greenwich Village?' He pulls a silver case from his jacket pocket, removes a cigarette, and lights it.

'Well, it's the first week of October, so the apples are in.'

He throws his head back and laughs. Nobody laughs like Delmarr; it's from the gut. 'With news like that, we might as well be in Ohio. What's next? A hayride through Central Park?'

'You never know.'

'So, your father will spend the day stacking apples into a pyramid, crafting a perfect display. Sometime I'd like to watch him,' Delmarr says sincerely. 'You know that's a talent. Presentation. That's a big talent.'

'I told you I come from artistic farmers.' I steal a cup of coffee from Delmarr's Thermos and head over to my desk.

Ruth Kaspian, my fellow seamstress, looks up from her drawing table. 'What's with the navy blue? It's positively funereal. Somebody die?'

'Not that I know of.'

'It's so severe. You're too pretty for severe. The dress has got to go.'

'It was a gift.'

'Give it back.' Ruth takes a stub of pink chalk and gently rubs it along the hem of the dress she has drawn.

'I can't. It came from family. My future mother-in-law.'

'Ick.' Ruth makes a face. She slides off her work stool and stretches. Ruth is tiny, compact really, maybe five feet one. We're both twenty-five years old, but she could pass for someone much younger. She has beautiful dark curls that frame her face in neat ruffles. Her pale skin and brown eyes are offset by her bright red lipstick. 'I get it. You're wearing it to impress Mrs DeMartino. The old soft soap. Let me know if it works. My future mother-in-law gave me an umbrella. Maybe I should open it indoors and scare the devil out of her. She's superstitious, you know. Russian.'

'Mrs DeMartino has been nice to me. I don't have any complaints.'

'Lucky you. Mrs Goldfarb is helping to plan our engagement party. She wants to do it at the Latin Quarter.'

'Could you try to sound a little more excited?'

'No,' Ruth says flatly. Her tone makes me laugh. 'I'm too practical to get all hepped up, you know that. I don't want to go to the Latin Quarter with either my relatives or Harvey's. They'll sit there like stumps. Like a bad breeze from Brooklyn.'

'Give them a chance.'

'Well, I guess I should just be honest. I don't want to be a

Goldfarb.' Ruth rolls up her sketch and stuffs it into a tube. She hands it to me and I place it in the bin behind my desk. Later we'll lay out all the drawings for Delmarr, and he'll choose a few to show our customers for next spring.

'But you love Harvey,' I remind her.

'I love him. Yes, I do. Since I was fourteen and he was fifteen and I danced with him at Morrie's Acres in the Poconos after he bought me a hot dog. But I've always hated his name. I can't believe I have to trade Kaspian, a name I love, for . . . Goldfarb.'

'Don't,' Delmarr says as he drops work orders into the bin. He takes a final drag off his cigarette and tosses the butt out the window. 'It's 1950. There are plenty of women who don't change their surnames.'

'Sure, they're called spinsters,' Ruth says.

'No, married women. Particularly in art and design. Actresses. Women in the public eye who had a life before meeting their future husbands.'

'Who?' Ruth wants to know.

'You've heard of Lunt and Fontanne?'

'Sure.'

'They're not Lunt and Lunt, are they?' Delmarr shrugs and goes into his office.

Ruth lowers her voice so Delmarr can't hear. 'Harvey is not going to go for Kaspian and Goldfarb, I promise you. It sounds like a fish market on the Lower East Side.'

'Maybe you should ask him what he thinks. He might let you keep your name.'

'Fat chance. I could never even bring up the subject. I'm his girl and I'm going to take his name, end of story. Harvey makes decisions ten years before he has to. He's already named our kids: Michael for his grandfather Myron, and Susan after his grandmother Sadie.'

Suddenly, I feel claustrophobic listening to Ruth talking about children and names and what Harvey wants and what Harvey doesn't want. Ruth is a brilliant artist, she can draw anything, she has excellent taste and an eye for what works. Delmarr believes she'll be a great designer someday. All this talk of Harvey and babies makes that seem like a faraway dream. Can't Ruth hear what she is saying?

'What, you don't like Susan?' Ruth looks at me.

'No, no, it's a nice name.'

'What's the matter?' Ruth keeps looking at me intently. She knows what I'm thinking, but I don't want to get into a big argument about her life. I love her too much to force my opinions on her. So I smile and say, 'Nothing.'

'Faker.' Ruth breaks off a piece of black chalk and begins sketching. 'Of course, you have nothing to complain about. DeMartino is as nice a name as Sartori. You're lucky.'

I look down at my engagement ring, one round carat nestled in a circle of gold on my left hand. I guess I am lucky. I'm engaged to a nice Italian fellow, whom I've known all my life. My parents like him. Even my brothers don't mind him.

'Dante's the kind of guy who would let you keep your name. He'd do anything you ask. I don't know how you did it, Lu. You ended up with a looker who has a good heart. Not many of those to go around.'

'Lucia, Ruth, I need to see you in my office,' Delmarr says from his doorway. Ruth and I look at each other. Delmarr's tone sounds official, and official usually means bad news.

'Okay, what did we do wrong?' Ruth asks as we take our seats in Delmarr's office. 'Mrs Fissé hated the collar on her opera coat?'

'There's no problem, which is why I went to Hilda Cramer and asked her to give you gals a raise.'

'A raise!' I look at Ruth.

'What did she say?' Ruth asks evenly.

Delmarr smiles. 'You got it. You go from forty-six, seventy-five a week to forty-eight dollars and fifty cents.'

'Thank you!' I clap my hands together.

'Thank you,' Ruth says solemnly, letting the good news sink in slowly.

'You two make my life pleasant around here. You work hard, you take on extra assignments when I ask, you even work weekends once in a while. You're professional, smart and can actually carry on a conversation. I'm glad Hilda Beast bit on my request. It makes me very happy.'

Ruth looks at me, I look at her. We stand to embrace Delmarr to show our gratitude and realize that's a line we've never crossed. She knows what I'm thinking and I know what she's thinking, so we cross the line anyway and throw ourselves on Delmarr. He pushes us away like eager puppies.

'That's enough, kids. We got work to do. Sartori, let's go. We got a date in B.'

I go to my desk, pull the pincushion over my wrist, grab the seamstress chalk, and follow him into the fitting room. Our favourite model, Irene Oblonsky, a six-foot blonde Russian beauty, all neck and legs and angular edges, stands in her slip on a pine block. From every angle in the three-way mirror, she looks like a rose, one lean line with a bloom at the top. The only curve on her body is the round descent of her shoulders into her long, slender arms. A cigarette dangles from her mouth. She looks bored. She is bored.

Delmarr gently takes the cigarette from Irene's mouth and places it in an ashtray. 'Scissors.' He holds out his hand. I place the scissor handles in his palm, like Kay Francis when she played a surgical nurse in one of her melodramas. I watch as Delmarr drapes white cotton muslin tightly over Irene's frame and begins cutting. Where he cuts, I pin. I follow his every movement, across her back, under the arms, over the décolletage, nipping in the waist, draping the skirt, closing the seams. Soon, Irene is totally covered in muslin, which now looks like a strapless gown.

'Take it in at the knee. Jacques Fath is showing the Mermaid,' Ruth says from the doorway. 'Make it so tight that she walks in short steps.' Delmarr nods in agreement and I pin the gown closely around her knees like a second neckline.

'Needs interest over the bust or we're just looking at another dull strapless.' With his scissors Delmarr creates giant petals from the muslin, handing them to me to hold. Then he takes a large runner of muslin and ties a giant bow over Irene's bust. He anchors the petals of fabric under the bow, creating a stiff base over the bodice. I pin them quickly. The slim silhouette works. It is bolder than the New Look, already passé with its giant circle skirts and tight waistlines. This is much more dramatic and modern.

'Done.' Delmarr steps back as I finish pinning.

'Now, that's interesting,' Ruth says.

Irene lifts and extends her arms, slowly turning. She stops and looks at herself in the mirror. 'Goot.' She shrugs.

'Let's do it in satin. Ruby red. Not cherry. Not garnet. Ruby. And make me a wide belt, let's say four inches with a simple square closure. The belt should ride over her natural waistline. Cover all of it in satin. I don't want to break the line. I don't want to see a black grommet, nothing but red from bosom to floor. Make one, complete and finished. By Friday.'

'Yes, sir.'

'Helen, Violet!' Delmarr calls, never taking his eyes off Irene.

Helen Gannon, the pattern cutter, a lanky redhead so lean she could be a model herself, breezes in. She stops when she sees the gown. 'Uh huh. Big bow the size of Jersey City. Nice, Delmarr,' Helen complains. 'Didn't your mother teach you simple is better? This thing has more layers than a tulip.'

'It's called *au courant*,' Delmarr tells her. 'Violet, where are you?'

Violet Peters, a small brunette in charge of assembly, comes running. 'I'm here. I'm here,' she says nervously. Violet worries about everything, but she needn't worry about her job. Delmarr trained her himself, so they have a shorthand. Violet looks at Irene. 'Whoa.' Then she says to Delmarr, 'This is labour-intensive.'

Delmarr disregards her. 'Uh huh.'

Helen and Violet hover around Irene like bees and remove the pieces of muslin, one at a time, placing them neatly on a long table off to the side.

I go directly to the fabric room next door to check our stock. As I flip through the tall tubes, bolts of velvet, wool, silk and gabardine, the only satin I find is a sheer beige, left over from a trousseau we built for a Greek girl from Queens (there's lots of money in those diners).

'Why the rush?' I ask Delmarr on the way back to my desk.

'The McGuire Sisters have a new show at the Carlyle. And they want Paris runway.'

'The McGuire Sisters!' Wait until I tell Ruth.

'Deliver three fabulous gowns and there may be some ringside tickets in it for you.'

'Please. My dad loves them!' I say.

'What about your fiancé?'

'What about him?'

'I was thinking a romantic evening out, just you and Dante.'

'He's not the nightclub type. Bakers are in bed by eight. The dough has risen by three a.m., so that's when they get up to make the bread.'

'I'll remember that the next time I order ham on a roll. I'll think of your Dante, who gave up all fun so that I might have fresh bread for lunch.'

'You do that,' I tell him.

After a day of hemming black satin opera coats with Ruth (the Philharmonic's fall schedule resumes this weekend), I am ready for a good meal and a glass of wine. This is the first time the DeMartinos and Sartoris have had dinner together since Dante and I announced our engagement. We see so much of the DeMartinos in the neighbourhood, since they supply the Groceria with bread and pastries, that an official dinner to discuss wedding details seems a little much. But Mama, who wants to do things right, insisted we sit down and discuss all the plans with both sets of parents. 'Respect,' Mama says. 'You'll find out it's more important than food on the table once you are married.'

Dante and I have been engaged for six months, so it's time to start planning the wedding in earnest. It's not easy when Dante works around the clock with little time off. At least Papa closes the Groceria on holidays. My future father-in-law challenged me when I suggested he close the bakery once in a while. He said, 'What day of the year don't people eat bread?'

After waiting a few minutes for the bus, I decide to walk home. I love my long walks in the city. Nature itself doesn't change as much as the store windows on Fifth Avenue, where there is always something new to see. The streets empty out after work hours. For several blocks it's actually quiet enough to think.

I take a right turn on Ninth Street towards Sixth Avenue, passing stately brownstones with wide stoops and bay windows bedecked with elaborate silk draperies. There are a couple of large apartment buildings with green-and-white canvas awnings stretched over the sidewalk on polished brass rods. I've wondered all my life what it would be like to live in one of those buildings, to have an elegant uniformed doorman hail cabs and help with the boxes after a day of shopping uptown.

The most beautiful homes in New York City are always situated near the parks, in this case, Washington Square. The doormen wink at me as I pass, and sometimes I wink back. Some days I get more winks than others, usually when I'm wearing this hat. There's something about turquoise velvet. As I wait to cross Sixth Avenue, a truck comes to an abrupt halt in front of me.

'Get in.'

'Exodus, for crying out loud!'

'Move it, Sis.'

I climb into the delivery truck with Exodus, the most rugged of my brothers, and the one who's usually in trouble for one thing or another. Exodus has light brown hair with some red in it. His face is shaped like Papa's and he has Mama's eyes. He's often mistaken for one of those tall, broad-shouldered Irish boys, but once you hear my brother curse in Italian (which he does often), you know he's one of us. I've always admired his bravado; he couldn't care less what anyone thinks of him and he's honest. He can also keep a secret, which is a plus in a large family.

'Ma's tearing her hair out. The DeMartinos are sitting there like marble statues. I just dropped off a case of soda, so it's an eyewitness account.'

'They're already there?' I should have known to get home sooner. The DeMartinos are always early. When Dante and I went to the movies with his mother, she arrived so early, she saw the end of the show before ours and ruined the movie for herself.

'Yep. I hope when you have a girl, it don't look like the old lady. *Faccia di* Bow Wow.'

'She's not that bad,' I tell him.

'Here's how I see things. A beauty like you marries into a tribe like that, and you have a baby girl and the beauty gets half cancelled by Dante's mother, automatically, no questions asked.'

'Thank you for pointing out that our children, your future nieces and nephews, won't get a fair shake in the beauty department. It gives me great comfort.'

'Why you wanna marry him anyway?'

'I thought you liked Dante.'

'He's a dolt. They're all dolts. They work in dough, for Christsakes. Yeast rises, and how? It's full of air. How smart can they be?'

'They run a very successful bakery.'

'Who can't make cookies and make a living? That's nothin'. I hope you know what you're doing, Lucia.'

'I absolutely do. Besides, nobody asked you.'

'Yeah, well. You should. I know you're gettin' old and all, but it doesn't mean you got to rush.'

'I'm not rushing.' If only Exodus knew how slowly I have taken things with Dante. I love my fiancé, but I wish I could stay engaged another year or two. I like the way things are.

When Exodus pulls up to our house to drop me off, Papa is waiting on the sidewalk.

'Lucia. You're late.' My father opens the door for me.

'Sorry, Papa. They weren't supposed to be here until seven.' I jump out of the truck. 'I have news. You'll never believe it. I got a raise!'

Papa claps his hands together joyfully, just as I did, and smiles broadly. 'That's my girl!' he says with pride. 'You deserve it. My mother would be so proud. See, all those sewing lessons she gave you paid off.'

'I wish she could see me put up a hem now. I hardly miss a stitch!'

'She sees you. She knows.' Papa puts his arm around me as we go up the steps. I am happy about the raise but the best part is making my father happy. His approval means everything to me. As we enter the house, I hear Perry Como on the phonograph. The sweet smell of sage, roasted onions, and basil greets me in the hall. I don't bother going to my room to freshen up. I open the door and walk into the front parlour.

'Mrs DeMartino, you look lovely.' I kiss my future mother-in-law on the cheek. She smiles at me. Exodus is right, this is a plain face with a touch of the bulldog. 'I like your hair.'

'I went to the beauty parlour.' She fluffs the curls in her jet-black hair. 'Why so late, Lu?'

'I walked home.'

'*O Dio*! Alone?' Mrs DeMartino looks at her husband.

'Yes. But don't worry about me. I stick to a safe route. I know all the doormen.' As soon as I say this, I realize I shouldn't have. I sound cheap, as if I collect doormen like racing stubs. Mrs DeMartino leans over and mutters something to her husband in Italian, which I don't catch.

'Mr DeMartino, it's wonderful to see you.' I extend my hand to my future father-in-law.

'How are you?' Mr DeMartino is wearing wool slacks and a shirt and tie. I've never seen him out of his white apron.

'Where's Dante?'

'He's locking up the store. He'll be along soon.' Mrs DeMartino looks at my dress intently.

'Oh, thank you for this lovely dress.'

'My cousin brought several back from Italy, my girls picked theirs, and I thought you might like one. I know you're fussy about clothes, but I figured this one would do.' She smiles.

'I like it very much. If you'll excuse me, I should go and help Mama.'

I go into the kitchen, where Mama is ladling tomato sauce over the *bracciole*, small bundles of tender beef stuffed with basil. 'They got here so early!' she whispers.

'I see.'

'I'm going to give you some advice. You're young. You can bend. Never argue with Claudia DeMartino. She will kill you.'

I laugh loudly. Mama shushes me. I say, 'It's not like when you were a young bride and Nonna lived here and you were practically her maid. Times have changed. I don't have to take orders from my mother-in-law. I'll do my fair share because I want to, not because I have to.'

'Have to. Want to. Doesn't matter. She's the *padrone*,' Mama whispers.

'Lucia?' Dante stands in the doorway. He looks so handsome in his suit and his smile is so warm, I am reminded why I love him. Dante bears a strong resemblance to the movie star Don Ameche, with black eyes, thick brown hair, a strong nose and a full mouth, and my Dante definitely has his broad shoulders. When I was a girl I made a scrapbook of newspaper clippings about all of Don Ameche's movies, and when I saw Dante for the first time, when we were kids, I thought it was fate that a boy from the East Village looked like my favourite movie star.

I throw my arms around my fiancé and kiss him on the cheek. 'Sorry I kept your parents waiting,' I apologize.

'It's okay. Mama's been waiting all day to taste your mother's *bracciole*.'

Mama grunts softly at the competition. We ignore it.

'Dante, I got a raise!' I tell him proudly.

'Good for you!' Dante kisses me. 'You work so hard. I'm glad they noticed.'

'Lovebirds, I need a hand here.' Mama hands a platter to me and a gravy boat to Dante. 'Congratulations, Lucia. I'm happy for you.

Now help me.' Mama kisses me on the cheek, then calls the DeMartinos to dinner. As we take our seats, I look out into the back yard. Right now it's not much of a garden, it's just a small patch of brown grass with a grey marble birdbath in the middle. At Christmas time Mama fills the basin with fresh greens and a ceramic Baby Jesus in His crib. Today there's no decoration, just an inch of black water. I wish Mama had scrubbed it out; it looks creepy. But Mama makes up for it indoors. She has set a beautiful table with a cluster of small white candles in the centre, which Papa lights as we sit down. Even Mrs DeMartino looks soft in the candlelight. Papa says grace. I help Mama serve the food.

'Where are your sons tonight?' Mrs DeMartino asks.

'They're unloading a truck at the store,' Papa tells her.

'We thought it would be nice if it was just us tonight,' I tell her as I smile at Dante, who looks as happy as I have ever seen him.

'Signore Sartori, are you aware your daughter walks home alone after work?' Mrs DeMartino ladles gravy onto her meat.

'I don't like it, but she's a grown woman and can walk wherever she pleases.' Papa says this pleasantly as he passes her the bread. 'Thank you for the bread, Peter,' he says to my future father-in-law.

'It's fresh,' Mrs DeMartino says.

As we begin to eat, the chatter is warm and friendly. This is the best part of marrying an Italian boy. There are no surprises. Our families are similar, our traditions are the same, the meal is delicious, and the conversation, peppered with neighbourhood news and gossip, is a lot of fun. This could not be going any better.

'So, should we get down to business?' Dante says. He puts his arm across the back of my chair and looks at me.

I begin. 'I was thinking Saturday May first at Our Lady of Pompeii Church—'

Mrs DeMartino cuts me off. 'No, no, St Joseph's on Sixth Avenue is better.'

'But it's not my home parish,' I say politely.

'But it will be. When you come and live with us, you'll come to our church. It's tradition.' Mrs DeMartino looks to my parents for support.

'I know that, but until I'm married, I live here on Commerce Street, and this is the church I was baptized in, confirmed in and attend every Sunday. It's where I met Dante. I know you had a falling out with the old priest but that was many years ago—'

'Father Kilcullen hated the Italians,' Mrs DeMartino says.

Mama shrugs. 'I thought he was all right.'

'We're getting off track. Ma, Pop, it's Lady of Pompeii,' Dante says firmly.

Mrs DeMartino looks at her husband. 'I think it's okay,' he says.

'So, good. May first. Our Lady of Pompeii.' Dante pats my hand. I don't know why, but the way he pats it irritates me. Dante goes on to tell a long story about the bakery truck getting lost in the Bronx, and how when the truck was returned to them, the driver had eaten his way through a dozen rolls. Mrs DeMartino laughs too hard at every detail. It occurs to me that I should be laughing at my fiancé's story, but somehow it just doesn't seem particularly funny to me.

'I'll have to get used to the trains on your side of town. Since you live farther east, I'll have to take the El to get to Thirty-Fifth and First and then I'll just have to leave early enough to walk over so I'm at work on time,' I say casually. A deep silence follows, so I try to fill it up. 'Ruth Kaspian is designing my gown, which should be very convenient, since—'

Mrs DeMartino interrupts me. 'You're not going to work at the department store.'

'I'm sorry?' I pretend I didn't hear what she said, but the truth is, I can't believe what she said.

'No, you'll be a housewife. You marry my Dante and you live with us and you help me at home. We're giving you the street-level apartment. We put in a new kitchen and it's very nice. You'll be very happy there.'

'But I have a job.' I look at Dante, who looks down at his food.

'You can sew from our house,' Mrs DeMartino says.

I look at my mother, who blinks at me as if she's trying to communicate something, but I don't know what.

'I don't take in sewing. That's not what I do. I'm a seamstress at B. Altman's in the Custom Department. I've been there for six years and some day I hope to run the department if I'm lucky and they choose me. Am I expected to resign?' I look around the table, but no one is looking at me. Now I pat Dante's hand, but not as gently. 'Dante?'

'Honey, we'll talk about this later,' he says in an authoritative tone I've never heard before.

'Why? We can talk about this now. I don't believe your mother should be misled. I intend to keep working.' Suddenly I remember my grandmother telling me the story of her betrothal and marriage, arranged by her parents in Italy. There was no mention of love or romance, just obligation and duty. Chores! Take in sewing? Not in 1950! Not in New York City! Claudia DeMartino is crazy if she thinks I'm going to put up hems for a pittance for the women on Avenue A. No thank you!

The only sound in the room is my father wrestling to remove the cork from another bottle of Chianti. The tiny squeaks fill up the silence. 'Let's not talk about work and jobs. Let's iron out the details of the wedding,' Papa says nicely.

Mrs DeMartino ignores him. 'What about when you have a baby?' She puts her fork down and lines it up carefully next to the knife and spoon.

'We'll be happy when that happens,' I tell her. Who isn't happy to have a baby?

'I am not raising your children while you're off at the store!' Mrs DeMartino bellows.

'Who is asking you to?' my mother suddenly wants to know. Evidently, Mama intends that only I make nice with Mrs DeMartino; she, however, can fight with her. Mama takes a deep breath and speaks slowly. 'Claudia, my daughter is a career girl. That doesn't mean she can't take care of a home.' She looks at me. 'That doesn't mean she *won't* take care of a home. These are skills she has had from an early age. She cooks, she irons, she cleans. She has been a full partner helping me here at home.'

'Thank you, Mama,' I say quietly.

'She has been trained.' Mama pushes her plate aside and smoothes her napkin. 'But she isn't like me and she isn't like you. I have tried to make her realize that a woman has enough to do at home without running to a job. In time, I believe she will come to understand this and make the necessary adjustments in her life.'

'This is all well and good *if* that is her intention,' Mrs DeMartino fires back. 'But this is not your daughter's intention! If she works, then she is not home and if she is not home, then who takes care of the children?' She slides her chair back and angles it towards my mother. 'You see my point, don't you?'

'That is not your business. Or mine. That is *their* business.' My mother gestures at Dante and me.

'Mama, I think Mrs DeMartino has a point.'

'See there? She knows! She knows that it's not right for a woman to work when she has children at home.'

'Mrs DeMartino, I didn't say that. And that's not what I mean. Let me be clear.' But I don't feel clear. I feel overwhelmed. Claudia DeMartino *is* a nightmare, just like Mama said, and she will only get worse. 'Let me explain.'

'I wish you would,' Mama says, wearily resting her face on her hand.

'I was hoping to take things one step at a time. To be married for a while, and then discuss the possibility of children—'

'Possibility? You spit in the face of God with talk like that. God sends babies when He sends babies, not when you want Him to send babies. You can't tell God when to send you a baby!' The tip of Mrs DeMartino's nose turns bright pink as her eyes fill with tears. 'I don't understand you. Do you love my son?'

'Yes, of course I do.'

'Then how can you put him after your job at a department store? It doesn't make any sense. A man needs to know that his wife puts him in first place. Otherwise she does not deserve him.'

'Mrs DeMartino, I know it wasn't that long ago that marriages were arranged—' Dante kicks me under the table. I see why. His parents' faces drain of all colour. They must have had an arranged marriage. No wonder she sees me as a selfish modern girl. Compared to her, I am. 'And that was a system that worked—'

'System? What system?' Mr DeMartino speaks up.

'But things have changed. We want to determine our future. We want a partnership, not a dictatorship.'

'I am not a dictator!' Mr DeMartino slams his hand on the table. The silverware jumps off the tablecloth with a jolt. 'I am the head of my household! I am the leader! The man is the leader!'

Mr DeMartino looks as though he may have a heart attack, so I take a deep breath and turn to Dante. He loves me and he would take me under any circumstances. Looking at him, I realize that I love him too, but I want things my way. If I join this family, it will be a disaster. I won't put my dreams behind those of my husband, mother-in-law and father-in-law. And why should I? I make my own living. I have always known if I walked out of my parents' home I could get my own apartment and live a good life. I stay here because I love my room with the window overlooking Commerce Street. And I love my mother and father, and until I marry I want to be with them. 'I'm sorry. I can't do this.' The words tumble out of my mouth so quickly, I don't know where they came from.

'What do you mean?' Dante is stunned. This is one moment when I wish I didn't have to be honest, but I look at his face and I see I cannot lie. 'I can't marry you. I'm sorry. I just can't.' I begin to cry, then swallow hard to stop.

'Lucia, don't say that.' Dante looks devastated. 'We'll do whatever you want. You can work, I don't care.'

'You say that now, but you don't mean it. Once we're married and

I'm living in your parents' home, they will have total say over our lives. I was kidding myself thinking that we would marry and I would move into your parents' house and keep my job and keep my life.' The buttons on the bodice of my dress feel like tiny carpet tacks punched into my chest. 'I'm very good at what I do. I got a raise today. A raise!'

'What is wrong with you?' Mrs DeMartino demands. 'Look at my son. He is a duke! How could you throw him off for nothing, for a job?' She says 'job' like it's the filthiest word in the world. 'How could you do that?' She stands and holds the wall behind her as though without it she would fall.

'I'm not doing anything. This is how I feel.' The tears are making my face itch. Papa gives me his handkerchief.

'You should feel ashamed! That's what you should feel!'

'*Basta, Claudia, basta.* Can't you see Lucia is upset?' Papa says quietly.

'You do not have control of your home, *signore*,' she says to Papa. Mama looks at Papa and almost starts to laugh; no one speaks to Papa in this manner. Then Mrs DeMartino turns to me.

'Lucia Sartori, you are young now and all the boys pursue you. You! The great beauty of Greenwich Village! All I ever heard was, "Lucia Sartori. *Bellissima*! You won't believe the face when you see it! Every good Italian son would give his eyes to marry such a girl." But you won't be a good wife! You are stubborn!' Mrs DeMartino shouts.

My father stands and faces Mrs DeMartino. He says calmly, 'No one says a word against my daughter in this house.'

I look at my mother, who shakes her head from side to side.

'Get the ring!' Mrs DeMartino says to her son.

'You want the ring?' I say in disbelief.

'You don't want Dante, you don't want the ring.' Mrs DeMartino extends her hand and holds it there steadily, waiting for me to drop the ring into it.

I look at Dante, who turns to his mother. 'Mama. Please.'

'She –' Claudia DeMartino sneers, '– loves her job more than she loves you.'

'That's not true,' Dante says softly.

'You may have the ring.' I twist it off my finger and turn to Dante. 'I thought this was yours.' Then I turn to his mother. 'Or does it belong to you?'

'It belongs to me.' Mr DeMartino stands and takes the ring. 'I bought it.'

Mr and Mrs DeMartino head for the hall and grab their coats.

'Lucia, this is crazy,' Dante pleads with me. 'Talk to me.'

'Oh, Dante.' I know I should reassure him, put myself in the path of his parents' exit and beg their forgiveness. I'd like to throw my arms around Dante and tell him we can go away, elope, come home, get our own apartment and start anew. How did this dinner party derail? How did such a wonderful day turn into this?

'Lucia, I'll call you later.' Dante follows his parents out the front door. Once they're gone I feel sick to my stomach.

Exodus comes in the front door, followed by Angelo, Orlando and Roberto. 'We're here for dessert,' Exodus announces. 'Where are they going?'

'Home,' Mama says weakly.

'They seemed angry,' Angelo says.

'Mrs DeMartino stomped the sidewalk so hard it looked like she was putting out cigarettes all the way to her car,' Orlando chimes in.

'What did you say?' Roberto asks me.

'I told them I was going to keep working and they didn't like it and Mr DeMartino took the ring back.'

Exodus shrugs. 'I told you they were dolts.'

'Do you want us to go after him? We could beat him up,' Orlando offers.

'Boys,' my mother says in her warning tone.

'Well, he made my sister cry.'

'No, your sister made *him* cry,' Papa says as he pours himself a glass of wine.

'Did they eat?' Roberto wants to know.

'There's plenty left.' Mama motions for the boys to sit.

My brothers take their seats as though nothing has happened, as though I didn't just return my diamond ring and defy Mrs DeMartino and change the course of my life. 'You're going to *eat*?' I ask.

'What else are we gonna do?' Roberto asks through a mouthful of DeMartino dinner rolls. 'Starve because the DeMartinos are idiots?'

I watch them in disbelief, as though I am watching a strange family on Commerce Street through their front window. When you come from a big family, it's almost as if you're one person; each brother or sister is an aspect of you, like an octopus with tentacles that move in different directions but are always part of the whole. Roberto is the eldest, so he's the leader; Angelo came second, and he's the peacemaker; Orlando is the middle child, so he is the dreamer; Exodus is the wild card, the free spirit, unpredictable. And then there's me, I'm the baby, I will always be the baby, no matter how much white is in my hair. Because I am a girl, I am my mother's helper and also their maid. Every shirt at this table is pressed by me on my Saturdays off. My brothers work at the market and, until they marry or I marry, I serve them.

Mama pulls plates from the dish server behind her and passes them out to the boys. Orlando loads *bracciole* onto his plate. 'I can't believe you wasted all this good meat on the DeMartinos,' he says. He is tall and thin, but the biggest eater in the family. His angular face looks like an intellectual's. He has soft, dark eyes and there is a gentleness to him.

'He'll come back,' Roberto says definitively.

'I don't think so,' Papa says softly.

'Aw, Pop. It's a lovers' spat. Everybody has those,' Angelo adds, winking at me.

'And if he doesn't come back, I wouldn't cry,' Exodus says, filling his plate. 'Look, men are like fish. You want a husband? You go out where there's lots of them, you throw out a line with some bait, and you reel him in. You check him out, and when he isn't the best, you throw him back. Throw Dante DeMartino back. You can do better.'

'He's a good catch,' Mama corrects him.

'No, no, *we* are the catches in Greenwich Village,' Exodus insists. 'Every girl in town wants to marry us. And why do you think we're prizes? I'll tell you why. Pop owns his own business and this building and we all work in it. People see dollar signs. They see the nice home Mama makes and the light bulb goes off in their heads and they think, "All that could be mine".'

'That's not a very trusting way to live in the world,' Angelo tells him.

'He's right. And you,' Roberto says, shaking his fork at me, 'better accept it.'

'Sis, don't listen to him. We aren't good judges of what love is all about. None of us is married,' Angelo says.

'Because you have it too good at home!' Suddenly my mother comes to life. 'The problem with this family is that you're all selfish. Nobody bends.' She points at me.

'Why should I bend, Mama? Bend to achieve what? To leave your home and go fifteen blocks east and do for Claudia DeMartino what I do for you, only if I go there, I have to quit my job? What would be the point of that?'

'Then don't ever get married. I should've been made out of rubber, the amount of bending *I've* had to do around here.'

'I gave you a hard life?' Papa looks at Mama.

'Not easy,' my mother fires back.

'See? You've been spared, Lucia. From a life of . . . well, this!' Angelo smiles.

'It's fine by me if Lucia never marries. I like the way she does laundry.' Roberto winks at me. My brothers laugh.

'You know what? You're not funny. Maybe you should do the dishes and *my* laundry once in a while.'

'Whoa, whoa. Now you're taking things too far. We don't want you to be unhappy, Looch. We're just protecting the family treasure.' Exodus pours himself a glass of wine.

'I am not the family treasure! But you, you're a pack of gorillas, the way you act! Everything is funny to you, isn't it?'

'Ma, the Caterina curse has kicked in,' Roberto says.

'Shut up!' Mama says to him.

'What are you talking about?' I ask him. I look at my mother, who withers my brother with a stare. 'What's a Caterina curse?'

'Roberto. Your mouth,' my father says.

'Papa. What is Roberto talking about?'

'Nothing. Nothing. Nothing.' My mother pushes her plate away and leans back in her chair.

Exodus rests his elbows on the table. 'Is there a curse on our baby sister? Is it Venetian like Pop or Barese like Mama?'

'The Barese one would involve some sort of gun play,' Orlando says. Again, my brothers laugh.

I look at Papa. 'Why didn't you tell me?'

'I wouldn't let him!' Mama interjects. 'Sometimes just knowing something like that makes it come true.'

'That's better than keeping secrets,' I say.

'Not necessarily. Secrets do a great deal of good. You take my Aunt Nicolette. One of her legs was shorter than the other. There was no need to tell her fiancé before they married. He might have run off. Instead they were married fifty-seven years.'

'Well, Ma, I'm different. I want to know everything.'

'What difference does it make? A curse is a curse.' Mama takes a sip of Papa's wine.

'It's Venetian,' Papa begins. 'Long ago, in Godega di Sant' Urbano, in the farm fields above Treviso and Venice, my brother, Enzo, and I were young men – about twenty years old. And we were farmers. Godega is a fertile valley beneath the Dolomites; you could grow anything there in the spring and summer. But we had a bigger dream. When we harvested the corn and brought it to market in Treviso, we admired the elegant *mercato* we saw there. It was a full city-block long, open, with vendors selling fruit, vegetables, fish, anything. So we saved our money, what little we had, and we came to America in 1907. We wanted to build our own market, exactly like the one we saw in Treviso. Enzo and I were a team. When we got here the shops were called grocery stores, so we made the English sound Italian and called our place "Groceria". Soon after, I met your mother at the home of my cousin. And Enzo met a girl named Caterina in Little Italy.'

'Papa, we know about your brother.' I don't want to listen to Papa's stories about the old country. 'We know you don't speak to him. We know he's a farmer in Pennsylvania and we've never seen him or met our cousins because you're still angry with one another. What does this have to do with a curse?'

'Mama and your aunt—'

'Don't call her aunt. She is not worthy of any title of affection.' Mama raises her voice.

'Mama and Caterina did not get along.'

'Pop, that's an understatement. I remember screaming fights,' Roberto adds.

Papa continues, 'It was very bad. It caused a rift between Enzo and me, one we could not repair. So, we decided we must end the partnership. We would flip a coin and the winner would buy out the loser. The winner would keep the Groceria and this building, and the loser would take his money and move out of New York.'

'We could have been a bunch of hilljacks in Pennsylvania.' Angelo clucks.

'There's a lot of dignity in farming,' Exodus corrects him.

'So, the day of the coin toss came, and your mother was expecting Lucia. This was the summer of 1925. When Enzo lost the toss, he wept. Caterina became so enraged she began to shout. That's when she placed the curse on you.' Papa turns to me.

'I don't believe in curses. That's Italian voodoo,' I tell him.

'What kind of curse, Pop?' Angelo asks.

'She said Lucia would die of a broken heart.'

'I hate that woman,' Mama mumbles.

'So, you actually believe my broken engagement is the result of that curse?'

'It looks that way,' Roberto says.

'Hold on! *I* ended my engagement. Nobody made me do it. No witch came to the door with a rotten apple, no strange bird sat in the window, and I've never walked under a ladder, so let's forget about this curse. It's irrelevant.' I wave my hand, dismissing the hocus pocus.

'You do seem to have some bad luck with boys,' Orlando says tenderly. 'There was the Montini guy. Didn't he go home to Jersey when you turned him away and threaten to drive his car into the ocean?'

'That wasn't my fault. He was nutty,' I say defensively.

'And whatever happened to Roman Talfacci?' Orlando asks.

'I beat him up. He said something untoward about Lucia, so that one was my fault,' Exodus explains.

We sit in silence for a few moments. No one knows what to say. Mama's hair has come undone and strands of white hang down around her face like string. Papa swishes the last swallow of the wine in his glass over and over again, as if he's looking for an answer inside the faceted crystal. My brothers lean back in their chairs. Maybe they believe the curse, too. Maybe they're wondering how they'll protect me in a world of spells and spirits.

The phone rings. Roberto excuses himself to answer it.

'It's DeMartino for you,' he tells me from the doorway.

My mother looks at me pleadingly. 'Talk to him. He's such a nice boy.'

I go into the kitchen and take the phone from Roberto. 'Dante.'

'I got the ring back from Papa,' Dante says.

I don't say anything.

'Lucia, I still want to marry you. Mama is all mouth. She doesn't mean half of what she says.'

I still don't say anything.

'Lucia, what's going on? Have you met someone else?'

'No, no. Nothing like that.' Although that's not exactly true. I did meet someone new: Dante DeMartino, the good son, so good he is weak, a man whose happiness comes from pleasing his parents.

'I've waited a long time for you, Lucia,' he says softly.

'I know.' I'm very aware of how long I have made him wait. Sometimes I feel guilty, but then I remember that complete surrender is for wives, not for betrothed career girls.

'I want to get married. Don't you feel it's time?' Dante says.

How can I tell him that when I'm at work, time seems unimportant, that I see my life ahead of me, full of exciting things to learn, and a world where the creative possibilities are endless? He wouldn't understand. I remember his face when I told him about my raise. He was pleased for me, but he wasn't proud.

'I'm sorry, Dante.'

Dante sighs as though he is going to respond, but he doesn't. He says goodnight and hangs up. We've been together for a long time and usually our spats are over quickly. But somehow, this argument feels like the end of us. I wipe my forehead with the dishtowel and go back into the dining room, where my father and mother wait at the table. My brothers have left.

'Lucia, what did you say to him?' My mother looks at me hopefully.

'I can't go through with it.'

Mama exhales and looks at Papa with a disappointment I have not seen before. In her eyes I have failed. I chose a good man from a fine family and now I've ruined it. How can I tell her that love should inspire me, not drain me? How can I tell her that I cannot, no matter how much I love Dante, marry him and live in his family home, where I know I am not valued beyond the chores I can do and the meals I can prepare? This is my mother's life, and to say those things would only hurt her. The idea that I have caused unhappiness to so many people in one evening upsets me and I begin to cry. Instead of making a scene, I climb the stairs to my room, two at a time.

When I get to my room, the collar on the dress Mrs DeMartino gave me feels like it's choking me. I yank it open, tear the buttons all the way down the bodice, and step out of the dress. I pull on my bathrobe, lie down on my bed, and look up through the skylight at the moon hanging overhead like a silver charm, far away with barely a glint of light coming from its surface. Here in my attic room, high off the ground, I am Rapunzel, though I know I am no princess. I sent the prince away tonight. Even though I believe I will not love any man more than I love Dante, I simply know I don't love him enough. I reach for the phone and call Ruth. The phone rings and rings. I hang up when I remember that she's out with Harvey and her in-laws. I hope she's having a better evening than I did.

'I'm tired,' I call out when I hear a knock at the door.

'It's Papa.'

He comes in and sits down on the stool of my vanity table, as he has done so many times when I've been hurt or disappointed or I've let someone down. No matter what happens to me, my father always knows what to say.

'Your mother is worried,' he begins.

'I'm sorry, Pop.'

'I am not worried.'

Hearing this gives me hope. 'You're not?'

'No. You know what you're doing. Why should you marry when you aren't ready? What good would come of that? I don't believe in the old ways when it comes to marriage. When I was a boy, our wives were chosen for us long before we even knew what a wife was. I was engaged to a girl in Godega. I knew I didn't want her, but my father insisted.'

I sit up and look at my father. 'I thought you came here to start the market. But you were running away, too?'

'I was.'

'So you do understand!'

'Your mother thinks I've put crazy ideas into your head. She thinks you're too independent. But I wish for you the same thing I wish for my sons: to work hard and live a good life. I hope you will always be independent. That means you will always be able to take care of yourself.'

'Mama is old-fashioned.'

'Her way works for her. It doesn't work for you. I tried to explain that to her but she doesn't want to hear it. She believes a mother and daughter should be the same.'

'But we're not the same, Pop. I can't get along with Mrs DeMartino just because I'm supposed to. I don't feel any duty towards her! How dare she tell me I must quit my job as though it's her decision to make! If she decides that, what else will she say and do? I'd be miserable on First Avenue with her. I want so much more. I have so many goals.'

'But you're a *woman,* Lucia. Listen to me. A woman is not like a man. She doesn't get to choose. She follows her heart and that's what makes the map of her life. You love to work and that's good. But to be a good wife and mother, that's a decision of the heart. If you don't feel it, you must not do it. You will be unhappy and your children will be worse. The unhappy man finds compensation outside the home. He works, he lives in the world, he can find joy outside of himself. But a woman builds the home and if she is unhappy there, she suffers and her children suffer. Your mother wanted a big family. She had a picture of this house, her kitchen, her children, long before she met me. She *knew*, you see. She was happy each time she found out she was having a baby. She wanted twelve! I told her five was plenty. It was in her to be a mother, like it is in you to work. You're a happy girl because you have a happy mother, a mother who wants to be a mother. And I'm a happy husband because she's a good wife. Do you understand what I'm saying?'

'I do, Papa.'

'Now, someday, you may meet a man who you will give up everything for. And when that happens, you will want to make a home for him. When that man comes along, you will know it. It isn't Dante because you didn't want to sacrifice everything for him.'

'I know, Papa. I didn't.'

'And . . .'

'And what?'

'And his mother is a *strega.*' Papa says this so nonchalantly, I can't help but laugh.

'You're right, she is a witch. But I could have handled her.'

'You say that, but I doubt it. I don't think a lion tamer for the Ringling Brothers could control that woman.'

'I know one thing, if I ever find a man who wants me to be happy as much as you, it will be a miracle,' I say.

'Maybe I'm not the best judge of what you should do. You know an artist should never stand too close to the canvas while he paints, because when he does he cannot see what he's doing. The same is true of a father. I am too close to you to truly understand what you are. If it were up to me, I would have you stay here with me and Mama forever. But I know that's selfish. You deserve your own life, Lucia.'

Papa goes to the door and turns to face me. 'Career girls.' He closes the door behind him.

I look down at my hand, where the white diamond nestled in gold used to rest on my finger. How plain my hand looks without it! These are the hands of a seamstress, not a wife, I think as I study them. Maybe there are times when the curse lands on the right girl.

Chapter Three

The sun is so bright in the Hub, Ruth has thrown clean muslin over the hot-pink bouclé suit she's finishing. 'Nothing worse than ordering a bright pink suit and winding up with faded Pepto Bismol,' she tells me.

'Should I close the shades?'

'No, no, I'm almost done. If you need refuge, Delmarr has his shades down.'

I haven't seen much of Delmarr this morning, so I knock on his office door. He doesn't answer, but I know he's in there. I can smell the cigarette smoke through the transom. I knock again.

'Go away,' he says.

I push the door open. 'Are you all right?'

Delmarr sits back in his chair with his feet propped up on the windowsill, staring out at Fifth Avenue. 'I've been shafted again.'

'What happened?'

'I brought the red gown to Hilda, she met with the McGuire

Sisters, they flipped for the dress, ordered three in red and three more in emerald green.'

'But that's great news!'

'For Hilda Cramer, the name on the label. For me? I get so little credit for designing the gown, I might as well be the bonded messenger who delivered the thing.'

'Some day you'll have your own label.' I take a seat opposite Delmarr.

'Not if I stay here.' Delmarr is right. In this business, the designer who does the work never gets the credit. Delmarr takes his orders from Hilda Cramer and follows through with her wishes.

Hilda Cramer looks exactly as I imagine the Head of Design for a major department store should look. She must be close to sixty years old, and she is long and thin, like a dress model, which she once was. She never made the leap to magazine work because she didn't have the face for photographs. She has a high forehead, a long nose and thin lips. She wears her hair in a short black bob, streaked with white. Hilda has the confidence and the aristocratic air that make her a good front man for the Custom Department. She fancies herself a Pauline Trigere or a Hattie Carmichael or a Nettie Rosenstein, a designer of refined elegance and Fifth Avenue style, but we all know Hilda hasn't picked up a sewing needle since the Great Depression. She's a figurehead, and short of having her likeness on the coin of a B. Altman charm bracelet, she rules us like the empress she is. And we obey. We know the rules. This is fashion, so it's about the dress and the name on the label, not the great mind who created it or the team that assembled it.

'She's old, Delmarr.'

'Not old enough. I'm looking at twenty more years of indentured servitude with good pay. She'll never retire.'

'Did she thank you at least?'

'You know how her eyes bug out of her head when she's pleased? Well, her eyes bugged. Then she grabbed the gown out of my hands and said, "I'm late." Then she was gone, and someone from retail placed the rest of the order.'

Delmarr swings his legs off the windowsill and swivels around in his chair. 'No matter how hard I try, and what inroads I make, I cannot get to the top. It's a conundrum. How does talent climb to the top? How did Hilda do it?'

'By sheer ambition.'

'Not enough. She figured out how to make the big cheeses around here believe she knew something. Or everything. How do you do that?'

'I don't know.'

'And that's why I've got the phoney title of Chief Designer when, in fact, all I am is Hilda Cramer's valet. A talented valet, but still a servant.'

'I think you should talk to her.'

'And say what? "Out of my way, old bag"?'

'No, you should tell Hilda that you want to start meeting clients to get their input, since you're making the adjustments and modifications—' I stop talking because Delmarr's face has turned as white as the bolt of cotton piqué propped behind his desk.

'Really, Miss Sartori?' Hilda Cramer's deep voice says from the doorway. 'Now a sewing-machine operator is weighing in on how I should run my department? Please!' Miss Cramer holds a pair of red beaded shoes. For a moment, I am shocked she remembers my name, then I feel as though I might throw up, so I grip my stomach with my hand. I look at Delmarr, who is standing but has closed his eyes. 'Out, Sartori,' Hilda orders. Then she turns towards Delmarr. 'I want to speak to you.'

I scurry out of the office and back to my desk. Ruth pulls me behind the changing screen. 'It was too late to warn you when I saw her coming. She moves like a python! What did she say? Did you see that suit? It's a Schiaparelli.'

I can't believe Ruth is thinking about fashion at a moment like this. 'She's going to fire Delmarr,' I whisper, 'and then me.'

'No, she won't. Who will do all the work? Do you know how hard it is to find talented people? She's not a fool. She knows we'd pick up our pincushions and head over to Bonwit's before she could say whipstitch.'

'Sartori. Kaspian. I need to see you,' Delmarr announces from his office. Hilda Cramer pushes past him and goes out through the Hub's double doors.

'I'm so sorry,' I tell Delmarr. 'Did she hear me?'

'Only the last part.'

'I'm fired, aren't I?' The thought of losing my job is like death to me.

'No, you're okay. For Godsakes, when you smell Je Reviens, she's in the area, so put a lid on it.'

'So, what did she say?' Ruth asks.

'Well, we have to make the gowns for the McGuire Sisters. And then . . . we have to build twenty-seven nun's habits for the novitiates at the Sacred Heart in the Bronx.'

'No!' Ruth flings herself against the wall melodramatically. 'She's trying to torture us.'

'That's right. Black worsted and white linen.'

'She overheard me and she's punishing us,' I say wearily.

'No,' Delmarr says, sounding more exhausted than consoling. 'Remember, this land is leased to Altman's by the Holy Roman Church and the least we can do is keep their devoted nuns in costume.'

'But she jobbed them out last year.' I look at Ruth. 'This is all my fault. I'm sorry.'

'No, it's much better than that,' Delmarr says. 'It's *my* fault. The McGuire Sisters know the truth.'

'They know you designed the gowns?' I am flabbergasted. No wonder Hilda looked mad enough to rip cloth with her bare hands. 'Who told them?'

'I was at El Morocco for cocktails after work and I had the sketch of the gown in my portfolio. I was sitting at the bar and a cute dish, who was there with a couple of friends, asked what I did for a living, so I showed her the sketch. Well, the dish turns out to be the hairdresser for Phyllis McGuire. She told Phyllis all about me, so when Hilda walked in for her consultation, Phyllis said, "I want to see Delmarr's gown".'

Ruth and I look at each other and squeal. What a coup! What luck that Phyllis McGuire remembered Delmarr's name and repeated it to Hilda.

'Ladies! Please,' Delmarr says, though he can't help smiling. 'So the nun's habits are Hilda's little way of keeping me in my place.'

Ruth and I go back to our desks. I look at her and know she is thinking what I'm thinking: Hilda Cramer won't be able to keep

Delmarr in his place for long, no matter how many nuns in the Bronx need new habits.

The first rule of life in a large family is that someone is always in trouble, but the turnover is frequent, so no one ever stays in the hot seat too long. When I broke off my engagement, Mama didn't speak to me for a while, but eventually she warmed up and now things seem almost back to normal. It helps that the ladies at our church are offering their sons as potential suitors, as if they were sweaters and all I have to do is choose the best cashmere. Mama is anxious for me to find a worthy husband, and when I hear her weeping in the kitchen, I worry that her tears are for me.

'Mama, what's wrong?' I ask, putting my arms around her. She cracks an egg into a bowl of ricotta cheese and adds a pinch of salt. 'I'm a terrible mother.' She motions for me to add the flour slowly as she beats the mixture with a fork, forming a dough to make pasta.

'Why do you say that? It's not true.' I take the bowl from Mama and finish folding the rest of the flour into the dough. She sprinkles more flour across the pastry board on the kitchen table and throws the dough onto the board with a thud.

'It is true. Your brother Roberto is getting married.' Mama kneads the dough, adding handfuls of flour to thicken it.

'What?' Roberto has not brought a girl home for Sunday dinner or announced that he was attending another family's Sunday dinner or made mention of any serious girlfriend. 'Mama, are you sure about this?'

'Yes. Tomorrow. At Our Lady of Pompeii. In the back.' Mama

shudders. 'In the sacristy.' She rolls the dough into a large circle, then takes a paring knife and cuts it into long strips.

'Oh my God! You're serious.' I sit down. Mama knows that she does not have to explain what this means. As they say in the movies, this is a shotgun wedding. A girl does not get the ceremony at the big altar in Our Lady of Pompeii unless she's earned it. 'To whom?'

'Rosemary Lancelatti.' Mama cuts the strips of dough into small rectangles.

'Who is she?'

'The girl carrying his child. He told your father and me this morning. We're supposed to shut up and accept it.' With two fingers Mama begins rolling the small rectangles one at a time into tiny tubes. She flicks the finished *cavatelli* into a pile. I sit down and begin rolling the pasta with her. We have spent so much time like this, the two of us, making macaroni. There's something soothing about mixing the dough, rolling it out and pressing it into shapes. 'I don't know, Lucia. I just don't know.'

A hundred things go through my mind at once. This is a fine way for the eldest son of the Sartori clan to start his family. What a bad example he sets for his brothers, though they are far from boys. They are men, but they act like teenagers. Not one of them has settled down. Why should they? They work at the market, eat their meals at home, have their laundry done by their sister, come and go as they please and stay out late without question. Mama takes care of them with the same zeal she did when they were children: she cooks and cleans and makes sure everyone goes to Mass each Sunday. Yet the boys have their freedom; most of their dalliances are never discussed, never mentioned. Occasionally I'd walk in on them discussing a girl, but they would clam up when they saw me. Now I wish Roberto had said something. Maybe we could have avoided this. This is awful. It's 1950. Girls know better, at least the girls I know.

'She trapped him,' my mother says, reading my thoughts.

'Oh, Mama, maybe not. Maybe it was a one-time—'

My mother bangs the bowl on the table. 'Your brother is weak. How many times have I told him to be careful? The world is full of girls who are looking for a home like ours.'

'Let's give her the benefit of the doubt here.'

'Why? We know what kind of girl she is, Lucia.'

'Sometimes things happen out of order.' I wish I could explain the world outside 45 Commerce Street, where there are all sorts of new rules and customs, where sophisticated people make their own decisions about their lives without checking with the parish priest, but that's a discussion for another day, and one I will never have with Mama.

'Out of *order*! What do you mean? Your brother knows better. Carrying on like that without being married is a sin! I better never catch you . . .'

'Don't worry, Mama.' I do my best to reassure her, but she is too angry to listen.

'I am so ashamed. I was so proud of Roberto! The first Sartori to serve his country. He was such a fine example, Orlando and Angelo followed him into the service. Even Exodus signed up when he was old enough, because he wanted to be just like Roberto. Your brother has ruined everything we built.'

'We aren't ruined. Roberto is going to marry her.'

My mother doesn't listen; she cannot hear me as she stays focused in her tirade. 'I worked so hard to teach my children to be decent, to have morals, to have standards, to be responsible and . . . aware. Stay awake, I told your brothers. Check the girl's background. What are her parents like? Where are they from? Be careful, Sicilians are different, I said. And what does he do? He finds a Sicilian and makes a baby!'

'I'm sure he didn't intend to do anything *to* us, Mama.' I make myself useful, transferring the *cavatelli* from the board to a tray lined with waxed paper.

'It's too late!' she cries. 'The story is all over Brooklyn already. Everyone knows you can't keep bad news secret. It's like trying to hide a dead body!'

'Mama, we'll get through this.'

'No, no, never. Where do you go to win back your good reputation, Lucia? I'll tell you, nowhere. It is gone forever.' Mama pulls open the utensil drawer and removes all the spoons, wooden, stainless and slotted, and rearranges them.

'What did Papa say?' I ask.

'He cried.' Mama shakes her head. 'Roberto broke your Papa's heart. He will never get over it.'

'Is she nice at least?' I ask. I correct myself. 'Nice is the wrong word. Is she a good woman?'

'*How* could she be a good woman?'

'I don't know. Maybe she's a nice girl who made a mistake.'

'Impossible! You think before you do these things!' Mama slams the utensil drawer shut and sits down at the table.

'Are they going to live here?' I ask.

'Where else?'

The last time the Sartori family processed to Our Lady of Pompeii Church on foot, with Mama in tears, was when our grandmother Angela Sartori died. We seem to have the same grim gait on Roberto's wedding day as we did the day we put Nonna in the ground. It's three o'clock in the afternoon. This kind of wedding gets the least desirable time slot. Mama already pointed out that it's at the exact time Jesus was hung from the cross on Good Friday.

Papa wears his good suit, a navy gabardine with a white shirt and dark blue silk tie. Mama wears her black funeral dress, a simple A-line sheath that buttons down the back. I decided not to put on a shroud, so I'm wearing a light brocade suit with a petal collar. The pattern of the brocade is autumnal, small gold leaves caught in an embroidered mesh of green. My shoes are simple gold satin pumps. In my purse, I carry a small orchid for Mama, who refused to pin it to her dress.

The name of our church seems appropriate today. Mama is convinced that the Sartori family is doomed and that Roberto's fate is worse than the people of Pompeii buried under the hot lava of Mount Vesuvius.

I love our church, situated on the corner of Carmine and Bleecker, nestled in the centre of a traditional Italian neighbourhood, with its cross high on the dome and, inside, the white marble walls with glittery gold veins, high ceilings and statues of saints peering out over the glimmer of candles lit for intentions. Father Abruzzi took pity on Papa and offered to do what he could under the circumstances. I've noticed that clergy can be oddly comforting once the deed is done; it's when the sin might happen that they become righteous.

I look for Roberto in the back of the church, but there is no sign of him. Mama, Papa, Angelo, Orlando, Exodus and I stand in a subdued clump near the holy-water font and wait. Mama keeps looking at the floor, hoping that when she looks up, she will have imagined this scene, and we will be at home, playing records and eating fried dough with powdered sugar as we do every Friday night.

The main doors creak and Roberto comes in, wearing a brown suit, holding open the door for his new family. The bride is a tiny thing, all of nineteen years old, with a high jet-black chignon and small features. She is pretty, even though she bites her lip and looks down at the floor. She's wearing a pale yellow suit (where she found it at this time of year, I'll never know) and black patent leather pumps. She has a whimsy net over her eyes on a small hairband. Her mother and father stand behind her, slight and birdlike, looking wounded. There are several small children behind them. Evidently, Rosemary is the eldest, like Roberto. The youngest, a girl, seems to be about eight or nine.

'Pop, this is Mrs Lancelatti and Mr Lancelatti. And this is Rosemary,' Roberto says.

'Nice to meet you,' Rosemary says too loudly. I can see she's scared.

'Hello,' my mother mumbles. The most my father can manage is a nod.

Father Abruzzi comes down the main aisle carrying a prayer book. He invites us to the sacristy, through a doorway behind the altar. We follow him in a group, and I'm sure every person who genuflects before the altar is having the same thought. 'Not good enough for the main altar.' Though Father Abruzzi tries to be pleasant, you can tell he doesn't like the situation either. He likes rules, order and a sense of organization in his parish, and he believes in announcing the banns of marriage in the church bulletin weekly for six Sundays prior to the wedding, another nicety we have not observed in this case.

Father Abruzzi wears his black cassock without the beautiful white-and-gold wedding vestment (we really are being punished!) and I take Mama's hand as he says the opening prayer. This is one of those moments when only a daughter can comfort a mother – sons don't understand piety and virtue, they are ruled by more earthly passions – so when Mama squeezes my hand, I feel useful in a situation that, for her, is hopeless.

Mr and Mrs Lancelatti gather the rest of the young children near. I'm sure they won't explain the details to them anytime soon. Angelo shakes his head in judgment. Orlando is trying to avoid getting the church giggles, a problem he's had since he was a boy. Exodus puts his arm around Papa in a gesture that says, 'Don't worry, Pop, this will be the last time this happens.' We shall live in hope.

Poor Papa. He can't speak to me about this because it would involve discussing the sexual relations of humankind, a subject he'd never bring up with his daughter. I know he's heartbroken, maybe more so than my mother who, even angry and disappointed, sees a child coming into the world as the ultimate miracle. With Rosemary's help, the workload in the house will lessen, so something positive will come of this for Mama. But for Papa, this is a personal failure, a violation of his code. How many times has he lectured the boys on respecting women; taught them by example? How many times has he disciplined them, trying to teach them how to be good men? This is a terrible ending to Roberto's story. Weddings are supposed to be the beginning of new life and love, but I can't see it here. Rosemary is too young to know what she is getting into, and Roberto, with his bad temper and immaturity, will be the worst husband in the world.

I wipe away a tear with my glove, and the advertisement in our store circular comes to mind: 'As the day grows long, so do her gloves.' I've always been taught that gloves are a sign of a true lady, but the bride isn't wearing any. She clutches the modest bouquet of yellow roses tightly, as though it's a rope she is swinging from over a giant pit. She has no idea what she's in for. I've lived with Roberto for twenty-five years. He's not easy. A wife with a moody husband never has an easy time of it. I feel someone staring at me, and I follow the feeling to Rosemary's mother. Her eyes are watery, too, but she manages a scant smile for me. Maybe it will bring Mama some consolation to know she isn't the only disappointed mother in this sacristy.

After the ceremony Papa takes us all out to eat at Marinella, a cosy restaurant on Carmine Street owned by a pal of his. I try to make small talk with the Lancelattis, who are as upset with Rosemary as my parents are with Roberto. Rosemary talks to Roberto, but I can tell that he doesn't really listen to anything she says. He keeps looking over at Papa. He still needs Papa's approval, but he knows it will be a long time before he wins it back.

*

After the reception, I change out of my suit and into a sweater, skirt and loafers. Mama and Papa are still too upset to show Rosemary the house. I was certain dinner would thaw them out, but it only made things worse. It reminded Mama that her eldest son will never have a proper reception in a big hall with a band. I hope Roberto is making his new wife feel at home. When I get down the stairs to the hall, I see a pile of stuff that must belong to her.

'Rosemary?' I call out.

'I'm in here,' she says from the living room. I find her sitting on the edge of the sofa alone. She is still wearing her wedding dress, and her veil is slipping off the back of her head.

'Wouldn't you like to change?' I ask her.

'I would love to but I don't know where to go.'

'Where's Roberto?'

'They have a delivery at the store.'

'Oh.' I smile but I'm furious. I can't believe my brother would leave his bride alone so soon after their wedding ceremony. 'Are those your things in the hallway?' I ask her. She nods. 'Well, come on, let's take them to your room.' I walk Rosemary through the dining room and show her the kitchen and the garden, which she loves. 'The living room, you know all about. Now, follow me.' I grab a suitcase and a box and start up the stairs. Rosemary tries to pick up a suitcase, but I stop her. 'Don't! No lifting!'

Rosemary smiles at me. 'Thank you.'

'I'll take care of it. Or Roberto will, when he comes home.'

I look down at her on the landing. She seems even tinier than she did at the church. 'I know this is hard for you,' I say softly. 'But everything is going to be all right.' Rosemary doesn't say anything.

She closes her eyes, trying not to cry. 'On with the tour!' I say cheerily.

'Can I bring Fazool?'

'What's Fazool?'

'My parakeet.' Rosemary lifts a scarf off a small birdcage, and a turquoise and yellow parakeet chirps when he sees her.

'That's Fazool?'

'Say hello to Lucia,' Rosemary instructs the bird.

'Pretty girl! Pretty girl!' the bird says.

'Well, that settles it. Fazool, you can stay,' I tell the parakeet as he flutters on his trapeze.

Rosemary laughs as she follows me to the first floor. I show her the door to my parents' room at the back of the house. It's closed. Then I push open another door with my elbow. 'This is it.' Rosemary comes into the room and immediately goes to the windows. She looks out on to Commerce Street. She turns and inspects the room, approving of what she sees. It's spacious, with two twin beds neatly made up in white linens, a large mirror and an old rocking chair. Mama has cleared the closet for Rosemary. 'Roberto and Angelo used to share this room, but we've kicked Angelo upstairs with Orlando. Exodus has the room directly overhead.'

'Where's your room?'

'My room is at the top. It's the attic, really.'

'So far to climb,' Rosemary says, sitting down on the corner of one of the beds.

'I don't mind it. Here's your bathroom. Luckily, you have your own.' I show Rosemary the bathroom. 'It's small but convenient.'

Mama has placed a stack of fresh white towels on the sink. 'Papa intends to make the street level into your apartment, so you'll wind up with the garden. Things happened so fast there wasn't time to . . .' I hear what I am saying and stop myself. 'Well, they'll get to it soon, I'm sure.'

'Thank you.'

'I hope you'll be comfortable here.'

Rosemary starts to cry. 'I hope so too.'

I feel so bad for my new sister-in-law, I put my arms around her. 'Don't cry. It's been a long day and you did very well.'

'Thank you,' Rosemary says again.

'I know it's far to walk, but you can always come upstairs and see me. If you need anything at all, you let me know.'

'I will.'

'Okay, I'm going to leave you to unpack and settle in. On Friday nights, we make fried dough. It's a lot of fun. I'll come and get you if Roberto works late.'

'I'd like that.' Rosemary blows her nose.

I close the door. Fazool says, 'Pretty girl.' I turn to go up the stairs, but instead go to my parents' bedroom and knock on the door. I push it open without waiting for an answer. Mama is lying on the bed with her arm thrown over her eyes.

'Mama?' I whisper.

'I'm awake,' she says without moving.

'I invited Rosemary to make *zeppoles* with us later.' Mama doesn't respond. 'Mama?'

'I hope you never have a day like this one. The look on Father Abruzzi's face. I wanted to die,' Mama moans.

'Father Abruzzi is not an expert on marriage and he doesn't have a family.'

Mama sits up. 'Don't ever say anything against a priest.'

'I'm not saying anything against him. But he can't understand what you're going through, not really. He didn't raise four wild boys and a daughter. He doesn't have any idea about your life. And by the way, it isn't very Christian to judge our whole family based upon one member's moment of weakness. What kind of nonsense is that?'

Mama turns away from me. An argument about the Church is one I will never win, but the truth is, I just want my mother to feel better. I can see this is a job that will take a long time and I have my own chores to do, so I move to go.

'Lucia? You're right. But don't tell your father I think so.'

At B. Altman's, Fridays are Delmarr's 'planning days', when he assigns clients and gives us an overview of the latest trends. We tell him what kind of progress we're making, and he adjusts our workloads accordingly. If we're done with most of our everyday duties – hemming, repairs, fittings and building garments – he takes us on field trips to shop for fabric or trims. Ruth and I love to go with him because he makes it fun. He buys us lunch and at the end of the day always takes us to have cocktails somewhere swell like the Pierre Hotel.

Every two weeks, Fridays are also the day Maxine Neal from Accounting hands out our cheques. When she walks into the Hub and gives me my envelope, she says with a big grin, 'Congratulations on your raise. You're lucky. You have a good boss behind you.'

Maxine's lipstick is the new coral shade the girls are showing on the main floor. Her skin is a deep brown, she is dressed primly in a navy-blue wool skirt and white blouse, and her nails are always done. Whatever difficulties Ruth and I have had pushing ahead in our department, it has been harder for Maxine in hers. She graduated from City College with a degree in business studies and had no luck in finding a job at any of the accounting firms in the city. Her uncle is in charge of shipping at Altman's, and he recommended her to our Accounting Department. She is overqualified, but I know she will prove herself and advance.

'Why don't you come down here and work with us? Get on the gravy train!' I tell her.

'I'm all thumbs when it comes to sewing and I'm colour blind. Now, you still want me down here?' Maxine walks over to Delmarr and places his cheque on the work table in front of him.

'Not to sew. Never! But you can bean count,' Delmarr tells her as he pours his third cup of coffee of the morning. 'And some day, when we blow this joint, you're coming with me, Max. I'm gonna need someone with a head for business when I set off on my own.'

'I'll be there!' Maxine says.

'I'm glad to hear I'm not the only career girl who *likes* to work,' I tell her.

'Oh, it's not a matter of like,' Maxine says. 'I have to work. When you see the M-10 heading downtown at six in the morning full of brown faces, it isn't because we're career girls with a dream.' She heads out through the swinging doors to deliver the rest of the wages.

Ruth, Violet, Helen and I usually brown bag our lunches. When the weather is good, we walk up to the open porticos at the New York

Public Library on Forty-Second and Fifth or head down to Madison Square Park, at Twenty-Third Street. Today, though, and on pay day, we meet at the Charleston Garden on the sixth floor of B. Altman's for the employee discount lunch with complimentary pie and coffee. The restaurant has a southern ambience, with floor-to-ceiling murals of rolling green Georgia hills, dotted with magnolia trees in bloom.

The four of us are practically a club. We call ourselves the Flappers because we were all born in 1925. We've been devoted to one another since we met six years ago at Katharine Gibbs Secretarial School, the first stop for any New York girl out of high school who wants to develop her business skills and put something official on her résumé. I knew I would sew for a living, thanks to my grandmother's careful training, but I didn't know the first thing about business. Taking a few classes that included typing, accounting and shorthand had made me irresistible to B. Altman's, which likes to hire a well-rounded girl. I was hired first, then I put in a good word for Ruth, Ruth recommended Helen, and then Helen recommended Violet.

'How bad was it?' Helen asks, eager for all the details of Roberto and Rosemary's quick wedding.

'Awful. My poor mother. She's still wandering around acting like she's in the middle of the Blitz.'

'Can you imagine? Mrs Sartori is so proud of her family.' Ruth shakes her head.

'Not any more,' I tell her. 'But I wish my parents could put aside their feelings and be nice to the girl. These things happen.' I stab a piece of lettuce.

'I'd kill myself if I ever had to get married like that,' Violet says solemnly. 'I'm Catholic and the only girl in my family who *had* to get married was my third cousin Bernadette. They made her live in the basement until the baby was born and then she was allowed in the yard. But only at certain times.'

'How grim.' Ruth spoons her pie filling onto the plate next to the crust. The crust, which will be forgone until Ruth has the final fitting for her wedding gown, looks like an empty beige shoe. 'She should have talked to me. There's no reason for a young woman to have a baby out of wedlock. She has to see a doctor and make a plan.'

'My mother's plan would be to shoot me,' Violet counters. 'Aren't your parents mortified?' she asks me.

'Sure. But what can we do? The baby is coming. You can't stop Mother Nature,' I say.

'Do you like her?' Violet asks.

'She's very young.'

'They always are,' Helen says, taking a drag off her cigarette. 'The Sartoris have taken two big hits lately. First their only daughter calls off a respectable marriage to the son of the best baker in the Village and then their eldest son brings home a bride with a baby on the way. What next?'

'If you ask my mother, she'd say locusts. She believes she has failed as a mother. Nobody's doing what she wants us to do. I feel guilty because I started it by ending my engagement.'

'Trust me,' Ruth says. 'You ending your engagement is not what got Rosemary pregnant. Right, Violet?' Violet blushes.

'Your mother thinks Dante is the ultimate catch,' Helen says to me. 'He's a baker, so you'd never starve. He works in a family business, just like your brothers, which means you have that in common. He's Italian. If we were to invent someone for you, we couldn't come up with anyone better. Shall I go on?' Helen loves to make lists and she loves to be right, and she's getting to do a lot of both at this lunch.

'Dante is a catch below Fourteenth Street, but Lucia has bigger fish to fry,' Ruth says in my defence.

'It's more complicated than that . . .' I begin, but then I stop. Good sense would tell me to go ahead and marry Dante because he'd be nice to me and provide well. But that's not what I'm looking for. Maybe I want to be Edith Head and create costumes for the movies, or Claire McCardell and design sportswear for the masses. But these girls have heard all that before, and they are as closed-minded about my dreams as my mother.

'I can't believe you gave the ring back.' Violet sighs. 'It was the whitest and hottest stone I ever saw. Not a speck of carbon, just clean, bright, white ice.'

'I don't care about the diamond,' I say, looking down at my hand, which seems downright juvenile with my garnet birthstone ring where a real diamond once was.

'You should,' Ruth says with conviction. 'When a man buys you a diamond, he's investing in you. It makes no sense that men have all the money because they have no idea what to do with it. They don't know what's good. The only way they find out what's good is if a woman tells them. They know nothing about how to make life beautiful. They don't decorate homes or make delicious meals or dress up with any level of creativity. Okay, they like their cars. What else is there to spend money on? What better cause for the average man than a wife who likes jewellery?'

'If only men came made to order. It's so hard to find a decent fellow.' Violet stuffs her handkerchief into the cuff of her charcoal-grey suit jacket. Then she smoothes her unruly eyebrows. 'If I ever met a good man and we fell in love, even if he was flawed or, say, had some physical defect like a club foot, I wouldn't break it off. I would try to find the best thing about him and hold on to that. I would overlook the negatives. Of course, my mother believes all the truly nice boys died serving our country in World War Two.'

'Well, now, that makes me feel much better.' I dump sugar into my iced tea.

'I don't want to be mean, Lucia. But you made a big mistake,' Violet says piously. 'There is nothing wrong with Dante DeMartino. I think you're going to regret what you did.'

'Oh, please, Violet. I will not. I felt like invisible hands were trying to choke me when we talked about the wedding plans.'

'Those hands weren't invisible. They were his mother's.' Helen sips her coffee. 'Who doesn't feel a little claustrophobic when they get engaged? I did. You give up a lot. Thank God I'm still working. How many times can you scrub the four rooms in your railroad apartment? It takes me all of a half hour on Saturday morning. I need my job.'

'You are *not* a romantic,' Violet says to Helen.

'Okay, okay, I'm making it all sound like drudgery and boredom, but it's not,' Helen says. 'Marriage is wonderful. Bill is a terrific husband. But I was nervous right before we got married. I thought, I actually have to live with this man, and it scared me a little. I like to be alone. I used to love to wake up in the middle of the night to read, and I figured, that's over. I made a list of the things I was giving up in exchange for a husband and the list of what I thought I was losing was longer than the list of what I thought I was getting. But then I got married and all the things I was worried about never happened. I like him being there when I come home from work. It doesn't disturb me when I'm doing something and he walks into the room. I like sharing my bed. Sorry, Violet, I know that's crude. But I do. He holds me all night like a rag doll. I feel safe. I love that.'

'Yeah, but don't you love Sunday night knowing the next morning is Monday and you get to come to work?' No one answers me.

After a while, Violet speaks. 'I do like working here. The job I had at Karastan, the carpet company, before Helen got me in here, was horrible. First of all, I wasn't even *me* when I was working there. I was Ann Brewster because the last girl who worked there got married and all the accounts she handled got mad and went elsewhere when she quit, so the boss decided that, instead of losing accounts when girls got married, he'd come up with a name, a character really, who sells the carpet. This way, if I got killed or married, Mr Zaran would hire a new Ann Brewster in my place. What a racket! I prayed every day I would meet a man and fall in love and get married so I could go into his office and say, "Find yourself another Ann Brewster!" Then my wish came true when Helen asked me to cut patterns with her at B. Altman's. So maybe it's not so much that I love my job, I just love it a lot better than the last one.' Violet sighs.

'Having a boyfriend doesn't even compare to working,' I insist. 'When my future in-laws came to dinner and were sitting there looking me over, I'm sure Dante's mother wondered how well I could iron and his father wondered if I could run the cash register at the bakery on Saturdays. I could see the wheels turning in their heads. That's when that little voice inside me said, "Don't do it. I don't care how much he looks like Don Ameche. Don't do it! That's not the life for you!"'

Violet looks at me solemnly. 'If that little voice was being honest, it would have said, "Lucia Sartori, you're twenty-five years old and you should get married because there will be no men left when you come to your senses and decide you need a husband."'

'God, Violet, you are such a sad sack.' Ruth pats me on the back like a display item. 'Just look at Lucia. She won't have any trouble finding a nice man.'

'Whatever you do, don't talk to strange men in the street,' Violet warns me. 'One time my sister Betty talked to a man in the street, and he took her around a corner, clubbed her and stole her purse.'

Whenever we have a few moments after lunch, Ruth and I spend them in the Interior Decoration Department and imagine what our lives would be like if we actually lived in the designer showcase rooms with their period furniture and beautiful art. Ruth stops at a Louis XVI dining-room table set for an elegant party with beige linens and pale yellow china that has a pattern of small bluebirds on the rim. 'This china is downright posh!' Ruth says excitedly.

'Do you think crystal stemware makes the wine taste better?' I hold up a goblet and twist it in the light of the overhead chandelier. 'At eight dollars a glass, it should,' I answer my own question. 'I love beautiful things. Why do I have to get married to have them?'

'Okay, here's what I want.' Ruth pulls me over to the display case and points at the place settings. 'See there? Spode buttercup china. Royal Crest sterling silverware in wildflower.'

'Pure silver. Look at that trim.'

'Ma says it will be a bear to polish, but that's okay. And by the way, that is real twenty-four-carat gold in the finish.'

'For somebody who isn't too excited about becoming Mrs Goldfarb, you're pretty excited about your dishes.'

'I'm trying to walk on the sunny side.' Ruth goes to look at the linen tablecloths and napkins displayed in an etagère in the corner. I become transfixed in front of a floor-to-ceiling mirror. The top of the frame is a gilt-wood flower basket with ribbons that drape the glass. It belongs in the foyer of a Park Avenue town house with black-and-white-checked marble floors. For a moment, I see myself in the hall of one of them greeting my dinner guests.

'Do you come with the mirror?' a man's voice says with just the right touch of humour.

'No, I come with the china. I'm the best little dishwasher in Greenwich Village.'

The man laughs heartily, so I turn to see the owner of the voice. 'Oh . . . hello . . .' If I were walking, I'd stumble, but I'm speaking, so I stutter until I find the grace to close my mouth entirely.

'Hello,' he says, looking at me as though he can see through to the very wheels that spin like the works of a timepiece in my head. 'You look familiar. Do you work here?'

I search for a witty comeback, but I'm too busy sizing him up to think of a good line. Ruth walks up behind me and says clearly, 'On another floor.'

My feet feel like they're melting into my shoes. I can't take my eyes off him. He must be six foot two. He's slim with broad shoulders and big hands. I notice the hands immediately because his shirt cuffs rest on the correct breaking point over the wrist. The suit, a warm grey tweed, is a European cut, so it fits without pulling or creasing the material and the pant cuffs land precisely on the middle of his polished oxblood lace-ups made of a fine Italian leather. I know these shoes, I've seen them on display on the main floor. His shirt is crisp and white, with a wide collar fastened with a gold hook and eye at the top button, and his tie is a bold stripe of black and white. His black hair is parted on the side and neatly combed. His eyes are grey, exactly the colour of his suit, and the thick black eyebrows, smooth and neat, taper off, framing his chiselled face. The jaw is square and strong; I'm sure by evening he could use a second shave. But it's his smile that has frozen me like a lump of tundra in the Arctic Circle. His white teeth and ever so slight overbite give him, if I can say the word, even think the word, a seductive smile. I have never seen a man like this, not in person anyway. And neither has Ruth. I hear her babbling about china and silver, but it all sounds like the low drone of a sewing machine. He nods politely and acts interested in what she's saying.

When I was a girl, Papa took me to a play on Broadway where an actress stood in the middle of the stage – a street scene jammed with buildings and people, city life in full swing – the music changed and the city began to pull away, piece by piece, wall by wall, person by person, until finally the girl was alone in a vast expanse of darkness, save for the spotlight shining from the rafters. I remember thinking that she looked like a pink pearl on a black evening glove.

This is how I feel. The world has gone away. There are no display cases or dressing rooms or mirrors. Not even Ruth. There is only him and me.

'Lucia? We need to get back to work,' Ruth says, yanking my elbow.

'Right, right.' I look up at the handsome stranger. 'We have to go back to work.'

'Don't let me keep you,' he says lightly.

Ruth and I lock arms and step onto the escalator. The handsome stranger leans over the half-wall as we descend.

'Lucia di Lammermoor. Like the opera.' He grins.

Chapter Four

Ever since I met the handsome stranger, I have found every possible excuse to return to the Interior Decoration Department in the hopes of getting another glimpse of him. Now I understand criminals returning to the scene of the crime. I need to relive the thrill, no matter how brief. And there's an upside to my curiosity: I'm buying all my Christmas presents in one place. Linens for Mama, leather cufflink boxes for my brothers, a satin bedspread for Rosemary, and a small marble statue of Garibaldi on a horse for Papa.

Christmas is very different this year, with a new family member in the house. If anyone were to ask what makes the Italians from the Veneto different from the Neapolitans like Rosemary (she is, it turns out, only half Sicilian), I would say the difference begins at Christmas. We put our tree up on Christmas Eve; Rosemary's family puts theirs up the day after Thanksgiving. Venetians fast on Christmas Eve and attend a midnight vigil; southern Italians have a banquet, including seven kinds of fish prepared different ways, and attend Mass on Christmas morning. The Venetians like bunches of fresh greens on the door, plain and simple, no glitter, no bows; the Neapolitans like to decorate the outside of the building as lavishly as the inside. Mama's people come from Bari, so they like the ornate as much as the southerners, but Mama, in honour of Papa, has always deferred to the traditions of the Veneto.

But Rosemary's presence has changed our household in ways that go far beyond Christmas. We've had to figure out how to include her in our family, and her task has been to try and fit in. Even though she's young, she's a good cook and a fine baker. She taught us how to make *tartufo*, creamy vanilla ice-cream truffles with a cherry centre dipped in hot chocolate then rolled in coconut. They're so delicious, Mama and Papa have almost forgotten that she 'had to' marry my brother. Rosemary gave me the recipe and told me to put it in a box. 'Start collecting recipes, because the day you get married, you'll need them,' she said. In beautiful penmanship she had written:

ROSEMARY SARTORI'S QUICK TARTUFO

(in America SNOWBALLS)

3 bags shredded coconut

1 cup heavy cream

1 gallon vanilla ice cream (softened)

12 maraschino cherries

For chocolate drizzle:

1lb dark chocolate

¼ box paraffin wax

Melt paraffin wax with the chocolate in a double boiler on stove until liquid. Set aside. Soak coconut in heavy cream. Set aside. Roll ice cream into baseball-sized balls. Bury maraschino cherry in centre of each. Drizzle chocolate sauce on ice-cream ball, then roll in coconut until covered. Place on wax-papered cookie sheet and freeze. Yields 1 dozen tartufo.

Papa and Roberto have been working diligently on the downstairs apartment. It will be perfect for a young family, with a new kitchen in the back that leads to the garden where the baby can take sun and play. They hope to have it done well before the baby's arrival in March, but it seems as if all they do is argue about details, from what kind of faucet to put in the kitchen sink to how many shelves should be in the closet. Roberto hopes to unveil the apartment for Rosemary on Christmas Day, so every spare moment the men aren't at the Groceria, they are downstairs, sanding, pounding and painting.

Christmas is Papa's least favourite time of year because the Groceria is jammed with tourists and surly customers, with everyone wanting special orders, whereas Mama embraces the holidays with gusto. When Papa was a boy, he didn't receive gifts at Christmas. He got a trinket and some fruit at Epiphany, 6 January. In Mama's family everyone received one special gift, and then they cooked a meal for a family who didn't have enough food to make a Christmas dinner. Every holiday card that comes into the house is displayed. Mama runs wide red ribbons around the living-room door frames and pins the cards to the ribbon. By Christmas Day the archways are covered in cards. I notice Mama has pinned up a card from my ex-fiancé's family. There was no personal message, just a stamp inside that said, 'Happy Holidays from the DeMartino Bakery'. Dante did send me a card with a handwritten note that said, 'I miss you. Love, Dante', which I pinned next to the one from his parents.

Mama stacks holiday records by Bing Crosby and Frank Sinatra on the record player, and the carols play night and day. The delicious scent of anisette, butter and coconut fills the house as Mama bakes. The pantry bulges with neatly stacked tins of home-made cookies. We'll tie satin ribbons on the tins and load up the car, delivering them to relatives and friends all over Manhattan and Brooklyn during the week of Christmas.

'Lucia, do you think it would be all right if I put lights in the front window?' Rosemary asks as she untangles a string of red, green and gold Roma lights for the tree. The blue spruce that we have hauled home touches the ceiling.

'We never have,' I say. 'But if it would make you happy, we'll ask Papa.'

'That's okay. I don't need the lights.'

'No, no, you're part of the family, you should have Christmas the way you like it.'

Rosemary begins to cry.

'What's the matter?' I climb down the ladder.

'I want to go home,' she whispers. Poor Rosemary. The whole time I was engaged to Dante I worried about Christmas and how I would have to spend it with Dante's family instead of my own. I will not share this with Rosemary at the moment. Instead, I guide my sister-in-law to the couch and sit down next to her. 'But this is your home now.' As Rosemary leans back against the cushions, I see how much the baby has grown. Ro's tummy is high and round.

'No, your father and mother look at me like I'm a *puttana*.'

'They don't feel that way at all,' I tell her, but she can see through the lie. She and I know the rules, and there's no getting away from them.

'My parents raised me the same way your parents raised you,' she says. 'I knew what they expected of me and I failed them. Worse, I brought shame upon them. They can't be happy for Roberto and me because we made a mistake. And they're not wrong. A good daughter doesn't *have* to get married, she waits for her wedding night. I didn't, and now I am paying for it. It's all my fault.'

'Wait a second. Roberto is just as responsible.' I hear Ruth's voice in my head talking about what sophisticated girls do. But Rosemary is as far from sophisticated as the Christmas lights she wants to string up in the front window.

Rosemary cranes her neck to make sure only I can hear what she is about to say. 'Roberto is a man, and they always said it and I never believed it, but it's true – a man is forgiven. The girl is always at fault. Forever marked. People say, "Roberto did the right thing." But that's not what they say about me. I'll never be able to make this right. Never. But Roberto already has. He married me, so his debt is cleared.'

'Do you love Roberto?' I ask.

'With all my heart.'

'In my mind – and maybe tomorrow Saint Ann will see that I am hit by a bus for saying this – I believe that love makes the difference.'

I hope Rosemary understands I am talking about making love itself, not just loving a man. 'Rules are rules. But I believe if you are going to marry the man, there is nothing wrong with making love to him before the ceremony. One God. One man. What's wrong with that?'

'Everything, if you get pregnant.' Rosemary exhales slowly.

'You know that I was engaged . . .'

'Dante DeMartino. So many girls in Brooklyn are in love with him!' Rosemary turns to me. 'All the mothers send their daughters to pick up the bread when he makes deliveries. They pour out of the apartment houses when the DeMartino truck comes through!' Just speaking about her old neighbourhood cheers her up. 'Did you and Dante . . .' Rosemary can't say the words.

'Make love? No. I *would* have married him if we had. But I knew it wasn't meant to be.'

'How did you know?'

'I always felt like there was enough time. And I guess what I'm waiting for, when it comes to love, is a man who makes time go by so fast that I can't hold on to it.' I prop my feet on the coffee table. I can't believe I'm confiding my deepest feelings to Rosemary. These sorts of revelations are usually reserved for Ruth. But I can tell Rosemary is a good egg and I want to be her friend, since she's already my sister.

I almost tell her about the mysterious man I saw at B. Altman's, the one with the smile and the beautiful hands. Besides my lunch strolls, when I look for him, I catch myself thinking about him a lot too. On the main floor one day, I thought I smelled his cologne, so I followed a man into Custom Shirts. When it wasn't Mystery Man, I felt like a fool. I told Ruth about it and she laughed so hard, I knew that what I was doing was crazy. Why can't I let go of the idea of him? And why was I hooked so fast? It was probably something as simple as the low sparkle of chandelier lighting or the panels of leather on the walls or the bowl of butter-pecan ice cream I had for dessert at lunch that made me feel full and woozy and a little wanton. Maybe the scene itself: the model dining room with the glistening silverware and fine linens and delicate china made me need a handsome stranger to enter stage left and take my hand and whisk me off into the future. I've been waiting my whole life to feel that magnetic attraction. But I can't tell Rosemary any of this, I'd sound ridiculous.

'We need to finish the tree.' I stand and stretch.

'Lucia?'

I turn to her. 'Yeah?'

'I thought you were so fancy, but you're just a girl.'

'Fancy?' I laugh and look down at what I'm wearing, corduroy pants and Papa's old wool sweater.

'You're so beautiful. Your hair is always shiny. And your clothes, I've never seen anything like them except in *Charm* magazine. You're always going out the door looking smart on your way to something important. I admire that.'

'Rosemary, I'm not fancy. I'm just a seamstress. I love clothes. I think they're art. That's all.' I extend my hand to Rosemary and help her up.

Papa and Roberto come up from the new apartment, where they've been working all morning. They chat with each other, oblivious to us. I interrupt them. 'Papa, Rosemary would like to put some lights in the front window. Is that all right with you?'

'Sure, sure,' he says without looking at Rosemary.

'Tell *her* then,' I say quietly.

Papa looks confused, but he knows what I mean. He hasn't had a conversation with Rosemary since the wedding day. I'm sure he doesn't realize it, but he avoids eye contact. Maybe he believes if he doesn't look at her, the whole incident will go away. But deep down Papa has a dear and tender heart. Despite his hurt, he does right by Rosemary as family: he plasters her walls, grouts tiles in her new bathroom, and gives Roberto a raise at the Groceria to ensure hers and the baby's future. But he doesn't acknowledge her. He's a traditional man and he cannot accept what has happened.

Now he turns to her. 'Rosemary, you may put the lights in the window.' He looks at her for the first time since he met her at Our Lady of Pompeii, as he stands here next to the half-lit Christmas tree. He even manages a smile.

Rosemary faces my father. 'Thank you, Mr Sartori.' Her voice breaks and she looks down at the floor.

Papa turns to go. I grab his arm and raise my eyebrows. He knows the look – my mother gives him the same one, the wordless prompt – and he obeys.

'Rosemary. You may call me Papa.' There is a moment of silence, then Papa goes into the kitchen. Roberto looks at me and then at his wife. He goes to Rosemary and holds her tenderly. Even temperamental Roberto has a soft side; maybe he's learning how to be a husband. I can see my brother truly loves his wife, and that all these weeks of whispering with Mama and worrying and praying for them were unnecessary. There is a real bond between them, the kind I hope to have some day. Roberto gives Rosemary his handkerchief, and she dries her tears.

I look at Rosemary and think that I could be her, I could be in Claudia DeMartino's living room tonight begging to have some part of Christmas the Sartori way, maybe to put the crèche in the fireplace, like we do here, negotiating Christmas as though it were a maze instead of a holiday. I'm sure she'd make me feel like an outsider. But I'm relieved not to be married, not to have to give this up, I want to be here, with *my* family.

'Where are the lights, Ro?' Roberto asks.

'Over there,' she says, pointing to a box near the base of the tree.

'Show me where you want them,' he says gently to his wife.

'You sure I look all right?' Mama asks me as she stands before my three-way mirror.

'Okay, how about, you look gorgeous?' She does. My mother has a beautiful shape. She is tall and broad-shouldered and she has great legs. It's hard to believe she's over fifty. It's not just her figure, though, it's her face that makes her stunning, her smile and her dark brown eyes, soft as sable.

'Thank you for making this for me.' Ruth and I made this dress for Mama in between commitments to finish luxurious gowns for the standard round of holiday parties attended by society matrons. I designed the off-the-shoulder blue velvet dress with a trumpet skirt and a long, slim silhouette, very Parisian. To finish the effect, Mama has pulled her hair into a chignon and wears a large cabochon brooch of faux sapphires, and glittery Austrian crystals cinched on her waist. 'Is this good enough for the McGuire Sisters?' she says as she twirls.

'They may have you come up onstage and model the dress.'

'You know, I heard them on the radio. On *Kate Smith.* And they were wonderful.'

'Now you'll see them in person.' I give my dress a final once-over in the mirror and tell Mama, 'Papa and Delmarr are waiting downstairs. Let's go.'

Mama puts her arms around me and looks at our reflection in the mirror. 'Lucia, thank you for this dress. And for everything. You always seem to know the right thing to say to me when I'm upset. You're a good friend.'

'Mama, it's easy. You're my favourite.'

'When I first saw you, right after you were born, you weren't blue and grey like the boys and your face wasn't smushed like an old apple. You were beautiful from the moment you breathed. You were a golden pink, and though your eyes were closed, the line of them curved up like a smile. You were peaceful and gentle. And I could see even then that you would grow up to be a great beauty.'

'Oh, Mama.' If I'm such a number, why do I have a platonic date on New Year's Eve?

'No, no, I mean it. I knew you would surpass me in every way and I wanted that. I prayed for that. And now you have.'

I thank Mama, and she picks up her purse to go. As I follow her down the stairs, I can't help but think how deep the ties in my family are. I wonder if outsiders would find it odd that I actually *like* to socialize with my parents. Maybe there are families in which the laces are loose and there is room to consider your own feelings first. But my brothers and I weren't raised that way. We are bound to one another. Maybe it's an Italian trait, or maybe it's just the way things took form in our home, but there's no way out of it. This truth defines my life. And I'm not unhappy about it.

Delmarr rises from Papa's easy chair and whistles, which makes Mama blush. 'Mr Sartori, we are the luckiest men in New York City.'

Papa takes Mama in his arms and kisses her. 'Yes, we are.'

'Hey, we haven't even had drinks yet,' Delmarr says with a grin. He looks at me. 'You and I are chaperones for these two tonight. No funny business in the back seat. Dem are da rules.'

'Aye aye, sir,' Papa says.

'I can't believe Lucia Sartori chose me for her escort tonight. Me, over all the suitors who leave notes on her desk and enquiries with the doorman at Altman's! I know how privileged I am!'

'Oh, Delmarr, it is I who am honoured.' I laugh.

'This is why we love you. All that beauty and still a streak of humility.' Delmarr takes my hand and opens the door. 'Come Cinderella, we're off to the ball!'

As we drive uptown, the dark winding streets of Greenwich Village give way to the bright broad avenues of midtown. As happy as I am to be with my good friend Delmarr on this special night, I wish I were in love. This is the kind of evening I've always dreamed of, and I know Dante would not have truly appreciated it. He would be as happy to sit on our stoop and toast the New Year with Papa's grappa. I think about the handsome stranger and wonder where he is and what he's doing. Does he ever think about me? I let myself believe that he might.

They still call the awning over the entrance to the Waldorf Astoria Hotel 'the carriage stop', even though it has been years since Park Avenue has seen a horse and buggy. Delmarr pulls up in his black Buick sedan (it's at least nine years old but in mint condition). One of several doormen races to the car and opens the door for me. I step out onto the sparkling sidewalk, which seems to have been poured with chips of diamonds in the cement. Delmarr comes and takes my arm while the doorman helps Mama out of the back seat.

My parents join us on the sidewalk, and I check Papa's tie, a gift from me, a soft silk in palest blue, cut just a bit wider for evening wear. It matches the handkerchief in his pocket. It took me hours to roll the hem of the silk on that handkerchief, but it was worth it. He and Mama look spectacular.

We blend into the crowd. Women in lavish satin gowns of the season's most popular colours, muted shades of charcoal grey, rose and chocolate brown, sashay through the doors on the arms of their escorts, handsome men turned out in tuxedos with starched white shirts and sprigs of green in their lapels. The chatter is sprinkled with laughter. As we climb the stairs to the lobby, a string quartet nestled on the landing underscores our entrance. This is what the society pages call uptown glamour – every detail is attended to, including the air itself which is filled with music.

'Come, revellers. Let us all welcome 1951 with a bang and say goodbye to 1950 with a raspberry,' Delmarr says as we go through the gilded doors of the nightclub. The Club Room is packed; as many as eight people sit round the small granite-topped tables. In the low smoky light, all I can see are red cinders from cigarettes and pale shoulders leaning into conversations. The scent of gardenia, orange blossom and rich tobacco lingers in the air as we are led to our table. And what a table! 'Ringside,' Delmarr calls it. He and Papa hold the chairs for Mama and me, then as they take their seats,

Delmarr whispers, 'Drink up. Tonight is on the house, courtesy of the McGuire Sisters.' Delmarr is in such a good mood, he hardly seems to mind that although the McGuire Sisters are onstage in his dresses, tomorrow the papers will give the credit to Hilda Cramer.

A combo takes the stage and begins to play. The percussionist, handsome and lanky with skin the colour of toffee, moves wire whisks across the drums so smoothly and quickly, they seem like wings. 'These guys are great,' Delmarr says. 'They usually play at the Village Vanguard.'

'Right near Commerce Street?' my father asks.

'You could walk,' Delmarr tells him.

Papa puts his arm around Mama. Maybe one of his New Year's resolutions will be to take her to jazz clubs in our neighbourhood. The waiter places flutes of champagne on our table, then with small silver tongs drops a raspberry into each glass, creating a pink fizz over the sandy bubbles. Papa pulls Mama close and kisses her ear. They are still in love, which seems like a miracle to me. Tonight they are carefree, away from the work, bills and children that give them headaches. I get a pang in my stomach thinking about how sad they were when I broke off with Dante. What good parents don't want their daughter to meet a fine young man and fall in love and get married? They just want me to have what they have.

'If you're gonna be my date, you'd better pep up. I don't need a lead anchor on my ankle on New Year's Eve.' Delmarr toasts me.

'Is this better?' I sit up straight in my chair.

'You're the only girl in the room in gold lamé.'

'That was intentional,' I tell him. After Ruth and I cut the material for this dress, I hid the bolt under last year's samples.

'You certainly stand out. I feel like I'm doing the town with Bathsheba. The way this spotlight is hitting you, it looks like you're in Macy's window.'

'Excuse me,' a familiar voice says behind me. 'Delmarr, how are you?'

I look up, but it's hard to see because the gentleman is standing directly in the beam of an overhead stage light. I shade my eyes. My dream man from Interior Decoration! It's him! I can't believe it! I was thinking about him so much today, I must have willed him here.

'Well, if it isn't young Clark Gable.' Delmarr stands and shakes his hand. 'Mr John Talbot, I'd like to introduce you to my date this evening, Lucia Sartori. And these are her parents, Mr and Mrs Sartori.'

'I'm pleased to meet you.' John Talbot extends his hand, first to my mother, then to my father, and finally to me. When he touches me, the same woozy feeling I had in Interior Decoration overcomes me. I can't wait to tell Ruth that it wasn't the butter-pecan ice cream after all.

John places his hand on Delmarr's shoulder. 'Well, I just wanted to say hello and wish you all a healthy and happy New Year.' He smiles and moves back into the crowd.

'My, my, he's handsome,' Mama comments.

'How do you know him?' Papa asks Delmarr. Uh oh, Papa already senses something. When it comes to me, he has radar.

'He's a jack of all trades. I did some business with him on an overrun of fabric out of the Scalamandre Silk Mills. He made me an excellent deal,' Delmarr tells Papa matter-of-factly.

Mama and Papa go back to their conversation and drinks. Delmarr looks at me and raises an eyebrow. 'Do you know him?'

'I saw him at the store one day.'

'He had the fish eye for you tonight.'

'Do you think so?' If only Delmarr knew how much that thrills me. *John Talbot.* At last I know his name. It's beautiful. I can see it engraved on a brass plate or the binding of book. It's an important name. It sounds upper crust, like the names of the girls who order opera coats for every fall debut of the Philharmonic and live in town houses on the Upper East Side.

'Don't get any ideas. He's a man about town. I see him at all the best places with all the best girls.'

'But—'

'Lucia, you're not meant to be one in a stable. You're better than that. You're a stand-alone girl.'

The lights dim further and the combo launches into an overture. There is a drum roll. In the pitch black, the McGuire Sisters take their places behind three microphones, the silver staffs shining in the dark. They begin to sing their smooth a cappella harmonies, and the crowd goes wild as the lights slowly come up. Delmarr says that the word is spreading about them; they are destined to be big recording stars. I can see why. They are stunning redheads, with fine features and big dark eyes. And those figures!

Mama and Papa watch the show with delight. To think that just last night, they were both wearing their reading glasses, poring over bills at the kitchen table and arguing about which ones to pay first. They never treat themselves. Mama sacrifices everything for her children. If I didn't bring home fashionable shoes and clothes for her, she'd wear the same old Oxfords for years on end. She refuses when I offer her money for the family till, though I make a good salary. She always says, 'Put it in the bank.' I will never be one third the lady my mother is. I close my eyes and make a mental picture. When I'm old I want to remember the two of them just as they are on 31 December 1950.

Delmarr nudges me when the McGuire Sisters walk offstage one by one after the opening number. The lights and music change and they reappear in Delmarr's ruby-red gowns. I wish Ruth were here to see our handiwork. After a few songs, the sisters go behind an upstage screen and emerge in emerald-green versions of the gown, singing, 'We're in the money!' Papa raises his hands high in the air and applauds, as do many in the audience. Delmarr leans back in his chair and says, 'Damn, I'm talented.'

Then Phyllis McGuire, the baby sister of the group, comes forwards. A man in a tuxedo hands her a papier-mâché clock and she shouts, 'Countdown to 1951: ten, nine, eight . . .' The crowd joins in and when we hit 'one', the room goes wild. From giant nets along the ceiling, multicoloured balloons and silver confetti rain on us. We're all on our feet, Papa kisses Mama, Delmarr kisses me on the cheek and spins me around. The McGuire Sisters applaud as the crowd cheers. As I'm shaking my head and the confetti is falling away like snow, Delmarr grabs me again, this time by the waist, dipping me almost to the floor. 'Delmarr, put me down!' But it isn't Delmarr, this is a cashmere suit, and it isn't deep blue, it's black, and the tie isn't Delmarr's hunter's green, it's a silver jacquard. And though I have no intimate knowledge of Delmarr's lips, I know these aren't his because this person doesn't smell like Delmarr. This man's neck smells like musky amber and cassia and fresh rain. It's John Talbot and I fit in the crook of his neck like a violin.

'Mr Talbot . . .' is all I can say to him. Standing nose to nose with him, the sounds in the room fade to a muffle, I feel his warm skin and look into his eyes. He looks at me with such intensity that I have to close my eyes.

'Happy New Year,' he whispers. He lets go of me and disappears once more into the crowd.

'What was *that*?' Delmarr asks, looking after him.

I don't answer. I just sit down in my chair.

Mama and Papa are chatting with the couple at the next table. I'm sure they didn't see the kiss. I put my hand to my lips so I will always remember how I spent the first seconds of this New Year. I look up at the stage where the huge foil numbers sway from the ceiling: 1951. In an instant, they look like lucky numbers to me.

Ruth and I stay after hours in the Hub to finish the buttons on her wedding gown. The cityscape visible from our window is pure black studded with tiny yellow lights like the combination of my favourite trim: jet beads and canary diamonds. Ruth's Valentine's Day wedding is a week away, and we're feeling the pressure to finish. Delmarr was sweet enough to leave us the key, so we can let ourselves out through the employee entrance on the main floor.

Ruth is built a lot like Elizabeth Taylor, so we took ideas from the actress's gown in *Father of the Bride* and merged them with a design by Vincent Monte Sano, who recently had a private viewing at Bonwit Teller's. We feel like traitors when we go to private viewings at other stores, but we can't resist when it's a designer we admire. We're copying Monte Sano's famous beadwork with small pockets in the skirt's layers of white tulle and a small crystal dropped in each. When Ruth walks down the aisle to the chuppah, she will literally dazzle.

I've had three dates since the New Year: one, a co-worker of Helen Gannon's husband from a stock brokerage firm (boring); another, arranged by my mother's cousin, with an architect from Florence (my Italian is far from flawless so we both nodded a lot without speaking); and a third with a friend of Delmarr's who served in the Army with him (a nice fellow, but not for me). I danced with several of Ruth's relatives at her engagement party, but those will never amount to more than a dance, because no good Jewish mother is going to offer her son in marriage to a Roman Catholic girl from Commerce Street. Or vice versa. And it's just as well; I haven't met anyone, Kaspians and Goldfarbs included, who I would set my permanent sights upon.

'Why don't you call Dante DeMartino? Tell him you need a date for my wedding,' Ruth suggests. 'Harvey always thought the world of him. He misses our double dates.'

'Sorry to disappoint Harvey, but Dante would think I wanted to get back together.'

'Don't you ever want to? Even just a little?'

'I have my moments,' I confess.

'I knew it!'

'Of course, Ruth. When I'm sad or lonely or bored to tears on a bad date I think about Dante. But then I remind myself why it didn't happen. He'll always work at the bakery, and that's fine, but it also means that he'll always live with his parents.'

'So you're right back where you started.' Ruth systematically pushes the straight pins into her cushion.

'Exactly. You see, Dante's life after our wedding day would not have changed one bit. We'd have a Mass and a dinner dance and we'd go to his home. I'd move into the room he grew up in, and into his bed, where I'm sure he'd be happy to have me for the next fifty years. But he wouldn't have had to give anything up. I, on the other hand, would be giving up *everything*. The day I married Dante, I would no longer work for B. Altman & Company, I would have signed on to Claudia DeMartino Enterprises: washing, cooking, cleaning and mending.'

'If John Talbot walked through that door right now, you'd jump at the chance to date him, wouldn't you?'

'It's not going to happen.' I should tell Ruth how tired I am of thinking about him. I wish he'd never kissed me. He ruined me for any men who might follow him. No one could live up to that kiss. Delmarr is right. Good-looking, sought-after men like John Talbot cause little thrills all over town, only to check their watch one day and decide to settle down, and when they do it's with a debutante.

I help Ruth into her gown for the final fitting. She stands on the model's platform and looks at herself from all angles. She looks like the ballerina on a music box. 'You're beautiful!' I tell her.

'I love the dress. Thank you. You've worked so hard.'

'I told you the boat neck with the cap sleeve was the ticket.'

'Look at those crystals.' Ruth turns slowly on the box. 'Some day we should open our own shop.'

'I would love to.' I flounce the tulle until it stands away from her body.

'I mean, why not? There are career girls in my family. My own mother works alongside my dad at the lumber store. When anyone asks my mom if she works, she says, "No!" But she's there every morning at nine, doing the books and the payroll. Of course, she'll tell you she's just helping out for the day.'

As I smooth the facing, I ask, 'Does Harvey want you to work for him?'

Ruth looks down at me. 'A couple days a week. You know, to do the books.'

'But you don't do books! You design clothes! You hate math,' I remind her. 'You always make me split the bill because you can't add.'

'I know, I know.' Ruth studies her gown in the mirror.

'Oh, Ruth. Can't you see what's happening? Everything is changing.'

'That's how it goes, Lucia.'

'It doesn't have to be like this! I hate what's happening to us, the way we throw our dreams away as though they're nothing. We're just a bunch of Ann Brewsters, a clique of nameless girls who come to work for a few years and bide their time till they're married. Then we leave, and right behind us is another young, hungry group of girls who come in with the same dreams, then their time comes, and they marry and *they* throw their dreams away. It goes on and on. No one ever stays and becomes the thing they imagined! And I can't believe you, of all people, don't see it. Ruth, we get married and lose everything.'

'You're upsetting me,' Ruth says quietly.

'Good! Get mad! Aren't you angry at a world that thinks so little of your talent? You're going to go and do Harvey's books, which anybody can do, and leave a job here that *nobody* else can do like you. Think of all the nights we've stayed here working overtime, not for the money, but because our department was the best, better than Bonwit's, Saks, Lord and Taylor's. We weren't just sewing. You were going to be the next Claire McCardell! Come on, Ruth.'

'I don't know what to say. You're asking me to choose.'

'Yes!' I yell. Ruth looks as though she is about to cry, and there is no sadder sight in the world than a woman in tears in a wedding gown. I breathe deeply. 'That's all we have. If you don't choose, believe me, there's a line of people starting with Harvey and ending with his mother who will choose for you. Do you want that? Do you want to give away everything you've worked for to make them happy?'

'Well, I can't *not* marry Harvey. I love him.'

'That's not what I'm asking you to do. I'm asking you to consider how you really feel. Do you ever think about *why* it's so easy for you to give up your dream?'

I help Ruth step out of her gown and place it carefully back on the dress mannequin. She doesn't answer my question, but why should she? It would only upset her more. I drape clean muslin over the dress, tucking it carefully under the hem, so dust can't get to it. Ruth puts our supplies away as I lower the window shades and turn out the lights. We walk down the escalators, since they are stationary after hours, to reach the employee entrance on the main floor.

'I'm sorry, Ruth.'

'It's okay.'

'No, it's not okay. You don't need more pressure from me.'

'It's not pressure. You make a lot of sense. You gave me a lot to think about.'

Ruth opens the door, a large gust of wind pins the door back, and it bangs against the building wall. Ruth motions for me to go outside first. She follows me out, then pushes the door shut, making sure it locks behind us. Snow has begun to fall. I bury my hands in my pockets to find my gloves. Ruth knots a scarf around her neck.

'I'm sorry I disappointed you, Lucia.'

'You've never disappointed me. I'm just looking out for you.'

Ruth looks towards Madison Avenue. 'It's hard to keep everybody happy, but I know there must be a way. I have to find it.'

'You will.' How can I tell my best friend that there is no way to keep everyone happy? I learned that first hand from the DeMartinos. The thought that I've hurt her makes me sad. I can't leave her tonight feeling sad. 'Thank you, Ruth.'

'For what?'

'For at least saying you wanted to open a shop with me.'

'I meant it.'

'I know you did.' I give her a hug and turn towards Fifth Avenue.

'Be careful getting home!' Ruth says to me as she heads east to her bus stop.

'I will,' I tell her. I look up Fifth Avenue. There's no sign of my bus. The wind is too cold to stand in, and I can pick up the bus a few blocks down, so I start walking. It's better to keep moving.

The tops of the skyscrapers disappear in a dense fog, and the light from the lower floors throws an eerie glow on the full clouds, which hang in grey ripples over the city like a ghostly meringue. I pull my black velvet rain hat with the wide brim over my ears and tie it under my chin with a bow. I bury my gloved hands deep in my pockets again and walk quickly downtown.

I wonder what will become of me. Ruth is being kind by offering to open a shop with me, but that's only a dream. Once she's married, she'll work for a while, and then she and Harvey will have a baby, and she'll quit and stay home to raise her family. I could open my own shop, I guess. But how? I'm not a businesswoman, I sew. Maybe it's because I grew up with brothers, but I see the business world as belonging to men. There are women who do it, though, women like Edith Head in Hollywood. I read in *PhotoScreen* magazine that Miss Head has a husband but no children. There aren't many women who work and have children. Motherhood is certainly difficult, but impending motherhood is not easy either. As Rosemary's due date draws near, I see how she struggles and how nervous she has become. Roberto stands by faithfully but helplessly. I'm sure deep down he's thinking, 'I'm glad she has to do this and not me.' Once again, it seems, women have to do everything.

Of all the people I know, men or women, the only one whose life I envy is Delmarr's. When he's not working, he's out on the town having fun. He dates interesting women, some intellectuals, some great beauties, some a combination of the two, and he always looks at life like a party. He tells fascinating stories of socialites and dances and nightclubs and nefarious characters and artists – the sum total of his experience is so colourful, even he can't believe his life sometimes. What a wonderful thing, to be satisfied and yet full of wonder.

I make the long crossing from the corner of Madison Square Park and continue down Fifth Avenue. The temperature seems to be dropping, and the snow is turning to sleet that hits my face like tiny daggers. I decide to hail a taxi. The trucks and cars whiz by me without a cab in sight. When I finally spot one, it's taken, no doubt coming from uptown, where at the first clink of a raindrop, the cabs fill instantly. I'm about to give up and keep walking when a car pulls over and the window rolls down.

'Lucia! It's John Talbot,' he says, leaning across the front seat of his new 1950 Packard painted a glossy midnight blue, with beige and cranberry accents on the running board. I remember this very model from Exodus's catalogue. My brother longs for one, but they're expensive and made to order. 'Do you need a lift?'

Quickly, I run through the mental checklist of safety precautions for the unmarried girl alone on the street. I throw out the rules when I remember that it is Delmarr who introduced me to John Talbot. Maybe this fellow has a lot of girlfriends, but he also has a car in the middle of what is turning into a terrible storm. 'Do you mind?'

'Not at all.'

'Don't get out,' I tell him as he attempts to open his door into moving traffic to come and open mine. I jump into the car.

'I'm going to have a talk with Delmarr. He's got a lot of crust having you work so late.'

'It's not his fault. I was helping my friend Ruth with her wedding gown.' I smooth my skirt and see that the car seats are made of the finest leather. The interior is clean and neat. This is a man who takes excellent care of his things.

'You make a lot of wedding gowns there, don't you?' John asks, easing back into the flow of cars.

'All the time.'

'Is that fun?'

'Well, as you can imagine, a lot of effort goes into a girl's wedding gown because she wants to present her very best self to the man who's chosen her. But when girls come to us to put together their very best selves, they turn into, well, to be honest, they turn into raging monsters.'

John laughs. 'But they look so sweet in the newspaper with their tiaras and veils.'

That's interesting. John Talbot reads the society pages just like Ruth and me. I don't think he's looking for the fashion, maybe just seeing which names have to be crossed out of his little black book. 'Oh, yes, we spend a lot of time bringing them back from beastly to demure. Sometimes I wonder if the grooms ever see the side of their fiancées that we do.'

'Probably not. You ladies have a way of duping us. We're suckers for you.'

'Then I would say you deserve what you get,' I tell him.

'Do you have a boyfriend?' John asks in a friendly way.

'Why would it matter to you? You kissed me on New Year's Eve like you knew me my whole life.' I can't believe I brought up the kiss. Instantly, I wish I could take my words back.

'I know. I want to apologize for that,' John says sincerely. 'I wasn't really behaving like a gentleman, though I can promise you, I absolutely am one. I just got carried away. That gold dress was something.'

'Thank you.' Now I'm glad I hid that bolt of lamé in the supply room. We sit in silence for a couple of blocks while I think of a way to get the conversation going again. 'Delmarr tells me you sell fabric.'

'It's one of the many things I do.'

'How do you have time to do more than one?' I ask.

'I figure, I'm young and I should try a lot of different things before I settle on one career.'

This is a terrible sign, I think to myself. If he's this noncommittal about his work, how could he ever settle on one girl?

'But I will settle on one thing eventually,' he says, as though he knows what's on my mind.

I exhale gently. Good. He's not a flibbertigibbet, he's just versatile. 'Oh, take that right onto Commerce.'

John misses the turn and continues down Seventh Avenue South. 'Sorry,' he says, not meaning it.

'Now you have to go all the way around the block to get me home.'

'That was the idea,' he says lightly. 'I like talking to you. I'm buying time. Is that all right?'

'I spent the day bending over a sewing machine, so you have to spell things out for me.'

'Okay. Let me spell it out, then. I want to spend time with you.'

'You don't even know me.'

'I see who you are.'

'Did you know I was born with a curse on me?' I ask. John laughs. 'Yes, I was. And my mother, God bless her, thought I dodged it when I was born without a birthmark on my face, because that was her biggest fear. But I think a curse is like a poisonous vapour – when it's released, it may not overtake you all at once but it will linger, and one day kill you. Do you know any Italians?'

'Sure.'

'Did you ever know any with a curse on them?'

'Only you.'

'And you're not deterred?'

'Not in the least.'

I point to my street. 'Okay, over there. This time don't miss it.'

John brakes and turns onto Commerce Street. There's one set of footprints on the sidewalk in the newly fallen snow. I point to them. 'When it snows I sit up in my window and watch it come down. And when I see the first set of footprints in the snow, I can't help but think they look like the cardboard feet in the dance kit from the Arthur Murray studio.'

'So you dance?' he asks.

'I love to.' I won't tell John Talbot that I used to pay my brother Angelo a nickel to dance with me.

'Sometime we'll go dancing.'

'I'd like that.' I point to my home. 'It's number forty-five.'

John pulls up in front. 'Wait. I'll come around,' he says. 'I feel bad I didn't get the door the first time.' Nice manners, I think, as he comes around the front of the car and opens my door. The snow sticking to his hair reminds me of the New Year's confetti from the night he kissed me.

'Where's your hat?' I want to know.

'In the back seat.'

'You ought to get it,' I tell him, pulling the brim of my own hat over my eyes. John opens the back door of the car and pulls out his hat. He puts it on, then takes my arm and walks me up the stoop to my front door.

We stand and look at each other for a moment, not long enough to lead to a kiss, but long enough to want one. Now he knows me a little, he knows I'm not the kind of girl you dip in a nightclub and kiss on the lips without asking. But I realize he's not the type of man who dips a girl in a nightclub and kisses her without asking first, either.

'Well, goodnight, Lucia.' He tips his hat.

'Goodnight, John. Thank you for the ride home.' I open the front door and breathe deeply once I'm inside. John Talbot exhausts me, but in a good way. This isn't a man who makes me feel comfortable. He's a man who keeps me on my toes. I never know what he is going to do.

The house is filled with the familiar scent of simmering tomatoes and basil. I climb the stairs to change into my slacks and one of Papa's old pullover sweaters. I want a nice dish of Mama's penne and then I will curl up in front of the fire with a glass of Papa's grappa and think about John Talbot.

Chapter Five

Once Papa finished remodelling the garden apartment for Roberto and Rosemary, he tackled Mama's kitchen. He hung a crisp red-and-white-striped wallpaper and installed pristine white enamel appliances, including the latest gas stove with four burners and a griddle. It inspired me to give my bedroom a new look.

When I tell Delmarr I want to redecorate, he takes me shopping at the D&D Building on Madison Avenue, where he introduces me to the finest selection of wallpapers in the world; English designs from Colefax & Fowler, French creations from Pierre Frey, and bright American patterns from Rose Cummings. After all our research, we end up going back to Altman's and up to the Interior Decoration floor, where we find a sample from Schumacher of yellow cabbage roses climbing a white trellis against a sky-blue background. Delmarr informs me that Altman's has won the commission to decorate the White House for President and Mrs Harry Truman. Delmarr's buddy Charles Haight, who started with him in Packaging, will be the chief designer. 'What's good enough for old Bess is good enough for you,' Delmarr tells me.

Now at home I've moved all my furniture to the centre of the room and opened the windows at both ends for a cross breeze. I spent most of the morning measuring out the wallpaper. The adhesive is tricky so I bought three extra rolls in case of mistakes. As I pour the paste into the tray, there's a knock at my door.

'Be careful,' I call out.

Ruth pushes the door open. 'Hi. Your mom said you were up here.'

'Up to my ears.' I put down the roller and sponge.

'Need a hand?'

'What are you doing here? You're getting married next week.'

'I'm in good shape. I need to relax a little.'

'Then sit over there and watch.'

'I'll go nuts sitting. Let me help.'

'Are you sure?' Ruth nods. I show her the plans and point to a spot on the wall. 'I'm starting right there.' I give her a roll of paper to unwind. She lays it across the floor, and just like the dressmaker she is, makes tiny pencil marks on the wall to correspond with the measurements of the paper.

'You already prepped the walls, I see.' Ruth smooths her hand over the wall with approval.

'Yep.' And then, as we do in the Hub, we go about our separate chores, quietly, efficiently, like the great team we've become. Whether we're wallpapering, conducting a fitting, or setting out the dinner we've ordered in for an overtime job, we know how to complete a task in the most efficient manner. We each seem to know what the other is thinking and we anticipate each other's needs and assist each other in reaching the goal. This is probably what a good marriage is like, I think. As we work side by side, I feel a pang of guilt. I was too hard on my best friend and I know it.

'Ruth, I'm sorry about what I said last night.'

'No, no. Don't apologize. You were honest with me. And I think you're right.' Ruth takes the straight edge and cuts the wallpaper to hug the baseboard. I hold it as she tacks the paper to the wall.

'I shouldn't have yelled.'

'You're Italian. You yell. It's okay.'

I carefully spread the glue on the back of the paper, Ruth helps me lift it from the edges, we walk it to the wall and ease it into position, smoothing it down with the grader. We step back to see the result.

'This is the ticket.' Ruth smiles. 'Good choice. I like it.'

The colours, the mood and the scale of the pattern suit the room, and the overall effect is just right. 'I do, too.'

'You ever wonder how we know?' Ruth takes the pencil and marks the next sheet. 'How come we just seem to know what works? It's like this wallpaper, you chose the right print for this wall, this room. How did you *know*? The rich girls who come in for fittings, they're always so . . . perplexed. They never know what colour is right on them, or what line looks good on their figures. They want to see what another client is having made, so they can copy it. They have no original ideas.'

'That's what they pay *us* for. To tell them what works. Maybe that's why God gave them all the money and gave us all the talent. It's good old-fashioned supply and demand,' I tell her.

Ruth helps me hang a second sheet of wallpaper. 'Harvey's cousin Jake is coming in from California for the wedding. He's a bachelor and he doesn't have a date . . .'

'Ruth, I will absolutely dance with him but I've already got an escort. I promised Delmarr.'

'Oh, right.'

'And besides, I have suitors galore. I can't possibly take on another. John Talbot picked me up in his Packard last night.'

'*What*?'

'Yep. And he drove me home and he almost kissed me.' I look at Ruth and smile. 'And next time, it won't be an almost.'

Mama asked Ruth to stay for dinner, since it's only right to feed the volunteer, but she has a date with Harvey. She's missing a delicious meal. Mama made Papa's favourite Venetian dish, a hearty fish stew from a recipe given to him by his aunt in Godega. Rosemary helped Mama prepare it, and wrote down the recipe for her collection (and mine).

VIOLA PERIN'S FISH BRODETTO

1lb shrimp, shelled and de-veined

1lb lobster tail cut into chunks

1lb sole cut into chunks

1 fresh lemon

1 large sweet onion, sliced

3 cloves garlic, minced

6 fresh tomatoes, chopped

¼ cup olive oil

2 quarts water

3 cups red wine

1 cup balsamic vinegar
3 tbsp fresh parsley, chopped
salt and pepper

Prepare fish, squeeze lemon juice over, set aside. In a large pot, sauté onion, garlic, tomatoes lightly in the olive oil. Add water and wine and balsamic vinegar. Stir well. Add fish and parsley. Add salt and pepper to taste. Cook on stove top over medium heat for 40 minutes or until fish cooks through.

Line soup bowls with thin slices of toasted Italian bread. Ladle stew over bread and serve. Yields 10 servings.

Rosemary and I help Mama prepare the bowls of stew. Mama takes her scissors and cuts a bunch of basil from her plant in the window. She rinses it, then cuts it in ribbons to garnish each bowl of stew.

'Maria!' Papa shouts from the living room. 'Maria, *presto*!' Mama throws down her dish towel and goes into the living room. Rosemary and I follow her. Roberto, Orlando, Angelo and Exodus are smiling mischievously. Mama eyes them suspiciously.

'What is it?' she asks. Papa picks her up and twirls her around. 'Antonio, put me down. You'll hurt your back,' she says.

'You won't believe it,' Papa says, covering her face in kisses.

'What? What won't I believe?'

'Zio Antonio left us the family homestead in Godega. My farm! The farmhouse where I was born. The barn where I kept our horse, the fields of wheat behind it, all of it. It's ours!'

'Who said so?' Mama demands.

'My cousin Domenic sent me a letter. Here. Look. You can read it yourself.' Papa gives Mama the letter, and the boys start talking over one another with plans for our inheritance.

Mama straightens her apron. 'What are we going to do with a farm?'

'We're going to visit!'

'When?'

'In August.'

'But I already rented a house at the Jersey shore.'

'Cancel it. Maria, *viva un po*! I don't want any arguments. We're going to Italy. The whole family is going home.'

Rosemary runs her hand over her stomach. 'I don't know, Papa. The baby will be very small and that's a big trip.'

'Please think about coming. I know it will be difficult, but this is my home, and my grandchildren will know it as their own! Besides, it's Italian law, we have to go in person to claim the property in court.'

'I am not spending my holiday in Italy feeding chickens and milking goats,' Mama says, putting her hands on her hips. 'I have enough to do around here.'

'You are going to Italy, Maria,' Papa says evenly.

'I am not going anywhere,' Mama counters.

It is so quiet in the living room, we can hear a taxi horn honking all the way over on Seventh Avenue. Mama and Papa stare each other down. My brothers back away, checking the exits. We all know what will happen next, a big fight that revisits every slight Mama has endured over the course of their long marriage.

'Mama,' I plead, trying to defuse the impending bomb. 'Can't you be happy for Papa?'

'Lucia, you don't know about farming. My mother's father was a farmer, don't forget. And that is a life of hell, I promise you. You work all day in the fields and all night in the barn. It's no fun, and your father and I are too old to take it on. We'll have to sell it,' Mama decides.

'I will never sell the farm!' Papa bellows. 'Never!'

Mama backs down when she hears the tone in Papa's voice. 'All right, all right, Antonio. *Basta*! I'll cancel the Jersey shore so we can see your farm. Wash up for supper. Are you happy now?' She turns and goes back into the kitchen.

Papa watches her go, shaking his head in disbelief. My brothers look at me, and I throw my hands up in the air. We may have been taught that Papa is the head of our household and the leader of the family, but the truth is, Maria Sartori runs the show.

I break the silence. 'Pop, I'm sorry. I think it's wonderful.'

'Me too, Pop.' Rosemary smiles at him. She squeezes his hand and then goes up the stairs.

During dinner Mama and Papa refused to look at each other. Afterwards Papa grabbed his hat and coat and slammed the front door on his way out for a walk. I told Rosemary to go and lie down, that I'd take care of the dishes. When my brothers and I were little Mama would tell us that if you eat when you're angry, the food turns to poison.

'Is Papa back yet?' Mama asks, coming into the kitchen as I dry the last of the dishes.

'No.' Mama sits down at the kitchen table. I pour a cup of tea for her and one for myself. 'Are you going to sulk all night?' I ask her gently.

'You don't know the whole story,' she begins. 'I read the letter. Your father got the farm and his brother got the money.'

'Zio Antonio had money?'

'Yes. And he knew of the feud between your father and his brother, so instead of splitting the land and money equally, he did his own division.'

'Maybe Zio was afraid that if he gave the farm to both of them, they would end up selling it.'

'Of course that's what he thought. Your father's family has never been anything but trouble.'

'Well, whose fault is that? You should convince Papa to make peace with his brother.' I can tell Mama is surprised by my tone. 'This ridiculous feud has gone on long enough.'

'We're better off this way,' she insists.

'Ma, what is so terrible that Papa and Zio Enzo haven't spoken in twenty-five years?'

'It was a lot of things.' Mama squeezes the teabag against her spoon so hard I'm afraid it will burst open.

'Let me guess. Money.'

'Of course it was about money. And it was also about character. Enzo's wife accused your father of making a pass at her.'

'*What*?' I can't imagine my father doing such a thing.

'Your father didn't do it, of course. I was there. But Caterina insisted that he did. She was so envious of Enzo and Papa's closeness she made up a terrible lie she knew would tear them apart. But that was simply the last straw. From the beginning she and I didn't get along.'

'Why?'

'She was a prima donna. She never worked! When we all lived in this house, I did all the cooking and cleaning and she never lifted a finger to help me. I was her maid. I did it because she was older and I wanted to prove to your father that I could make a nice home and get along with everyone, so in a sense I didn't mind. But Caterina was a very insecure woman. In my mind, the most dangerous people in the world are insecure women. They can do more damage in a day than an army.'

'What did she do?'

'She spent a lot of money on things for herself and didn't mind that the rest of us went without. At the end of the month, when we paid the bills, there would always be a royal battle between Papa and Enzo. Those arguments alone would have caused a rift.'

'You shared expenses?'

'Papa and Enzo put everything they made at the Groceria into a pot. Both families ate from that pot. Of course, there was a debt to the bank. And Caterina knew it. I've never been a woman who wanted a lot of fancy things, I'm happy with very little. Caterina, however, needed lots of things to make herself happy. She was furious when she was banished from New York City but that was the deal: whoever lost the coin toss moved, and the other brother bought him out. It was the only way.'

'So Papa chose you over his brother, and that's when Caterina put the curse on me.'

'Right. She had to make one final scene. But your father and Enzo were determined to make the deal stick. There was no way one of them would have backed out. A deal is a deal. And I don't think Enzo minded so much. He always missed the country. I think if he could have, he would have gone back to the Veneto and had his own farm.'

'Uncle Enzo probably would have liked to get the farm in Godega.'

'It's done now, Lucia. I'm sure Caterina will be very happy with her pile of lire.'

Ruth and I have a deadline to finish a travelling ensemble for a Park Avenue lady who's spending the spring touring Europe. This is Ruth's final big job before her wedding and honeymoon. As we wrap up, Ruth pulls a long sheet of butcher paper off the roll, tears it across the blade, and lays it down on the cutting table. She takes a piece of black chalk from her supply box and writes, 'John Talbot', then stands back from it. 'Now, that's a distinguished name. Sounds like a scholar or a banker or something grand.'

'If he's so grand, why hasn't he called?'

'That, Lucia, is the million-dollar question.' Ruth smiles.

'Ladies, for your bulletin board.' Delmarr throws a letter down on my work table. 'The Mother Superior of the Poor "We're Barely Scraping By" Nuns of the Bronx would like to thank you for their habits. They will keep you and yours in their prayers.'

'That's nice,' I say sincerely.

'Write Mother back, would you, Lucia, and tell her that I would like her entire Order to pray that my hair stays in. I saw a touch of scalp in the back this morning. It's small but it has the potential to spread and I'm too vain to lose my hair.' Delmarr twists to look in the three-way mirror, patting the back of his head. 'Is there a saint for the prevention of hair loss?'

'Don't look at me. I don't know from saints,' Ruth says.

'I don't think there's a saint, but there surely are novenas for desperate situations,' I offer.

'Then include Harvey,' Ruth says. 'Do they pray for Jews?'

'Why wouldn't they?' I ask.

'Then tell them to pray for the shiny bald spot on the crown of Harvey's head. It's already the size of a postage stamp, but it's okay, I told him I would love him no matter what.'

'That's how it is when you get married.' Delmarr leans against the wall. 'Which is why I never will. What honest person could stand up before a group of people and promise that in sickness, yech, poverty, they've got to be kidding, and whatever else comes down the pike, that you would *never* leave? The wedding vows are a licence to be a complete jerk with full knowledge that the person you married has agreed, no matter how large a horse's ass you are, to stay by your side until death. A fool could tell you this is a bad deal.'

'Could we change the subject, please?' Ruth says pleasantly. 'I am almost a bride.'

'Lucia, I'm going to lunch with John Talbot. You want to come along?'

Before I can answer, John comes through the doors. He's wearing a black pinstripe suit with subtle stripes in the palest periwinkle. His tie is watermarked Chinese silk in off-white, against a bright white shirt. Why is he always so well turned out and therefore irresistible?

'Would you like to come?' Delmarr asks me again.

'I can't. I have plans.' I look at Delmarr and smile politely, but I want to wring his neck. I'm not a tagalong on his business lunches, not with John Talbot.

'Okay, no problem,' Delmarr says casually.

John looks down and sees his name in chalk. 'Someone sending me a message?' he asks, pointing to his name.

Ruth and I look at each other with slight panic. Delmarr picks up on it immediately. 'Oh, that was me. I asked Ruth to make a note to remind me about our lunch.' Ruth and I are thinking the same thing: Delmarr is a stand-up fellow who can catch a fastball.

'How are you, Lucia?' John says, smiling.

'Just fine. Have you met Ruth Kaspian?'

'Sure, upstairs. Remember? It's a pleasure to see you again.'

'Thank you,' Ruth says with a smile. 'It's a pleasure on my end, too.' Delmarr shows John out. Once they are gone, Ruth leans across her drawing table. 'He's magnificent.' She sighs. 'His teeth are whiter than his shirt!'

'That's what they mean when they say movie-star looks,' I tell her.

'You may well end up with him after all. You're a beauty match. My Aunt Beryl always says money marries money and pretty marries pretty. When she's tipsy she also says poor marries poor and ugly marries ugly.' Ruth pours herself a cup of coffee out of her Thermos and refills my cup. 'Guess what Uncle Milt is?'

'Pretty?'

'Nope. Poor.'

The afternoon goes by with no sign of Delmarr. The booking secretary finally delivers a message to us at about four o'clock that says he'll see us Monday morning, he's gone to an appointment outside the office. There's nothing unusual about this – we spend a lot of time running errands to fabric houses, trim shops and notions stores. I'm just dying to ask Delmarr about John Talbot, but it will have to wait till after the weekend.

I take the bus home, anxious to start my weekend. Sunday is Ruth's wedding, but I will spend tomorrow admiring the wallpaper in my room. I also have a new book I can't wait to crack open, *Mr Blandings Builds His Dream House,* and a new shoe shop on East Fifty-Eighth Street to wander through. When I get off the bus and make the turn from Seventh Avenue onto Commerce, I feel comforted by the lantern twinkling over our stoop.

'Mama, I'm home,' I call out from the vestibule. I'm starting up the stairs to my room when she appears in the doorway.

'You have guests,' Mama says, meeting me in the doorway.

'I do?' I try to see around her. 'Who?'

'Delmarr and that fellow John we met on New Year's Eve.'

Mama turns and goes into the kitchen. My heart races. I'm sorry I didn't apply my lipstick before I started home, but I wasn't expecting company. Without taking my coat off, I check my face in the mirror by the door and go into the living room.

'What a surprise,' I tell Delmarr and John, as they rise to greet me. 'So the longest lunch in history led you to my house?'

'I went by your papa's store for some superior olive oil and he invited us to dinner,' Delmarr explains. 'Go take your coat off. Your mother convinced me to make a vat of Manhattans, and they're iced just right.'

'Great,' I say.

'Pop and the boys are on their way home, honey,' Mama calls from the kitchen.

Back in the hallway, I take off my coat and hang it up next to John's. His overcoat carries the spicy scent of amber I remember from New Year's Eve. I hear Delmarr and John chattering inside, so I take a moment to examine the coat. It is tailored with the finest details, a smart black satin lining, leather backing on the collar, chamois lining on the cuffs. The vent in the back is reinforced with silk cording, an old technique that lets the coat fall to the back of the knees without wrinkling. On the shelf over the coat rack is John Talbot's hat. It is a Borsalino; it, too, has a custom touch, a gusset in the crown to fit the owner and no one else. The gloves that rest on the brim are made of black kid leather with a rollover cuff. John Talbot is particular and I like that. I pull my lipstick out of my purse and apply it. I look down at my simple camel wool skirt and wish I had dressed in something more festive, but this will have to do. Plus, I don't want this man to think I'm trying to impress him.

I join them in the living room. Delmarr hands me a glass. Rosemary comes out of the kitchen after Mama. She moves slowly, the weight of the baby, due any time, evident in her every movement. John asks her lots of questions, how she has prepared for the baby and where she's delivering and all about her doctor. Rosemary asks John why he is so interested in babies. He tells her it's the only miracle in the world. Mama looks at him with approval.

'We're home!' Roberto calls from the doorway. My brothers are laughing, joking with one another. Papa leads them into the living room, giving Mama the zippered canvas money-sack from the store. He kisses her on the cheek.

'I see you got here just fine,' Papa says to Delmarr and John.

'Not without a compass,' Delmarr says. 'These Village streets are as twisty as rolatini.'

'Did you meet my brothers?' I ask.

John points. 'That's Roberto. That's Angelo. That's Orlando. And the bruiser who looks Irish is Exodus.'

'Hey, I'm all Italian,' Exodus retorts. 'Don't make me prove it.'

'Oh, I won't,' John jokes back. 'I hope that by the end of the evening, you'll have taught me all the Italian curse words I can retain. I'm visiting Capri as a guest of the Mortensons come Easter and I want to shock them with foul language.'

Delmarr laughs. 'Believe me, you'll need them after a week with Vivie Mortenson. She's a piece of work.'

'Well, these are the boys to teach you,' Papa promises. 'They know more bad words than me and I grew up in Italy.'

'How do you know the Mortensons?' I ask John.

'They're old friends.'

'I made Sally Mortenson's debutante gown,' I tell him. John smiles politely. I wonder if he'll be less interested in me now that he knows I make his friends' clothes.

Delmarr reads my mind. 'All the girls request Lucia when they come in for a fitting. They know she's the best.' He winks at me.

As I watch the men joke and spar, it occurs to me that for most of my life I've been the only girl in the room. When I began my career I was relieved to be with women. There's an understanding and a language among a group of women which I treasure. As much as I love my brothers, I've never been able to tell them things I could have told a sister. Mama was sensitive to that and tried to compensate. But there are some things I would have felt more comfortable saying to a sister instead of Mama. Being the only Sartori girl has made me more confident, though. I don't think I would have had the guts to take my sewing samples to Altman's Custom Department had I not had brothers who taught me about competition. And I don't think I would have even tried to *get* a job had Papa not encouraged me to take care of myself. He told me I would make better decisions if I made them out of want and not need.

I help Mama serve the meal – polenta and roasted Cornish game hens. Delmarr gets a kick out of my brothers and talks to them about working in the Groceria. He asks lots of questions about how the operation is set up. John says he can't imagine what would happen if someone weren't pulling his weight – how do you fire your family? As we eat, John tells funny stories about characters he has met in his extensive travels. Even Delmarr is fascinated. While we clear the dishes, Papa gets down to business.

'So, John, what is your trade?' Papa asks as he pours himself a glass of wine.

'I'm a businessman. I'm interested in starting new ventures in several areas. I like importing. Lately, I've been working with a textile manufacturer in Spain. I'd like to provide goods to the fabric houses on Fifth Avenue. Among other things.'

Papa raises an eyebrow. 'Other things.'

'Yes, sir. I like to be useful. I have connections, and I like to use them to do some good. For example, Bishop Walker Sullivan called me recently to arrange a couple of buses for an upstate retreat—'

'You know the bishop?' Mama says, impressed.

'For many years. Anyway, he needed a hand with transportation and I helped out.'

'I'm sure he appreciated it.' Mama smiles, then nods at Papa. 'So, you're Catholic?' she asks hopefully.

'I am.' John Talbot doesn't know it yet, but he's just won my mother over.

'Antonio,' my mother says. 'The port.'

'I'll get Ro's sesame cookies,' I offer.

'I make them by the pound, they're my only craving,' Rosemary says to Delmarr apologetically. 'I hope you like them.'

Roberto returns to talk of the Groceria and his dreams of expanding and modernizing it. Papa, in his wise way, lets Roberto go on and on about attracting new customers, opening a second store uptown and someday having a chain of Grocerias. Rosemary has heard these dreams in detail many times, so her eyes get a tired look as she nibbles a cookie. Mama likes to hear Roberto's ideas of progress; she takes pride in our ambition. John listens carefully to Roberto spin the dream.

'If you have one business going gangbusters, you *should* expand,' John tells him. 'You can't grow if you don't envision the bigger picture.'

'Tell Papa that. He likes the old ways,' Roberto says.

'I'm not against the new,' Papa says pleasantly. 'I just don't understand how to have two stores and meet the quality standards I have set for myself. I'm one man, who can inspect one piece of fruit at a time. If the crates come in and I dump them in a bin and stick a price on them without checking, then I'm no better than the store up the street. My customers know they're buying the best, because I have chosen it for them. My fish is fresh from Long Island Sound, my meats are from the farmland of Pennsylvania, and my fruit comes from all over upstate New York and from as far as Italy. I still buy my blood oranges from the same Italian family I met as a boy in the open market in Treviso. The farmer wraps each orange like a jewel, crates them all, and sends them for sale in my shop.'

I squeeze Papa's hand. 'I used to wait for those crates from Italy. The whole block smelled like sweet oranges!'

'I am not saying that everyone in the world has to be as fussy as me, but my customers trust me, and that is a bond I take seriously.'

'Sir, I respect that.' Delmarr toasts Papa with his port. 'Like you, I believe in quality. But I think we must face the fact that the world is changing. Since the war, in my business, the mandate has been, "How many can we make and how quickly can we make them?" There was a time when the store said you could say no to a customer if you knew you couldn't turn out a quality garment. Now they tell us to take every order. There's a lust for profit, at the expense of quality. They'd like us to work seven days a week, with double the output. I don't know where all of this is headed, but it isn't good.'

'Since the boys came home from the war, our customer base has expanded,' Mama says. 'We used to be a neighbourhood market, but now we get more and more people from uptown.'

'Two reasons,' Roberto explains. 'Lots of guys were stationed in Italy and got a taste for fresh basil, the best Parmesan, good olive oil . . .'

'And where were they going to get it uptown? These bluebloods don't know from authentic Italian. So they began coming to us,' Exodus adds.

'But it was more than just what we are selling,' Papa says. 'When I came to this country, the Italians were not embraced. But after we sent our sons to go toe to toe against Hitler, everything changed. We were able to bring honour to our people. It altered the way people in this city looked at us.'

'All the Sartoris served?' John asks.

'I'm the only one who didn't make it overseas. I enlisted near the end and got as far as Fort Bragg,' Exodus says.

'You still defended your country, Ex.' Mama puts her arm around him.

'Did you serve?' Papa asks John.

'Yes, sir. I was stationed in France.'

I smile, knowing that this matters to Papa.

By nine o'clock the conversation wanes, since we're all tired from the work week. The only person with pep is John Talbot, who becomes more animated and engaging as the evening wears on. He's a night person, I think to myself, the opposite of me. I like to be in bed early and wake up before the sun rises, so I have the full benefit of a long morning. I imagine John Talbot at the clubs until all hours. He probably does a lot of entertaining in his business, so late nights are a requirement. It's something for me to think about, though. It's a small negative in the sea of delightful qualities I am finding in John. I'm a girl who hardly shows her feelings (maybe that's another result of living with brothers) but deep within me, I feel a quake of falling for Mr Talbot. I look across the table at him and wonder how I would feel if he were mine.

'You're tired,' John says to me.

'It's been a long week. Seems that every custom order these days is a rush. Ruth and I can barely keep up.'

'It is definitely the busy season,' Delmarr agrees.

'You tell those swankies to wait,' my mother instructs us. 'There's no sense killing yourself over a party dress.'

'Yes, Mama.'

'Yes, ma'am,' Delmarr assures her as he and John stand. Delmarr shakes my father's hand and says goodnight to everyone.

John Talbot turns to my mother. 'Thank you for a delicious dinner.'

'Come by any time,' Mama says warmly.

'I promise I will.'

I show John and Delmarr to the vestibule. While John puts on his coat, I take down his hat and gloves and hand them to him. 'Borsalinos are very chic.'

'And durable. This hat will last a lifetime.'

Delmarr holds out his hat before placing it on his head. 'I hope my hat passes inspection.'

'Impeccable as always, Monsieur Delmarr. Lilly Dache would approve.'

'Ah, thank you, thank you. I'll pick you up around two on Sunday, Lucia. I can't wait to see Ruth in her Elizabeth Taylor wedding gown. She wouldn't let me look, even though I designed it. Evidently men are bad luck in general. Please thank your mother again for dinner.'

Delmarr opens the door and steps outside, leaving me and John in a brief moment of silence, which I break. 'Goodnight, John.'

'Lucia? Are you busy tomorrow?'

My mind files through my chores. I picture myself curled up with a book.

'Not very,' I tell him.

'Would you like to go for a ride?'

'That would be nice.'

'I'll pick you up at one.'

After I close the door behind him, I watch through the pink panes of glass as he and Delmarr walk up to Barrow and turn off.

'He's a looker,' Rosemary says from behind me.

'Do you trust lookers, Ro?' I ask her.

'Never.'

'Me neither.'

'But I like him. And he likes my sesame cookies, which shows good judgment.' Rosemary hands me an index card. She has already written out the recipe for me.

ROSEMARY SARTORI'S SESAME SEED COOKIES

3 cups flour

dash salt

1 tsp baking powder

2 sticks real butter (warmed to room temperature)

¾ cup white granulated sugar

3 jumbo-sized egg yolks

1 tsp vanilla extract

large handful sesame seeds

1 tbsp heavy cream

Take the flour, salt and baking powder and sift together into a small bowl.

In a large bowl blend the butter into the sugar with a fork. Add in the egg yolks, one at a time, then add the vanilla. Take the dry mixture (from the small bowl) and pour into the large bowl of wet ingredients. Mix well, with hands! Make into a ball, should be doughy.

Cover with saran wrap and put in refrigerator for a couple of hours. After this time has passed, lightly flour cutting board. Roll dough into long strips and cut into 2-inch pieces.

Wet sesame seeds in heavy cream. Take each cookie and dip into seeds. Put the cookies on a greased cookie sheet. Bake for 9 minutes at 400°. Yields 3 dozen cookies.

I spent the morning pressing my brothers' shirts in the laundry room. I never mind the job. The fresh scent of cotton when the steam iron hits the shirt is comforting. I get satisfaction when I look at the freshly starched shirts on hangers arranged in order on the rack, from my eldest brother to my youngest. Between housework and Ruth's wedding tomorrow, I almost wish I hadn't made a date with John for this afternoon. It's unlike me to accept a last-minute engagement, but there's something about him that makes me want to throw out my rules.

When he comes to the door promptly at one, Mama is waiting with a couple of wrapped turkey sandwiches and a small sack of Rosemary's sesame cookies for us to take on our ride.

'Have you ever been to Huntington?' John asks as he opens the door to help me into his car. I notice a fringe of cloudy white salt on the bumpers, the only sign the car has been out of a garage since the winter began.

'No,' I tell him.

He goes around to the driver's side, gets in and settles into the seat. 'Long Island. It's building up. You know, there are only so many views of the ocean. Finite real estate. That's where the money is.' He looks at me and smiles, turning the key. The Packard engine hums evenly like a church organ. 'I have a real estate plan. You know, the entirety of the American economy is built on real estate. I plan to buy a home, then borrow against it to build another, and so on, until there's a development with my name on it. What do you think?'

'I think . . . it sounds great.' I don't know what else to say. Real estate is not something I have given much thought to. As we head over to the East Side, cross the Manhattan Bridge over into Brooklyn and sail onto the highway, John Talbot tells me about his big dream to use the money he makes from real-estate development to open an elegant hotel with all the trimmings in Manhattan. He sees a nightclub, a restaurant, rooftop views, the works. His enthusiasm is contagious. I imagine the women at such a hotel in their mink coats and pearls. I see the men who accompany them, dapper New York business tycoons, and I see John Talbot in their midst, entertaining them with his wit and charm.

Huntington Bay, Long Island, still has the kiss of the last snowfall on its trees and sloping lawns. The homes are new, dotting the hillsides in a mix of styles, brick colonial, Connecticut farmhouse and my favourite, English Tudor. There's something about the bricks, casement windows and castle doors that makes me feel secure.

'You love the Tudor, don't you?' John looks at me and stops the car in front of the house.

'Italians like English design. Mama has family in Forest Hills. They're crazy for the Tudors.'

John pulls the car over in front of an empty lot. 'Let's go,' he says and jumps out of the car. He opens the door for me, offering me his hand. 'I want to show you something.' John leads me up a hill. It's icy, so I slide back and we laugh, but he moves me in front of him and pushes me up the knobby hill until we reach the top. Through the trees, I see a silvery expanse, hung low with white clouds.

'That's the bay,' John says.

A feeling comes over me, one I've never experienced before. I connect with this place, deeply and instantly, as if I have been here before. What would it be like to live near the water? To be able to walk to the ocean and hear the waves and smell the sea salt every day? Fancy Upper East Side Manhattan, dressed in black velvet, has always been my idea of sumptuous living, but now I imagine having a view of the ocean. I can see the blue summers and the petal-soft springs when the driftwood bleaches from dull grey to eggshell white in the sun. Papa told me stories of going to Rimini on the Adriatic coast below the Veneto where the sand was the colour of snow, and, against the blue water, it could blind you in the noonday sun.

'You should live on the water, some day,' John says, as if he knows something about my future that I do not.

My feet get caught in the dry bramble of some old branches. John kneels down and helps me out of the twisty mesh. I look down at him and I can't help imagining the precise moment he will propose marriage to me. He looks up at me and I swear he is thinking the same thing. Quickly, I pull my foot loose and extend my hand to help him up. We go back to the car without saying a word.

Once we're back on the highway, I feel sad about leaving the ocean behind. I look out the window because this isn't something I want to talk about. I need to think about it before I can articulate it. Plus, I want to run all of this by Ruth. She is wise in these matters.

'Would you like to meet my mother?' John Talbot asks.

'Well . . . of course.' I'm surprised John wants me to meet his family. After all, this is only a first date.

'We don't have to. We could do it another time,' he says, sensing my discomfort.

I change my mind. The more clues I have to understanding John, the better. 'No, no. I'd like to. Does she live out here? With your father?'

'No, he died when I was seven. She remarried when I was twelve. My stepfather was a nice man named Edward O'Keefe.'

'Do you have any brothers and sisters?' I ask.

'Nope.'

'So, it's just you taking care of your mother.'

John Talbot doesn't reply, and for whatever reason, I don't press him. I'm already beginning to read his signals. He is not direct. When he is uncomfortable or doesn't want to talk, he ignores the question. He doesn't volunteer information. But all interesting men are evasive, aren't they? He's an enigma. So, I'm not terribly surprised when he turns into a circular drive with an arch over the entrance with a sign that says Creedmore.

If you'd never heard of Creedmore, but stumbled upon it, you might think it was a private estate with its grand driveway lined by hundred-year-old oak trees with ivy growing up their trunks like long gloves. But it's not an estate, it's a hospital for the elderly, the infirm and, occasionally, the troubled who need a respite from the noise of the world. This is how it was explained to me when I was a girl.

'Does your mother work here?' I ask John as we walk under the awning that leads to the main doors.

'No, she's lived here for the past three years.' John opens the door for me. Beyond the small foyer is an enormous visiting room ringed with the elderly in wheelchairs, some alone, others with weekend visitors. The centre of the room is curiously empty, like a circus ring before the show begins.

As we approach the reception desk, I can see that the patients are clean and well cared for, but that doesn't compensate for the sadness I feel when I look into their eyes. The nurse greets John as he signs in. He shows me through the set of doors leading to the rooms.

'My mother had me late in life. She was nearly forty. Three years ago she had a slight stroke,' John explains as we walk. 'I took care of her myself for the first year, but then she suffered another stroke, that one massive, and lost her speech. Her doctors suggested a convent hospital on Staten Island, but my mother never liked Staten Island. I asked for alternatives and one of the doctors recommended this place.'

John opens the door to his mother's room and motions for me to enter first. The room is fairly spacious, painted mint green, and sparsely furnished. Its saving grace is a large window on the far wall that overlooks a garden with a rolling field behind it.

There are two patients in the room. Closest to the door, sleeping in a bed with the pillows propped almost to sitting position, is a small white-haired lady. In the far bed, looking out at the view, another petite white-haired lady is eating her lunch. Her hair is coiffed with marcel waves; her fingernails are short and painted bright red. She wears a pressed pink housecoat with a zipper front.

'I brought a friend today,' John says as he kisses her on the cheek.

She smiles and looks up at him, then grabs his arm with her hand. He reaches down and gives her another kiss. 'I would like you to meet Lucia Sartori.'

'Hello, Mrs O'Keefe.' I smile at her.

She looks me up and down without smiling and goes back to her soup.

'I brought you some chocolate-covered marshmallows.' John places the box of candy on her bedside table. 'Are they treating you well?'

She can't answer but she does not seem frustrated by this. Obviously, they are treating her well. Her bed is neat and the room is spotless.

John pulls up a chair and indicates that I should sit. He sits on the edge of the bed and takes his mother's hand and chats with her. John has the same strong jawline as his mother, but her eyes are light blue instead of grey. Around her face are touches of faded gold in her white hair, indicating that once upon a time, her hair was red. 'Mrs O'Keefe, were you a redhead?' I ask.

'Yes, she was. A real Irish girl with a genuine Irish temper,' John replies.

Mrs O'Keefe looks out the window and sighs. She reaches for the candy John brought, unwraps it, and offers John and me each a piece. We sit with her for half an hour as John recaps events happening in the news. She doesn't appear to listen, but he presses on, trying to entertain her.

I have never known anyone who lived in a place like Creedmore. When my mother's mother came to live with us after my grandfather died, we took care of her ourselves. It was unheard of to seek help outside the home. As I look at Mrs O'Keefe, I wonder if she knew her life would come to this. John is very attentive, checking with the nurses and making sure she is comfortable. My mother always told me to observe how a son treats his mother. What I see today impresses me.

The drive back to Manhattan seems short, except for the theatre traffic outside the Midtown Tunnel. It's only six o'clock but it feels much later. We spent the whole day together, a day so full, it seemed to last a month. I am tired from the ride, from all the things I saw and learned, and from John himself. He is intelligent and needs more than an eager listener. He needs a confidante with whom he can share the flurry of ideas that seem to come so easily to him.

John pulls up in front of my house, gets out, and opens my door. He extends his hand and helps me out of the car. Then he lifts me up by my waist. I place my hands on his shoulders because my feet are barely touching the ground. Without a word, he gently kisses me. He holds me so tightly, I feel bound to him. I lean back a little to look into his eyes, but they are closed. I wonder what he's thinking. The cold February twilight sends a chill through me, but his face is warm and I bury my nose in his cheek.

'Thank you,' he says softly.

'Mr Talbot?'

'Yes?'

'Are you ever going to ask me before you kiss me?'

'Probably not.' He laughs.

'Just so I know the rules.'

I go up to the stoop and take out my key. John Talbot waits by his car until I am safely inside. I watch him through the windowpanes and hear the low tweet of his whistling as he climbs back into the Packard. He flips open his cigarette case, pulls out a cigarette, taps the tip on the dashboard, and lights it. Then he drives off down the street. The moment the car turns the corner and is out of sight, I feel sad. There it is, the first sign of falling in love, the great longing that comes from even the slightest separation. When I look at him I don't feel that I deserve him, rather that I aspire to him. This will be a love I will have to earn, but something tells me John Talbot is worth it.

I sit down and pull off my snow boots, thinking the house is awfully quiet. When I go to the foot of the stairs, I see a note taped to the banister: 'Come to Saint Vincent's Hospital! We have a girl!' I rush to put my boots back on and run the fifteen-plus blocks to meet my new niece.

Inside the warm hospital I find the stairs to the third-floor maternity ward and take them two at a time. The waiting area outside the new mothers' rooms looks more like a train station than a hospital. Happy fathers corral the newborns' siblings, not quite sure how to handle the children on their own. I see the occasional grandmother or aunt pitching in to help, but it's mostly the overwhelmed daddies, who try to make the children settle down and behave. A nurse, used to the fray, manages the proceedings with patience. I rush to the desk and enquire about the Sartori baby. The nurse smiles and points to the nursery. There is quite a crowd pressing against the large window. Hogging the front are my brothers, my parents and the Lancelattis.

'Excuse me,' I say to the people waiting to get at the window. I squeeze in next to my parents. 'Where is she?'

'Oh, Lucia, Rosemary did so well,' Mama brags. 'She's six pounds three ounces. She's tiny but strong.'

'Which one is she?' I want to know.

Roberto points to an infant swaddled tightly in a white flannel blanket. 'Can't you tell? Look at that head of hair.' Her face peeks out of the cocoon, a pink rosebud with a head of thick black hair.

'She's an angel!' Papa says proudly. 'Not since you were born, Lucia . . .' He gets tears in his eyes.

'That hair reminds me of Mr Castellini's toupee. A lot of hair on top and nothing on the sides,' Exodus comments. The boys laugh.

'That's not funny!' Mama says. It occurs to me that the phrase she utters most often to them is that one.

Papa has his arm around Mama. They look at the baby with such adoration that I can understand why Mama had five children. There's nothing like this moment, nothing as hopeful as the face of a newborn. 'Hey, let's give the other families the window,' I tell everyone.

'*Andiamo*!' Mama says, giving Papa a gentle nudge to move the boys to the waiting area.

The nurse comes in with a chart and looks at us. 'Let me guess. Italians,' she says with a half smile. 'You folks really know how to pack a joint.'

'Are we being too noisy?' I ask her.

'No, no, I'm teasing. Rosemary would like to see her mother, Mrs Sartori, and Lucia.'

'That's Aunt Lucia,' I tell her.

'Boys,' Mama instructs, 'we'll see you at home in a little while.'

'Roberto and I will be in the waiting room,' Papa tells her.

In single file, we follow the nurse down a quiet corridor to Rosemary's room, Mama, Mrs Lancelatti then me. Mama takes Mrs Lancelatti's hand as they enter the room. Rosemary is exhausted. She looks even smaller than usual, and the way she's propped up in bed reminds me of Mrs O'Keefe at Creedmore.

Mrs Lancelatti goes to the opposite side of the bed and kisses her daughter. She cradles Rosemary's face in her hands. 'I am so proud of you,' she says.

'It wasn't bad, Ma. We've decided on her name and we wanted you to hear it first. She is Maria Grace, in honour of our mothers.' Ro smiles. Both Mama and Mrs Lancelatti begin to cry. 'Okay, now you go. I need to sleep.'

'Grace, I made a roast,' Mama says to Mrs Lancelatti across the bed. 'You must all come to dinner.'

'Thank you. That's very kind of you,' Mrs Lancelatti says to Mama. They kiss Rosemary and go out into the hallway together.

'Sleep well, Ro,' I tell her and turn towards the door.

'Lu?'

I take Rosemary's hand. 'Are you all right?'

'I just did one of the most important things I'm ever going to do. And it's so strange . . .' Rosemary looks out the window, but there is no view, only the brick airshaft of the next building. 'It doesn't feel right to take any credit for it.'

'What do you mean?'

'You know, it happened so fast, they couldn't give me anything for the pain.'

'No!'

'It's okay, I'm glad they couldn't put me under. I wanted to see her born. My friends who have babies have told me that one moment they were asleep and the next, they were mothers. I didn't want that. I wanted to see her come into the world with my own eyes.'

'What was it like?'

'She came out, arms in the air, like she was reaching for something. The doctor snipped the cord, and the nurse was about to take her away, and I shouted, "No! Give me my daughter!" They're supposed to check them out first, but I must have scared the nurse because she handed Maria Grace to me. And my baby knew me. She nuzzled me immediately. Then the nurse took her away to clean her up.'

'Were you afraid?'

'A little.' Rosemary smooths the sheets and smiles. 'And then I felt . . . I feel . . . redeemed.' If only she had seen the Lancelattis and the Sartoris as they stood outside the nursery window, she would know that her wedding day will not be the defining moment of her life. Today is the day everyone will remember.

'You're so calm,' I tell her.

'You know, it wasn't what I thought it would be. Not at all. It was as if I was a parachute and Maria Grace was a sky-diver who made it safely to the ground. I got her here, and my job was done.'

'Your job is far from over,' I say with a laugh.

'I know. But I also know it's not my world any more, it belongs to her.'

The nurse comes in the door carrying my new niece. 'It's time to feed her,' she says to Rosemary.

'I'll be right outside,' I tell my sister-in-law.

The nurse gives the baby to Rosemary. Maria Grace seems so much smaller than she did in the nursery, and her hair much darker and thicker, as if she is wearing a black velvet tam.

'Do you want to hold her?' Ro asks. 'That's okay, isn't it?' she says to the nurse.

'Just for a moment,' the nurse replies.

Ro leans down and whispers to the bundle, 'Meet your Aunt Lu,' then hands the baby to me. How warm she is! I hold her like a piece of delicate china.

'Nice to meet you, Maria Grace. When you get big we're going to go to Broadway shows and to get our hair done. We'll buy lots of fancy shoes and purses and paint our nails rose red!' I whisper. 'May God bless you all the days of your long and happy life.' I kiss her and give her back to her mother.

The smell of the baby's skin, coupled with the look on Rosemary's face, content and at peace, makes me cry. This is a moment so rare and beautiful, I cannot hold it. And yet I want to preserve it, because I know that the birth of the first child of my eldest brother is a once-in-a-lifetime event. We go on, I think to myself. We go on and on and on.

Roberto stays at the hospital with Rosemary. When Mama, Papa, the Lancelattis and I arrive at home, we can't believe our eyes. My brothers, who have never set a table or washed a dish in the sum of their collective lives, have the dining-room table set with Mama's best china. The long white taper candles are lit and there's a small centrepiece of pink carnations in a glass bowl. I decide not to rib the boys, because this kind of largesse should be encouraged. Angelo has poured champagne into a series of flutes on Mama's best silver tray and he serves each of us a glass.

'To Maria Grace!' Orlando toasts.

'May she grow healthy and strong!' Mr Lancelatti adds. '*Cent'anni*!'

Dinner is good fun, with my brothers teasing and playing with Rosemary's younger brothers. After dessert they go out back in the garden and Angelo and Exodus toss the younger boys about while Orlando makes up ghost stories to entertain them. Rosemary's little sister stays behind to help clean up after dinner. At the end of a lovely evening, Mrs Lancelatti calls for my brothers to bring in her boys. They're taking the train home to Brooklyn, but first they will stop over at Saint Vincent's and say goodnight to Rosemary, Roberto and Maria Grace.

What a day this has been, I think as I climb the stairs to my room. The five flights, which I usually take at a clip, seem like twice the distance. So much to think about: John Talbot, his mother, the ocean, and now my new niece. And tomorrow is Ruth's wedding! As I change for bed, I glance at the book I was supposed to begin reading today and figure there will be lots of time for that later.

I climb into bed and turn off the lamp, and the room fills with the yellow haze from the streetlights. I think about Sylvia O'Keefe at Creedmore and how happy she was to see her only son. When Ruth and I have a fitting for a young debutante, who is plain, with a so-so figure, we realize the clothes can't make her beautiful; only her inner light can. When people are filled to the brim with love, they are their most beautiful.

Before I go to sleep, I pray for baby Maria Grace, that life will bring her all she desires, that she will grow strong and tall and have big dreams. And then I thank God for sending me a niece. After all these years, it will be nice to have another girl around to help with the dishes.

Chapter Six

After the most exciting Saturday of my life, I not only managed to stay awake through Ruth's wedding but threw myself into the hoopla. I was pulled into the inner circle for the hora, a traditional Jewish dance, and I danced with Ruth's and Harvey's cousins and with Delmarr more times than I could count.

It was a little lonely at work for the next week. I told myself it was because Ruth was away on her honeymoon, but the truth is, I was disappointed that John didn't call.

On Ruth's first day back, she catches me checking the Hub's telephone message board one time too many.

'He hasn't called, Lu. Relax.'

'I can't. I miss him.'

'Oh, please. What do you miss exactly? You had one date with John, a car ride to visit his mother. For Godsakes, why don't you skip the courtship and go directly to marriage? That's how I'll be spending my dreadfully dull Saturday. We just got back from the honeymoon and we're already "spending time with Mother".'

'Lucia, Ruth, come here for a second,' Delmarr calls from the fitting room.

When we get there, Ruth lets out a low whistle. For once she is impressed. 'Where did you get the loot?' she says as she circles around a rolling rack, hung with three gowns, each a confection of white.

'Paris.'

'I'll say.' Ruth nods in approval.

I gently lift one of the hangers off the rack. The gown is as light as whipped cream, but structured as if an architect had had a hand in it. Two dainty silk straps hold up a straight sheath of white satin with a subtle pattern of Medici bumblebees. A row of tiny gold-and-white silk butterflies is daintily sewn up the right seam of the skirt to the waist. Anchoring the left strap is a larger version of the butterfly. I have to know the artist behind this masterpiece. 'Who made this?'

'Spies.' Delmarr laughs. 'Hilda had a sketch artist attending the shows with her and this is a version of a Pierre Balmain. He's starting a ready-to-wear line, so Hilda didn't feel bad pinching the concept. She also pinched one of Balmain's top seamstresses to make the prototype.'

'She's ruthless!' I hold the dress up to my body in the mirror. 'Nothing could ever go wrong for a girl wearing this dress.'

'You'll find out. Try it on.' Delmarr smiles.

'Can I?'

'Come on, I'll help.' Ruth takes the dress, and I follow her behind the dressing screen. I unzip my skirt and step out of it.

'No slip,' Delmarr says, turning his back on the screen as he lights a cigarette.

'Delmarr,' Ruth calls, 'I can't believe the construction. The zipper is hidden under the arm right in the seam. And it's the tiniest zipper I've ever seen!'

Ruth helps me step into the dress, which floats over my hips and falls to my ankles in one smooth drape. I lift my arm as Ruth zips me in. I close my eyes and, twisting gently from side to side, feel the garment on my body. This is a fitting technique taught to us by Hilda Beast, who said that once a woman is in her dress, she shouldn't feel it on her body. If a dress is designed and constructed properly, it should either mould to the woman's figure, or stand away from it without pulling, binding, or tugging at any seam.

'I can't come out,' I shout to Delmarr.

'Why? Doesn't it fit?'

'No, it fits so well, I feel like I'm not wearing anything.'

'Love the French!' Delmarr laughs. 'That's the idea.'

Ruth pushes me out. Delmarr is waiting by the model box and helps me onto it. Ruth grabs a pair of size-seven pumps we keep on hand for fittings and holds the shoes while I step into them.

'I like to think I'm good, but I ain't this good.' Delmarr squints at me in the mirror. I look at myself, but I don't see me, I see a girl transformed by the perfect dress. I hold my arms down by my sides and study my reflection.

'Oh, Lucia,' is all Ruth can say.

'Hold this moment, Miss Sartori.' Delmarr stands on one side of me and Ruth is on the other. 'This is youth. Your star is high in the sky. You may never be this beautiful again. Enjoy it.' He winks at me.

'I wish I had somewhere to go in this number,' I say into the mirror.

'You do. I'm taking Nancy Smith to the cotillion at the Plaza. Her brother is in town and he needs a date.'

'You want me to go?'

'Gee, I'd come,' Ruth says, 'but I'm playing canasta with Harvey's parents and after that we're going for seventeen-cent hamburgers at White Tower. Yippee!'

'Sorry you're busy, Ruth.' Delmarr turns to me. 'You need shoes, stockings, a clutch. You and Ruth go borrowing.'

Ruth and I spend our lunch hour going from department to department currying favours from Delmarr's connections. The managers are happy to loan to Delmarr because he sends our customers to them for accessories. In the Evening-Shoe Department, Ruth picks a white closed-toe mule covered in *peau de soie* with tiny seed pearls on the vamp. We find an ornate Indian clutch made of embroidered tone-on-tone shantung, and over-the-elbow evening gloves with tiny opal buttons from wrist to elbow. I stay so busy all afternoon, I hardly give a thought to John Talbot, though I do wish he could see me in this dress.

I leave work early to have my hair put up for the gala. On the way home I stop at Saint Vincent's to see Maria Grace, but she and her mother are both napping. I stop at the florist's and pick up a gardenia for my hair. My escort will probably bring me a flower, but a girl can never have too many.

Christopher Smith picks me up promptly at 7.30. I find out his life story between the Village and Fifty-Ninth and Fifth. He's an engineer, he graduated from Princeton and left college for two years to serve in the Navy (even though his father could have procured a deferment, Christopher felt strongly that he must serve), and is now working for his father's company, an iron-ore-mining firm. Blond, tall and blue-eyed, Christopher is a typical Upper East Side son of privilege. But he is gracious and warm, with a good sense of humour. This will be a terrific evening. 'I'm going to be honest,' Christopher begins. 'The girls on fix-ups, at least in my experience, never live up to the description beforehand. You're beautiful.' I thank him. In this one instance I do believe the dress is doing all the work. I'm lucky to be wearing it.

The town car pulls up at the main entrance of the Plaza. As we walk up the stairway to the Grand Ballroom, it's as if high society is announcing the coming of spring. The ladies are dressed in pale silks, neutral tones of beige, shell pink and butter yellow. So far, mine is the only white gown (leave it to Balmain to create a trend instead of following one). Christopher seems to know everyone in the outer reception area. A few girls run up and say hello – warmly to him, politely to me. I'm certain they're wondering what he's doing with me. I may look the part, but they know I am not one of them. Society types are one family and each member is known. Anyone new sticks out like a red shoe with a green gown.

While the society girls have not changed, the young men have. In the wake of World War Two, walls have come down. Customs and rituals normally reserved for the select few of a certain lineage have become more inclusive. The line between uptown and downtown blurred as men returned home from the services with young brides from all over the world. Ten years ago, a Catholic girl like me wouldn't have been welcome at the Plaza Hotel, and Christopher would never have agreed to take me. The war changed all that. The uptown boys matured from carefree dandies to sober thinkers. The downtown boys, having fought for their new country, were respected and not treated like second-class citizens. I hold my head high as Christopher leads me into the ballroom. After all, I am the sister of four veterans and the daughter of a successful Manhattan businessman. I belong wherever I want to go and can accept the invitation of anyone who wants to take me.

The superb Vincent Lopez Orchestra is playing as we cross the dance floor to our table. Garlands of daisies and cherry blossom hang from the ceiling like ribbons. Hand-painted murals of country gardens stand out against the room's ornate gold moulding. The tables are set with crisp white linens, and the centrepieces are goldfish bowls with actual fish swimming in them! Ruth won't believe it.

Delmarr waves to me from across the dance floor. He makes his way through the crowd. 'Christopher, nice to see you again,' he says as they shake hands. Then he looks at me. 'What do you think?'

'It's a wonderland,' I tell him as he gives me a twirl.

'You're the prettiest girl here,' Delmarr says. He leans into a small cluster of talking people, and takes a girl's hand and turns her towards us. 'Nancy, come and meet Lucia.' Nancy Smith is the feminine version of her brother, long and lanky, with sky-blue eyes, beautifully complemented by her pale grey gown.

'Nice to meet you. Thank you for taking a charity case tonight,' she says to me, flashing a dazzling smile at her brother.

'It's my pleasure—' I begin, but Nancy is whisked away by another couple.

'You have fun!' she calls over her shoulder.

Delmarr whispers in my ear, 'Her divorce was just made final. This is her first night without the ex. It's like I'm chasing a runaway train.'

'Lucia, I'd like you to meet some of my pals from Princeton.' Christopher puts his hand on my arm. Standing behind him is a group of immaculate young gentlemen, the kind I see in group photos on the society pages. Christopher introduces me to each young man, and they pay me compliments about my dress and hair.

'Are you a princess?' one of them asks.

'No, why do you ask?'

'Your dress has the Medici family symbol in the fabric.'

'You're sharp,' I tell him. 'Do you know what the bumblebee means in Italy?' He shakes his head. 'Royalty.'

'Did you graduate from Vassar?' another of the young men asks me.

'No, I didn't go to college. I went to Katie Gibbs Secretarial School and then got a job as a seamstress at B. Altman's,' I say with pride.

'Oh, to find an old-fashioned girl who likes to sew,' one of the fellows says kindly.

'Back off. She's mine until midnight,' Christopher says as he leads me out onto the dance floor. He's a very smooth dancer. I could get used to a life like this, I think as he pulls me closer. When I look over his shoulder, I am surprised to see John Talbot. In his arms is Amanda Parker, *the* society deb of the moment. As the music changes, John lifts her by the waist, then kisses her just as he kissed me outside my house less than one week ago. The picture stings so, I close my eyes. When I open them, she's still draped on him like fox trim on velvet. The monologue in my head begins: he's not really your beau, well, he did take you for a drive; you have met his mother – but you have no stake, no promise from him; you hardly know him. But then I remember his kiss. Isn't a kiss a promise? A show of intent?

'Are you all right?' Christopher asks.

'I'm fine,' I lie. Then, I decide to turn this buggy around. I am not going to be any man's throwaway girl. John Talbot needs to know I'm not some nobody who's pretty but unconnected. 'Christopher? Do you know Amanda Parker?'

'Sure.'

'I would love to meet her.'

Christopher leads me across the dance floor to Amanda and John. When John sees me coming towards them, he stares at me in disbelief, as though this is a dream and I'm emerging from a Scottish mist with a battalion of poor townsfolk behind me, seeking justice. Then he blanches when he realizes it's really me and I'm really coming to talk to him.

'Amanda, I'd like you to meet my date this evening. This is Lucia Sartori,' Christopher says.

Amanda dips her head down and smiles at me, brushing the shiny flip of her curls behind her ear. This pose, the very same one captured on the society pages, is meant to make her dark patrician beauty into something more vulnerable, when it is clear that she is anything but. Amanda introduces John and then she and Christopher tease each other a bit, but I keep my eyes steadily on John Talbot, who still can't look at me.

'John?'

'Yes?' At last his eyes meet mine, then he looks me up and down, not in a cheap way at all, but rather in admiration.

'It's good to see you again,' I say.

Christopher takes my arm and excuses us, and we go for drinks. I am tempted to turn to see if John Talbot is watching me, but I don't. It wouldn't do any good. He's taken. I should have known he couldn't possibly be available. As angry as I am, I also understand him. He aspires to be a part of this world, too. But what he doesn't know is that the best he and I can do is pass through it on someone else's arm.

As soon as I'm home, I call Ruth and tell her about the dance. She listens thoughtfully to everything I say and decides that I'm overreacting about the kiss John planted on Amanda Parker. I disagree, and when I hang up, I think about that kiss again and again. Each time I replay it in my mind, it drives me further and further away from the idea of John Talbot. 'It's over,' I say to myself aloud as if the intonation makes it official. I get ready for bed, wishing I hadn't gone to the cotillion at all. I see John's face and wish I had never met him.

'Lucia! Wake up!' Mama shakes me.

'What is it?'

'Get dressed. Hurry!'

I look at the clock. It's quarter to five in the morning. 'What's going on?'

'The baby!'

I hear Mama's footsteps click down the stairs. I jump into my slacks and sweater from the day before, forgetting my socks, and run down the stairs. Papa is waiting by the door, and Mama is pulling on her coat and sobbing uncontrollably. I put on the boots that I left near the bench last night, grab my coat, and follow my parents out into the street.

'What happened? Papa? Mama?'

'She's gone. The baby is gone.'

'Gone? What do you mean?'

'She died.' My mother sobs. 'Lucia, she died.'

I don't believe it. We find a cab on Hudson Street and the driver gets us to Saint Vincent's quickly. Mama has not stopped crying. Papa holds on to her but she is inconsolable. I'm certain there's been a terrible mistake. I held Maria Grace in my arms. She was fine. What could possibly have gone wrong?

Instead of waiting for the elevator, we find the stairwell to the maternity ward. We run down the hallway to Rosemary's room but it is empty. A nurse directs us to the room where Maria Grace was taken. Through the glass I see my brother and his wife holding each other. A doctor stands close by. We push the door open. Mama is screaming now. Papa tries to calm her down, but nothing he says can make her stop.

The expression on Rosemary's face is so devastating that I have to look away. Roberto is crying, but the tears are of frustration – he doesn't understand. None of us does. I go to the doctor and grab his arm. 'What happened to the baby?' I ask him.

The doctor has already been through all this with Rosemary and Roberto, and I'm sure he'll have to go through it all again when the Lancelattis get here from Brooklyn, but he explains everything patiently. 'The nurse called me to the ward. Maria Grace was having trouble breathing. I checked her thoroughly and found that her heart rhythm had slowed. I ordered oxygen, but she went into cardiac arrest anyway. Her heart failed. We tried to revive her, but nothing worked. I can offer you no reason for something like it. She was a small baby, but that didn't have anything to do with it. I believe she had a congenital condition, a weakened heart from birth, so weak that there was nothing we could have done to save her.'

Roberto lunges at the doctor, but my father intercedes and holds Roberto tightly. 'My son,' he says. 'Son.' And Papa begins to cry.

'I'm sorry. I'm truly sorry,' the doctor says.

Mama holds Rosemary, whose arms are stiff at her sides. She squeezes her eyes shut as if trying to change the picture of what has happened, hoping that this is just a dream. Maria Grace Sartori died at 3.32 a.m. on 22 February 1951. She did not live two weeks.

Even if I live to be an old lady, I will never experience anything worse than the funeral of my niece. Each word Father Abruzzi utters at the altar of Our Lady of Pompeii in the Mass of the Resurrection sounds like a lie. Heaven, the peace that lives in the heart of Christ for those who believe in Him, and the idea that the baby is safe in the loving arms of the Blessed Lady seem like empty promises made to people in a hopeless moment. I don't believe any of it. It is so cruel when a child dies, and then, adding to the horror, the random blame begins. Who is to blame? The doctor? The hospital? The mother and her milk? The circumstances of Maria Grace's conception? Oh, the guessing that goes on trying to understand the will of God.

At the end of the funeral Mass, our families walk out behind the casket. I can't leave my pew. When Orlando reaches for my hand, I pull it away and shake my head; I want no part of the recessional. I can't bear to look at Rosemary as she walks behind her daughter, knowing that she can never hold her in her arms again. Nor can I stand to see Roberto, who blames himself, certain that some defect in his character made God take away his precious child because he was not worthy of her.

Mama prays and Papa does, too. I can't. I sit in the pew and wait for everyone to leave. I don't want to listen to words of comfort, and I can't offer any. When the last of the mourners are outside on the sidewalk, I look up at the altar, covered in a haze from the incense.

The past couple of days have been so horrible, I've decided I will never have a baby. I couldn't risk this happening to my little girl. I told Papa and he said, 'You can't do that, Lucia. It's not your decision, it's God's.' But it seems to me that if God made the decision to take this baby, He cannot be trusted. I am haunted by how Maria Grace felt in my arms. The newness of her was unlike anything I ever experienced. I feel a hand on my shoulder, but I don't turn to see who it is. I can't.

'I'm sorry, Lucia,' Dante says in a whisper. I reach up to take his hand. He comes and sits next to me. He hugs me and I cry. 'What a terrible, terrible loss,' he says.

'I'm afraid Rosemary and Roberto will do something to themselves. They can't bear to look at each other. We were so happy when she was born. I don't understand why this happened. For what? Why?'

'Maybe the baby came to bring everyone together.'

'But why was she taken when she brought so much joy?'

'I don't know, Lucia.'

'Nobody does. That's what makes this so horrible. There isn't any sane reason for it. Dante, can you think of any reason why this should have happened?'

'I can't. There is none.' Dante takes out his handkerchief and wipes away my tears. 'Your brother and sister-in-law need you. You've got to be strong. I know you can do it,' he says. 'Come on. I'll walk you to your car.'

The church is empty, but the crowd on the sidewalk is still there, comforting Rosemary and Roberto and embracing my parents and brothers. I hold Dante's hand as he walks me through the doors and out into the sunlight. Ruth steps forwards and hugs me. Behind her I see Delmarr, Helen and Violet, who are every bit as devastated as I would be if this terrible thing had happened to one of them.

It is a cold day, with mounds of grey slush left from the last snowstorm piled in the gutters. How ugly the Village looks, how rude the horns blaring in the traffic jam. Where are all the people going anyway? Don't they know what we have lost?

The wind cuts through me. I sob from the pit of my stomach, not caring who hears my weeping. I lean against Dante and give him all my grief. I'm only twenty-six years old, and in one moment, this exquisite world with its possibilities and joyous details went from a lustrous valley to a dark pit. Maria Grace took all the beauty with her.

I look up and see Dante's mother, his father and his brothers and sisters. They encircle me and hold me without saying a word. I feel their strength, and I am not ashamed to take what I need. Sometimes when the worst happens, the only people who truly understand are the ones who have known you since you were small. The DeMartinos are practically family, and they know what to say and do.

Dante helps me into the hearse to travel with my family to the cemetery in Queens where the baby will be buried in the Sartori plot. 'I'll follow you out there,' Dante says. Before he closes the door, he reaches out and takes Roberto's hand. Roberto pulls Dante inside and embraces him, weeping on his shoulder. Dante looks at me and lets my brother cry for a few moments. Finally, Papa puts his arms about Roberto and Dante goes.

Dante stays with me through the burial, which is worse than the funeral, if that's possible. It is so bitterly cold we can hardly stand outside. The priest says his final prayers, but Rosemary will not let go of the casket to put it in the ground. We don't know what to do. Finally Roberto kneels and joins her and, for a long time, both of them hold on to Maria Grace. Orlando and Angelo finally get down on their knees and help Roberto and Rosemary stand. I look for Exodus, but he is over on the road with his back to us, his shoulders heaving as he weeps.

In the days that follow Maria Grace's death, we are like ghosts in our house. There is no music or conversation. Meals are silent ordeals. Dante has stopped by every day since the funeral, either before or after work. Sometimes he sits with me for a couple of hours, sometimes he comes in for a few minutes. He seems to know exactly what to say and do. His compassion extends beyond me, to my brothers, Rosemary and my parents.

At the one-week anniversary of Maria Grace's funeral, there's a knock at my bedroom door.

'Hi, honey.' Dante opens the door. 'Can I come in?'

'Sure.'

'So, this is your room,' Dante says, drinking in the details. He looks at my bed, as though he has imagined me there, or imagined himself there with me, then he turns away in embarrassment. 'It's exactly as I pictured it.'

'Really? I always thought if a man laid eyes on my canopy bed, he'd burst into flames like Saint Lorenzo.' I pat the bed and invite him to sit down.

Dante sits next to me. 'So far, so good.'

'So, how do you like it?'

'It looks as though a princess who likes to read and sew lives up here. Honey, I'm worried about you. You need to go outside.'

I gaze out the window and think about going outside. Every day I try to go, and every day I stay in my room.

'The longer you wait, the worse it will be. Come on. I'll take you.'

Dante sees my suede loafers by the vanity table. He brings them to me, then kneels and puts them on my feet. He stands, gently pulls me off of the bed, and gives me a hug. He walks me to the door and puts a hand on my back as we descend the stairs. When we get to the hall, he helps me into my coat and wraps a scarf around my neck. Then he takes my hand and opens the door. I follow him out onto our stoop.

'See, that wasn't so bad, was it?' he says.

I look back at my house. 'It's so quiet in there.'

'I know. It's very strange.' Dante takes my hand as we head towards Grove Street. I stop him and put my hands on the lapels of his coat.

'Dante, thank you for being there for all of us. I don't know how to repay you. I don't think there is any way.'

Dante puts his arms around me. 'You're family, Lucia.'

'Almost was.'

'You'll always be my girl. You were from the first moment I saw you. You were sitting in church with your brothers. You were eight years old and I was twelve and I thought, I hope she waits for me. Lucia, I'll wait forever if I have to.'

Dante pulls me close. We stand by the wrought-iron gate in front of the McIntyres' brownstone. It's the very spot where he kissed me for the first time when I was fifteen. I wonder if he remembers. He leans towards me and kisses me softly on each cheek and then finds my mouth. I'm so sad from all that's happened that I fall into this familiar place like the old chenille pillows I've had on my bed since I was a girl. I wonder how many times he kissed me during our time together. A thousand? More? How many times have I buried my face in his neck and breathed in the smell of his skin?

'You must hate me for the way I broke off our engagement.'

'How could I hate the girl I used to stare at in church?'

'Well, I was staring back. I thought you were the best-looking older man I ever saw.' Dante laughs and takes my hand again, and we walk for a long time in silence. The only people in the world who have known me longer than Dante are my own family. 'Dante . . .' I say after a while.

'You don't have to say anything, Lucia,' he tells me. 'I understand.'

The only thing that could get me back out into the world is the thought of returning to work. I miss my friends and the comfort of our routine in the Custom Department. I've taken two weeks off, something I was only able to do because Hilda Cramer was in Paris for the runway shows and had no idea who was in the shop and who wasn't. Now Hilda's back, and I'm ready to return to my routine. My room at home is beginning to feel a little like a prison.

There is a rolling rack of debutante gowns to hem by my desk. As I flip through them, I see Helen has pinned them up nicely. I take the first white silk shantung gown off the hanger and fit it onto the mannequin. I get out my needle and thread and begin to stitch, following the perfect line of pins.

How can I describe how much I love to sew? It's as though my hands have known what to do from the first moment I held a needle. My left hand pulls the edge of the fabric taut while my right hand pedals in and out with the thread. I'm so good at it, and I've done it for so long that the tiny stitches are invisible. Hems were the hardest thing for me to learn. It takes precision to keep the hem even as you sew, and a lopsided hem ruins an entire garment. Nonna Sartori used to say to me, 'No one has to know how many times you rip out the hem.' Sometimes I ripped out a hem fifty times to get it right. Now, it's second nature. I get it right the first time.

Ruth bursts in the Hub and makes a beeline for me. 'He's here! Talbot. He's on his way in.'

'So?' I ask calmly, without taking my eyes off the hem.

'If you want to skedaddle, you've got time.'

'If he's coming to see me, I'm ready for him,' I tell her.

Ruth sits down at her drawing table and waits, keeping her eyes on the doors. 'He's in,' she whispers. I don't look up. I keep my eyes on the hem.

'Hello, Lucia. How are you?' John Talbot asks.

'I'm better. Thank you for the lovely flowers you sent. They were beautiful.'

'It was a small thing, but I wanted you to know I was thinking of you . . . and your family.'

'It was very kind.'

'I want to explain something,' he begins.

Ruth clears her throat, picks up a sketch and goes into Delmarr's office.

I sense a big wind-up for a dissertation about why John chose Amanda Parker over me, but the truth is, I understand it in a way. As much as I may aspire to be a part of the world I make costumes for, there are certain elements of high society that I find repugnant. I could not live by their code. Marriage has a different meaning above Thirty-fourth Street. Affairs are tolerated and blue-bloods are loyal to a family crest instead of the bond between a man and a woman. I may like the lifestyle, but I don't approve of the morals. I think more of myself than that. 'Please, John, I don't need an explanation. I believe you should see whomever you like. And good luck to you.'

'I broke off with her, Lucia. I don't want Amanda. I want you.'

It seems as though Papa and his cousin have written hundreds of letters back and forth planning our August holiday in the Veneto. Cousin Domenic and his wife, Bartolomea, sent Rosemary and Roberto a beautiful icon, a silver picture of the Blessed Lady, when Maria Grace died. Ro keeps it on her nightstand and prays her rosary, begging for strength.

'I have an idea,' Papa says to me as I help him count the change at the store. 'I'm going to convince Rosemary and Roberto to come to Italy with us. What do you think?'

'I think it's a great idea.'

'A change of scenery might help them.' Papa lowers his voice. 'How do you think Rosemary is doing?'

'I don't know. She seems a little better sometimes, and then she starts to cry and she can't stop. Mama tries to console her, but it's so hard.'

'I'm going to lock up,' Papa tells me as he starts his nightly ritual. Since I was a girl, I loved to be in the store at closing time, to watch him put a final mist on the fresh vegetables, feed the 'mouser' cat, Moto, and turn out the lights.

'Dante stopped by today,' Papa says casually.

'How is he?' Since John Talbot's slow return to my life, Dante has slipped away again.

'He's all right. He wonders why you won't see him.'

I can't believe Dante confided in my father! I haven't said a word to Pop about him.

'And don't get mad at him,' Pop goes on. 'He didn't say anything. I asked him what was happening with you two.'

'Why would you ask?'

Papa is spraying the vegetables and he doesn't turn around. 'Maybe I like him. And maybe I think he's right for you.'

'Oh, Pop.'

I wish I could tell my father why I've avoided Dante since the night he kissed me. I felt myself fall back into the well of him, and with it the same old feeling of being trapped returned.

'Papa, do you like John Talbot?'

'Why do you ask?' Papa walks over to the counter. 'You aren't seeing him again, are you?'

'We go to lunch.' I sound vague, but the truth is, John and I see each other most days. We have lunch, go for a drive or visit his mother. He is slowly proving to me that I am the only girl in his life.

'He's not for you, Lucia.'

'Papa!'

'You asked me! So I tell you the truth. Mr Talbot is a mystery to me. And I don't understand what he does with his time,' he says as he takes off his apron, folds it and places it under the counter. Then he comes around and stands right in front of me.

'He's a businessman, like you,' I assert.

'No, he's a snappy dresser with a fancy car who seems to have big plans and no job.'

'I like a man who presents himself well and has polish. It shows a certain confidence. As for his plans, he has big dreams, and you of all people, Papa, someone who came to this country with nothing and built a business, should understand aiming high.'

'Lucia, watch what men do, not what they say.' Papa places his hands on the counter and leans back against it.

'What am I missing, Papa? What do you see that I don't?'

'All people have blind spots. And you have a blind spot about Mr Talbot. You are too enamoured of the surface. You like his clothes and his lifestyle, the ease of it. This is a weakness in you, but it is also your talent. You make wonderful garments and you have an eye for beauty. But you also have a way of covering flaws with skill. You told me about the lady built like an eggplant who needed a new dress. You performed a magic trick: you dropped the waist of the dress and padded the shoulders, giving the illusion of a figure in proportion. When it comes to John Talbot, you cannot see what he really is, because you admire him too much. And if he does have some defect of character, you are confident you can fix it. This is no good.'

'Papa, I know what I want. I do admire him. I don't see anything wrong with that.'

'I know that you will overlook his flaws in favour of his strengths. But when you marry someone, you must understand the flaws in order to appreciate the strengths. Lucia,' Papa says wearily, 'who has known you since the day you were born? Have I ever discouraged you based on my own weaknesses?'

'No, Papa.'

'I will never tell you what to do or who to love. I only ask that you stay alert. Stay awake. Don't rush.'

'I can promise you, Papa, that I won't rush anything.'

I have a sick feeling in my stomach. I want Papa to like John. If I am to continue seeing him, it's important to have my father's support.

'Lucia. Invite the man to Sunday dinner.'

'Do you mean it, Pop?'

'Let's see what he's made of.' Papa smiles and gives me a stick of cherry candy like he used to when I was a girl. 'Let's go home.'

After three consecutive Sunday dinners at my house, John Talbot and I are officially a couple. Mama adores him. Papa is unconvinced, but at least he's trying. John and I have begun to see each other exclusively, so Ruth and Harvey have invited us for their first Seder supper in their own home. Usually, I spend all of Easter week in church, beginning with Holy Thursday, then Good Friday and the Easter Vigil at midnight on Holy Saturday. Easter morning has always been my favourite holiday, but this year I won't attend any of the festivities. I haven't been back to Our Lady of Pompeii since Maria Grace died. Sometimes I want to pray, but when I try, I can't. I'm still angry at God, and to pray when I feel this way is false. Mama is worried about my faith, but I can't pretend to feel comfort in a place that continues to bring me pain and reminds me how easily God abandoned us when we most needed Him.

I've never been to a Seder, but I know that for the last couple of weeks Ruth has been preparing the traditional Passover foods, which symbolize the journey of the Jewish people out of Egypt. The newlywed Goldfarbs (Ruth lost the battle to keep her own name) found a quaint apartment on Gramercy Park, across town from Commerce Street.

'Are you sure you want to walk?' John asks as he takes my hand on the stoop.

'Do you?'

'Sure.' John looks handsome in his navy gabardine suit. 'Do I look all right for a Seder?'

'I'd say so.' I find it endearing that John is a little worried about whether my friends will like him. 'You look perfectly appropriate. Sharp.'

'You look beautiful,' he says. 'I love you in yellow.'

'I made it myself,' I tell him. Delmarr got some soft wool crepe on a buying trip to Montreal. From it, I built a day suit, with black-and-white herringbone trim and gold buttons on the jacket. My favourite part is the peplum, which ruffles in a subtle way in the front and is cut deep in the back to give the jacket movement. I found matching shoes on sample sale at the store, black *peau de soie* pumps.

'I love a girl who can make her own clothes,' John says.

'Just any girl?' I'm instantly embarrassed to be acting so coy. John and I are well beyond this.

'Not just any. You.' John stops and pulls me close. He kisses me on the corner of Cornelia Street. A cabbie whistles at us as he goes by.

'Thank you. You make me feel good when you say things like that.'

'I love you, Lucia.'

I close my eyes to savour the words. John Talbot loves me! 'I love you, John,' I tell him.

'I was hoping.' He smiles.

We walk for a while and stop at the liquor store, where John buys a bottle of wine for Harvey and Ruth. Rosemary made macaroons which I'm carrying in a pretty tin. John takes my arm as we cross Fifth Avenue.

'Lucia, one thing concerns me.'

I feel a pang in my stomach. He told me he loved me, but here comes the bad news. 'What's that?' I say as lightly as I can manage.

'Your father doesn't like me.'

'He likes you,' I lie. Surely John can't see through Papa's excellent manners.

'No, he doesn't. He thinks I'm a phoney.'

'A phoney?' I wave off the idea. 'John, listen to me. Papa is old-fashioned. He understands things in a basic, simple way. He believes there are only three businesses to be involved in: food, clothing, and shelter. You dabble in other areas, ones he doesn't understand. That's all.'

'You understand what I do, don't you?'

'You're an entrepreneur.' If I'm honest, I don't think much about what John does for a living. I know he's very busy, he travels a lot, and he makes good money. He dresses well and takes me to the best places. He has a regular table at the Vesuvio on West Forty-eighth Street. What else do I need to know? Papa's apprehension is the reaction of an overprotective father.

'I wish you'd talk to your father and explain that I'm trustworthy.'

'Put yourself in his place for a minute. I'm his only daughter. You know he's been protective of me all my life, and as I get older, it gets worse. There seems to be more pressure from him.'

'What about the pressure on me? He makes me feel like I'm trying to take advantage of you.'

'You know that's not true, so don't worry about it.' I tighten my grip on John's arm.

'I'm old-fashioned myself. I'm not looking for his approval. I want his respect.'

'Give it time,' I say reassuringly.

'I know you're the biggest catch in Greenwich Village.'

I laugh. 'You're crazy!'

'Don't you see what happens when you walk down the street? Heads turn. Literally. Heads turn because people want to get a look at you. You're not a small person with a small life. You have a big destiny.'

I don't know what to say. Nobody has ever seen me this way before. Maybe Delmarr a little, but certainly not Dante, who saw me as the baker's wife. 'I never think of myself like that. How far can a career girl go without the right address and surname?'

'You can do anything you want.'

I stop John and kiss him. I love that he believes in me and understands what I want. He sees me in the context of a big world, not simply of the neighbourhood. John sees what I will become.

Ruth and Harvey's apartment is railroad-style. The rooms are small but Ruth has decorated boldly, using paint, wallpaper and draperies made from overstock fabrics at work. She has set a beautiful table; the choices from her bridal registry were the best of the best. Though the fine china and faceted stemware are too grand for the one-bedroom apartment, it doesn't matter. Ruth is happy. She and Harvey, after the world's longest courtship and engagement, belong to each other, and while there were no surprises in what they were getting, they clearly relish the novelty of a life together.

During the meal, John squeezes my hand under the table. It's almost as if we have a secret from the world. We love each other and we said it aloud. If he is crazy about me, I'm even more crazy about him. I would do whatever is necessary to make John Talbot happy, anything in the world.

When I arrive at work early and see that Hilda Cramer's assistant has left a pile of new work for us to do, it occurs to me that the Custom Department is like the fairytale with the shoemaker (Hilda) and the elves (us). A mysterious messenger drops off assignments at night, we make the clothes, and then the messenger whisks them away to see if they pass muster. I imagine Hilda sitting in her sleek Upper East Side penthouse as the messenger holds up each piece and she approves or rejects our efforts.

'What are you doing here so early?' Delmarr asks when he spots me at my desk.

'I'm not sleeping well,' I say.

'I could think of a thousand things to do that are more fun than getting to work early.'

'Well, I can't think of any. That's why I'm here.'

'Fair enough.' Delmarr pours himself a cup of coffee and freshens mine.

'Thank you,' I say, reaching for the cup. 'What are *you* doing here so early?'

'The truth?' Delmarr lights a cigarette. 'I'm planning my next move.'

'You're not leaving B. Altman's, are you?' My insides go into panic mode. If Delmarr left, what would happen to me, Ruth and the Flappers? He's our leader. This place would have to close without him.

'Maybe.'

'But—'

'Shhh, Lucia, I wouldn't leave you here. You'd come with me.'

I feel a sense of relief but also sadness. I love Altman's. How could I ever leave? But how much of my love of this department is about my respect for and awe of Delmarr? In an instant, I decide I would follow him.

'So, would you go with me?' he asks.

'Anywhere. Anytime. You just have to name it.'

'Really?' Delmarr sits back.

'Yep. And you don't even have to marry me.'

'Sorry, I couldn't do that anyway. Not to you. Not to anyone. I love spending my Friday nights at El Morocco drinking Manhattans and talking with the regulars, getting home at sunrise, and sleeping through most of Saturday. I ain't husband material.'

'No, you aren't.'

He smiles. 'I came here for the bachelor life. If I'd wanted to be trapped I would have stayed on the farm in Ver-sales, Indiana. It's spelled Versailles, like the French palace, but they pronounce it like it rhymes with 'yard sale'. I figured that was reason number one to move. Never live in a town with a name the natives can't pronounce.'

'You've never talked about where you're from.'

'I didn't think you could handle the excitement,' he laughs. 'It was rustic. With one movie theatre. My salvation. I loved the movies. Especially Park Avenue comedies where a young heiress falls for the butler and you find out he's a prince. The men were swell. They were charming and funny and well dressed and got the girl – always got the girl. I wanted to be like that, not like the farmers I saw around me, who worked outside and never said much. I lived for conversation. And then I found my talent. I would draw scenes from the movies, you know, tableaux of characters. A teacher of mine saw the drawings and began to encourage me.'

'You were a prodigy.'

'Oh yeah. Nobody could draw like me, at least not in Versailles. But it wasn't my talent that separated me from the folks I grew up with. It was curiosity. I really wanted to see the Atlantic Ocean. I know that sounds nuts, but I wanted to know what sand felt like on my feet, and what waves looked like. I had a list of things I wanted to see. I wanted to find places like that ballroom where Fred Astaire and Ginger Rogers danced in *Top Hat*.'

'You're a regular at El Morocco. That's pretty close.'

'I worked on the farm and as an illustrator at the local paper. When the war came, I went into the navy with the express purpose of getting to New York City. An old teacher submitted my drawings and that's how I wound up at the New York School of Design on a G. I. Bill. Imagine that. I had to serve in the worst front of the Pacific theatre to get my shot at the big town. I wanted to see an ocean and by God I got to see one. And when the war was over, I was so happy I hadn't got killed, I promised myself I would take big risks. So that's when I dropped my last name and invented the suave man you see before you. Delmer Dickinson of Versailles, Indiana, became Delmarr.'

'Delmarr definitely sounds more uptown than Delmer.'

'Hilda wanted to know if I was French when she interviewed me. I was going to lie and say yes, but then I reconsidered and said, "Miss Cramer, the only thing French about me is the croissant I had for breakfast." She laughed and I got the job.'

Chapter Seven

Most people love autumn in New York City, but to me June is the most beautiful month. Girls' hats change from felt to straw, winter boots go back in the closet and are replaced with breezy sandals, and wool skirts are traded in for glorious billows of crisp cotton piqué. Everywhere you turn, women look like bright blooms bursting in a garden.

Weddings are on everyone's mind. The society girls call this June Swoon; Delmarr calls it Bitch Witch Month, since we are deluged by cranky brides and their demanding mothers. We work round the clock to finish gowns in all categories, for the brides themselves, their mothers, the attendants, down to the flower girls. Most brides have their final fittings about ten days before the wedding, so the work schedule in the Hub is feverish.

Delmarr ordered up bolts of crisp voile by the ton in pastel shades of pink, blue, mint green and butter yellow. By the end of June, we will have used every inch of it. 'Stick with the classics,' we hear Delmarr say a thousand times a day in his office to yet another nervous bride leafing through swatches. After she's made her decision and left, he comes out and ceremoniously declares, 'Another wedding party. Pink voile.' Delmarr may be a great designer, but he is an even better salesman.

Due to the volume of clientele moving through, gossip is rampant. While Ruth was doing a fitting for a society bride, she overheard the girl swapping stories with her maid of honour about Amanda Parker, who was recently betrothed to a lawyer at one of the city's big law firms. Hearing she is off the market for good made me smile. I don't need any of John's old flames re-igniting and ruining our courtship.

A mere fifty blocks separate my life in Greenwich Village from the grandeur of the Upper East Side of Manhattan but, in truth, they are worlds apart. There's a lustre and history to uptown life that we first-generation immigrant girls aren't part of, and we know it. As an Italian girl, I'm welcome in the posh private clubs only if I'm on the arm of a member. Ruth is Jewish, so she's out entirely. Helen Gannon's father was a beat cop in Brooklyn so she's out, too. And poor Violet is the daughter of a widow on public assistance, so she never had an opportunity to secure the right connections and rise above her station. Still, I would choose my friends over any of the daughters of privilege I have sewn for. My girls have the kind of character that comes from having earned their place in the world.

Helen measures out three and a half yards of white dotted swiss on the cutting table. I'm on my way over to help anchor the fabric when she stands and turns towards us. 'All right, I can't keep this secret any longer.' Her tone is uncharacteristically chipper. 'Girls, I have news. There's going to be a baby Gannon.' We gather round and congratulate her.

'Is it okay if I have news, too?' Violet says meekly. 'I don't want to take any of the lustre away from Helen's.'

'You won't,' Helen says. 'Spill it. I have nine months to regain the lustre.'

'I'm happy to announce that I have been seeing one Officer Daniel Cassidy. I met him when I reported a lurker at the Fifty-Ninth Street subway station. We're on our third date. I think he likes me.'

'Are you smitten back?' I ask her.

'I'm hopeful,' Violet says with a sigh. Then she beams. 'Let's say I have a very Presbyterian view of things even though I was raised Roman Catholic.'

'Let me guess, the cop is a Presbyterian,' Ruth says, turning back to her work.

'Yes, he is, but that's not why I'm opening up to new religious ideas,' Violet explains. 'Instead of believing in the sin ladder, with its steps of venial, mortal and fry in hell, I have come to embrace the belief of predestination. The stories of our lives have already been written and we're simply following a divine plan. The good things that happen to us were meant to happen, and the bad things that happen are lessons meant to teach us to be better.'

'You're kidding, right?' Ruth says. 'I need a drink.'

'The only one allowed to drink on the job is Hilda Beast Cramer.' Helen moves closer. 'And I know, because I had to fix the facing on her suit jacket and it smelled of Eau de Gin at three in the afternoon.'

'That's why she never married,' Ruth says, sweeping fabric remnants off the cutting table and into a bin. 'She's too busy pitching woo with Tom Collins,'

'Hey, don't knock the original career girl,' I say, feeling the need to defend the old battle-axe. 'What's wrong with being a lifer, a career girl first and always? Without her, we wouldn't be working at Altman's.'

Violet trims the edges of the waxy pattern paper. 'Get you. You're the last person who would wind up like Hilda. You have more beaus than buttons. Has your father thawed towards John at all? Is he going to Italy with your family?' She pins the pattern pieces to the fabric. Helen hands her the shears and Violet begins to cut the material.

'You know my father would never allow me to bring anyone but a husband on a trip that involves any sort of sleeping, anywhere.'

'Don't worry,' Helen says. 'It may take time but, once you're married, your father will come around.'

'First he's going to make it hard on you,' Ruth says. 'It's all part of Papa Sartori's master plan. He wants to get you out of the country and away from John, so he can tempt you with a continental type.' She hands me a stack of drawings for filing. I laugh at her comment, but I don't find it funny. Though Papa is cordial to John, he still isn't warm, and no matter what John does or I say, Papa is not budging. Well, I'm as stubborn as Pop. I'll have a whole month in Italy to convince him. When he sees that I love John more after a month of separation, he will surely accept him.

I sit down at my work desk and begin to sort through Delmarr's sketches. We'll build some dresses for the fall, and the rest of the sketches, never realized, will be filed. As I lay out his work, I see themes emerge. Delmarr is easing fashion from Dior's New Look, with its tight waists and opulent skirts, into what will surely come next, very feminine, unstructured dresses in fabrics that women can care for with little effort. The structure, the pleats, tucks and padding, is gone, to be replaced with simple lines. Delmarr is offering convenience to the new post-war career girl as well as to the busy housewife. In the margins he has written words like 'easy', 'low maintenance' and 'washable'. He understands the needs of career girls and homemakers better than we do ourselves. Time is the new luxury, and Delmarr knows it.

Sometimes, if I have a couple of hours before a date, I pull my sewing chair out onto my tiny terrace, put my feet up, and let the fresh air put pink in my cheeks instead of Max Factor. The view is one of my favourite things about my room. When I look across the way at the back yards of our neighbours, separated by fences and the occasional low tree, I see every interpretation and style of garden, from an ornate rococo sculpture garden of marble angels to a rustic country bench under a lone oak tree. Life on Commerce Street is as layered as one of Rosemary's Napoleon pastries.

Delmarr says the longest wait in life is when you're waiting for someone to die, but I disagree: it's when you're waiting for a man to ask you to marry him. Since the night of Ruth's Seder, when John told me he loved me, I have been waiting for a proposal. What else do we need to know about each other?

With John there's never any talk of me quitting my job, no assumptions like Harvey has about Ruth's career, only ideas about how he and I can work in tandem, partners in all things. Of course, I would make him a beautiful home. We could summer in Huntington Bay and, for the rest of the year, I picture a penthouse on Fifth Avenue with a wrap-around terrace where I can grow roses. I imagine elegant dinner parties by candlelight and long lazy Sunday afternoons reading on our chaises longues until the sun begins its descent over the Hudson River. I thought I would never leave Greenwich Village, but now I want to live uptown.

I don't think our future will include children. Maria Grace's passing changed my perspective on that forever, and John doesn't show much interest in child rearing either. I can see him taking my nieces and nephews for ice-cream sundaes at Rumplemayer's and carriage rides in Central Park. Our lives will be filled with socializing and our careers. Where would children fit in that picture?

While John is attentive and warm and kind, our conversations about the future end abruptly when we get beyond the summer of 1951. Surely John knows that if we were engaged I would have invited him to Italy. But he hasn't asked me, so he'll stay behind and work while I see the Veneto for the first time. As of tomorrow, 30 June, I am still unmarried and unintended. John has business in Chicago during the month of July, and we leave on the first of August, so I won't see him for two whole months. He must realize I'm disappointed, but I am determined not to bring the subject up. There's nothing worse than a woman who has to pry a marriage proposal out of a man.

The aspect of his Italian upbringing that my father holds on to most is the 'holiday', the month of vacation he takes each August without fail. Every year since Roberto was born, Papa has closed the Groceria and taken our family out of the city. We've rented a lakeside cottage in Maine, a house on the Jersey shore and a bungalow on Rehoboth Beach in Delaware. Once we arrive at our destination, work is never mentioned. We swim, eat, laugh and play board games. I've never seen Papa as excited as he is this year, knowing he'll be returning, with his entire family, to his boyhood home.

To make our last day together special John is driving me all the way to the beach on the eastern tip of Long Island. I'm taking extra care dressing for our date because I want to leave him with the best picture of me until we meet again in September. I wear a new white cotton bathing suit, with a vent of illusion netting around the waist. Ruth and I bought suits wholesale when Cole of California came through with their trade sale.

John is due to pick me up in a few minutes, so I dress quickly. Over my white swimsuit, I button on a full tulip skirt with bold alternating panels of bright white and hot pink. I wear matching pink espadrilles with ballerina ties around the ankles. I load wide gold bangles on one arm. I attach a coral-and-pearl starfish brooch, the only piece of jewellery John has given me, to the crown of my wide-brimmed straw hat.

When I look into the mirror on my vanity table, I see an exhausted girl. A month of working day in and day out does not make for a serene countenance and bright eyes. I hope my bright pink-and-white ensemble will make up for the grey half moons under my eyes.

'John's here!' Mama shouts from the bottom of the stairs. I grab my beach bag and go downstairs, where he's waiting for me in a pair of white chinos and a pale blue cotton shirt. He's already tan and, with his black hair, he looks like one of those rich playboys you see in *Life* magazine on the terrace of a villa on the Isle of Capri.

'You look pretty,' he says and kisses me on the nose.

'So do you,' I tell him.

John takes my beach bag from me while resisting Mama's endless pleas to bring some food for the drive. 'No, thank you, Mrs Sartori, we'll get a bite out at the beach.'

'All right,' Mama acquiesces as she sees us out.

In the car John chats excitedly about a deal he has brewing with a plant nursery in New Jersey. Apparently, the contract for supplying trees to Manhattan's parks has expired and John wants to get in on it.

'Is there any kind of business you won't do?' I ask him.

'What does that mean?' John shoots me a wounded look, then turns his attention back to the traffic.

Papa still believes that John is frittering away his time in nightclubs and prefers a good party to an honest day's work. Papa told me that John needs to settle on one kind of business instead of dabbling in anything that comes his way. I tried to tell Papa that a hotelier in Manhattan needs connections, and those are made in restaurants and nightclubs frequented by the elite. 'Honey, you're very eclectic in your business dealings. That's all I'm saying.'

'Oh. Well, yeah.' John's posture relaxes a bit. 'It's a big city and there's a lot to be done. I met one of the Mayor's aides in the dining room at the Taft Hotel – that's where all of them have breakfast – and I started a conversation over scrambled eggs at the buffet. He mentioned the parks contract and I made a couple of calls, and here we are. I'm doing a little business with the city.'

'That's fantastic,' I tell him, giving his arm a bit of a squeeze.

John smiles at me, relieved that I approve. I never tell him what I'm really thinking when it comes to his business life and he never questions my attitude. I wonder if this is a bad sign. He doesn't instinctively know how I feel, and I'm becoming reluctant to tell him. I'm sure these silly fears will disappear after we marry.

As a girl who's worked since I was twenty, I have a pretty good head for business. I'm no expert, but I agree with Papa: the only way to get results is to focus on one product, make the best item you can and then sell it to the widest possible audience. Papa taught me the importance of serving the customer and giving them a pleasant experience when they're shopping. The Groceria is artfully laid out, and the customers enjoy the displays as much as the food he sells, and he gives away small samples while people shop. When I told Delmarr, he imitated Papa and made sure that when customers came in for a fitting, we offered them coffee or tea with a pastry. It's the personal service that's important.

John drives us all the way out to Montauk Point. We have hot dogs and soda at a roadside stand and take a long walk on the beach. We climb to the top of the lighthouse and stroll through its gardens. As we walk along the streets admiring the homes with an ocean view, John points out the different styles of houses and asks me which one I like best. I appreciate that he pictures us in homes I've only seen in magazines. I think of Dante DeMartino, who would have been content to live with me in his parents' home all his life, with an occasional weekend trip to Coney Island. The life I'll have with John Talbot is beyond anything Dante could have imagined.

As we drive back towards the city, we pass a yard sale in front of an old Victorian house. I see a rocking chair painted pale yellow that would fit nicely in my front window. I crane my neck to survey the goods as we go by, and John suddenly stops and turns the car around. I start to object, but he cuts me off. 'I saw that look. You can't tell me you don't want to have a go at that sale.'

We're not the only ones who have taken a detour on the way back from the beach to see what treasures the old house might be hiding. Cars are parked on the lawn and dozens of people are milling about. The rocking chair has a small 'sold' sticker on it. 'That was a lure,' John says quietly. 'Who doesn't love an old rocker?' He goes over to a folding table packed with personal items from handkerchiefs to shoes and holds up a small turquoise enamel vanity mirror with a matching hairbrush.

'You must have this,' John says, pulling out his wallet as he turns to the gentleman overseeing the sale. He hands a bill to the man, who promptly hands it back, explaining, 'I don't have that kind of change.'

John shuffles through the bills in his wallet; they all seem to be hundred-dollar bills, nothing smaller.

'How much is the set?' I ask.

'Two dollars.'

I open my purse and give the man two dollar bills.

John shrugs at the salesman, then kisses me on the forehead and says, 'I owe you, honey.' I can feel the salesman watching us as we go back to the car. We drive through a series of small seaside towns separated by fields and make our way down quaint main streets, passing an old-fashioned ice-cream parlour and boutiques holding sidewalk sales of clothes, books and handmade crafts. The twilight sky turns from bright blue to purple as the sun meets the water in an explosion of hot pink clouds. As we near Huntington John turns off the main road and heads to our favourite spot.

He pulls up in front of the open field where he took me last winter, gets out of the car, and opens my door. 'Here we are,' he says, helping me out.

'Look, more houses going up.' I point to the field behind us, where two more homes are being built. 'Soon we won't be able to park here.'

'Why?'

'Because this land will be sold and somebody will put a house on it.'

'You're right,' John says. 'It has been sold.'

'I knew it,' I say, sighing and looking out at the bay. 'How could land with a view like this sit for long? They're very lucky.'

'You are,' John says with a grin.

'What do you—'

He pulls me close and kisses me. 'This is where I am going to build you a house, Mrs Talbot.'

'*Mrs Talbot*?' I am thrilled by the sound of it. This moment goes beyond what I imagined it would be.

'You will be, if you say yes. Will you marry me, Lucia Sartori?'

John Talbot gets down on one knee and opens a velvet box. Inside is a ring with an emerald-cut diamond, simple, spare and white, in a magnificent platinum setting.

'Yes, I will marry you.' I rest my hand on John's shoulder.

He stands. 'Go ahead, put this ice rink on your finger.' He pulls the ring out of the box and places it on my hand. I begin to cry. 'Now you're legit, Mrs Talbot. Two carats worth of legit.'

I laugh. 'Legit? What a word!'

John continues holding my hand in both of his. 'Well, it's not all that you are. You are everything to me, Lucia. You believe in me, and no one has ever really believed in me before. I'm a successful man, but I've always had to scrape and fight and push for my place. I've travelled a lot, and everywhere I went I looked for the girl who would be mine for life. After all that, I found you right here in New York. I wouldn't have believed it could happen. I'm the luckiest man in the world.'

I imagine John travelling alone without me and the thought makes me sad. I have such empathy for him, I want to take care of him. And now I'll have a lifetime to love him. He covers my face in small kisses, and then moves to my ear and down my neck.

I know the rules. I am supposed to wait until my wedding night, but I can't. I won't. I would give John Talbot everything I have in this moment, my heart, my mind, my home, all of it, and it would be the right thing to do. John's hands slide under my skirt, and he carries me to the far side of the field, where a hill leads down to a dune. The sky is a veil of orange haze. I look up into John's eyes and I see what I have prayed for. This man loves me and only me. He slowly undoes each button of my skirt and then uses it to make a blanket beneath us on the sand. He gently slides on top of me. 'I love you,' he says.

All my life I've wondered what this moment would be like, and now that it is here, it's as though I'm not in my body, I'm somehow floating above this romantic scene, savouring details, but not feeling as though it is entirely mine. Then John's kiss reminds me why I'm here and why he's chosen *me* out of all the girls in the world. In the rise and fall of his breathing, and his gentle caresses, this feels right.

Slowly, all sound and scenery fall away, as in the moment I met him. When something is right, there's no need to be afraid, and there is no reason to question it.

I run my hands through his thick hair, and the dazzling stone of the ring catches the last bit of light before the sun buries itself behind the dune. The best day of my twenty-six years turns into night, and if the sun never returned, I wouldn't mind.

John and I don't say a word as he drives me home to Commerce Street. I sit close to him as he drives with his arm around me, and every few minutes, he leans over and kisses me. The art of conversation isn't an art at all, it's the silence that has meaning. When he pulls up in front of my house, I invite him in.

'They'll be so happy for us. We have to toast our engagement, it's tradition!' I kiss John on the cheek. 'You're going to marry an Italian girl. We toast everything, even laundry day!'

John laughs. 'Okay, okay, you're the boss.'

'And don't you forget it.'

As we climb up the stoop, the stairs feel different. I've changed, and the world I live in feels different. These are the steps I played on as a girl, but I get an odd feeling that this is no longer my home; my place is with John now.

'Mama?' I call out as we enter the foyer.

'She's in the kitchen,' Papa says from the living room. I throw my bag down on the bench and take John's hand and lead him into the living room. 'Did you eat?' Papa asks, looking up from his paper. He checks his watch. 'It's late. You must have had dinner.'

'I'm not hungry, Pop,' I tell him.

'How are you, sir?' John asks, leaning down to shake Papa's hand.

'Fine. How are you?' Papa replies.

Mama comes out of the kitchen. 'Oh, you're home. Can I get you a sandwich or something?'

'No thanks, Mama. I have something – *we* have something to tell you.'

Mama can sense what I am about to say but she tries to contain her excitement to let me deliver the news.

'John has asked me to marry him and I said yes.'

Mama shrieks and runs to us, embracing us, and kissing me on both cheeks. As she hugs me, I look over her shoulder at Papa, who is staring at the floor. 'This is wonderful! Wonderful!' Mama says. 'Congratulations! Antonio, get the glasses. We have to toast them!'

'I told you.' I wink at John.

Papa stands up and goes to the kitchen for the glasses. He returns with them and a bottle of port. He pours the port and gives each of us a glass. 'Lucia, you're my life.' He raises his glass.

'Pop?' My father's eyes are wet with tears. 'Papa?'

Mama quickly fills in the silence. 'Oh, he's fine. He is overwhelmed – his little girl is getting married, that's all.' She shoots Papa a look.

'No, Maria, I'm not fine and I'm not overwhelmed,' Papa says. He looks from Mama to John. 'I'm disappointed that this young man asked my daughter to marry him without discussing it with me first. What kind of a man does such a thing?' He turns to me. 'And what kind of daughter accepts under those conditions?'

There is a dreadful pause. Finally John speaks. 'Mr Sartori, I apologize. I didn't think to ask you because Lucia has already been engaged.'

Mama looks at Papa. John doesn't realize that by making such a statement he has brought my virtue into question. The implication that I'm used goods, and therefore a separate entity from my family, is not what my father and mother need to hear.

'He doesn't mean it like it sounds, Papa.' I move to John's side. 'It's just that John is leaving on a business trip tomorrow and we won't see each other for a couple of months. It slipped his mind to come and seek your permission.'

'Yes, yes, that's what happened,' John says. Papa regards John with what seems like pity, as though my fiancé is hiding behind my skirts while the gun is aimed at his head.

'You're twenty-six years old, Lucia,' Papa says. I wish he wouldn't say my age like that, I sound like the oldest maid on Commerce Street. And I feel like one as I look around this living room, with its faded chintz slipcovers, outdated lace doilies and ceramic lamps with fringe on the shades. Don't they know that I was looking at mansions today? Estates with an ocean view? I may have been raised here but I want more. My father came to America for the very same reason. Can't he see that a man cut from the same cloth has walked through the door? John will give me all the things I desire, but he's not enough? 'You can do what you want. But don't expect me to be happy for you.' Papa puts down his glass and starts to leave the room.

I am furious. I follow him. 'Papa, how dare you ruin this moment for me? You say you want me to be happy. *Stai contenta*! *Stai contenta*! You say it every day, but you don't mean it. "Be happy, Lucia! But you can only be happy if I tell you to!" You couldn't care less what I want! Nobody is good enough for me, but when I find someone to love, someone I truly love, you humiliate him. He didn't do anything wrong! This is 1951, and your silly peasant traditions belong back on the farm where they came from! I can take care of myself and I don't need your blessing!'

'Lucia!' Mama is more shocked at the way I'm speaking to my father than angry about what I am saying.

'And I don't want to hear anything else against this man. I don't care what he does for a living, I don't care what kind of family he comes from, and I don't care what you think of him! He's mine and I want him.'

Papa's temper ignites. 'You will not speak to me in—'

'Won't speak to you how? Honestly for once? And Mama, you were more than happy to pass me off to Claudia DeMartino as a scullery maid, so you aren't blameless either. You just want me married. It could be John Talbot or any man in a suit with the proper hat.'

'That is not true!' Mama says indignantly.

I take John's hand and walk him to the door. Mama and Papa do not come after us. 'Goodnight.' I kiss John briefly but tenderly on the lips. He seems confused. 'I'll handle this.'

I go back into the living room. Mama has sunk into her chair and Papa is looking out at the garden with his back to me. 'You know something?' I say, talking to Papa's back. 'If one of your sons had come home with a girl tonight and she was wearing a new diamond ring, you would never have behaved towards her the way you did towards John. You ruined the most beautiful day of my life. Rot in hell.'

I take the stairs up to my room two at a time. I hear my father calling to me angrily from the bottom of the stairs. No matter how old I am, he is still the leader of this household and will not tolerate disrespect. But I can't tolerate his disrespect of me either. I go into my room and lock the door. I go to my vanity table and turn on the small lamp and open the drawer. I pull out my savings register from the Chase National Bank and remind myself that I have the means to live my life outside this house. The long row of deposits written in blue ink soothes me. I'm an independent woman, I tell myself, and when I look in the mirror I believe it.

Ruth and I take our bag lunches to the garden behind the library for a change of scenery and some much-needed fresh air. Helen took a personal day to rest her swollen feet. Violet spends all her lunches with Officer Cassidy at the White Tower on Thirty-first Street.

It's a beautiful day so we linger on the lawn after finishing our sandwiches. Ruth has her legs stretched out in front of her and is leaning back on her hands, her face turned up to the sun, eyes closed. 'Your father still hasn't spoken to you?' she asks.

'I haven't spoken to him,' I tell her, running my hand over the few blades of grass that haven't been matted down. 'Mama is so angry she won't even look at me.'

'Do you want to fix it?'

'Either I fix it or I don't go to Italy.'

'You should go to Italy. Once you're married, and I can tell you this from my own experience, a trip to Queens becomes a big deal in a household budget.'

'Really?' I want to tell Ruth that may be true of Harvey and her, but I'm marrying an up-and-coming businessman. I don't think travel will be strictly a luxury.

'Trust me. Here's what you should do.' Ruth sits up straight and pulls her legs up alongside her. 'Call your priest. Set up a meeting. Bring your parents in and make peace.'

'Are you sure *you're* not Italian?'

'When Harvey and I hit the wall with his mother about the wedding plans she heard me call her a not-so-nice name to Harvey. She shouldn't have been eavesdropping, but the damage was done. So I had the rabbi come over and settle the dispute. Parents are impressed when you have the maturity to go to the clergy.'

'Ruth, how is it you always know what to do?'

'I just got to this marriage thing first. That's all. How's John handling everything?'

'He delayed his trip to Chicago for a week.'

'What's he doing out there anyway?'

I wish I could answer Ruth, but every time I ask John about the business in Chicago, he gets impatient and mumbles something about a potential partnership. Evidently, there is a wealthy man who wants to do a project with him, and John needs to go out and form a potential partnership. I start to clean up the remnants of our lunch and answer, 'Oh, you know, some deal is brewing.'

'Have you had the talk yet?' Ruth asks, as she screws the tops back on our Thermoses.

'What talk?'

'The money talk. About how much you have and how much he has, and what you're going to do with it.' We stand and begin to fold the fabric we brought to sit on.

'No!' I find Ruth's suggestion tacky. There will be plenty of time later to set budgets and talk about saving.

'You'd better talk to him now. You don't want any surprises.'

'I could never bring up the subject of money with John!' He's always flush with cash, he lives at one of the best hotels in the city, he bought me a stunning diamond and he takes me to the nicest places. I can't imagine haggling over every dollar the way I've seen my parents do, bills covering the kitchen table, negotiations taking place well into the night.

'What are you going to do when you're married and you need something?'

'I suppose I'll go and buy it, Ruth.'

'Nooo. You have to *ask* him if you can go and buy it.'

'But I have my own income!'

'Doesn't matter. You're a team now, and one half of the team can't be writing cheques the other half has no knowledge of.' Ruth brings her end of the fabric up to mine, then gives the material a final fold. I don't say anything more as we begin the walk back to Altman's.

I know Ruth means well, but the rules for her marriage don't apply to John and me. I may still have questions about his career, but he doesn't like answering them, and as long as he's happy, I'm happy. That's all that matters.

'Promise me you'll have the talk,' Ruth admonishes me as we turn down Fifth Avenue.

'I promise.' But I don't mean it. Ruth is my best friend, but she has her way of doing things and I have mine.

*

Mama, Papa, and I kneel in our living room as Father Abruzzi says a blessing over our heads. We spent an hour and a half discussing our disagreement, and Father Abruzzi sorted it all out, with the conclusion that what's done is done. I am engaged. My parents have to accept it, and I have to accept their concern. Father Abruzzi then calls John in from the street, where he has smoked his way through a pack of Camels. John seems relieved when Papa shakes his hand and Mama kisses him on both cheeks.

'Lucia, when you return from Italy, I want you and John to come for instruction. When you choose a date, we will print the banns of marriage,' Father Abruzzi tells me. Personally, I think our priest is obsessed with the banns of marriage. As far as I'm concerned, the only people who need to hear about my marriage are those I will invite to the ceremony. The banns of marriage open up my private life to the entire community of Italian nonnas, who will insist on making a home-made hope chest for me, crocheting everything from blankets to shoe bags to commode seat covers for my future home. All I have to do is give them a colour scheme and the needles will commence their clicking from Carmine to King Street.

'We'll be there, Father,' John promises. For a non-Italian, my fiancé learns quickly.

I thought the rest of July would drag without John in town, but between work and getting ready for the trip to Italy, the time flew. On the morning of our departure Roberto, Angelo, Orlando and Exodus leave early to take the heaviest luggage to the airport. Papa is carrying the rest to a taxi waiting at the kerb, while Rosemary and I finish getting ready and Mama takes care of the breakfast dishes.

'Lucia!' my father barks from the bottom of the stairs. 'How many hatboxes do you need to take to Italy?'

'Three, Papa.'

'But you only have one head,' Papa says, holding all three boxes up in the air.

'And it needs to be covered in the hot Venetian sun. It wasn't my idea to go in the hottest month of the year to a place warm enough to grow olives.' I skip down the stairs and kiss Papa's cheek. 'You want me to fry over there?'

'Take them,' Papa says, giving in.

Mama pokes her head out of the kitchen. 'She can twist you like a *mapeen*,' she says, wringing out her dish towel.

'So can you,' Papa says.

Rosemary squeezes my hand as we drive through midtown to the Queensboro Bridge, heading to the new international airport. 'Look at this as one long shopping trip for the wedding and your new home,' my sister-in-law says. 'We'll be back in no time.'

The first thing I did, at Mama's insistence, was register for my gifts at B. Altman's. She wants my home to be furnished with the finest of everything, from Irish linens for the bed and Egyptian cotton towels for the bathroom to English china and silver for the dining room. John hasn't had a real home since he sold his family house on Long Island and put his mother in Creedmore. The Carlyle Hotel is elegant, but I know I can do better.

Mama and I plan to buy furniture and all the fabrics we need for draperies in Italy. I will buy as much Murano glass as I can ship.

John has shown me the plans for the house in Huntington, and I want a dazzling multi-coloured chandelier like the one I saw in the Milbank mansion when Ruth and I went to give the matriarch a private fitting.

Delmarr's gift is my wedding gown, so he will be sketching while I'm gone. The girls have agreed to help, and Helen's last day of work is the week I return. They are saving me a tremendous expense by making my gown, the attendants' and Mama's. That will be money I can save for furniture.

It's hard to believe that I've saved $8,988.78 in the six years I've been working. I never went on vacations other than the ones with my family, or splurged on jewellery or a car. I made most of my clothes, and the things I couldn't make I bought at Altman's sales with my employee discount. I knew that someday I'd need a nest egg. I plan to spend about a thousand dollars on furnishings in Italy and I will keep five hundred dollars in the savings account as a little emergency fund. The rest I put into the down payment for the construction of our house in Huntington Bay. My share is a pittance compared to what John is spending, but I gave it to him gladly, knowing I am half of this team. Besides, I got to choose all the tile work, help design the kitchen, and push for an enormous bay window that overlooks the ocean, so my investment is worth every penny.

When we disembark the airplane in Rome, Papa actually drops to his knees, kissing the earth.

'Your father, just like the Pope.' Mama throws her hands up. Then she helps Papa stand. 'You'll ruin your pants,' she says, brushing him off.

Papa gathers us round and begins speaking to us in Italian, but he speaks so fast, we have a hard time understanding.

Orlando says, 'Papa, please, we're Americans. Give it to us slowly.'

Papa explains, more calmly this time, that we will take the train to Treviso and spend the night. 'Then we will drive home. Home to Godega di Sant' Urbano.'

Delmarr told me that Rome is a lot like New York City, but I don't see it. New York doesn't have parks of ancient ruins or the Coliseum or three-hundred-year-old fountains like the one in the Piazza Navona. Yes, there are thousands of people and the same crazy traffic, but for me that's where the similarities end.

I have no trouble with the flirtatious Italian men because I'm travelling with Papa and four brothers, who guard me like a Brinks truck delivery. When I meander a few feet from the family to look at shoes in a shop window, men seem to gather like pigeons ready to peck a stale hunk of bagel. Then Papa joins me and gives them the eye and they scatter instantly. I'm not the only one they're after. Mama gets her share of whistles. And when a man made an advance towards delicate-looking Rosemary as we were boarding the train, she barked in her finest Brooklynese, 'Buzz off, buster, before I belt ya!'

As the train takes us from Rome to Venice, my first sight of the Adriatic at Rimini makes my heart pound. The roads curl down to the ocean like ribbons, and the white sand is barely visible: every inch is covered with people and umbrellas in bold stripes of orange and white and green and pink. The water meets the shore and ripples onto the sand, forming a glittery hem. The houses, painted coral and sky blue, are set into the hills like sequins on silk. The air, though hot, is breezy and clean, leaving an end note of citrus from the blood oranges growing on the trellises of nearly every home we pass.

Living in the middle of a city, surrounded by bricks and pavement all my life, I never knew that the water would matter so much to me. As I look out over the Adriatic, I think of my new home in Huntington. I wonder if John is pushing the workers, whether they have poured the concrete base for the sub floor or mounted the support beams for the walls. John has assured me it will be ready well before we move in on our wedding night.

As the train brakes slowly to a stop in Faenza, children run alongside it, frantically collecting the coins passengers throw out the window. The war ended six years ago, but you can see the Italians have not recovered. We look downright opulent in our simple cotton dresses and white gloves, while they, though neatly dressed, wear shoes that are tattered and clothes that are obviously hand-me-downs.

There's a little girl, barefoot, in an undershirt and white pants, the cuffs rolled to her knee. Her skin is the tawny colour of caramel, and her black hair and eyes shine in the sun. Rosemary puts her hand on the window and rests her face against it, studying the girl while the train waits to take on more passengers. I know she is thinking about her daughter, wondering what Maria Grace would be doing, sitting up, eating pastina, cutting her first tooth.

'The candy!' Rosemary sits up and grabs her purse from overhead. 'I have a bag of candy! Lu, open the window.' I stand and unhook our window. As the train begins to pull out, Rosemary calls out, '*Vieni qua! Vieni qua!*' The children follow her voice and run to our window. Rosemary tosses handfuls of gold foil hearts filled with hard cherry candy. They jump and catch them like falling stars. The little girl in the white pants reaches for the candy but misses it; another boy grabs the piece that landed closest to her and runs away. I call out to her, '*Corri! Corri!*' As she runs towards our window, Ro throws her the last piece of candy, and she catches it. We look back at her as the train pulls away, her cheeks round with candy as she smiles.

Treviso has always been Papa's dream city. It is surrounded by a wall and a man-made moat, giving it the look of an island. It is softly lit and gauzy, with lacy willow trees surrounding deep canals filled with mossy rocks and gurgling water.

The homes that line the moat are made of brick which has faded to a pale gold sepia. They have long windows with simple black shutters. Small footbridges span the moat. The feeling in Treviso is that everyone and everything is connected. There are no free-standing buildings; the city is a fortress.

The streets are cobblestone, but not the typical grey colour we have on our Dutch settlement streets in Greenwich Village. These have a smoky blue-green patina reminding me of turned copper, maybe from the moss that comes from being so near the water. The moss makes Treviso quiet, as though it is lushly carpeted.

When we arrive at the hotel, the manager greets us with such enthusiasm, I wonder if Papa is long-lost Italian royalty.

'Who is Lucia?' he asks, looking at Rosemary, Mama and me.

'I am,' I say.

'You have a telegram, signorina.' With great flair, he gives me the yellow envelope.

Have a wonderful time.
I wait. Missing you.
Love, John

'How romantic!' Rosemary says wistfully. My brothers laugh. 'Oh, you're a bunch of lugs,' she tells them.

The manager makes a fuss about giving us rooms with a view of the canal and recommends a nearby restaurant for supper. After we have a nice nap and dress for the evening, Papa leads us to the open-air market by the river and explains that at the end of the day, the vendors throw the unsold produce and fish into the curve of the river and it is carried away downstream. Very different from how things are in New York City where Papa spends a fortune to have his garbage hauled from the Groceria by truck.

The maître d' at Lavinia Stella, the best restaurant in Treviso, happens to be the brother of the manager at our hotel. It's clear from our reception that he was expecting us.

'My sons,' Papa says once we have taken our seats, 'you see how it is in the homeland? Everybody works together. I want you to take a lesson from this.'

'Pop, we already work together,' Roberto says.

'Yes, but you fight too much.' Papa holds out his arms, drawing attention to the mood in the dining room. 'See, here you never hear fighting.'

I whisper, 'That's because they're duking it out in the kitchen.'

Orlando hears this and laughs, but Papa means what he says. His greatest goals in life are to leave a good business to his sons and for his sons to get along. '*Niente litigi*,' he always says. 'No fighting!'

Our meal begins with a delicate fish salad of sweet white bream and baby shrimp nestled in greens. Afterwards, the waiter brings us orecchiette pasta in a rosy sauce made with basil, tomatoes, sweet cream and butter. Then we have a platter of grilled lamb chops dusted in breadcrumbs and olive oil. For dessert is a small custard for each of us, spilling over with caramel crust.

'If every meal is going to be this good, I'll have to put elastic in the waist of all my skirts,' I tell Rosemary, crossing my hands over my stomach and leaning back in my chair.

'I wouldn't worry about it. Today we walked about five miles on top of the train ride. That's like walking from Commerce Street, over the Brooklyn Bridge, to my mother's house.' Rosemary smiles and takes another spoonful of custard.

Papa raises his glass. '*Mia famiglia.*' I smile at him. No matter how much I miss John, I know that one day I will be very glad I had the chance to make this trip with my father.

'Jesus, Pop, could you stop crying? We're gonna get a reputation,' Exodus says, playfully looking over his shoulder.

'I'm sorry. I toast you, my family, who I love more than anything in this world. Tomorrow, we see Venice, and then to my home. *Salute!*'

We raise our glasses and say, '*Cent'anni,*' a hundred years of health and happiness for all. Now even Exodus has tears in his eyes, but I don't tease him, because I have them too.

Chapter Eight

There are three ways to get to Godega di Sant' Urbano: by car, by horse, or by foot. Our car resembles a turn-of-the-century model with a rumble seat you could see at the Smithsonian. 'Any minute I expect Teddy Roosevelt to crank the engine,' Mama says when she sees it. The only member of our group excited by the A-Type Citroën is Exodus, who knows the make of this Swiss nightmare and calls it vintage. The rest of us call it a wreck.

We pile into the car on what has to be the hottest day in Italian history. The trip is so arduous, Mama says her rosary three times, asking God to let the car last long enough to get us to Godega safely. Godega was a small farming town until the community built a new church and convinced Pope Urban XXI to come and bless it. This brought prestige to the town, renamed Godega di Sant' Urbano, and in all of Italy the poor farmers were held up as an example of piety and perseverance.

Finally, after passing what seems like the tail end of civilization itself, we see a sign that says, 'Godega di Sant' Urbano'. Godega has a very short main street, which looks even smaller against the expanse of the farm fields behind it. There is the church, of course, one dry-goods store, one open-air café with tables and grass-green umbrellas, and a war monument, a sleek, engraved marble obelisk in the middle of a square of grass, enclosed by a chain draped on posts. A couple of horses, untied and unsaddled, stand near an open portico, where a few chickens scratch in the dirt.

'This is rustic,' Mama says, her voice lilting upwards hopefully. Poor Mama. Raised on the rowdy streets of Brooklyn, she doesn't quite share Papa's feeling of excitement for homecoming on the farm. Yet I feel like Papa's stories over the years have prepared me. Godega is exactly as he described it.

'I love it,' Orlando says, reading my mind. 'I feel like I'm home.' While the other boys horsed around, unable to sit still, Orlando would sit with me and listen to Papa's tales of the Veneto.

The sky is a canopy of Mediterranean blue, not a cloud anywhere to break the brilliant colour. The hills and pastures roll out like raw silk on a cutting table, as wave after wave of wheat blows gently in the breeze. In the distance we see the Dolomite Mountains, their rocky faces the smudged grey colour of a pigeon's feathers, their peaks the colour of salt.

'*Domenic! Eccoci qua!*' Papa waves. His cousin, who is driving an open flatbed truck, another old wreck, honks the horn when he sees us. Domenic pulls up and jumps out of the driver's seat to embrace my father. He is about Papa's age, with a full head of close-cropped grey hair and the broad shoulders of my father's people. Two stunning girls follow him out of the cab, along with a woman his age.

'Wow-ee.' Angelo whistles under his breath when he sees the

girls. One is tall and slender, with hair that hangs to her waist in a shiny cascade. She wears a sleeveless navy-blue cotton dress with sandals. The confident way she holds her head leads me to believe she may be older than she looks. If she came to New York, our model Irene Oblonsky would be out of a job. 'This is my neice, Orsola Spada,' Cousin Domenic tells us. My brothers make jackasses of themselves trying to get introduced at once, and poor Orsola is completely confused. 'And this is Domenica,' Domenic says proudly. She is equally beautiful, petite and curvy, and obviously has guts.

'And I am Bartolomea, Domenic's wife.' Bartolomea, oddly enough, is a redhead with deep brown eyes. She has a lovely shape too. Whatever they eat on the farm, it shows up well on the women.

Domenic helps us up into the back of the truck, where he has built two benches that we sit on, and there's plenty of room for all of us once we put our luggage in the centre. I wave to Papa and Roberto, who follow behind us in the car.

'This is quite an adventure,' Mama says to me pleasantly.

I nudge her and direct her gaze to Angelo and Orlando, who bookend Domenica and Orsola and are suddenly full of questions about the Veneto and in desperate need of tour guides to show them the sights.

'Idiots. They act like they've never seen a girl before,' Exodus huffs.

As the truck makes a turn down a dirt road, we are jostled like bales of hay. The road is lined with stalks of wheat so high it's like being in a tunnel. I look up at the sky. The sun hangs low, burning pink in the surrounding blue. Everything is different in Italy: the food, the heat, Papa's emotions, my brothers' antics, my mother's newfound patience, everything but me. My heart is back home with John Talbot.

Domenic pulls up at a three-storey stucco box in the middle of a clearing and helps us out of the truck. Papa has not seen his home since he was seventeen years old, and he begins to cry. Domenic pats Papa on the back forcefully, as though he is trying to dislodge something from Papa's windpipe. Only once Papa has dried his tears and blown his nose does Domenic stop patting. Bartolomea and the girls gather fresh vegetables from the garden while Domenic conducts a tour.

'Come, I show you the inside.' It doesn't look like any farmhouse I've ever seen before. We follow Domenic into the house through two wide wooden doors and into what can only be described as a stable. The floor is covered with straw and the windows are covered in blinds made of thin wood slats, which have been raised. Even though it is midday, the room is dark. 'The animals are at my farm. The donkey, two pigs,' Domenic thinks. A very thin chicken rustles under the hay in the corner, startling Mama. 'Oh yes, the hen. For some reason, she stays.'

'The living quarters are this way,' he goes on and begins climbing a rough-hewn ladder up through a hole in the ceiling. We follow him like ants climbing a branch.

'Not bad!' Roberto, who is ahead of me, says. Papa helps me through the opening, then Mama.

'Zio Antonio lived here until the day he died,' Domenic tells us.

There is one enormous room with a long table, simple and homemade, and twelve chairs that have woven seats. The stucco walls are washed in a pale peach colour that turns to rose on the ceilings and baseboards. A nubby beige sofa and two chairs, low and deep, sit under the windows. The entire far end of the room is taken up by a fireplace made of grey fieldstones, some as large as a hatbox. I have never seen a hearth so large – I could stand in it! A collection of old farm tools hangs over the fireplace. The black tools against the gold background give the effect of tintypes in shadow boxes. There is one floor lamp with a simple rose glass shade. After seeing the stable downstairs I'm relieved to see they have electricity.

'See, Maria. Simple. No knick-knacks,' Papa teases her. 'My wife has more dishes than a restaurant,' he says to Domenic.

Ignoring the joke, Mama asks, 'Where do we sleep?'

'Upstairs.' Domenic points.

'Another ladder,' Mama remarks cheerfully, climbing up to the third floor. I follow her. There are two large bedrooms. Each has two twin beds, which seem like our beds back home until we sit on them. Instead of using a box spring and mattress, the beds are large open wood crates, stuffed with straw-filled sacks. With sheets and a blanket over top, they look like normal beds.

I sit on one and smooth the blanket. 'It's not too bad.'

'Now we know how the chicken feels.' Mama rolls her eyes.

Papa and Mama take one room, and Rosemary and I take the other. My brothers will sleep down in the stable. Before Roberto goes downstairs with my brothers, he embraces Rosemary, who buries her face in his neck. Their loss has made them even closer.

The garden is full of ripe tomatoes, yellow peppers, arugula, radishes and potatoes. Domenic has brought prosciutto, thin strips of sweet ham, and bresaola, lean beef in paper-thin slices, both of which he cured in his own smokehouse. He has also brought some of his own olive oil in a black flask and plenty of wine, a hearty red Chianti, in ceramic jugs.

Bartolomea takes Mama outside and shows her the outdoor hearth, made of stone with a tall chimney. There is a short stone wall next to it (for cooling whatever has been baked, I'm guessing) and another table behind it, longer than the one indoors, with a bench to sit on, on either side.

'It's too hot inside to cook, you cook here,' Bartolomea tells Mama and shows her the utensils stored neatly below the oven, which is open at both ends. Italian ingenuity, I think as I look through. You keep the uncooked dishes on one side and then serve the finished product from the other!

'You are hungry now, no?' Bartolomea drapes a bright yellow cotton cloth on the table, anchoring it with small black flasks of olive oil. Orsola puts a plate, a fork and a small wooden cup at each place setting. Out of a basket brought over from Domenic's truck Bartolomea unloads trays of delicacies: tiny sandwiches made with crusty bread, anchovies, a platter of blood oranges splashed with olive oil and pepper, fresh figs sliced in half with hunks of hard cheese, succulent smoked sardines, curls of Parmesan cheese and shiny black olives. There are big, puffy oil biscuits for dessert. Orsola places bunches of fresh grapes beside each plate. It's a feast.

Bartolomea calls us all to lunch. As we take our seats on the benches, time seems to stop; we could be any generation of Sartoris gathering to eat under the Venetian sun.

After a week of sleeping on sweet straw, walking to and from town for an afternoon cappuccino, resting and napping and reading

Goethe's notebook about his Italian travels, my farewell gift from Delmarr, I decide I could get used to the Italian lifestyle. But not without my fiancé. My heart aches for John, and every time I see something wonderful I wish he were here to share it with me.

I received my first letter from Ruth, who tells me that Helen is getting bigger by the second – she has let out Helen's work skirts twice already! Violet is pressuring the cop and expects a ring by Labor Day. Delmarr seems preoccupied; they are going to lunch, and Ruth will write with the details. She then mentions that John has been to the store a couple of times and came in to say hello to everybody. He told Ruth he was up in Interior Decoration to find the right drawer pulls for a walk-in closet he is designing for our bedroom suite.

'Lucia!' Ro calls, and from the sound of her voice I can tell that something is terribly wrong. I run around the house, where she kneels next to Papa, who has fallen to the ground.

'Mama!' I yell. She comes running out of the house with Exodus. I kneel down next to Papa and feel his pulse, which seems faint. 'Get water,' I tell Ro. 'We have to take him to town.' Exodus and I try to revive Papa. He opens his eyes but he doesn't know where he is. 'Keep him awake!' I tell Mama as we lift him into the back of the truck Domenic left for us. The rest of the boys are at Domenic's farm this afternoon, helping him fill his silo with hay. It's about a mile away in the opposite direction to town, so we decide to take a chance and find a doctor in Godega.

Exodus drives over the pits of the old road as fast as he can. The movement is okay because it helps Papa stay awake. We pull into town and I see a group gathered at the café and scream, '*Dottore,*

Dottore!' The waiter rushes into the restaurant and calls for help. Mama, always calm in a crisis, asks for a cool rag for Papa's face.

The doctor arrives, a man of about forty who directs us to a bench in the shade. He mixes a packet of powder into some water, and makes Papa drink it. He explains that the powder contains potassium and other minerals, including some salt. It must taste terrible, because Papa makes a face as he sips it.

'What happened?' he finally asks, clearly restored by the bitter concoction.

'Signor, you must stay out of the sun.' The doctor smiles. 'Every time an American comes here, they faint in the heat.'

'It didn't feel hot,' Papa defends himself.

'Signor, if a place is hot enough to grow oranges, it's too hot for people.'

Exodus helps Papa stand and we begin to walk back to the truck. Mama stops us. 'Oh, no. You're not going anywhere. Not until the sun goes down!'

'Maria,' Papa starts to argue.

'No, we are going to sit in church. Right over there in the back pew of Saint Urbano's. We'll sit in the cool shade and say the rosary and thank God that it wasn't anything worse.'

Papa throws his hands up. With Mama on one side and Exodus on the other, he enters the church. Rosemary and I exchange a smile.

Papa invites the whole family to the courthouse in Godega to secure the final paperwork on his inheritance. Though the building is very small, it also seems to be the police department, because the only *carabiniere* in town stands out front. I sit with Roberto and Rosemary.

Orlando and Angelo wait by the door, as if to guard it; from whom or what, I have no idea. Exodus leans against the wall whispering with Orsola. Mama turns and motions for them to be quiet. Orsola gets up and moves away from Exodus so as not to get in any more trouble.

As the officer reads the will aloud, Papa closes his eyes and listens to the words carefully. When Enzo's name is mentioned, Domenic leans over to tell Papa that Enzo signed off on his portion of the estate. Papa nods. I can see that the severed relationship with his brother still bothers him. It's the one thing about my father that I find mysterious. He's a peaceful man. How can he bear to be angry with his brother for all these years? At the end of the proceeding the officer rises and kisses Papa on both cheeks – it turns out that he is a third cousin to Papa on his mother's side.

After ten days at the farmhouse we make plans for our side trips. I want to shop in Venice, so Rosemary and I come up with an itinerary. We pack a week's worth of clothing for our trip. It is no small feat to wash clothes in the hot sun, hang them on the line, and press them with an iron that looks like a door stop. But there's no other choice.

A package from John arrives before Ro and I are about to leave. It's from Bonwit Teller's, sent one week before we left for Italy!

'I can't believe he spent money at the competition!' Ro says, laughing. I open the box and lift out a small tiara made of white satin roses with leaves made of pale green velvet on a band of dazzling Austrian crystals. 'How delicate!' Ro squeals. The note reads:

My dearest love,
For your veil.
I love you, John

'Boy, you are getting a prince.'

'Don't I know it,' I tell her. I pack the tiara away.

Most Italians are on holiday in August, so it takes a lot of bartering to get a ride down to the train station in Treviso. Papa negotiates with a car service, commenting that these rides are as expensive as our flights over. But the car trip has an upside for Papa, since the driver is like a built-in chaperone. It's all worth it, when Ro and I join the throng walking across the Rialto Bridge into the city of Venice. She points to the gondolas sailing underneath us. We stop in San Marco to look at the Palazzo Dario, its façade inlaid with colours of marble I didn't know existed: red with turquoise veins, gold with white, green with orange, all cut and configured into a wild Byzantine pattern. The guidebook says Venice was the gateway of trade for the world from Africa to the Orient, and the influence of many cultures is apparent.

'Scusi,' a man says in Italian. He pronounces each word carefully. *'Puo prendere una fotografia di me con mia moglie? Grazie.'*

'Prego,' I answer. 'Are you American?' I ask as I take the camera from him.

'Yes,' he says in English as he stands beside his wife. 'You too?'

'Finally, some of our own!' his wife says from under her wide-brimmed hat as she poses. She is about fifty years old and is lean and tall. Her blonde hair is twisted into a long braid. She has a patrician beauty, with wide-set blue eyes and a high forehead.

'That's how we feel,' I tell them as I snap their picture. 'We've been staying up in the country. I'm Lucia Sartori and this is my sister-in-law, Rosemary.'

'I'm Arabel and this is my husband, Charlie Dresken.' Charlie is about Arabel's age, but he is her physical opposite, small and muscular, with red hair and a beard.

Charlie takes the camera from me and asks, 'Where are you from?'

'New York City. Greenwich Village.'

'Commerce Street!' Ro adds.

'Small world,' Charlie says, smiling. 'We're from Long Island. Syosset.'

'Really?' I ask. 'My fiancé and I are building a house in Huntington.'

'Oh, Huntington is fabulous!' Arabel says. 'They're building some gorgeous homes over there. What does your fiancé do?'

'He's a businessman. Importing,' I explain.

'Where are you girls staying?'

'We're at the Pavan Pensione at Campo San Marina,' Ro reads off our itinerary.

'We're at the Giudecca. Actually, we were about to have lunch. Would you like to join us?'

'We would love to!' I say.

'Meet us in the hotel lobby at two,' Arabel says as she writes down the address on our itinerary.

Rosemary and I are so excited to be able to dress up and have lunch we practically run through the streets to find the Pavan Pensione. We are given a room on the second floor, sparsely furnished but clean, with a shared bath down the hall. We don't even mind sharing the bath, as all we have in Godega is an outdoor shower, which is like bathing in a wooden barrel. We put on stockings and gloves and hats, something we haven't done since getting off the plane in Rome. I think we look very Italian; I wear a black cotton circle skirt with a white blouse and a bright red sash, and Ro wears a beige linen skirt and a pink blouse with a pink patent leather belt. When we reach the Guidecca we're glad we made an effort. The lobby is marked by an old-world elegance; there are ornate crystal chandeliers and heavy Victorian furniture with velvet cushions.

Arabel greets us and ushers us into the busy dining room, where Charlie has gotten us a table overlooking the garden. We find out that she is an art professor at Marymount Manhattan and Charlie is a lawyer. They've been married for ten years and have no children.

'Her children are her books and her antiques from our travels.' Charlie laughs.

'And so are yours.' Arabel pinches his cheek, and he smiles at her. 'You see, Charlie and I come to Venice every year, and each time we come we visit the same churches to look at the same works of art because we find something new every time we look at them.'

'Photographs in books don't do the trick,' Charlie adds.

'You must join us at Saint Stae. There is a series of paintings there that was commissioned by Andrea Stazio—'

'A very wealthy man,' Charlie interjects.

'Very wealthy, who wanted the lives of the twelve apostles interpreted by twelve young artists. So he selected the best around. My favourite in the group is by a young man named Giambattista Tiepolo. He painted *The Martyrdom of Saint Bartholomew.*'

'It will take your breath away,' Charlie tells us.

Arabel continues, 'The painting always moves me. I think it has to do with the image of this man, Bartholomew, emerging from what looks like a black pool, into the light. He is surrounded by evil and doubt, but he persists in his determination to die honourably and see the face of God. It is the best interpretation of suffering I have ever seen. You feel his agony.'

Rosemary, who has done her best to listen to a conversation she has no interest in, is in need of a nap. Her eyes have glazed over. All this talk of art is too much for her. But it has the opposite effect on me. I am now ravenous for more details, so I ask questions, and Arabel and Charlie are happy to answer them.

As I watch the two of them interact, I see they love each other, but there is also a discourse between them, an intellectual connection I never think about in my relationship with John. When Arabel speaks about the history of Venice and the masterpieces on display here, I wonder what I might have missed by not going to college. The only girls from my high school who went were extremely intelligent and wanted to become teachers or librarians. I knew I would work with my hands, but I see that the work I do would be enhanced by an education in art and literature. Arabel seems to know a little something about everything. What I know about the world, I know in detail, but my view is not expansive. It is limited to Greenwich Village and B. Altman's. Perhaps the right connections aren't simply social, but a world of deeply layered ideas, shared by people who care about them. Being around Arabel makes me want to be a part of this world. We make plans to join them as they tour Venice. Arabel has lots to show us.

*

Arabel and Charlie show us as much of Venice as we can take without falling over in exhaustion. What a coup to have an actual art historian explaining things. Today Arabel insisted we see the glassworks of Murano. On the ferry across to the main island, Arabel explains that the glassworks were moved out of Venice because of the smoke and heat produced by the ovens. When we tour the main factory, it reminds me of the Hub at B. Altman's. Each person completes a specific task, after which they pass the work along to the next person, until the garment, or in this case, the goblet, sconce, bowl, or chandelier, is finished.

'Isn't it hard to pick a chandelier when you haven't seen the house?' Arabel asks me. Maybe because I'm a seamstress, I can envision things as they'll be in their final form. In my mind's eye a swatch of fabric becomes a full skirt, a handful of beads, a jewel-encrusted bodice, a piece of black velvet, a collar. When I walked the acre and a half of our lot with John, I could picture each room, each doorway, point to the exact spot the bay window should go so the afternoon sun would suffuse the downstairs with rosy light. What an odd thing, I think, to need to build something so you can visualize it. I couldn't do what Arabel does, but I think perhaps she couldn't do my job either.

I barter with the salesman when I find a stunning chandelier, one I could never afford in the States. The base is burnished copper, and the arms have leaves of gold. The glass ornaments are fruit, in every conceivable colour: smoky quartz grapes, peridot pears, garnet apples and pink cherries. He promises that he will wrap each piece of fruit carefully and tells me not to be shocked when the chandelier arrives in a box the size of a room.

'Just so it gets there without breaking,' I tell him. What a spectacular vacation! Everything I see feeds my creativity and gives me ideas, from the coral buckle I saw on a lady's shoe to the silk moiré tent we dined in at the hotel. Even the cooking utensils are works of art in Italy, with their enamel handles in vivid colours.

Arabel arranges a car the next day for a drive down to Florence to buy silk. I learned about Antico Setificio Fiorentino from Franco Scalamandre, a purveyor of silks on Fifth Avenue. I will be able to repay Arabel's generosity with some of what I know about textiles and fabric. When I bought silk taffeta from Scalamandre to make a gown for a mezzo soprano at the New York Grand Opera Company, he told me about the factory where the silk was woven. He painted a detailed picture of the place, from the silkworms spinning the thread, to the chuff of the looms operating from morning till night, to the drying room, where the freshly dyed fabric is stretched on wooden frames so the colour dries evenly. As we go through the factory, I realize the materials we work with at B. Altman's are only a small sample of what they create here. If I had some of these stripes and plaids, I could design a whole season around the variations of pink.

Arabel points to an off-white taffeta that has a delicate watermark in the design. She says, 'I don't know what I could ever do with it, but it's exquisite.' She holds it up, and I can see from the way the fabric drapes and the regal simplicity of the tone-on-tone weave, delicate with a sheen for dramatic effect, that it could only be used for one thing: my wedding gown. Arabel and Rosemary agree, I buy ten yards, plenty for whatever Delmarr will create.

When we have to say goodbye to Arabel and Charlie the next

morning, I'm sad to see them go. I've never spent time with such an educated woman, and I see what I've missed by not furthering my education. I'm proud of my training and schooling, but I see now I could have done more. I remember the night at the Plaza when Christopher's friend asked me if I'd gone to Vassar. How I would have loved to go away and live in a dormitory with lots of other smart, ambitious girls. I've done very well with my talents, but I haven't pushed myself. I have ideas and the passion to execute them, but there is a whole world I haven't experienced, and it would have allowed me to rise to the top.

Mama is thrilled to see us when we return safely from our trip. I give her the strands of Murano glass beads I bought for her. When I watch her try them on in the mirror I notice she tilts her head just as I do when trying on jewellery. Mama takes her eyes off the beads and looks at me in the mirror. 'Are you all right?'

'I'm okay, Mama.'

She examines my reflection closely, studying me as she has done all my life. I can see from her expression she knows something has changed. My mother has always been my closest confidante, so there isn't much I can keep from her.

'Why are you so serious?' she asks.

'I don't know,' I lie. How can I tell her that this trip has changed me? I met Arabel, who lives in a world of literature and art and infused me with her passion. I saw craftsmanship so exquisite that it made me think about how I could become a better seamstress. Why, though, do my aspirations sadden me? Why do I always feel that I have to give up something I love in order to climb higher?

*

We spend our last weeks in Godega eating and laughing and enjoying one another's company. This will be my last family holiday as a single daughter. Of all the things I learned and all the places I saw, not one has meant more to me than these precious days here in Papa's family home. These are the moments I will treasure, my mother laughing as she sits in Papa's lap, Roberto walking with Rosemary through the fields, Angelo, twenty years too old to be an altar boy in Saint Urbano Church but serving Mass anyway, Orlando baking pizza in the outdoor oven, Exodus fixing the engine of the old car for the twelfth time, and me, digging my bare feet into the grass where my father played as a boy.

As we load up the truck to go back down to the Treviso train station, Cousin Domenic seems preoccupied. He mashes the tobacco into his pipe as though he's angry at it.

'Are you all right, Cousin?' I ask him.

'I will never see you all again,' he says.

'Sure, you will. You'll come to America, and we'll come back.'

'No, you're young, you don't know. You have so much ahead of you that you think you have all the time in the world. I know this time will never come again. You won't come back.'

I smile at Domenic and give him a hug. As gay and funny as Italians can be, they can brood and turn dark in an instant. Nothing in life is certain, I want to tell my cousin. This month has been wonderful. Stop complaining! This is easy for me to say, since I've been counting down the moments until I see John.

Roberto loads the last of the bags into the car. Domenic, Bartolomea, Orsola, and Domenica have come to see us off.

'Where's Exodus?' Mama asks, counting our heads as though we are chickens.

'Mama,' Exodus says in a tone I barely recognize. His sarcasm and humour have been replaced by a serious timbre.

'Let's go. We have two trains to catch before the plane.' Mama moves towards the truck, her purse over one arm and a small satchel in her other hand.

'Mama . . . I'm not going back,' Exodus says.

Mama grips the door of the truck with her free hand. 'What do you mean you're not going back?'

'I'm staying here,' he says firmly.

'But what about New York?' I ask him. I am stunned! I could almost expect a half-baked idea like this from Orlando or Angelo, but not from the brother I've been closest to all my life.

'What about it?' Exodus says evenly.

'It's your home!' I tell him.

'My heart is here.' Orsola moves to Exodus's side. 'We're going to get married.'

'*O Dio*.' Mama plops down on the bench in the truck. 'Antonio Giuseppe, you handle this.'

We know Mama means business when she calls Pop by both of his names. We back off as Papa and Mama face Exodus, and ready ourselves for the fireworks.

'Ex, what are you doing?' Papa says gently.

'Pop, you know I love the store and working with you. But all my life I wanted to be outdoors. I always wanted a farm. I like working from the minute the sun comes up till it's suppertime. This is what I'm cut out for. I want to grow things in the earth, not just sell them. I like how quiet it is at dawn when I go to milk the cow. I like the way my boots sink into the dirt after I've ploughed it. I don't want the noise any more. I want peace.' Ex extends his hand and we listen to the soft rustle of the breeze moving through the wheat. 'That's music to me, that sound. I feel like I've found what I'm supposed to be doing.'

'But I need you back home,' Papa says quietly as he looks past his son to the fields beyond.

'You have three other sons, and you could always hire somebody from the outside.'

No one in a family business ever utters the words 'hire somebody in from the outside'. They are considered the highest insult, because the whole point of having a place like the Groceria is to leave your children a profitable enterprise, so that the family can stay close and work together.

My mother stands up and raises her voice. 'We will never hire outside our family. We will close the place down before we hire from the outside!'

'Maria, please.' Papa turns to his wife. 'There is a tradition here for him.'

'And a girl! A beautiful girl! Let's not forget that!' Mama jabs. Orsola looks at the ground. I want to go to her and tell her that this isn't her fault, it's just the way our family operates, but once she marries my brother, she will see all of this herself.

Ex turns to Papa, who is the reasonable one in this fight. 'There's nothing that would make me happier than being in charge of my own life. Growing my own food, chopping wood for the fire, all of that. That's what I want to do. It's how I want to live.'

Mama throws her hands in the air. 'Thank God, at last we know what Exodus wants. Well, tell me then, son, who is the imposter that

I birthed, nursed, raised and took care of like an angel all these years? Where is he? Maybe *he* can make some sense to me, because you, you're like a drunk right now – drunk on romantic wheat fields, Italian moons and Domenic's wine!' she bellows. 'You get in this truck and you come home to the United States of America where you are a citizen! Now!'

Exodus doesn't move. Orsola weeps and Papa, who isn't supposed to be in the sun, is beginning to fry.

'Maria. Let the boy go.'

'Antonio!'

'Let the boy go. If one of my sons has to leave me, this is the place I would want him to go. The Sartoris have been here farming for hundreds of years. I am proud to have a son return to my homestead, where I grew up, and I will be happy to see his children grow up in this house.'

The only sound we hear is the thin chicken walking on the straw in the stable. Mama holds her head in her hands and sits down again on the bench, but she knows Papa is right. Exodus climbs up into the truck and puts his arms around her. 'In my heart I will never leave you, Mama.'

After a moment, Papa seems to remember that there is another aspect to all of this. He made his mistake with Rosemary's entrance into the family, and he won't make the same one twice. He turns to Orsola. 'Orsola, welcome to the family,' he tells her. She embraces Papa and then each of us, and finally Mama. Papa gives Mama his handkerchief. She blows her nose and says, 'Is anybody in this family ever going to have a normal wedding?' Roberto cranks up the truck, Domenic and his family climb aboard with us, and the last thing we see as we take the turn to the road to Godega di Sant'Urbano is Exodus with his arm around Orsola's waist and one very thin chicken peeking out the door of the farmhouse, their new home.

Chapter Nine

John is waiting at the gate when we get off the plane in New York, holding a dozen red roses tied with a white satin ribbon. He's dressed impeccably as always, in a beige linen suit, a blue-and-white-striped shirt, and a navy tie. As many times as I took out his picture in Italy, seeing him here so handsome makes my heart beat so fast I can't breathe. I know ladies aren't supposed to run, but I don't care. I run down the gateway and into his arms. I bury my face in his neck and breathe in the smell of his skin, which I have missed so desperately.

'How's November fifteenth for a wedding day?' he whispers.

'November! We've got invitations to send, a band to hire, a meal to cater, a dress to make! It's crazy!' I tell him. By now my family has gathered, though they are hanging back like a clump of moss on an old rock.

'I don't want to wait,' he says, smiling.

'I don't either!'

'We can be ready by November fifteenth,' Mama says with a hint of panic. I know her well enough to realize she thinks it's too soon, but since our meeting with Father Abruzzi, she's tried hard not to shoot down every idea John and I have about our wedding. Instead of arguing, she gives John a kiss on the cheek. Once my mother has spoken, my brothers become animated once again and they greet John with handshakes. Only Papa, dear Papa, has to force a smile. He will never say another word against John again because he promised Father Abruzzi and he doesn't want to lose me. But why can't he see how happy I am?

Roberto and Rosemary ride in the Packard with me and John and most of the luggage, while Mama, Papa, Orlando and Angelo follow in a taxi. I tell John about Exodus's decision to stay, and Rosemary regales him with stories of our trip to Venice. When we all reach Commerce Street, John helps my brothers unload the luggage, weighed down with Italian books, candlesticks, leather purses and silk. The chandelier and all the housewares were to be shipped by boat. John has things he needs to do, so he kisses me, and promises to pick me up for dinner that evening.

The first thing I do is take a shower. I stand under the luxurious, pulsating hot water for fifteen minutes, enjoying every second. It feels decadent after a month of washing in tepid water without any pressure. I step out of the shower and throw on my robe. When I go into the hallway, Ro hands me a glass of lemonade. 'You didn't have to do that,' I say.

'The hell I didn't! I haven't seen an ice cube in thirty-one days. I wanted you to know they really exist.' She clinks her glass against mine and goes back downstairs, leaving me to get ready.

*

I grab a sweater on my way out the door with John that night. New York City is still warm in the evenings, but it feels downright chilly compared to the Veneto. John has made reservations at Vesuvio.

'How much did you miss me?' I ask once we're settled in our booth.

'Every second. And you?'

'Every half second.' I lean across the table to kiss him.

'I was scared to death you'd meet some Italian count or duke or whatever they have over there and decide not to come home.'

'They could have lined up Italian bachelors from the top of the Alps to the heel of the boot and I wouldn't have been even mildly tempted. I have the best fiancé in the world. Why would I even look?'

'Beautiful girls can have their pick.'

'And I pick you.'

'I got you something while you were gone,' he says with a grin. 'When I saw it, I said, there's only one girl in the world who could do this justice.' John motions to Patsy, a tall, dapper Italian and the owner of the restaurant, who brings a large box to the table.

'Honey, what is it? I, I thought we were saving for the house . . .'

The box is as big as the table and about a foot deep, fastened with a pink satin ribbon so wide, it takes me a moment to untie it. When I lift off the lid, I am stunned. I pull out a mink coat of the softest, deepest black. It has a stand-up collar, square-cut shoulders, and deep cuffs.

'Check the lining,' John says. I open the coat and see my name embroidered in glittery gold thread. 'There's no mistaking who this coat belongs to.'

'Lucia is a noble name,' Patsy says, looking very proud of his role in this whole thing. 'It means light. You are such a lovely girl, you don't need a mink coat. Many women, they need the mink coat.' He walks back to the bar.

'Honey, can we afford this?' I ask John.

'What do you mean, can we afford it? You get the first fur coat of your life and you're worried about how much it costs?'

I should tell John that this is not my first fur. Papa bought me a wool coat with a fox collar when I got my job at B. Altman's, but John doesn't need to know that. 'It's just that the house is such an investment. It's our dream.'

'The house is covered.' John takes a sip of his Manhattan and taps the table with the stirrer impatiently.

There's something odd about the way he says that, as though the house is covered but other things are not. I think of Ruth, who made me swear that I would have the money talk with my fiancé. I never did. I never thought money was something we would quibble over.

'Look. I didn't buy you this coat to upset you. I can take it back,' he says.

'No, no, I love it.'

'You don't act like you love it.'

'Of course I do. You gave it to me. I'm sorry if you think I'm ungrateful.'

'That's the message I'm getting here. Do you think I ride through midtown and roll down my window and throw a thousand bucks out into the street like it's confetti? Do you think I go out and spend money like a fool to impress people?'

'No, that's not—'

'You don't trust me, do you?'

'What are you talking about? I'm going to marry you.'

'But do you *trust* me?'

'I wouldn't be here if I didn't trust you.' I can't believe that this beautiful evening, with this extraordinary gift, has escalated into an argument. I take a deep breath. 'Oh, John, come on. I'm jet-lagged, I'm not myself. I love this coat and I'll wear it every day I can.'

John relaxes. 'You're my girl. I just want you to have the best.'

'I do. I have the best.'

'Well, try it on,' he says, pulling the coat out of the box and holding it like a towel for a swimmer just emerging from the surf.

'Now?'

'Yes, now. I want to see you in it.'

I stand up and slip into the coat. It is sumptuous, soft and light. Patsy gives a low whistle.

'Thank you, honey.' I lean over and kiss John on the lips. When I open my eyes, I catch my reflection in the serrated mirror behind the booth. In the faceted squares of glass, I see hundreds of me in the mink coat.

'John, are you hungry?' I ask.

'Not really. Are you?'

'Not at all. Why don't you get the car?'

John smiles and leaves the table. I meet him under the awning in front of the restaurant. He tips his hat. 'Where to, ma'am?'

'The Carlyle Hotel please,' I answer, playing along. November 15 cannot get here fast enough.

Delmarr and Ruth covered for me during the month of August, since Hilda Cramer never likes anyone to take over two weeks' vacation at a time. But after such a long absence, I'm thrilled to push through the doors and be back in the Hub. I have the silk for my wedding gown, and stories galore for Delmarr and Ruth. I come early to get my desk organized before the gang gets in. I check the calendar on the chalkboard.

Instead of the usual system of fittings in yellow chalk and final delivery in pink, there are symbols I haven't seen before. Ruth's drawing table seems the same, but the storage bins are different. I push open the doors to the supply room, and see the fabric folded flat and stacked from floor to ceiling rather than standing on end. A feeling of panic goes through me. I go back into the Hub and into Delmarr's office. The signed photo of the McGuire Sisters is still on the wall and his colour wheel is still on the desk. I exhale, relieved.

'Corporate spy?' Delmarr says from behind me.

His voice startles me and I jump. 'Don't do that!' I tell him and then I throw my arms around his neck.

'What, Talbot withholding the sugar?' Delmarr hugs me back.

'Not at all. What's going on here, Delmarr? Everything looks different.'

'Not everything, just a little thing from corporate called inventory. They want to know what we have here, every yard of fabric, every inch of trim, every jet bead in every size. I think Hilda Beast is on the ropes.'

'They're going to fire her?'

'Ease her out.'

'Then you'll be the name on the label?'

'Noooooo.' Delmarr sits down and puts his feet on the desk.

'Don't you know anything about the ways of the retail world? The underling of the person they're putting out to pasture never gets the job. No, they'll bring in some hot shot.'

'But you're a hot shot.'

'Thank you. I could be, but I'm not. Not in their eyes anyway. And they told me as much.'

'Bastards.'

'And it doesn't help that Helen quit.'

'Quit?'

'She's swelling up so badly she can't work. Violet is in woo woo land with that cop she's seeing and can't focus on anything. She sent out three day suits without hemming them last week. We looked like fools. And then Ruth—'

'What's wrong with Ruth?'

'Harvey wants her to quit so they can have a baby. He thinks the job is too stressful. And then there's you. I'll lose you as soon as John Juan puts the ring on your finger.'

'No, you won't,' I say.

'Come on, Lucia. Be serious, just for a moment. I get you girls bright-eyed and bushy-tailed out of high school—'

'Katie Gibbs.'

'Or Katie Gibbs, and you come in here, guns blazing, ready to take on the world. By the time you hit twenty-five you clear out like somebody dropped a bomb. You rush to get married and when you do, you leave me.'

'*I* won't, Delmarr. *I* won't.'

'Talbot isn't going to let you work. He's going to polish you like the hood ornament on his Packard and set you in a china closet in

Huntington. That's your fate, kid.' Delmarr fills a mug with coffee and hands it to me.

I was raised with men, so it never occurs to me that there are any limitations to what I can do. But this isn't just about what I want. John has a say. 'Why does this have to be so hard?' I know now that Delmarr is right. Nobody can be both: career woman and housewife. I kept hoping I would figure out a way to do both. But only men get the luxury of a magnificent career and a good home life.

'He loves you, but he loves you if you're there for him every minute. You're only allowed your dreams if they are his dreams too. Trust me. I'm older than you, and I've seen this a hundred times.'

I stare down into my coffee cup, which looks like a black pit I'd like to jump into. 'It stinks.'

'Yeah, it does. But what are you gonna do? That's love.' Delmarr swings his legs off his desk and jumps to a standing position. 'But for now, in the waning days of the B. Altman Custom Department, I'm going to beg you to finish the Ashfield order. Two evening dresses and a hostess pantset. She's a chub so keep the flow loose.'

'A Madame Rouge.' That's one of our code phrases back at the shop. It refers to our larger lady clientele. Delmarr came up with it when he took a lady's measurements and the numbers went as high as the red mark on the tape measure.

'The rouge-ee-est.' Delmarr laughs.

'Welcome back, Lucia,' I say aloud.

'Oh yeah, and that too, kid. Welcome back.'

Every year when I leave for vacation I harbour a secret fear that when I return my desk will be cleaned out and my job will be gone. And now, the thing I feared the most has happened: I left for a month and came back to my gleaming castle on the third floor of the best department store in New York City, only to find it in ruins. I go to my desk and pull my handbag from the drawer. Inside the zipper pocket, I pull out my little red pass-book from the Chase National Bank. On 5 July 1951, I wrote a cheque to John for $7,500.00 for the house. My nest egg is gone. If the department closes, I will have to rely on John for money. I don't want to rely on anyone! The thought that I will never work again peels through me like a sudden chill.

'How was Italy?' Ruth booms as she sweeps into the Hub.

I quickly put away my bank book. 'Hi!' I say too brightly.

Ruth gives me a kiss on the cheek. 'What's wrong with you?'

'I missed you!'

'No, you look shaky. What happened?'

'We're going to lose our jobs.'

'You already spoke with Delmarr? We're too high-end for the new B. Altman's. They want ready to wear on every floor. Can you imagine the crap they'll roll in here? The workmanship will be shoddy, the fabrics will be cheap, the kind that never lose the smell of the dye! Yech! New York class is going to take a powder.'

'Ruth?' My voice quivers as I say her name, alarming her. She puts down her pencil. 'I gave John all my savings.'

'You did what?'

'All my money.'

'What did he do with it?'

'He's putting it into the house.'

'Oh, okay.' Ruth breathes a sigh of relief and clasps her hands behind her head. 'You scared me.'

'Well, he wasn't going to squander it,' I say defensively.

'Okay, okay. I believe you. Lucia, honey. I've got something to tell you,' Ruth leans in.

'What?' I try not to panic, but my mind instantly goes to Amanda Parker and how the society girls make sport of stealing men from one another.

'You know Harvey goes to the track once in a while for fun. Since the Seder he's invited John a couple of times. Last week Harvey came home and told me John is a serious gambler. Harvey bets a buck on a horse. He said John puts down fifty, a hundred dollars.'

My heart sinks. From the minute I looked at my bank book and saw that one red withdrawal after pages and pages of deposits, I've been gripped by fear. 'You don't think he's gambling *my* money, do you?'

'No, no, I'm sure he would never do something like that. But I know you, and you've been saving every penny since the day we started here.'

'Why would he need my money for the house if he has so much of his own?' I wonder aloud. I look at Ruth. She is thinking the same thing.

'Sweetie . . .' I know what Ruth is going to say before she says it. 'You never had the money talk, did you?' I shake my head. She continues, 'Hold on. Before we go off half-cocked, let's think this through. You gave him your savings, for *your* house.'

'Eventually, we would combine all our money anyway,' I tell her, justifying my position. 'I wanted to be a full partner in everything. Is there anything wrong with that?'

'Of course not. And he's going to be your husband. You have to trust him.' Ruth looks at me kindly. 'The gambling thing I wouldn't worry about. You know, sometimes Harvey goes out with the boys and has a few drinks and comes home slightly ploughed. I accept it. One guy's cocktails are another guy's horses. What can you do? Everybody has a weakness. You just don't want the weakness to turn into a habit.'

On my way home from work that night, as I cross Fifth Avenue, I turn and look back at B. Altman's and burst into tears. The happiest days of my life have been in that building and now everything is changing.

What will I do without seeing Ruth every day? She knows everything about me, down to such detail that when I confided that I made love to John, she sent me to her uncle, a respected gynaecologist on the Upper West Side, so I would be responsible and 'use protection'. I'll also miss Helen Gannon, who cut fabric so precisely, it was as if she was cutting glass with a diamond. It was never hard to assemble a garment Helen had cut; she'd look at the measurements and the fabric and then cut to the flow and drape of the customer's figure . Nobody does that any more, but she did, and now she'll use that talent making drapes or baby clothes. Violet, even though she can be annoying, was always loyal. If you needed help on anything and had to stay late, you could always count on Violet. And Delmarr took me under his wing back when I didn't know a Chanel from a Schiaparelli.

But it's not all about losing my friends. The world itself is losing something. The kind of quality I believe in will no longer be valued. A hand-stitched hem is no longer a study in precision and detail; a garment is slammed through a machine, pulled off the bobbin, and thrown in a bin with the dozens of others assembled that day. There's no Delmarr meeting with a client and asking her what she likes or studying her colouring and shape to create clothes that make her gorgeous. There's no personal service in ready to wear. Do women really want to paw through a swinging rack jammed with garments in every size and colour? The gentility of my working world will be as woefully out of date as a snood, come the spring of 1952.

'Why the face?' Papa asks as I'm hanging my coat.

'The store. The Custom Department is getting overhauled.' I don't want to get into the details with him, so I go into the kitchen. But he follows me.

'What about your job?' he asks.

'I don't know yet,' I tell him in a tone meant to indicate that the discussion is over.

Mama comes downstairs and joins us in the kitchen. 'Lu, I think I've decided to wear coral at your wedding. I was sold on the turquoise blue, but then I thought, I want something brighter, happier. What do you think?'

'Lucia is losing her job,' my father tells her.

'Papa!'

'So, she's getting married,' Mama says lightly. 'She doesn't need to work. She'll have more than enough to do at home.'

'Now you sound like Claudia DeMartino,' Papa says to her.

'Why bring her up?' Mama counters.

'Because she has the same ideas about Lucia that you do.' Papa spears a meatball from the pot of sauce simmering on the stove.

Mama gets him a small plate, and says, 'Antonio, I want you to listen to me. Lucia has chosen a very nice, sophisticated man to marry. They are not going to live like we live. He is a worldly type, he travels, he is part of –' she waves her hand in the air '– uptown. They are going to live in a suburb, okay? With a view of the ocean. In a house with a chandelier from Murano in the hall. You see what I have? I have the lamp in the hall that was there when we moved in. This girl is different from us, and you need to accept it.' Mama puts her arm around me. 'We have one daughter, and I don't want to lose her because you think that no man she brings home is good enough.'

'No man *is* good enough,' Papa says, 'but some are better than others.'

'Papa, what is your problem with him?'

'I don't understand him, Lucia.'

'Why do you need to understand him?' Mama interjects. 'You don't have to live with him, she does.'

'You just don't want me to marry anybody!'

'That's not true. I accepted Rosemary and have grown to love her. I left my son Exodus in Italy with Orsola because I saw in her many of the things I saw in your mother. They are a good match. If I felt that John Talbot had the qualities of a good husband, I would support you. I don't question that he is in love with you, but I worry, that's all. I worry. I'm sorry. I can't help it.'

If only Papa knew how much I needed to talk to him about my fears, today of all days. But he makes it impossible. It is as though I have to defend my feelings for my fiancé constantly, so I can't be honest. I'm afraid, terribly afraid that I won't be able to keep up with the pace of John's world, that I'll have to turn a blind eye whenever he wants to invest in another venture or buy something we can't afford. I don't even know how much money he has. I'm afraid to ask and make him angry with me. I grew up watching my parents share all the responsibilities involving finances, but John acts as though those sorts of questions are insignificant, irritating, beneath him. Maybe this is what I'm really scared of: I'm not enough for John Talbot.

'Papa, please don't worry. I need your support. Please.' I must look pitiful, because Papa puts his arms around me.

'I will always be here,' he says.

'And some day, he will love John,' Mama promises.

'That would make me very happy,' I say. Papa looks so weary in the bright yellow light over the kitchen sink. I'm making my father get old before his time.

As I climb the stairs to my room, I wish the floors would never end, that I could keep climbing until I found some kind of peace. I especially miss my brother Exodus tonight. Somehow when we were all together under one roof, I believed no harm could ever come to us, curse or no curse.

In the final days before the wedding, I find myself waking up earlier and earlier (today it was three a.m.) and being unable to get back to sleep. I lie in bed and think of John.

This morning, I replay a scene from last July in my mind. I'm in John's car and he's driving me home from work. I ask him to come into the house and he can't because he has a business meeting. I'm about to get out of the car, and he says with a big smile, 'Do you have the cheque?' I pull out my chequebook and write out a cheque to John Talbot. I fold it at the crease and gently tear it out. 'This is all the money I have in the world, honey,' I tell him. He takes the cheque without looking at it, folds it until it is a small rectangle, and then slides it into the handkerchief pocket of his suit jacket. 'It ain't much baby, but it's all you've got,' he says, laughing, and then he kisses me. I know its a joke, but it stings like a slap.

'Lucia!' Mama calls up the stairs.

'Yes, Mama?'

'Can you stop at the Groceria on your way to work?'

I take my purse and go downstairs. Mama has prepared the bank envelope. 'Bring this to Papa and let him go over the figures. The caterer sent a list of hors d'oeuvres you need to look at for the reception. How's Delmarr doing on your dress?'

'Fine, Mama. How many responses have we gotten?'

'We're going to have about three hundred at the reception when all's said and done,' Mama says. 'Where are you having the gifts sent?'

'Out to Huntington.'

'How's the house coming?'

'I haven't seen it, Mama. John wants to surprise me. We'll stay there on our wedding night.'

'As it should be,' Mama says proudly. Thank God she never asks me anything else about my wedding night. Then I'd have two sins on my hands: mortal (making love) and venial (lying about it).

When I arrive at the Groceria, Papa is hanging wheels of Parmesan cheese from the ceiling like a mobile. 'Now, that's original,' I say.

'Where do you think you get your talent?' He smiles.

'Have you gone to rent your tuxedo yet?'

'Nope.' He walks over to the register and I follow.

'The boys have all got their tuxedos. The least you can do . . .'

'Is show up and give away the most beautiful girl in Greenwich Village.' As he methodically places the change in the drawer, he assures me, 'I know my role. Your mother goes over it with me every night. She wants the best wedding anyone has ever seen. Finally, one of her children is having a Mariani-style Italian wedding. You know the Barese, they go for the glitz.'

'Papa?'

'Yeah?'

'Don't give me any money when I get married. The reception is enough of an expense. Okay?'

'Why do you say that?'

'I want you and Mama to take care of yourselves. I want you to rest.'

He closes the register, comes around the counter, and kisses the top of my head. 'Sure. Sure.'

'I mean it,' I tell Papa firmly.

'Go to work,' he tells me as he picks up a crate of tomatoes and goes to create his next display.

I walk through the store and wave goodbye to Angelo, who is pouring ice chips on the fresh fish. I'm about halfway up the block when he comes running after me, calling my name.

'Lucia, come back! Something's wrong with Pop.'

When I get back to the Groceria, Papa is sitting on a stool. Roberto is trying to give him a cup of water. 'Please, Pop. Drink it,' Roberto pleads.

'Let me see.' I lift Papa's head and look into his eyes. 'You're going to Saint Vincent's.'

'The hospital? Ba!' he says.

'You're going. And right now,' I order him. Papa's colour is terrible. He hasn't looked this bad since he fainted in Italy.

'There's nothing wrong with me.'

'Hopefully not, but if there is, we're going to make it better.'

Roberto goes for the truck while Angelo and I wait with Pop. 'I wish you wouldn't make such a big deal out of it,' Papa says to me.

'Papa, if anything happened to you, I would die,' I say, kneeling beside my father and holding him in my arms.

The worst part of calling home with bad news is that Mama drops the phone and then you're never sure if she heard it all, and if she did, whether she's all right or in a state of shock. When I tell her Papa is in a room at Saint Vincent's, she drops the phone but picks it back up quickly. She isn't that surprised. She told him his colour was poor at breakfast, but he disregarded her completely.

By the time Mama gets to the hospital, she is calm. 'Antonio, you've got to take better care of yourself.' She stands beside his bed and holds his hand.

Dr Goldstein, a heart specialist, joins us in Papa's room. He is lanky and young, with a kind face. 'Mr Sartori, I've been to your market many times.' Papa beams. 'The best prosciutto in New York City in my opinion.'

'Make my husband better and you get free prosciutto for the rest of your life,' Mama says.

'My wife, always giving away the store,' Papa jokes, squeezing Mama's hand. Then he looks at the doctor with a serious expression. 'You want to tell us what's wrong with me?'

'The good news is that you didn't have a heart attack,' says Dr Goldstein.

'And what's the bad news?'

'We're not sure exactly what happened to you.'

Angelo speaks up. 'Doc, Pop was lifting a case of crushed tomatoes when he passed out. Could that have anything to do with it?'

'It could.' The doctor smiles. 'In the meantime, we want to run some more tests.'

'Is there anything Papa can do to make things better?' I ask.

'No lifting. No stress. And in terms of your diet—'

'I know all about it: give up butter and eggs and my Manhattans.'

'Do you smoke?'

'One cigarette after dinner. That's all. Never during the day.'

'If you were well, I'd say one won't kill you. But you should stop smoking altogether.'

'I'm throwing out those cigarettes!' Mama says.

'Your days of strenuous labour are over. No loading or unloading trucks, no lifting period. I want you to walk about a half mile a day, but no more. And I'd like you to follow this diet. It may seem bland at first, but in time you won't even miss your old way of eating. We'll need you to stop by for a heart monitor once a month.'

'Give up food, work, smoking and spare time. Anything else, Doc?'

'A good attitude would be helpful. We're going to keep you overnight to do some more tests.'

When Dr Goldstein leaves the room, we try to perk up Papa's spirits. He laughs with us, but I can tell that he is frightened. It's devastating, seeing the leader of your family full of fear.

'We're going to follow the doctor's instructions exactly,' Mama declares.

'Who wants to live like that?' Papa says.

'You do! You want to live, Antonio Sartori, and don't you forget it!' Mama kisses him and lets her cheek rest against his.

'Okay, okay,' he tells her. 'I'll eat cottage cheese and lettuce for the rest of my life. Soon, I'll grow ears and be a rabbit.'

Mama stands up straight and says sternly but tenderly, 'I don't care what you turn into as long as you're here and healthy.'

Rosemary has thrown herself into my wedding plans like a genuine *comare*. She's put herself in charge of the favours for the guests, traditional Italian confetti and tiny bags of candy almonds. She has tied each little bundle with a lace bow; how delicate they look lined up in an open box in the living room. Not to be outdone, Mama's cousins in Brooklyn have made cookie platters for each table. Mama cleared her pantry next to the kitchen and filled every shelf with round platters loaded with baked delicacies – apricot cookies, coconut drops iced in pink buttercream frosting, fig and date bars stacked in pyramids, wrapped in cellophane, and tied with crisp white satin bows. Whenever Mama opens the pantry door, we get a blast of sweet vanilla, cocoa and lemon sugar through the living room. It reminds me of Christmas. Mama bakes whenever there's something to celebrate.

'I don't know if you like this, but it's something we always did in Brooklyn,' Ro says, lifting a beautiful bride doll out of a box. The doll is sitting in a pool of lace with a long tulle veil. Her eyes blink when Rosemary moves her, her lips are hot pink and she has a mole drawn on her chin. 'See, we put her on the lead car.' I must have a puzzled expression, because Ro sounds a little exasperated as she goes on: 'We'll tape her right to the hood ornament of John's Packard.'

'It's cute,' I tell her, forcing a smile of approval. My Venetian side comes out. I prefer simple adornment. Dolls on cars are pure Neapolitan.

'I knew you'd love it.' Rosemary pulls another doll out of the box. This one is dressed in caramel satin, like my bridesmaids, Ruth, Violet, and the doll woman herself, Rosemary. 'This is for the attendants' car.' Ro looks at me hopefully.

'Did you make those doll dresses?' I ask her.

'Yeah.'

'They're pretty. Nice trim work on the lace. Strap her on the second car.' Rosemary looks relieved. 'And thank you. You've worked so hard on this wedding and I want you to know that I appreciate it.' I give her a big hug.

'Thank you, Lu. You've been so good to me.' Rosemary turns away.

'What's the matter?' But I know there's no need to ask. 'It's Maria Grace, isn't it?'

Rosemary fusses with the bride doll, straightening the veil and smoothing the skirts. 'I'm having another baby. But keep it a secret. I haven't told Roberto yet. I'm waiting until after your wedding.'

I hold her tightly. 'Congratulations. Maria Grace will be the baby's guardian angel.'

She brushes away a tear. 'You know, besides Roberto and our parents, you were the only family who ever held her.'

'I know. And I'll never forget what she felt like in my arms.'

Sometimes I think about the baby, how sweet she smelled and how easily she fitted in the crook of my arm.

'What's wrong?' Roberto asks as he comes in and drops the boxes of programmes on the front bench.

'Nothing,' I tell him. 'What's a wedding without a crying jag? Best man, have you picked up the rings?'

'I have it under control.'

'Where's the bachelor dinner?'

'The Vesuvio. Where else? That fiancé of yours thinks it's the only restaurant in New York City. Of course, they treat him like a king over there. That's all right. The food is good.'

'We're home!' Mama shouts from the hallway when she and Papa arrive back from his follow-up visit with the doctor. Rosemary, Roberto and I rush to the hall.

'What did the doctor say, Pop?' Roberto asks.

'You're looking at a healthy man. My heart is strong. That caveman diet your mama has me on is working.'

'Thank God!' I throw my arms around my parents. 'I knew you'd be fine if you listened to the doctors.'

'I'm going to put on some tea,' Mama says and smiles.

Papa and Roberto follow her into the kitchen. 'Thank God,' Rosemary says to me. 'Now you'll have a happy wedding day.'

'It's the day before your wedding, Mrs Talbot. Any wish you have, I will grant,' John says as I stand on the stoop and he reaches for my hand. It occurs to me that this is the last time he will call for me here at my parents' house. It's the last day that 45 Commerce Street will be my home.

'I know it's against the rules,' I begin.

'Doesn't matter.'

'I want to go to our house.'

'Hmmm.' John thinks. 'Is that what you really want?'

'Yes! I'm dying to see it!'

'Let's go then,' he says, pulling me close.

John and I don't say much as we speed along the expressway to Huntington. As we turn onto the road to the Cascades housing development, I lean over and kiss the man who, this time tomorrow, will be my husband. Suddenly, I don't want to see my house.

'Turn around,' I tell him.

'What?' John brakes and pulls over.

'Let's go back to the city.'

'I thought you wanted to see the house.'

'You've worked so hard on it. Let's stick with our plan.' John's intention was for me to see the house for the first time on our wedding night. I want to save something special for tomorrow night. I don't want to ruin the surprise for him, or for myself.

'Are you sure?' John raises his eyebrow.

'Absolutely,' I tell him.

John makes a U-turn and gets back on the highway. I look over at his profile, studying every detail as though it were a pattern for a garment. Each feature has beauty and definition, the straight nose, the strong chin, the square jaw line, the clear forehead. It's the face of a man without a worry in the world. I catch myself imagining the faces of our children, hoping our daughter will inherit those long black eyelashes and that our son will have that sweet smile. I've almost changed my mind about having a baby. I think I would like to have something only John and I could create together.

'You made the right decision.' John seems pleased.

'I did?'

'You need to have some surprises in this lifetime,' he says. 'Otherwise, what's the point?'

I turn on the radio and, as I search through the static for music, I look up and see Manhattan stretching before us. My home, the city where I was born, the place where I've spent twenty-six happy years. I never thought I'd leave, never thought I'd say goodbye to Commerce Street. But now I have to. I *want* to. I'm going to begin a new life with my husband.

Delmarr is surprised when he sees my bedroom. 'You *are* an Italian princess. What a room! It's bigger than my apartment. If I were you, I'd just move Talbot in here. What do you want to move all the way out to Hauppauge for?'

'Huntington.'

Delmarr makes his way to the back window overlooking the gardens. 'Whatever. It's still the suburbs. You ever lived in the suburbs?' I shake my head. 'The "sub" is in there for a reason. *Sub*tract excitement from your life and replace it with boredom.'

'I could never be bored with a view of the ocean.'

'You'll see.'

Ruth, who's lived in elevator buildings all her life, huffs and puffs through my doorway. 'Every time I climb those stairs I understand why you're so slim.' She lays her dress bag over a chair and plops down on my bed. I examine her slacks and sneakers. 'Don't worry,' she says. 'All I have to do is jump into my dress.' She sits up. 'Your hair is amazing!'

'Mama put it up,' I say. She did a beautiful job. We copied a high chignon out of *Vogue*, then Mama anchored the tiara John gave me on it.

'You look stunning,' Ruth says.

'Well, homeliness was never this girl's problem.' Delmarr says. 'The Talbot family won't know what hit them.'

'John has no family. There's only his mother and she's too sick to come. But he'll have my big Italian family soon enough.'

'All right, let's get you into your get-up.' Delmarr removes the muslin balloon from my gown. I have never seen a more beautiful dress. It's a sculptured ball gown, strapless with a fitted bodice. Delmarr designed a series of tucks under the waist that leads to sweeping flounces that attach over the bustle with a single button.

'My God, it looks like it's made out of cotton candy,' Ruth marvels.

'Straight from the runways of Paris,' Delmarr says proudly.

'Here are the gloves.' Ruth hands me long white satin evening gloves.

'Remember, as the day grows longer . . .' Delmarr begins.

'So do her gloves!' we all finish in unison.

'Okay, where's my matching bolero for the church? No priest has seen a woman's arms since the Crusades.'

'Lu, I didn't make the bolero,' Delmarr answers.

'Oh God, no. I don't have anything that will go with this gown and I can't go sleeveless!' I'm about to cry, when Delmarr grins.

'This is my gift.' From the muslin sack, Delmarr pulls a floor-length white satin evening coat with a portrait collar. The deep sleeves have wide cuffs covered in tiny seed pearls nestled in beads that shimmer like pavé diamonds. 'No girl from B. Altman's Custom Department is going to get married in a tacky bolero.'

Like a queen, I put on the dress and Delmarr's coat, this royal robe, and descend the stairs. Papa sees me as I turn the corner of the first landing to greet him in the foyer.

'*Stai contenta*,' he says to me, taking my hands.

'Oh, Papa. I am happy.' I have never said a truer thing in my life.

I wanted to walk to Our Lady of Pompeii but Mama wouldn't hear of it. 'The hem of your dress will be black in half a block!' So we ride over in Papa's car, with the bridesmaids following in Roberto's car, complete with the doll in the caramel taffeta dress on the hood. Roberto gave John the bride doll for his car last night. The thought of him taping a doll to the hood of his car makes me chuckle.

I peek into the church to see how well it accommodates our three hundred guests. Every pew is practically full. The pew markers, bouquets of white carnations and miniature pink roses tied with caramel-coloured satin bows, look lovely. I breathe in the smell of incense, Chanel No. 5 (evidently the perfume of choice for my cousins from Brooklyn) and beeswax from the tall candles surrounding the altar.

Helen Gannon, ready to have baby Gannon any moment, turns and winks at me from the end of her pew. She is wearing a fuchsia satin swing coat, a glorious contrast with her red hair. It's a wonderful feeling to see everyone you know and love under one roof for the happiest day of your life.

'The priest said to wait in the baptistry,' Ruth says. 'As if a Jewish girl would have any idea where the baptistry is.'

'Don't worry,' I say. 'We'll go in a second.'

I kiss Mama and Papa and wave to Exodus and Orsola. They've been home nearly a week but I've hardly seen them because I've been so busy tending to last-minute details.

'Come on, Lucia. You're supposed to be in hiding,' Ruth chides me.

She and I join Violet and Rosemary in the room off the vestibule. There is a waist-high marble font for baptizing babies under the stained-glass window. A large statue of Saint Michael, patron saint of the angels, carrying a sword and shield, stands in the corner. 'Rugged,' Ruth comments as she looks him up and down.

She busies herself fussing with my hem, while Violet smears on another layer of lipstick. 'I'm getting so many good ideas for my wedding,' Violet says earnestly. 'I wonder if Presbyterians use pew markers.'

Rosemary paces back and forth, trying to see out the crack in the window to the street. I stand patiently, holding my bouquet of calla lilies (modelled on Claudette Colbert's *It Happened One Night*). I put the flowers in the font and fluff my skirt. There is an ornate gold cross on the wall, the centre of which is a mirror with the sacred heart of Jesus painted on it. I catch the reflection of my eyes in it. Then I look closely. My eyes are blue like my father's, and they are clear, since I slept well last night, but something is wrong. I can feel it, and I can see it in my own eyes.

'Ro, what time is it?'

'It's ten thirty,' she says brightly. 'But my watch is always fast.'

'At the rehearsal last night, I told John to be here by ten, didn't I?'

'Yes, you did. I heard you,' she tells me.

'Is he here yet?'

'I don't see his car. But that doesn't mean anything. You know what? I'm going to go back to the sacristy. I can go outside and through the side entrance and I'll see if John is there.' Rosemary grabs her coat and goes out the door.

'Men are always late,' Violet complains.

'Don't forget. It's a weekend,' Ruth says. 'Traffic is horrible. John's driving to the Village from the Upper East Side and it's impossible to get across town on time unless the guy has wings.'

We stand in the quiet for what seems like a very long time. I hear the organist pause and begin to play the same tune over again.

Finally, Rosemary pushes the door open and smiles. 'He's not here yet, but Roberto did his duty as best man and talked to him at about eight o'clock this morning. He was having breakfast and I'm sure he'll be here any minute.'

'What time is it now?' I ask.

'It's exactly a quarter to eleven,' Rosemary says as she looks at her watch. But it's not fast. I made Ruth check the clock in the sacristy a few minutes ago.

'Well, there's nothing to do but wait,' I tell them. They don't say anything but they don't have to. They're worried. And so am I. Where is he? Has something terrible happened? My heart begins to race. I've been dating John Talbot for one year; not once in that entire year was he late. I'm sure Ruth would tell me there's a first time for everything. But suddenly, my stomach flips and churns. I feel sick. I need air. It's funny how a church that's always seemed so ornate and polished can suddenly seem like a hall. When I enter the vestibule, I notice the collection baskets are stacked off to the side, the bulletin board is tacked with handwritten announcements, and the rubber rain mat with its series of holes, reveals muddy marble underneath.

'I'm going outside,' I tell the girls. I go out to the street. The air is cold, and I inhale slowly to steady myself. I'm amazed that, on the most important day of my life, nothing has changed in Greenwich Village. Across the street, a man in overalls pumps oil off his truck through a wide hose, down into a valve on the sidewalk, and there are three young women at the corner news-stand buying magazines, and in the diner, an old man is being served in his booth by the window. Don't they know what day it is?

'Look, Mommy, the snow queen!' a little girl says to her mother as they pass me. The mother smiles at me, but in her expression, I see who I am. She puts her head down, tightens her grip on her daughter's hand, and keeps walking. The stranger sees it, she knows. And I know too. She does not want her daughter to see anything so sad.

I wait outside as long as I can, hoping that if I stare at Bleecker Street long enough, a car carrying my future husband will pull up in front of me. I don't know how many times the cycle of red, yellow and green is repeated before it becomes clear to me that the car I'm praying for is not coming. I go back into the vestibule. My bridesmaids look at me with forced smiles. Only Ruth looks away. She knows. John Talbot is not going to marry me. Not this morning. Not ever. I've been jilted.

Chapter Ten

What happens after a jilting is probably a lot like what happens after a murder. The clues are gathered, the crime scene is cleaned up, all the ugly details are removed, and then life goes on. I don't know what happened in the immediate aftermath, like the seven-course meal at the Isle of Capri restaurant, or who told the band, the Nite Caps, to go home, or where the trays of cookies went. It's been a week and I haven't asked. My gown is in the closet and my bouquet is in a shoebox under my bed. I can't find the tiara. It must have gotten lost between the church and home.

The attendants and I waited at the church until three o'clock. I insisted on it. Somehow, I convinced myself that three o'clock was the magic time, that John would come to his senses and rush into the church apologetically. The guests, however, left after two hours. My brothers went, pew by pew, and told them they could leave, that we would be in touch.

Roberto and Orlando went up to the Carlyle to find that John Talbot was still registered. Orlando cooked up some story about

John being ill, and because my brothers were clean-cut and well dressed, the general manager relented and let them into John's room. They found the room clean, the bed made, but no sign of John. Not even a toothbrush. The general manager asked my brothers if they were going to take care of the bill. John Talbot owes the Carlyle Hotel $2,566.14. My brothers explained they weren't family. The general manager didn't believe them.

On the way out, Roberto thought to ask the garage attendant about the Packard. The attendant said he hadn't seen the car in a week or so. Odd. But what isn't odd about a man who disappears?

We called the police, and they issued a missing person's bulletin after forty-eight hours, mostly as a formality. They had seen this sort of thing before, they told Roberto. It brought me no comfort to know other girls had endured this humiliation. In fact, that made it worse. I provided the police with pictures of John and the tickets for our honeymoon flight to Bermuda. They took everything and promised to return it later.

There's a knock at my bedroom door. I don't answer it. I haven't for a week, why should I now? Mama pushes the door open.

'Lucia?'

I feel guilty for putting my mother through this. It wasn't what she planned for her only daughter. 'Hi, Ma.'

'I brought you something to eat.'

'I don't want it.'

'Please, please eat,' Mama begs. 'Our hearts are broken seeing what that man did to you. Don't die for him too! He's not worth it.'

Papa's right, Mama is dramatic Barese down to her soul.

'Mama, I'll eat. But I want to come down to the kitchen.' I've been lying in bed long enough. The more I stew about John, the angrier I get. I'm not a girl who is content to let things lie. I want to know why he did this to me. And the answers won't come here in my room.

Papa beams when he sees me coming down the stairs. Then he looks up to heaven and thanks God. 'I prayed you would come downstairs! And I prayed you would get angry!'

'Well, Papa, both of your prayers have been answered.'

'Are you sure you want to do this?' Ruth asks as she turns off the highway to the Cascades housing development.

'Are you getting cold feet?' I ask her. I realize it's an ironic choice of words but Ruth doesn't let it throw her.

'A little. I lied to Harvey and told him we were going shopping. He was afraid if we drove out here we might run into John. It's possible he's hiding out here.'

'The police checked already,' I say.

'Let's have a plan anyway. If he *is* here, we won't get out of the car.'

'Fine.'

'What do you think happened to him?' Ruth asks tenderly.

'I don't know.'

'Lucia, I want to help you, you know that. But I don't understand why you want to see the house. Why would you torture yourself that way? You just have to forget about him.'

'Ruth, you know how we make clothes?'

Ruth looks confused.

'It's the only thing I know how to do. You make a drawing, I break it down into pieces, those pieces are made into a pattern, the pattern is placed on the fabric, the fabric is cut, we stitch the pieces together, and then we have a garment.'

'Okay, but—'

'Listen, Ruth. I sat down in my room with a notebook and made a list of everything that I knew for sure about John Talbot. First I described him, that's the drawing. Then I went through my date book and wrote down every place we'd ever been, especially the places we went more than once. Huntington Bay, Creedmore, Vesuvio, all of them. Those are the pieces.'

'Okay, I get it. Now you're sewing it together.'

'And when I'm done, maybe I'll have something to look at that will help me understand what's happened to me.'

'You haven't been out here since . . .'

'Actually, we drove out here the day before the wedding. But at the last minute, I told him I wanted to save the surprise for our wedding night.'

'What's the address?'

'It's the last lot on this street.' I point to the end of the block. 'With a view of the bay.'

'What a neighbourhood,' Ruth says as she passes the new homes, with their two-car garages and straw on the ground where the grass will grow eventually. 'No wonder you loved it so much.'

'There, Ruth!' I point to the hill that would have been my front yard.

Ruth pulls the car over in front of the lot. But there is no house, only a 'FOR SALE BY OWNER' sign on the tree where the driveway was supposed to be. There's a phone number printed on the bottom.

Farther back in the empty field I see a man searching for something in the back of his pickup truck.

'Are you sure this is the right place?' Ruth says, obviously hoping I'm wrong.

'Yes. This is it.' I get out of the car and climb up the hill to the man. 'Sir?'

'Yes, miss?' He smiles.

'Is this your property?' I ask.

'No, it isn't. I work for the man who owns it.'

'John Talbot?' This is the first time I have said his name aloud since I was left at the altar, and my icy tone is not lost on the caretaker.

'No. His name is Jim Laurel. Do you know him?'

'No, I don't.'

'Well, if you know Huntington, you know Jim. He owns this entire development.'

'So this property wasn't sold to anyone else?' I don't even want to know the answer, since it makes John's lies so much worse, to know that he *planned* to ruin my life.

'No, it just went on the market. You interested?'

'Maybe.' I can barely speak, I'm so upset.

Ruth joins us. 'We're looking at, um, lots of lots,' she tells him.

'Take my card.' The man gives Ruth his card and gets into his truck. As soon as he is gone, I sit down on the ground.

Ruth sits down next to me. 'Come on, Lucia. Let's go.'

'He lied about *everything*,' I say, not so much for Ruth to hear it as for me to believe it.

'I'm so sorry,' she says.

I look over the lot, and instead of seeing a sandy hill covered in patches of wild bamboo, low brush and clumps of old seaweed, I see my home. Each detail is as I imagined it, the Tudor castle door at the entrance, the glazed brick, the boxwood trimmed low on either side of the slate-and-concrete sidewalk, the rose taffeta draperies blowing in the breeze, and the chandelier, which I took hours to choose in Murano, twinkling in the hall. The sights and sounds of my first home are as real to me as the sand I dig into with my hands.

'Come on, it's getting late,' Ruth says, walking to the very spot where my front door would have been. 'You've been through enough for one day.'

I start to follow Ruth down the hill but stop and point to the bay. 'See that orange haze? It sort of settles over the water like sheer chiffon. The first time I made love to him, that's what the bay looked like. Just exactly like that.'

Ruth takes my hand. I turn around as I walk to the car with her. I know I will never see this place again.

Ruth and I don't say a word as we drive home. We're almost at Commerce Street when she breaks the silence.

'There's one thing I really don't understand. Do you mean to say that John Talbot drove you all the way out to Huntington the day before you got married and there was *no house*? How did he think he'd get away with this? And what made you change your mind?'

I sit and think about this for a few moments. Ruth pulls over, puts the car in park, and it idles as I search for an answer. 'Somewhere deep within me, I must have known the truth. I knew he wasn't who I thought he was. But I thought I could make him into the man I knew he could be.'

'Oh, Lucia,' Ruth says sadly.

'And somehow, I believed I was better because he loved me. You know how it is, Ruth. You think a man can give you what you want, so you surrender. Papa was right. I loved the way John looked, the places he took me and the life he promised to give me. It was all on the surface.'

Ruth nods. She understands, and I surely do too, what my attraction was to John Talbot. Now I have to figure out the rest of the puzzle, so this never happens again.

Papa's Veneto traditions have once again lost the Christmas wars. We won't be fasting on Christmas Eve. Rosemary has prepared the feast of the seven fishes with Mama, and we're all together. Even Exodus and Orsola decided to stay for the holidays. I think Mama had something to do with that. She convinced my brother that I needed him, and Exodus still wants to make up to Mama for staying in Italy.

Mama set a beautiful table with silver candelabras filled with white candles and her best china on a red tablecloth. After we sit down, Rosemary clinks her wine glass with a spoon. 'First of all, Merry Christmas, everyone!' What a change this is from last Christmas when Rosemary was the meek new bride who had to ask Papa if she could hang lights in the window. This year, she not only put lights in the windows, she also strung them through evergreen garlands down the railings and wove them through the front fence. Orlando calls it Sicily North. 'Second,' Ro continues, 'Roberto and I are expecting a baby in May!'

All of us leap out of our seats to hug and kiss the ecstatic parents-to-be. In the hubbub we hear the tinkling of a spoon against glass again. Everyone turns to look at Exodus.

'We have news too!' Exodus announces.

'You're moving back home?' Orlando asks.

'No, we're having a baby too! Ours is due in June!'

We cheer the second bit of happy news, but I can't help feeling sad in the midst of all this joy. My brothers seem to know how to pick good partners and create a life. Why can't I?

'Somebody get the door,' Mama says when we hear the bell.

'It must be Delmarr. I invited him for dessert,' I tell them as I go into the hall to answer the door. Usually I peek through the glass, but Rosemary's garlands obstruct the window. I throw open the door.

'Lucia . . .' John Talbot is standing in the rain on our stoop wearing his blue cashmere overcoat. I don't move. At the bottom of the stoop are two policemen. I try to close the door, but I'm not fast enough. John pushes it open.

'Please, Lucia. I need to talk to you,' he says softly.

'What are you doing here?'

'I came to tell you I'm sorry.'

'*Sorry*?' The word sounds so weak and empty I wish he hadn't said it.

'I have to tell you what happened.' John looks at me nervously. 'I know you don't have to listen, but please give me a chance to explain.'

I look at his face, still possessed of the fine features that I loved so, but there's something in his eyes that frightens me. His shoes are scuffed and unpolished, and even the coat is shabby-looking. He is clean-shaven, but I can smell liquor on him – a first. I look at what a mess he has made of himself, of me, and I can't believe it. Where were the signs that we would come to this?

'Where have you been?' I ask as I let him in and close the door behind him. He'll never be able to explain what he's done, but I might as well learn what I can.

'It doesn't matter.'

'Lucia, are you okay out there?' Roberto calls out.

'Sshh. Don't say anything,' John whispers. He puts one hand on the doorknob to go back outside.

Roberto comes around the corner. When he sees John Talbot, he becomes enraged. 'How dare you come here!'

'I need to talk to Lucia,' John says with as much bravado as he can muster.

At the sound of his voice, all my brothers, as well as my father, rush into the hall. The women stand behind them like a front-line battalion, present and ready to protect me.

'You want to talk to my sister? Are you crazy? After what you did?' Roberto shouts.

'I don't owe you an explanation. I owe your sister.'

'You have *that* fucking right,' Roberto says. I hear my mother gasp at his language. 'Where's her money?'

He pushes past me, grabbing John by the collar and pinning him against the wall. John, clearly weakened and unable to fight back, slumps against the wall. Roberto slams John's head into the plaster. '*Where's her money*?' John doesn't answer. Roberto slams his head again. 'You thief!' John still says nothing. Roberto hits his head on the wall a third time. 'Where's her fucking money?'

Part of me wants Roberto to keep hurting him, as payback for the humiliation I endured on our wedding day. But I can't bear to watch my strong brother beat this pitiful man.

'Stop it, Roberto!' I say. My brother steps back and John slumps against the wall. 'Please. I want to talk to him.'

The policemen, who had been waiting on the stoop, push the door open and put John in handcuffs. 'That's all the time you get. I'm sorry, ma'am. He told us you were his wife and it bein' Christmas, we gave him a gift.' One of them gives John a shove. 'Don't push it.'

I reach for John. 'No, Lucia,' my father says, holding my arm.

My brothers stand guard, as they have done all my life, until the police car bearing John Talbot disappears around the corner of Barrow Street. I cannot move.

'The bastard even ruined Christmas,' Roberto says.

'Yes,' I say quietly. He ruined our wedding, our future and even Christmas. And I would like to know why, even after all that, I still love him.

The days off between Christmas and New Year are usually my favourite because my work is done. Whoever needed a new dress bought it, and by Christmas Eve it has been altered, pressed and delivered. But this was supposed to be my first Christmas as a married lady. I am full of unanswered questions about what happened with John, and I haven't been able to sleep since he showed up at my door. If only I could understand why he left me, I would be able to press on.

Most of my friends try not to bring up the subject. It could be they want to spare me the embarrassment, but I suspect that they believe it was due to some flaw in *my* character that I didn't anticipate it. I was asleep at the wheel of my own life and I deserved what happened to me. I made this bed, and I lie alone in it.

I've been called in for questioning by the police which, on top of the personal shame of the situation, fills me with fear and dread. What if they think I had knowledge of John's business dealings? I called the only lawyer I know personally, Arabel's husband, Charlie Dresken. He assuaged my fears and told me he would be there with me, and that I should fully cooperate with the investigation. 'You have nothing to hide,' he told me. That may be true, but why is it that all I want to do is hide?

The police didn't give Charlie all the details of John's illegal activities, but they did say they were extensive. The police have asked me for a complete list of all the gifts John gave me. They also requested a calendar of our social life, including times and places, as far back as I could remember. It wasn't hard to assemble, since I collected keepsakes from the moment I met him; the McGuire Sisters programme from New Year's Eve, menus from restaurants, matchbooks, scribbled poems, even a dried rosebud plucked off a trellis in Montauk from the day we first made love. Putting it all together, though, was almost unbearable.

While the police gather their information, I begin to gather my own. There's one person whose face has haunted me over the last several weeks. I had grown fond of John's mother, Mrs O'Keefe, and she had begun to look forward to my visits, too. Even though she couldn't speak, she was alert and aware of everything going on around her. I've been worried about her through the holidays.

John Talbot is still in jail, and I doubt she knows what happened to him.

As I walk from the train station to the entrance of Creedmore, I wonder what I will say to Mrs O'Keefe when I get there. The regular receptionist is on duty, but when I greet her, instead of waving me in as usual, she asks, 'How can I help you?'

It dawns on me that I've always come here with John, so she might not recognize me on my own. 'Could I go inside and see Mrs O'Keefe?'

Her expression changes from friendliness to a look of concern. 'Didn't anybody tell you?'

'No.' I get a pain in my stomach.

'She passed away.'

'When?'

'Let me check the date.' She studies a log behind the desk. 'Sylvia O'Keefe died on November sixth.'

I don't thank the nurse. I simply turn towards the door. But before I can walk away, I need to know one more thing.

'I'm sorry to bother you again,' I say, turning around. 'But . . . was she alone?'

The receptionist reaches out and pats my hand. 'That nice son of hers was with her.' November sixth? Why didn't John tell me his mother died? What kind of man withholds such information?

On my first day back at work after the Christmas vacation, Charlie Dresken waits for me during my lunch hour outside the police station on Sixty-seventh Street. When we go inside, Charlie speaks to an officer at the front desk then I follow him to a small office, where we are greeted politely by a detective, a nice Italian man about Papa's age, whose badge identifies him as M. Casella. I begin by telling him that I went to see Sylvia O'Keefe. He was already aware of her death.

'Miss Sartori, how long did you know John Talbot?'

'One year.'

'Was that the only name you knew him by?'

'Are there others?' I ask, my dismay mounting.

'He used five aliases, all with the first name John. The other surnames are: O'Bannon, Harris, Acton, Fielding and Jackson. Sounds like a law firm, doesn't it?' He smiles but I don't. 'Hmm. He used his real name with you.'

I don't respond to the detective's comment. It does not make me feel better to know that John's name was the only true thing he shared with me.

'Did he live with you?' the detective asks matter-of-factly.

'We were engaged to be married. I live with my family. And always have,' I tell him in a tone that lets him know my character is not to be disparaged, despite my poor taste in men.

'Did you ever know a woman named Peggy Manney?'

'No.'

'She's Sylvia O'Keefe's daughter. She and her mother were not on speaking terms, which created a perfect situation for John Talbot, as you called him, to move in and take control of Mrs O'Keefe's finances.' My mind goes back to the day John told me he was an only child. 'Mr Talbot spent the last several years bilking Mrs O'Keefe out of her savings, cash and goods.'

'What?'

'John Talbot is a con man, Miss Sartori. He made his living by what we call negotiated theft. He'd build up trust with people and pretty soon he'd be in business with them. They provided the money, and he'd use it to fund whichever scam he had going at the time. When things didn't work out, he'd run. It worked for a long time, because most people are too embarrassed to report when they get taken.'

'But you think he stole from his own mother?' I can't believe it. I saw their close relationship. He loved her.

'She wasn't his mother.'

'*What*?' Was there anything I knew about John Talbot that was true?

'Talbot found her at church, can you believe it? Went to Saint Anthony's Parish Church in Woodbury and tagged her. She was a perfect victim – wealthy, lived alone, estranged from her daughter, eager for companionship – so he set about charming her and ingratiated himself into her life. She more or less took him in as her own. In time, he convinced her to let him manage all her finances. When she got sick, he put her in Creedmore. As far as we know, he never physically harmed the old lady, but he certainly brainwashed her. Her home in Woodbury became his base of operations.'

'But he lived at the Carlyle Hotel.'

'Sure, he had a suite there on and off, depending on what he was up to in the city. Guess whose money was bankrolling it? Sylvia O'Keefe's. That's why we need an accounting of whatever he gave you, in case any of it technically belongs to her rightful heir. Peggy Manney has made a list of jewellery her mother owned that's missing.' Detective Casella hands me the list, and I pass it to Charlie.

My head begins to pound, and I rest my face in my hands.

'I know, it's unbelievable.' The detective shrugs. 'And if Mrs O'Keefe hadn't died and the money hadn't run out, he'd still be fat and happy.'

'And married to me,' I say softly.

'You're lucky. So are a string of other girls he almost victimized. Amanda Parker for example.'

'What's she got to do with this?'

'Talbot tagged her too. He wanted her father to bankroll some construction scheme he had going. We tracked this story down through a developer out on Long Island . . .'

'Jim Laurel?' I ask weakly.

'How do you know Jim Laurel?'

'John had supposedly purchased land in the Cascades Development from him. He said he was building our house on it.'

'That was never going to happen. Jim Laurel is a smart businessman. Talbot told him that he was in business with Daniel Parker and Laurel wanted in. But it turned out to be all smoke and mirrors. Did Talbot ever get any goods or cash from you?'

'Almost all of my life's savings. Seven thousand five hundred dollars.'

The detective makes a note of my loss. 'Do you know John Talbot was with Mrs O'Keefe when she died?' I ask him.

'That was the least he could do.'

'I think he genuinely cared about her.'

The detective shakes his head as though I'm an idiot. 'We found a storage unit filled with stuff. Boxes and boxes of stuff from B. Altman's. You work there, correct?'

'Yes. Our bridal registry was there too.'

'So, this stuff, you think . . .' He hands me another list, which I scan quickly.

'These were for our wedding. I had all the registry gifts sent to a post-office box in Huntington. John said he was picking them up and taking them to our house.'

'These goods aren't stolen then. They should be returned to you.'

'I don't want any of them.'

'You can decide that when we return them. By law we can't keep this property if it belongs to you. You're not the one under arrest here.' He jots down some notes and then looks at me. For the first time Mr Casella softens. 'Take the stuff back. He owes you.'

The detective goes on to ask me more questions, mostly about places John and I had been.

'There's one more item Mrs O'Keefe's daughter asked about. Did Talbot ever give you a two-carat emerald-cut diamond in a platinum setting?'

'For our engagement.'

I can tell the detective doesn't want to say what he has to say next. 'You need to return that. It was stolen from Mrs O'Keefe and rightfully belongs to her daughter. You understand, I'm sure.'

Charlie nods at me. 'It's okay,' he says and pats my hand.

I open my purse and give the detective the ring, which I have kept in a ring box. I get up to leave.

'If we need to get in touch with you . . .' the detective begins.

'Call my office.' Charlie gives Mr Casella his card.

Out in the street, I become so angry I can't think. 'I'm such a fool!'

'No, you're not a fool. John Talbot was an excellent con man,' Charlie insists. We hail a cab and ride in silence until Charlie drops me off at work. 'Lucia?' he says. 'Forget him. You're a young girl, and dwelling on this won't do you any good.'

'Thank you for coming with me today, Charlie.'

As I enter the store, even the smell of exotic perfumes can't revive my spirits. Ruth is waiting for me in the Hub, ready with a cup of hot coffee and a cinnamon bun from Zabar's. 'So, what happened?'

Delmarr comes out of his office and motions to me.

'Come on, Ruth,' I say. 'I might as well tell the story once.'

'Jesus, I heard the whole story down in the islands,' Delmarr begins.

'What?'

'John Talbot went after Daniel Parker's dough. Tried to get a loan, then tried to get a job in his brokerage firm. But Parker had someone run a background check on him and they found a lot of holes in his stories. They also wanted a complete report on what he had in the bank. Before things went too far, Talbot ditched the whole plan, even if that meant ditching Amanda too. To mess with a guy like Dan Parker . . . I don't know if that makes Talbot courageous or an idiot.'

'Did Amanda Parker talk to the police?' I ask, knowing the answer. 'Of course not. Girls on the Upper East Side don't get dragged into police stations to have their integrity called into question. No need to make it worse for *her*.'

'It is worse for her,' Ruth says quietly. 'It made the paper.' She hands me an article from the morning *Herald*. The headline reads, 'Society Poser Nabbed'. I close my eyes, not reading another word. I give the article back to Ruth.

*

After returning all John's gifts, including the starfish brooch (another beautiful piece that belonged to Sylvia O'Keefe), there's only one other bit of business to attend to before I am finished with John Talbot for good. I must talk to Patsy Marotta at the Vesuvio.

The cabbie gives me a roguish grin as I climb into his cab with an enormous muslin sack. 'For me?' he asks.

'Nope,' I say flatly.

'It ain't a dead body, is it?'

'No, sir,' I say, a touch of impatience creeping into my tone.

'You got enough room back there?'

'Yes, sir.' I give him the directions to the Vesuvio. I'm not feeling very chatty.

The restaurant doesn't get busy until about eight o'clock, so I've planned to arrive around six. As I push through the polished brass door I can't stop myself from thinking that this is the first time it wasn't opened for me by John Talbot.

I stand in the doorway and look around the dark restaurant, which smells of fine tobacco, sweet wine and prime rib roasting in rosemary, which must be the special tonight. Patsy is where he always is, at the bar, half propped on the stool, one foot resting on the brass rail and the other extended out, as if he's ready to jump up and run to the kitchen. The bartender gives Patsy a look when he catches sight of me. Patsy puts out a cigarette, then turns to face me. 'I thought you'd come see me eventually.'

'I won't take too much of your time,' I say.

'Would you like something to drink?' he asks.

'No, thank you.' I glance at the empty tables. 'Could we talk over there maybe?'

Patsy rises and shows me to a table.

'Did you know about John?' I ask him. 'Do you know he's in jail?'

'The police spoke to me.' He shrugs.

'Well, Mr Marotta, since John Talbot gave me this mink coat in your restaurant, I'm returning it to you. I figure you would know where it came from.'

'I do know where it came from.'

'Where?'

'From Antoine Furriers of New York City and Toronto. It's totally on the up and up.'

'Antoine Furriers may be on the up and up, but I'm sure this particular coat was stolen.'

'It wasn't. He earned it.'

'I doubt that.'

'No, really. From time to time I would hear of jobs and pass along the information to John because I knew he dabbled in lots of business. Or so I thought. The owners of Antoine Furriers have lunch here a few times a week. They told me they were looking for someone to transport furs between New York and Toronto. They had a driver and a truck but they needed a more experienced businessman to accompany the goods over the border and make the transaction. John did it for several months, and he asked for the coat in lieu of cash. It was entirely legit.'

There's that word *legit* again. It makes my skin crawl.

Patsy continues, 'You keep the coat. It's yours.'

I stand and pick up the unwieldy bundle. 'You know, everybody keeps telling me to keep this stuff, as though it's the stuff that matters. Like a coat or a ring or a chafing dish can make up for all that's happened to me. I can tell you, Mr Marotta, that they don't make up for anything. I get no comfort from these *things*.'

Patsy doesn't answer me. He just gazes towards the kitchen before lighting another cigarette.

I thank him, and knowing that I won't come to his restaurant again, I say goodbye.

'You're a good kid,' is the last thing he says to me.

The official closing of the Custom Department at B. Altman & Company is set for 1 November 1952. They graciously informed us this morning by a mimeographed letter on each of our desks, signed by someone whose name we've never seen before. The letter said we have exactly seven months to wrap up any outstanding work, but first, dear employees, kill yourselves through another June Swoon so you're too exhausted to find yourselves a new job outside the company.

Ruth swears closing the Custom Shop is the first step to luring us all into retail, where we will sell off the floor and oversee alterations from time to time. The rats are jumping off the sinking ship on a regular basis now. Every day someone else comes in and announces his or her resignation. Violet left to become a housewife on her wedding day. Only Delmarr, Ruth and I hold out. When we have lunch with Helen, we tell her that baby David came at just the right moment. She is spared the painful details of disassembling our shop. It started with the high-end fabric stock, for which no further orders were to be placed. Then they began to take our best machines and send them God knows where. And now we're actually supposed to refer our private customers to a new department called In-Store

Consultation, where girls right out of high school run around the store gathering garments they think the customer will like. This is what B. Altman's now calls 'personal service'. We hear it was the brainchild of Hilda Cramer, who wasn't fired, but given a sweet deal that moved her out of Altman's and into her own private salon in White Plains. Occasionally we'll hear her on the radio with the style expert Ilke Chase talking fashion for the working woman. Ruth and I joke that we may call and make an appointment with her, since we're unemployed career girls who could use some good advice.

I turn in my seat and look out the window. This morning I felt okay – not better, but on my way to better. It's been a month since I was questioned by the detective. I know I have to stop dwelling on the past year and start thinking about my future. Last night I made a list of the designers I most admire, and even went so far as to look up their addresses and phone numbers. I intend to call every one of them, even Claire McCardell, and see who's in need of an experienced seamstress with a specialty in the application of beadings and trim.

Ruth calls to me from the front desk. Even our receptionist is gone, so whoever is walking by picks up the phone. 'It's for you, Lu.'

I pick up the phone. 'Hello?'

'Lu? It's Roberto. It's Pop again. He fell.'

'Is he at Saint Vincent's?' I ask.

'No. Come home.'

I jump in a cab and rush home. I run up the stoop and find Rosemary waiting at the door. She looks miserable, six months pregnant, standing with tears streaming down her face. 'It's not good, Lucia,' she tells me.

The boys have carried Papa up one flight and into his bedroom. When I enter, I blurt out, 'Has anyone called Exodus?' It must be the sight of my Papa in his bed in the middle of the day, something I've never seen before, that makes me want all of us together again. Maybe having one of us missing weakens Papa's resolve, maybe all of us together could pull him through.

The bell rings downstairs. Rosemary and Roberto go to let Dr Goldstein in. Mama is sitting on a footstool at the head of Papa's bed.

I take my father's hand and sit down on the bed next to him. 'Papa, are you okay?' I ask him, knowing he is not. 'I love you, you know. With all my heart.'

'*Grazie*,' he murmurs weakly.

The doctor asks us to wait outside, but Mama stays put. After a few minutes the doctor joins us in the hall.

'I'm sorry to have to tell you this. But your father is very sick. We've known it for some time now.'

'But his heart . . .' I can barely speak.

'It's not his heart. He has cancer. We believe it began in his pancreas, and it has spread to his liver.'

'Cancer?' I say softly because I don't believe it.

'It was diagnosed in November. We've known for some time that we'll be able to do something for his pain, but that's all.'

I turn to my brothers in disbelief. 'Did any of you know?' They are as shocked as I am.

My mind goes back to the month of November, to the night that Papa came home from the doctor while we were preparing confetti for the wedding. He and Mama gave us a good report. They said he was healthy. They lied, so I would have a happy wedding. I begin to cry. Orlando puts his arms around me.

'Is he in pain?' Roberto asks.

'Soon, we can give him morphine, which we administer through an IV drip. I've spoken with your mother and she'll arrange for a nurse to come and take care of that.'

'How long does he have?' Angelo asks.

'It could be days. Maybe less.'

We hear a muffled cry from the bottom of the stairs. We look down at Rosemary, who weeps into her hands, feeling the loss as keenly as we do.

'What can we do?' Orlando asks.

'Stay with him, be strong for him. That's all you can do. And I'll come back and see him, whenever I'm needed.'

I say, 'Angelo, call Exodus right away. Roberto, take care of Rosemary. Orlando, go back to the Groceria, keep it open, and make sure everything's running smoothly. Papa would want that. Okay?' Orlando nods and goes. I stand on the landing for a moment, say a quick prayer pleading with God to save my father, and then go back to my parents' bedroom.

I tiptoe in. Mama has not moved. She holds Papa's hand and looks at him, as though the intensity of her gaze could cure him. Papa has gone to sleep. I put my hands on his face and kiss his cheek. I whisper to him, 'We're here, Papa.'

The boys, Mama and I take turns sitting with him day and night. I don't know how many days; we have stopped counting. Sometimes I look at Roberto's face and know he feels guilty about his fights with Pop. I'm so ashamed of the night I told my parents to 'rot in hell' that I beg God to wake Papa up just so I can apologize for my terrible behaviour. If I could have that moment back, I would never have said those things. I didn't mean them. And now, I know Papa was right about everything. He was right about John Talbot.

Taking care of Papa becomes the focus of life in our home. It's been two days since the doctor visited. Papa takes broth and weak tea, and while the morphine dosages are small, they help him sleep. He knows he is dying, but he is determined to wait until Exodus arrives. We tell him repeatedly that Exodus is on his way, though Orsola will have to stay behind due to her pregnancy. When I speak to Papa, I try to lift his spirits with talk of his grandchildren. 'Papa, you will have two grandchildren by summer time!' This makes him smile. When he naps, I cry, knowing he will never see his grandchildren.

Exodus should be here by tomorrow morning. Papa is weakening; his fight to stay alive is really the fight to see Exodus one last time. Mama is amazing. She doesn't cry and she never leaves him. At night, she still climbs into their bed, and he sleeps in her arms.

The boys alternate working at the Groceria and being here with Papa. There is none of the usual squabbling or bickering, so I'm surprised when I hear the low tones of a tense conversation at the bottom of the stairs. I look at Mama, who motions for me to see who it is. 'Maybe Ex made it sooner!' I tell her. Papa's eyes open and he smiles.

Roberto comes up the stairs, followed by an older man whom I've never seen before. 'Lucia, this is our Uncle Enzo.'

Roberto steps aside. At first I extend my hands as one would to a stranger, but when I look into his eyes and see my father, I throw myself into his arms. The two men are so alike. The broad shoulders and delicate hands, the large head and curly salt-and-pepper hair, the paunch, not enough to require a diet, but enough to consider it from time to time. 'I'm so happy to meet you. Thank you for coming to see Papa,' I tell him.

'I came as soon as I heard.' He sounds like a healthy and strong version of Papa.

I take Uncle Enzo into my parents' room. Mama stands when she sees him and for the first time in three days she begins to cry. Her sobs awaken Papa. I don't think he initially believes his brother is really here, not until Uncle Enzo kneels next to the bed and takes him into his arms. Papa looks so small. He makes a sound, a deep moan, as if he has finally released a sadness he has been carrying since before I was born.

I motion to Mama that we should give them some privacy. I put my arm around her and lead her out of the room. Before I close the door, I look at the two of them, two boys who came such a long way to fulfil a dream. Years of estrangement and hard feelings fall away as my uncle holds my father.

Angelo gives up his room for Uncle Enzo. The nurse comes and tells us that Papa's system is starting to shut down, but that he has a strong heart. She wants to increase the morphine dosage. Mama explains to Papa that more morphine will ease his pain. Papa shakes his head decisively. Mama assumes he doesn't want to go to sleep until Exodus arrives, so she tells the nurse to keep the medication level where it is.

None of us can sleep. We stay in Papa's room, and when we need a break, we go down into the living room, where Rosemary puts sandwiches and cookies and there is always a fresh pot of coffee. What a Sartori she has turned out to be. My brother Roberto is a lucky man to have such a splendid wife.

We're all relieved when the front door opens and Exodus bolts in. 'Where is he?' Exodus drops his bags and runs up the stairs. We follow behind him and pile into Mama and Papa's room, as we used to do every Sunday morning before church. Mama would make us come to their room to see if there were shoes to be polished or hair to be slicked down with a touch of pomade. Uncle Enzo is on one side of Papa and Mama is on the other. Exodus hesitates when he sees Uncle Enzo, trying to make sense of the situation. Uncle Enzo gets up and steps away. Exodus puts his hand on our uncle's back and then moves in and kneels next to Papa. 'Pop, I'm here. Can you hear me?' Papa hasn't opened his eyes since last night. 'Squeeze my hand, Pop. It's Ex. I'm here. I made it. I made it.' Papa must squeeze my brother's hand, because Exodus yells, 'That's it, Pop! Squeeze my hand! Good!'

Mama runs her hand through Papa's thick, curly hair. Then she pulls her handkerchief from her pocket. Papa's eyes are closed and a tear rolls down his nose and off his cheek. As Mama gently wipes it away, I hear her say, 'He's gone.' Her eyes never leave his face. 'My love is gone.'

When the funeral home comes to take Papa away, the boys insist that Mama, Rosemary and I stay in the living room until he's in the hearse. Uncle Enzo stays with the boys; it's as if he has been a part of our lives all along.

'Mama, when did you call Uncle Enzo?' I ask.

'I didn't call him.'

'I called him,' Rosemary says softly. 'I couldn't bear for Papa to go without saying goodbye to his only brother. I hope it was all right.'

Mama embraces Rosemary. 'It was exactly right.'

In the weeks after Papa's death, our family came together as never before, and we found out what Antonio Sartori meant to people in Greenwich Village. Over the years, Papa would come home with funny stories about customers, sad stories about families who needed food, which he'd send over, or poignant stories about what it was like to be an old-fashioned grocer in a world of chain supermarkets. The only frozen item Papa allowed in the store was the ice to lay the fresh fish on.

I always thought I was like my mother's people, but when Papa died I saw how much I am like him. He was a perfectionist. 'To you, they are a crate of oranges, to me, they are a sculpture!' he'd say as he stacked oranges into a glorious pyramid with waxy leaves in the spaces between. He made topiaries out of boxes of pasta and ceiling treatments out of dried herbs. The ropes around the casings of salamis were works of art, knotted a certain way and at a certain length, so the customers could see what a delicacy they were buying. I have the same feeling about sewing. Perfection was my problem and the customer's right – after all, she was paying. Papa felt the same way.

We had one strange request before Papa's funeral. When we called Domenic to tell him of Papa's passing he was devastated, but then he asked us a favour. He wanted us to take a photograph of Papa in the casket. When Mama heard, she said absolutely not! But I told the funeral director, who agreed to take the picture, and I sent it off to Cousin Domenic without telling Mama.

Uncle Enzo comes back to the city to visit and to see if there's anything we need. We put on a big dinner for him, and Rosemary is hoping that some day, the families can reunite. She's working on it. Mama is happy to see Uncle Enzo, but she hasn't quite warmed up to the idea of seeing Zia Caterina. We're not going to push her. Mama will let us know when she's ready, and then we'll go for the full-blown reunion.

After the dishes are cleared, I ask Uncle Enzo to come into the kitchen.

I say, 'Do you remember the curse Zia Caterina put on me before I was born?'

'Oh, she didn't mean it!'

'I'm sure she didn't,' I say. Clearly, he is as upset by the memory as Mama was when Roberto confessed the family secret. 'Still, what exactly did she say?'

'She said she wanted you to be beautiful but unlucky in love.'

'Well, Zio, you can tell her the curse worked out fine.'

'Lucia, she didn't mean it. Caterina has a temper. I've lived with it for forty years. She curses everything, the priests, you, me, the cow. Everything.'

'It's okay. Really, it's okay.' I embrace him. 'Once a curse comes true, it's over.' I look my uncle in the eye. 'It's *over.* Right?'

'*Si, si, finito, finito.*'

Chapter Eleven

Antonio Giuseppe Sartori II was born on 1 June 1952. Mama wept when Rosemary told her the baby's name, but there's nothing like a new baby in the house to alleviate grief. He's a good baby with a sweet temperament.

About a month later Delmarr invites me to lunch as a thank you for getting him through the final bridal season of the Custom Department. He takes me to the cafeteria at Saks Fifth Avenue, partly as a joke but mostly because the food is delicious.

'Kid, you've had one helluva year.'

'Don't I know it.' I shake my head slowly. 'The worst was losing Papa.'

'The Talbot fiasco was terrible too. I still blame myself a bit for that. I'm sorry I introduced you. I'm sorry I couldn't see him for what he was. I should have done a better job of protecting you,' Delmarr says sadly.

'It's not your fault. Let me tell you how I *know* it's not your fault.'

'Okay.'

'After all that has happened, I still love him.' Delmarr is the only person in the world I could admit this to, and I am relieved to finally say it out loud.

'Why, Lucia? Why do you still love him?' Delmarr says tenderly.

'Why does anybody love anybody who has hurt them? Because there's always hope. Papa didn't talk to his brother for thirty years. At the end of his life, his brother came to see him and they forgave each other. All my life there was this impossible family burden we were hauling around, and then in the final moments, Papa got the best gift of all, his brother's forgiveness. I know that's why he went like an angel.'

'I don't think Talbot's going like an angel.'

'Probably not.'

'I have a proposition for you,' Delmarr says.

'You know I'm a nice girl,' I half-heartedly tease.

'Yeah, my loss, kid. Anyhow, I got a new job and I want you to come with me.'

'I knew Claire McCardell would hire you!' This news is a huge relief. I won't have to leave behind everything familiar if I can continue to work with Delmarr.

'No, I'm out of retail, custom, all of that. I'm going to Hollywood to work for Helen Rose.'

I'm flabbergasted. 'Helen Rose who made Elizabeth Taylor's wedding gown when she married Nicky Hilton?'

'The very one.'

'Delmarr, how on earth did you meet up with Helen Rose?'

'Her second-in-command went to the competition and she heard about me, get this, from Hilda Cramer, who was out there on radio assignment to interview the great costume designers of film.'

'*Hilda* got you a job?' I thought I had already heard the most amazing news, but this is even better.

'Oh, she told Helen Rose I was the cat's pyjamas, socks and night-cap.'

'Well, you are, and it's about time everybody important knows it!' I'm so happy for Delmarr. He belongs in Hollywood, where glamour and elegance still matter.

'She asked if I had any talented staff I'd like to bring along and I told her all about you.'

'You did?'

'Absolutely. Come with me, Lucia. You'll go right on staff making a salary.'

'Are you serious?'

'Yep. Pack your bags, kid. We're going to California. If ever there were two New Yorkers who needed a fresh start, it's us. There's one thing, though. I want your personal guarantee that when I tell you to drop a guy, you'll drop him *pronto*. That's Italian for fast, you know.'

'I'll do whatever you say.' I throw my arms around Delmarr's neck. 'Thank you, thank you!'

'One more thing. I'm thirty-six, if anyone asks. We're going to the land of youth and beauty, and forty isn't a number anyone wants to hear. It's like the failing grade that puts you out of school. Forty and you're out.'

'No problem. But Delmarr . . .'

'What?'

'I thought you were thirty-four.'

'Even better.'

*

'Who's gonna take care of Ma?' Roberto whines.

'I can take care of myself!' Mama counters. 'I'm not some old lady.'

'You're not old, but you are a lady. And there are some things that a mother needs her daughter around for, okay?' Roberto smacks the table lightly with his fist, just like Papa used to do.

The change in Roberto since Papa's death is noticeable. Though he's assumed the unelected position of patriarch, life was so much easier when Papa was the leader. Despite the fact that Papa was from the old country, he had a progressive way of looking at things. Roberto acts like God has personally selected him to keep traditional family roles established in medieval Italy thriving and intact in America. I'm sorry that I announced my job opportunity to the family during Sunday dinner. I should have known better.

'I think Lu should go,' Rosemary says as baby Antonio, wrapped in a soft blue blanket, sucks on the tip of her little finger. 'You boys might not know this, but she's very talented. She doesn't take in mending or make curtains. She's an artist in a custom shop.'

'We know where's she gone every Monday through Friday for the last eight years, Ro,' Roberto tells her.

'Hollywood is so far away,' Orlando says sadly.

'There's always the *Super Chief*, the fastest train in America, and it runs both ways,' I remind him.

'Last fall was horrible. We don't want anybody to hurt you ever again. Okay?' Roberto says as he tears off a piece of bread. 'You're too good, Lu. It's always been your problem. You get sucked in by bad elements. It's not your fault. But it happens and we gotta stop it.'

'I'm getting older. If I'm going to make a new start, I need to do it *now*.' I wish I could explain to my family what it's been like since

John Talbot left. The changes are subtle, but I feel them deeply. I used to be pursued by young men from good families, but no more. The kind of suitors who have approached me lately aren't men my family or I would ever consider. The other morning, when I passed the school yard on my way to the Groceria, the young men didn't even call my name. When I smiled, they didn't acknowledge me. I need to go somewhere I can begin anew.

'We'd like it if you'd find a nice guy in the neighbourhood and start a home. Now, if you don't find a nice guy, we love having you here. You're a big help to Mama and Ro, and the new baby.' Roberto beams with paternal pride.

I'm grateful when Mama changes the subject. Roberto may believe that he has the final say over my life, but he doesn't. I'm a modern woman and I'm going to do what I want to do. I haven't worked this hard for so long to stay home and be the maiden aunt to my nieces and nephews, no matter how much I love them. It's time for me to think about how *I* want to live, and if giving up my glorious room and life in New York City is part of the package, then that's how it must be.

After dinner I help Rosemary wash the dishes and put them away.

'Thanks for speaking up at dinner,' I say.

'Listen, Lu, there's enough help around here. I know you feel a duty to your mother, but this is the good thing about being in a big family: many hands make light work.'

I laugh. 'I noticed that. Since you moved in, taking care of the house has been so much easier.'

'I love it here.'

'You don't miss Brooklyn?' I ask, wondering if I'll be homesick in Hollywood.

'Only the Promenade. There's something about water. I used to walk along the river every night after dinner. It's very soothing.'

I never got to show Rosemary the spot that would have been my home on the water, but I remember the feeling of peace I'd have whenever I looked out on Huntington Bay. 'I wonder if I'll like the Pacific Ocean?'

Mama yells, 'Telephone for you, Lucia!'

I dry my hands and go into the living room to take the phone from Mama. 'Hello?'

'Lucia, it's Dante.' I haven't seen him since Papa's funeral. We didn't get to talk much, but once again, when we needed them, the DeMartinos were there. My heart melts a little at the sound of his voice.

'Dante, how are you?' I ask warmly.

'I'm fine. How have you been?'

'We're muddling through here. It's not the same without Papa. Thank you again for the beautiful flowers you sent to the funeral home. And to your whole family for coming to be with us.'

'I'd do anything for you, you know that.'

'I know.' I've been asking myself since November why I couldn't be content with a nice fellow who loved me. Why did I have to go for heat and danger, the slick John Talbot types? What was I thinking, going above Fourteenth Street for love?

'Would you like to go out to dinner on Saturday?' he asks. His voice breaks a little, just like it did the very first time he asked me out on a date.

'I'd love to,' I tell him.

*

The last gown we build in the Custom Department is Violet Peters's lace fantasia wedding gown, rows of lace and ruffles over a full skirt with a bodice of illusion netting and long sleeves that come to a point. The gown is too silly for Delmarr's taste, but he designs it to please Violet, who's ecstatic when she sees the final result. It's appropriate for a girl who will recess out of the church under the honour guard of the New York City Police Department, their swords forming a silver canopy in the air.

I have to say, I can't wait to get to California and make movie costumes. I'm tired of wedding gowns and all that comes with them. If I ever marry, I'll wear a suit, like they did in my mother's day. The world has gone too crazy for big weddings. Maybe it's still the postwar glow, a glorification of true love and men coming home to devoted women, but enough is enough.

Ruth, Helen and I throw Violet a bridal shower at the Plaza Hotel, just the four of us over high tea. The place is posh, with its flower arrangements of long-stemmed roses and pink lilies spilling over their tall pedestals like fountains. Everything comes to the table on polished silver, cookies and tea sandwiches served on a three-tiered tray by a waiter wearing white gloves.

Violet cries when she opens the three-piece leather luggage set we bought her and finds her new initials embossed in gold on the handles: V. P. C. 'I'm gonna be Wallis Simpson on my honeymoon!'

'And then there was one!' I toast myself with champagne and say loudly, 'What's to become of the old maid?' I'm feeling a little tipsy.

'Come on, you've got plenty of time,' Ruth says kindly.

'Girls, let's face it. I'm a very poor planner. I chose a career that's becoming obsolete and a man who, last time I heard, was in jail. And now, I've agreed to go out on a date with my ex-fiancé.'

'First of all, the closing of our Custom Shop is not your fault,' Ruth begins.

'And how could you have known John Talbot was a con artist?' Violet adds.

'Grab Dante DeMartino. We all loved him and you should get it over with and marry the man,' Helen says.

'I want to go to Hollywood more than I want a husband,' I announce with such conviction that the ladies at the next table look at me.

The girls stare at me. I realize too late how rude I've been. Three career girls now making jobs of being wives don't need to hear about my big plans in movie land. What do they care about palm trees, convertibles and sunsets on the beach, and worse, enjoying all these things alone? But it's clear to me: I'm the left shoe, the oddball, the sideshow. I want to work like a man. No one puts it that way, but that's the truth. That's my dream. When I look back on all I've been through, my working life is the only thing that's never let me down.

None of the fancy things I have been given in my life, from Papa's gift of a coral necklace on my sixteenth birthday to John Talbot's mink coat, meant nearly as much to me as the things I bought myself with the forty-eight dollars and fifty cents a week I make at B. Altman & Company. There isn't a man who can come along and buy me anything that I cannot buy myself. 'Never let the man know that,' Mama used to say to me, but the lesson didn't take. I've spent wisely and never splurged. I remember my first radio, my first hair dryer with the deluxe bonnet and the canopy bed from Interior Decoration I bought with my own money. I calculated how many hours I had to work against the value of the purchase. I could practically tell you how many stitches I'd need to sew to walk out of B. Altman's with whatever item my heart desired.

My biggest problem when it comes to the opposite sex is that I know how to be happy on my own. It's in my nature to make the best of a bad situation. Even now, with the department closing, there are opportunities to pursue for a worker of my calibre and experience. I may have to travel across the country to seize the opportunity, but still, it's mine for the taking.

'Who says everybody has to get married?' Ruth says.

Violet takes a bite of her cookie. 'It's the building block of society.'

'Well, you girls may have to be the blocks,' I tell them.

'You don't sound sad about it.' Violet looks sad enough for all of us.

'I'm not,' I say.

'Violet, Lucia has her happiness coming. In fact, she's owed it,' Ruth says to me and smiles. How I will miss her when I move to California. Her friendship has shaped me, made me feel safe and given me a confidante I could laugh with. I am so lucky I met her when I most needed a partner. 'I hope you're never sad again,' she tells me. 'You've had enough of that for a lifetime.'

It's that funny time of year in New York City, the week in September when it's neither hot nor cold, and there's a mugginess in the air that ruins the best hairstyles. I leave the curlers in an extra hour to keep the humidity at bay. Dante has invited me to the San Gennaro

Festival. I haven't seen him for a couple of months, and I'm looking forward to catching up with him.

Dante picks me up promptly at seven (men who are late have never been my problem). He whistles when I come down the stairs. 'Do I have a date with Ava Gardner?' he asks.

'I'm her stand-in,' I say.

Little does Dante know, I copied this outfit right out of *Photoplay* magazine. Ava Gardner, during one of her brawls with Frank Sinatra, was wearing black capri pants, a white blouse and a wide waist-cinching red belt with matching flat sandals. I copied it down to the smallest detail, including the delicate gold hoop earrings nestled against her dark hair.

Commerce Street is jammed with cars, every parking spot taken, which is rare. The festival brings families from all the boroughs, and even though we're twenty blocks from Little Italy, cars have overflowed into the Village. As we walk over, Dante doesn't take my hand, but he guides me when we cross the street by placing his hand on the small of my back.

'How's work at the bakery?' I ask.

'Good. Papa's cranky, but he's always cranky. And Mama's taking care of the house as usual.'

I look at Dante and envision how close I came to living with his family on First Avenue and East Third Street, with bleached white diapers hanging on the line in the back yard, and his mother making home-made pasta on the farm table in the kitchen. For one moment I reconsider what life with Dante DeMartino might have been like. He's handsome, and so mannerly and sweet. He has deep roots like mine, and Papa thought we were a good match. Dante is not a shallow man who flits through the world having a good time at the expense of others. Ruth would call him the genuine article. As we walk through the crowd, men tip their hats to him, and women smile and ask about his family. John Talbot might have elbowed his way into society, but Dante has a common touch. I wonder why I never appreciated it before.

As we walk under the glittery white arches over Mulberry Street, I ask myself how I can bear to leave Greenwich Village. It has been my home all my life. I know my people well and they know me. For every gentleman who tips his hat to Dante, there's one who throws me a kiss. We're not only welcome here, but celebrated. Will the movie stars in Hollywood treat me with such affection and respect? This is where I belong, in the heart of Little Italy with people just like me. All around us window boxes are stuffed with small red, white and green Italian flags and I wonder if I'll ever see anything like this again. Will it be enough to stick flags in the urns outside my Hollywood bungalow?

This morning I ate only a banana for breakfast because I want a sausage-and-pepper sandwich and then a sack of *zeppoles*, fried dough rolled in sugar, which I am not sharing. Dante waits in line for our sandwiches, while I watch the Italian men from Faicco's flip the sausage on the grill and shovel the steaming peppers and glistening onions onto the soft white bread and into a wax-paper sleeve. Papa and I would eat these sandwiches every year at the festival, and holding on to this tradition makes me feel like he's still with me.

After we've covered every inch of the festival, I watch as Dante gambles at the roulette wheel, which, unfortunately, reminds me of Ruth's story about John Talbot losing a bundle at the track. With each spin of the wheel, I recall more clues that should have steered me away from John. Why didn't I listen to my father? Poor Papa, who finally gave in to the idea of John Talbot so he wouldn't lose me altogether. What a silly girl I was. If Dante DeMartino loved me before, he'd really love the new Lucia Sartori, sadder but wiser. Dante quits the wheel after losing five dollars and buys me my sack of *zeppoles* before he runs out of cash. 'Good thing I can walk you home,' he says with a smile. 'Because the cab fare went to San Gennaro Church.' As we walk out of Little Italy and head back towards home, I suggest we sit on the post-office steps and eat our *zeppoles*.

We sit quietly, watching as people leave the festival, carrying balloons and stuffed animals won at games. Then Dante brushes the powdered sugar off his hands and says, 'Lu, there's something I want to tell you.'

Sitting there with Dante, with the drone of the crowd behind us, the lights spilling down the street, and the taste of sugar on my lips, I'm reminded of all the feasts I have gone to with him. Suddenly I want to lean over and kiss him. Instead, I sit back. 'So, what do you want to tell me?'

'I'm getting married, Lucia.' Dante stares down at his hands.

I'm glad he's not looking at me, because I need a moment to compose myself. Then I say warmly, trying to sound upbeat, 'Oh, Dante, congratulations. Who is she?'

'Juliana Fabrizi.'

'I don't think I know her. Is she from the neighbourhood?'

'Yeah, they live near us on First Avenue. Her father has a deli on East Tenth Street.'

'Oh. Well, maybe if I saw her, I'd know her.'

'I don't think so. She didn't go to school with us or anything. She's younger. She's eighteen.'

'Eighteen.' I whistle low in disbelief. I can't believe this day has come so soon – I am not the youngest girl on the dance floor any more. Who would have thought that Dante DeMartino would be the man to point it out to me? 'What's she like? I mean, besides the fact that she's eighteen,' I say pleasantly.

'She's very easy going. Pretty. Sweet.'

'Does your mama like her?' I ask.

'Very much.'

'Then she must be a great girl.'

'You think so?' Dante still seeks my approval.

'You know, Juliana is very lucky. You're the best. They don't make 'em any better than you.'

'That's exactly what I say about you. You have just one flaw.'

'Only one? This I've got to hear.' I put a big smile on my face, but what I really want to do is cry. I liked it better when I controlled the situation, when I knew that Dante loved me, and no matter where I went or what I did, he was there in the bakery pining for me. He was my security, as much as Papa was, a man who would love me and wait for me no matter what. That has all changed now he has fallen in love with someone new. 'So, what is my one flaw?'

'You're not the marrying kind.'

Dante looks at me at last, but he can't hold the gaze. He seems to be trying not to cry. I can't cry about the truth. If I did, the person I would betray is me. I stand and brush the sugar off my capris. I extend my hand to Dante, and he takes it and stands up. We look at each other.

'I'm sorry, Dante,' I tell him. I know that if I told him I wanted him, he would probably drop Juliana Fabrizi and return to my arms. He's waiting for me to say the word but I'm not going to. I will not hurt him again.

'I know you are,' Dante says sadly. And on this, my last date with Dante DeMartino, he holds my hand all the way home.

Closing down the Custom Department should be a simple operation, since we've been dismantling it since last February, but there's still a ton of paperwork to finish. The most difficult chore is the final inventory of the fabric supply room. Each remnant represents a memory of some dress we made, suit we built, or coat we tailored.

'Look, Lu. Nun's wool!' Delmarr lifts the flat board over his head. 'How do those girls live in this material? I wouldn't cover a car seat with it.'

'They take a vow of poverty, you know. It wouldn't be the same if their habits were made of silk chamois.'

'Here. You should have this.' Delmarr brings me a yard of gold lamé.

'New Year's Eve!'

'You know, we did a lot of work in here. I'm surprised we still have fingers.'

'Do you ever wonder what it will be like when we walk out those doors for the last time?' I point to the Hub's swinging doors, which have marked every coming and going for seven years.

'You don't have to worry about that.'

'What do you mean?'

'They're taking the doors off tomorrow.'

'Taking them off?'

'Oh, yes. They're reconfiguring the floor, so the doors are going, and then these walls, and soon the third floor will be one big open space full of racks and racks and racks of machine-made crap. Won't that be pretty?'

'We won't be here to see it.'

'Thank God,' Delmarr agrees.

I'm so happy Mama has a new grandson to coo over on our first Christmas without Papa. Sometimes I see her cry, and then she pulls herself together and throws herself back into holiday preparation, but I know it's not easy for her. And it doesn't ease her mind to see me packing for California.

Delmarr is astonished at our Christmas Eve feast and moved (spiritually, I'm not sure, but definitely aesthetically) during Midnight Mass at Our Lady of Pompeii. 'You realize all the things that have happened to you in this church,' he whispers. 'And you keep coming back. That's the part I can't believe!'

'It's called faith,' I whisper back.

'It's called fear of hell.'

Mama nudges us to stop whispering. When I look at the altar covered in red poinsettias, and the pew markers, white carnations with red ribbons, I close my eyes and imagine how I must have looked on my wedding day. It's been over a year, but it seems like ten years have passed, and then there are those moments when it feels like yesterday. I have the very same feeling about Papa's passing. Sometimes it feels like he's been gone for a long time, and other times, I half expect him to pull up in the truck and yell from the street for Mama to come with him for ice cream.

Delmarr kisses me on the cheek after Mass and gives Mama a big hug. As he turns to cross Cornelia Street on his way home, he looks back and shouts, 'Monday morning, six a.m., Grand Central Station. Connection to Chi-town. Then the *Super Chief* to Hollywood.'

I wave. 'See you there!'

I have only one week to finish my packing. It's the hats that are causing me *agitazione*. The California sun is bright and I don't want it to ruin my New York complexion.

I'm doing laundry in the basement when I hear a loud thump. At first I think it's the machine, but I realize the sound came from another room. I sprint into the next room, afraid the baby fell, but Antonio is napping quietly in his crib. I run upstairs to the kitchen and find Mama on the floor. She has collapsed, and there is a pool of blood next to her face from a gash in her forehead. I grab the phone and call for an ambulance. I get down on the floor next to Mama and try to listen for her heart. Soon the paramedics arrive and load her into the ambulance. I pray aloud to God, 'Please don't take her.'

Here we are again, I think as we wait for a report from the doctor at Saint Vincent's. The boys were bereft when Papa got sick, but this is even worse. This is Mama, and I don't think her sons can picture the world without her. Neither can I.

After a while, the doctor comes out to talk to us.

'Is she all right?' Roberto asks him.

'Your mother had a small seizure. At first, we assumed it was a stroke but it's more like the precursor to a stroke. We're going to have to spend some time figuring out what happened to her, but hopefully we can prescribe some medication that will prevent any such episodes.'

My brothers are silent and every bit as bewildered as I am. As she herself pointed out, our mother is young. 'How bad is it, Doctor?' I ask.

'We won't know anything for twenty-four hours. She's responding to stimuli, which is a positive sign. I'm sorry. We have to wait and see.'

Angelo fights back tears. I gather my brothers in a circle and reassure them, just as Mama did with us when Papa got sick. 'We're going to stick together and we're going to wait and see what the tests tell us. And then we'll figure out what to do.'

The boys stay in the hospital most of the afternoon, until I send them home. I remain by Mama's side. Sometimes I sit on the bed and wipe her face gently with a cool washcloth. When I cry, I try not to make any noise to wake her.

When the morning comes, my body feels like a bent wire. I slept sitting up in the chair and woke up whenever Mama moaned or a nurse came in. But I'm seized with panic when I open my eyes to find her bed empty. I run out into the hallway and grab the first nurse I see.

'My mother, Maria Sartori, where is she? Is she okay?'

The nurse answers in a soothing voice. 'She's been taken down for tests.'

'Thank you,' I tell her. Please God, don't let me lose my mother.

I go back to Mama's room to wait. The doctor gathers us together as soon as my brothers arrive.

'I have hopeful news. It definitely wasn't a stroke. She's sustained some damage to her heart, but it's minimal. Basically, your mother has a rapid heartbeat, which has probably been there all her life, which caused her to short circuit. The blood supply to her brain was affected. Luckily, you found her almost immediately.' Roberto puts his arm around me as if to thank me. 'But she'll need physical therapy and a lot of help at home.' The doctor leaves us, and we embrace one another, feeling relieved. We are very lucky.

Mama is able to communicate by suppertime. She speaks slowly, and sometimes has to stop and search for a word, but she understands everything we're saying. She's hungry, and in our family that's always been a sign of good health. Rosemary sneaks a first-class dinner of spaghetti al burro and chopped greens into Saint Vincent's.

Roberto insists I go home. The long, hot shower feels fantastic but all my clothes are in suitcases, so I have to unpack to get dressed. I pull the stool from my vanity table out onto the terrace, yank the long telephone cord out the door, and sit down to make a call. 'Delmarr?'

'How's your mother?' Delmarr says with concern. 'Rosemary called me.'

'Mama almost had a stroke.'

'Jesus. But Rosemary said she'd be okay.'

'Eventually.' And then I bite my lip because I'm starting to cry. 'I can't go to California.'

'That's okay, honey, you can join up later. Helen Rose isn't going anywhere. She'll understand. I'll explain the circumstances.'

'Could you?'

'Of course, she's a human being, not a cold cookie like Hilda Beast.'

'Thank you.' I wipe away my tears and exhale, knowing Delmarr will always look out for me.

'No problem, honey. You take care of yourself. And Mama Sartori. I'll call you when I get there and we'll make your plans then.'

I hang up the phone. It was sweet of Delmarr to say we'd make our plans at a later date, but we both know the truth. I'm never going to California, I'm never going to work for Helen Rose, and I am never going to sew the costumes of the stars. I'm going to stay here at 45 Commerce Street and take care of my mother for as long as she needs me. When that duty is done, and I hope it won't be for many years, I'll think about my life and what I want. For now, I am the daughter my parents raised, and I will put my family before anything and anybody else, including Delmarr, Helen Rose and a glamorous life in Hollywood. I must find a way to be here, to take comfort in doing my duty. Zia Caterina's curse has real teeth. Yes, I am broken-hearted, but not by the loss of a man. It's the closing of the Custom Department that broke my heart, and the loss of quality, style and service that went with it.

Chapter Twelve

Lucia and Kit's tea party has lasted past suppertime and blended into evening seamlessly. The silvery afternoon rain clouds have gone and left behind a sky the colour of indigo ink. I've been sitting here for hours, Kit thinks to herself, but what a story. She shivers. The rear apartments on 45 Commerce Street are evidently cooler because they aren't over the boiler. Kit looks over at Aunt Lu's mink coat and considers asking if she can try it on just to warm up.

'Aunt Lu, if the Custom Department closed in the early fifties, what did you do at B. Altman's until 1989?'

'I took a position in Evening Wear. The hours worked well with taking care of Mama. Look at this.' Lucia shows Kit a framed article from *New York* magazine featuring the B. Altman bridal shop. The headline reads, LUCIA SARTORI, MOTHER TO THE BRIDES. How ironic that a jilted bride-to-be became a mother of sorts to hundreds of New York girls seeking the perfect wedding gown.

'When did your mother pass away?'

'Not until my forty-seventh birthday.'

'That's why you never made it to Hollywood?' Kit asks.

'That's why.'

Kit leans back in the chair and looks at the wall. 'Aunt Lu . . . this wallpaper, it's the wallpaper you put up with Ruth, isn't it?'

'It's the very same.' Lucia smiles.

'*This* was your room?' Lucia nods. Kit asks, 'Where's the sewing alcove and the bay window?'

'I lost them when they divided the floor in half,' Lucia says quietly.

'They chopped your room in half? That's criminal! Who did it?' Kit realizes she has raised her voice and takes a deep breath.

'My nephew, Tony.'

'Oh, that's rich. You mean to tell me that *my* Tony Sartori, Duct Tape Tony, is the sweet little baby who came after Maria Grace? He hacked your room in half?'

'He's the one. Each floor was divided, if it wasn't already, into two apartments. More rentals, more income, you see.'

'What a sleazebag! I'm sorry, Lucia, but there's no excuse for such a thing.'

'The worst part was that he did it as soon as my brother died. Roberto hadn't been gone a month before Tony took over the building and changed everything.'

'Lucia, I don't mean to be rude, but shouldn't you own this building? If all your brothers are gone, how come you didn't end up with the building?'

Lucia shakes her head slowly. Clearly, this is something she's still struggling to understand. 'When Papa died, he left everything to my mother. When Mama got sick, she turned everything over to Roberto. Roberto had four sons. He was very traditional, much more so than Papa, and he believed the family property should always remain in the hands of the men. That's how I got cut out. Of course, Roberto insisted his sons take care of me, and they believe they do take care of me. And I suppose this apartment would be expensive today. If I ever have a real problem with them, I pick up the phone and call Rosemary and she straightens her boys out. It could be worse.'

'But that's not fair! You took care of your mother! The family should have thanked you or repaid you somehow.'

'Roberto didn't look at it that way. A daughter's duty in those days was always to her family.'

'What about Rosemary?'

'She wasn't in the immediate family. And she's a woman too. I don't believe my brother left anything to her – just the order that the children take excellent care of her. Besides, she had her own mother to look after.'

Kit stands and paces, fuming at the injustice. 'Did they cut you out of the sale of the Groceria too?'

'I never worked there like my brothers, but when they sold it, they split the sale among themselves. That was fine, it was their company,' Lucia says evenly.

'I think it's terrible! You're as much a Sartori as they are.'

'You're of a different generation. These were the rules. I don't like them but I understand them. It all goes back to Italy and the way property is passed down in a family. It's not a good deal for the women, but that's the way it is.'

'Well, it's a raw deal.' As Kit sits down again, she notices the stacks of B. Altman gift boxes. 'Lucia, what's in all the boxes?'

'Dishes and things.' Lucia pauses. 'They're my wedding presents.'

'Oh my God.' Kit wonders how Lucia has lived with a daily reminder of John Talbot in her home all these years. 'Why did you keep them?'

'The police kept them as evidence after they apprehended John. They convinced me to take them back. And then I tried to return them to my guests, but they wouldn't take them. Bad luck, they told me.'

'So the Caterina curse? It was for real.' Kit shudders.

'Maybe I believed it and that made it real. We'll never know.' Lucia puts the empty teacups on the tray and stands. 'I'm exhausted. Are you?'

'Totally.'

'I hope I didn't bore you,' Lucia says.

'*Bore* me? Are you kidding? It was riveting. Every morsel of it. Thank you.'

'Come back another day and we'll go through the boxes. There are some lovely things in there that I think you'd like. A hand-painted urn. Some crystal vases. Enamelled teaspoons.'

'Thank you, Aunt Lu. I'd love that.'

As Kit descends the stairs back to her own apartment, the deep compassion she feels for Lucia is surmounted by a hunger for the truth. She goes into her apartment with a plan. Although she would like to know what happened to Delmarr and Ruth and Violet and Helen, she has to find out what became of John Talbot. She stays up late into the night making a list of as many dates, places and names as she can remember from Lucia's story. Perhaps tomorrow, before getting back to the play she is writing, she can make a trip down to the New York Department of Records.

John Talbot's aliases were all common names, and searching through the records of 1951 and 1952 brings up hundreds of documents. It would take Kit a lifetime to sift through them. She goes to the information desk in the outer office and waits in line. When it's her turn, Kit follows the research assistant back into the main library, where he makes copies of all the police records from the Greenwich Village and Upper East Side precincts. There are several pages with references to a John Talbot. Kit takes the voluminous material home to read.

A few phone calls, a long session on Google, and three Starbucks visits later, Kit has the John Talbot dossier.

Lucia Sartori's old flame is alive. The problem is, he's in prison again. After a twelve-year stint for various theft charges, he seemed to go straight. When he got out, he looked up his buddies who'd found him work before, including Patsy Marotta at the Vesuvio, who got him a job out on Long Island with a restaurant-supply company. Talbot stayed clean for a long time, but about twenty years ago he slipped back into his old ways. He got involved in a stolen-car operation, shipping parts from Germany to the United States. Kit figures this most recent conviction will probably keep him in prison for the rest of his life.

Once Kit has uncovered all the facts, she knows she must share them with Aunt Lu. She's pretty pleased with herself for the successful detective work, and excited by the prospect of helping Aunt Lu find a resolution, but she's also dreading having to deliver such monumental, and potentially upsetting, news. In the end, she decides Lucia has been living with the aftermath of John Talbot for fifty years, and deserves to see how he turned out.

The walls of propriety have come down after Lu and Kit's tea. Kit feels absolutely at ease charging up the stairs to the fifth floor and banging on Aunt Lu's door. 'Lucia?' she calls out.

'How are you, Kit?' Lucia says, opening the door in her bathrobe. She must also feel that their long afternoon has put them on a familiar footing.

'I'm great, thanks. But busy. Really busy. Let's see, first, I wanted to know if you'd like to go out to dinner with my friend Michael and me tonight? Just Chinese. At Ma Ma Buddha.'

'I'd like that, dear. Thank you.' Lucia beams.

'Okay, I'll come get you around seven.' Kit turns to go.

'Kit? You said first.'

'Oh, yeah, that means there's a second. I also wanted to mention that I've found John Talbot.'

Aunt Lu looks at Kit. Then she steps back into her room and sits down in the nearest chair.

'Lucia, are you okay? Are you upset with me? I just had to know and I wanted to share what I found, but if it makes you unhappy, I won't . . .'

Lucia doesn't answer.

'Lucia?' Kit says nervously.

At last, Lucia breathes deeply and closes her eyes. 'Where is he?' she says.

'Oh, Lucia. I'm so sorry. I didn't mean to—'

'Where is he?'

'He's in the slammer,' Kit says honestly.

The way Kit says 'slammer' makes Lucia smile. 'Well, he always had a difficult time with the up and up.'

'No kidding. I googled him, I mean, went online and found all sorts of articles about him. And I got some of his police records too. He's in Sing Sing. The state prison in Ossining, right up the Hudson.'

'Kit, I hope you won't be offended if I ask you to leave. I'd like to be alone. I need to think.'

'Absolutely,' Kit tells her. She pulls Lucia's door closed and goes down the stairs with a heavy heart. What had possessed her to go digging in the graveyard of Lucia's lost loves? She should have known that Lucia was not the kind of woman who goes looking for closure. If she was, she would have looked for John Talbot herself.

As Kit is settling down with her laptop to try and make some headway on her play, there's a knock at the door. She is surprised to find Aunt Lu standing there, still in her bathrobe.

'Come on in.' Kit ushers her in and closes the door, knowing that under normal circumstances Lucia would be far too proper and modest to wear her robe outside her own apartment. She's not herself, Kit thinks, and it's all my fault.

Lucia looks at Kit. 'I want to see him. But I can't make the trip alone. Will you come with me?'

'Of course,' Kit tells her. 'I'll take care of all the arrangements and we can go this weekend.'

'This weekend?' Aunt Lu touches her hair.

'Yeah, Saturday is visitors' day. But we can leave at lunchtime, so you can get your hair done as usual.' Kit knows Aunt Lu's Saturday rituals as well as her own. The smell of Aqua Net lingers in the hallway every weekend after Lucia's visit to Village Coiffures.

'That would be nice,' Lucia tells Kit. 'I would like to look my best.'

Kit waits for Lucia in the vestibule before they leave to take the subway to the train. She looks at the old bench, imagining Lucia and John Talbot saying goodnight. She then looks at the panes of pink glass in the door, and she pictures young Lucia peering out, waiting for her date to arrive. Kit has never paid attention to the building in such detail before. She looks up at the ceiling and sees an ornate chandelier; studying it more closely, she sees that the multicoloured crystals on it are glass fruit.

Lucia calls from the landing, 'I'm coming, Kit.'

'Take your time!' Kit calls out pleasantly. She continues to look around the vestibule with a new awareness until Lucia joins her.

'Lucia?' Kit points. 'Is that your chandelier?'

'Yes, it is,' she answers simply. 'No sense storing that in a box. It's to be enjoyed.' She shrugs.

The view from the train to Ossining is so tranquil that Kit isn't surprised when Lucia tells her there was an entire movement in painting called the Hudson River School. It turns out that Lucia took courses in art at the New School for Social Research with the encouragement of Arabel Dresken. The clefts of the hills, the wide pewter-coloured river, and the Victorian homes, make Kit feel as though she's speeding through another era. She needs all the soothing visuals she can get. Her stomach is churning with the fear that Lucia and John Talbot's reunion will be a disaster.

'Why are *you* so jittery?' Lucia asks Kit.

'I'm scared to death that John Talbot will be a creep.'

'He won't be a creep. He'll be what he always was, slick and confident and full of vinegar.'

'How do you know?' Kit wonders.

'I'm an old girl and I've been around a long time. There's one rule that applies to everyone from the time they're born until they die: people don't change. Maybe slightly, but never deeply. We are what we are, I guess. And I'm glad about that, because I have a lot of things I want to ask John.'

'I have more questions, too. But not for him. For you,' Kit says, seizing an appropriate opening.

'Well, then. Ask me.' Lucia sits up and smooths her skirt.

'What happened to the other girls at Altman's, like Helen Gannon?'

'Dear Helen. She had another son, Albert. And her husband did very well on Wall Street. They moved to Scarsdale. I used to take the train out to see her and spend the weekend with them. We still chat on the phone quite often.'

'How about Violet?'

'Violet died two years ago. She was married to Officer Cassidy up until the end. He has since remarried,' she says sceptically.

'Boy, that was fast.'

'That's what we thought.'

'Did they ever have kids?'

'No.'

'And how about Ruth?'

'Ruth Kaspian Goldfarb,' Lucia says tenderly. 'She and Harvey moved to Florida. They have three girls, all of them quite accomplished. One teaches fashion design at the Fashion Institute of Technology. I see Ruth once a year when she comes up to celebrate Rosh Hashanah with her sister. And I still talk to her at least once a week.'

'Oh . . . and Delmarr! What happened to him?'

'He made it big in Hollywood. He did costumes for television. All the big song-and-dance specials. Every time he was in New York he would come to see me and say, "Kid, when are you coming out west to make it big?" It wasn't meant to be. He never married, and he always had a grand time. He left a string of broken-hearted women coast to coast. I never knew anyone who refused to be pinned down like Delmarr. To the end, he was a solitary man in a very social business. He died last year. I took his passing very hard.'

'And how about your brothers?'

'You know about Roberto. Angelo became a Brother in the Maryknoll Order. Orlando married a nice Jewish girl, Rachel, and they had a daughter, Rafaella. And then my dear Exodus, he and Orsola had seven children, four girls and three boys, all of whom are still in Italy, doing well. I made many trips to the Veneto to stay with them. The kids loved it when Zia Lucia brought them Yankee baseball gloves and Hershey's chocolate. Sadly, the men in my family didn't have very long lifelines. None of the boys lived much past Papa's age.'

'Aunt Lu, did you ever marry?'

'No. But there was a man in my life for a long time. He was already a widower when I met him, even though he was only in his forties. He and his wife never had any children. I wasn't the love of his life, and he wasn't mine, but we had a lovely, uncomplicated relationship. We did love each other in our own way. He was a wonderful companion.'

As the train pulls into the station, Kit watches the wives and children of prisoners, dressed in their Sunday best, disembark and walk towards the visitors' entrance. The mood is surprisingly happy even though the travellers are on their way into a depressing place.

Lucia pulls her compact out of her purse and goes over her face with a round powder puff, never lifting it off the surface, but pressing the colour against her skin. Then she freshens her lipstick. She offers Kit a mint and then puts one in her mouth. 'How do I look?' she asks.

'Beautiful,' Kit tells her. Lucia is wearing a black skirt and a white blouse with a long mint-green scarf. She wears her mink coat. Her hair is done.

'Let's see what John Talbot has to say for himself,' Lucia says.

The women follow their fellow passengers down a sidewalk marked with bold arrows and the word 'VISITOR' showing the way. Kit's nervousness returns tenfold. Horrible scenarios race through her mind. What if John Talbot is a lunatic? What if they get caught in a prison riot? What if something terrible happens to Aunt Lu and Kit has to explain it to Duct Tape Tony?

Kit and Lucia are patted down and put through metal detectors (not too different from going to a Knicks game at the Garden, Kit thinks), and then asked to wait. After almost half an hour, they are shown into a large room filled with visitors and surrounded by guards.

'How will we know him?' Kit asks as they find a place to sit.

'I'll know him,' Lucia says.

Metal doors, extending from ceiling to floor, swing open, bringing to mind the Trojan horse. As the metal scrapes the concrete, there is a low rumble, followed by the entrance of a sea of prisoners in orange jumpsuits. Lucia looks over the crowd for a few moments.

'There he is.' She points.

Kit sees a tall man with thick white hair standing near the doors, away from the rest of the men. 'Wait here,' she tells Lucia. She walks quickly through the crowd and approaches him. 'Are you John Talbot?'

'Yes. Are you Miss Zanetti?'

'Yes, sir.' Kit blushes. No one ever calls her Miss Zanetti, and she finds it a little bit provocative.

'Where is Miss Sartori?' His voice breaks. He clears his throat and leans on his cane.

'She's right over there.' Kit motions over the crowd to Lucia. 'I'll take you to her.' She turns and begins to walk, then realizes she's moving too fast. She slows down and takes his arm. He walks fine on his own, but he's slow.

'I see her,' John says.

Lucia stands. Kit can tell she's trying not to reveal any emotion. As Lucia and John exchange greetings, she seems to warm up. John takes Lucia's hands into his own. They look at each other with the wise knowing only old lovers can share. For a moment the years seem to melt off them, almost as if a vapour has lifted off the present and left behind their youth, when men were gents and women were girls, and as the days grew longer, so did a lady's gloves. 'Lucia, as beautiful as ever,' John says grandly.

'Thank you, John.'

'I'm going to leave you two to chat,' Kit says.

'No, no, sit right there.' Lucia points to a chair nearby. Kit slides down into it, embarrassed to be as eager to hear what John Talbot says as Lucia is. John helps Lucia into a chair and then takes a seat across from her. Lucia sits up straight, her spine like a steel rod, and John leans towards her, resting his hand on the top of his cane as they talk.

John asks, 'How is your family?' While Lucia tells him, Kit can't help but smile. The last time he saw them, Roberto beat him up.

'Did you ever marry, Lucia?' John asks.

'No.' She takes a deep breath. 'Did you?'

'Four times,' he answers. Lucia smiles as John puts his hand to his head as though he is pounding a message to his brain. 'Twice to the same woman but four total.'

'Any children?' Lucia asks.

'No children.' Kit notices that the look on Lucia's face is almost perplexed, as if she's trying to connect this old man to the dashing fiancé of her youth. He's probably thinking the same thing.

'John, I came to thank you,' Lucia says, to John's obvious astonishment. 'Back in 1979, you sent me a letter. It was a lovely letter and you enclosed a cheque for seventy-five hundred dollars.' John nods slowly. 'I thought it was very brave of you to get in touch with me after all that time and honour your debt. I wanted to thank you in person for that.'

'It disturbed me that I took your money. I know, that's funny, isn't it, coming from a man whose current address is the state penitentiary?' John laughs. 'But I knew what that money meant to you. I always knew what I had done was terribly wrong. A good woman can make a man do the right thing. And in my lifetime, you were that woman.'

Lucia bows her head. 'Thank you,' she says. They sit in silence, then Lucia looks up again. 'John, we have a few things to clear up. I always wondered why you came to my house that Christmas. What did you come to tell me?'

John stares out the window while he considers her question. 'It was simple, Lucia. I came to tell you I loved you.' He straightens the collar of his prison uniform. 'I know you probably won't believe it, but I didn't set out to hurt you.'

'Oh, John, you had me marked from the minute you saw me,' Lucia says. 'Didn't you?'

'Sure, in the beginning I thought you could help me. I suppose my initial thought was always about advancing myself in some way. But you were so lovely and accomplished that I really fell in love with you. That's how things got as complicated as they did. I'd never been in that boat before, believe me. I even tried to convince your father, who was dead set against me, to see the light. He offered me ten grand to leave, and I turned him down.'

'My Papa offered you money?' Lucia is stunned.

'He was surprised when I turned him down. But, see, I wanted to marry you. You wanted the same things I did. But then I had a bad run. The worst of my life.'

'A bad run?' Lucia says the words slowly, apparently not quite sure what to make of a man who has dismissed the happiest year of her life as a bad run.

'See, one thing after another went wrong when I was with you. Everything I touched went south. Jim Laurel backed out of our

Huntington deal. And Daniel Parker ruined me all over the Upper East Side. He got it in his head that my business wasn't legit. And your father was never going to trust me. I saw that he'd never make me a part of your family or allow me to help expand the Groceria. The last straw was Sylvia dying a week before our wedding. No matter what the police told you, Lucia, she was like a mother to me. She wanted me to have that money. I took good care of her. I deserved it. *We* deserved it. But that rotten daughter of hers took everything.'

Lucia watches as John spins this fable, this strange version of the truth. Kit can tell she'd like to stop him, but he has a certain look in his eye. He must have had a similar look in 1951, painting the dazzling picture of their future together. It's a manic look, one of daring and wild intent, but it's also the face of a salesman. John is so convincing, he is almost irresistible. But Kit can see that Lucia is right, John Talbot hasn't changed. He can justify every crime that landed him in this prison. The only thing he's guilty of, in his mind, was trying to better himself, to become an important businessman.

'To be perfectly honest, I was overwhelmed. And then there was you, and the wedding, and the life with your family, and I couldn't face it. I couldn't pretend for one more minute that I could pull off a traditional life with the mother-in law-and the father-in-law and the kids running all around. I needed a good streak and it wasn't happening. It was as though I was cursed, I couldn't catch a break. So, I took the coward's way out. I left.'

Kit watches Lucia's eyes reveal the pain from so long ago. The excuses must seem weak, much like the character of the man she was to marry. Lucia holds her hand up to stop his story. 'John. I've heard enough.' He looks surprised. Evidently, there aren't a lot of people who stop John Talbot in his tracks. 'There's just one more thing I need to know.' Lucia takes a deep breath. 'The day before the wedding, when we drove out to Huntington to see the house, how on earth were you planning to get out of that? *There was no house.*'

John shakes his head slightly. 'That was my one piece of good luck in a long while. You gave me an out, Lucia. I think you knew you gave me an out, too. You made it easy for me to walk away. If you'd pushed me to show you that house, I would have had to tell you the truth. But you gave me an extra twenty-four hours to figure out what I was going to do. And I couldn't see a solution, so I walked away.'

Lucia thinks for a moment. 'And to think I would have followed you to the ends of the earth.'

John fishes in his uniform for cigarettes and offers one to Lucia, but she declines. 'But, you see, I didn't have to worry about you, Lucia. You didn't need me.'

'What are you talking about?' Lucia leans forwards in her chair.

'You had a life without me. You loved your job. You had a home. A family. You were an independent career girl. You were going to be just fine. Believe me, I've known women who need a man to take care of them. You can't leave those girls at the altar.'

The din from the conversation in the room escalates. Since there isn't much time for the prisoners and their visitors, people talk loudly, as if what they're saying to one another will matter more. A loud and frightening buzzer goes off, signalling the end of visitation.

Lucia, John Talbot and Kit rise to their feet. He whispers something in Lucia's ear, kisses each of her cheeks, and then lightly kisses her lips. He holds her, his eyes squeezed shut as if he's trying to see the picture in his memory more vividly. John goes back through the huge metal doors without turning back.

'Are you okay?' Kit asks.

'That was just fine.' Lucia says softly.

As they join the herd going back to the train, Lucia stops to take in the view of the prison, set beside the Hudson River.

'What is it?' Kit asks.

'He told me that every night before he goes to sleep, he pictures me in a white cotton dress standing in a doorway. We're alone and he takes my hand and says to me, "Come out and see the ocean, Lucia. It's all I have to give you." And you know what's funny about that?'

'What?'

'I'm seventy-eight years old and I never did have a home near the water, but John does. He's in a cell with no window, but he's still on the water.'

Kit helps Lucia into a window seat on the train and takes the aisle. They ride in silence for a while, each one thinking about the distinguished white-haired man, once the most dashing man at the spring cotillion at the Plaza Hotel in New York City. Kit turns to Lucia. 'Do you regret anything? You know, with all that's happened to you, the turns of your life, do you wish things had been different?'

'You can't keep bad things from happening,' Lucia says. 'And the good things, I don't think you can take any credit for them – they're just luck.'

'So it's a no. No regrets,' Kit says, leaning back in her seat.

'I don't regret anything that's happened to me, because somehow those things were meant to happen. The one thing I wish is that I had reacted differently to some of the events. I let things get me down and keep me there, sometimes for too long. And I believed I could somehow control the bad things, and that was a big mistake. Things turn around when they're meant to. You can't force it.'

When they arrive back on Commerce Street, Lucia invites Kit upstairs to her apartment. 'It will take a minute,' she promises as she opens her door. 'I want you to have something.'

She crosses the room and comes back with a dress bag. Kit opens it and takes out the gold lamé dress Lucia wore at the Waldorf on New Year's Eve.

'Of all the things I ever wore, this was my favourite.'

'Oh, Lucia,' Kit says, and embraces her. 'I will cherish this all my life.' She holds the dress up against her body. 'And if anything will keep me at my goal weight in this lifetime, it will be *this* dress.'

Kit climbs the stairs slowly. By the time she reaches her apartment, she has opened all her mail. After visiting John Talbot, Lucia and Kit fall back into their routines, with one difference: Kit now checks on Lucia frequently and takes her out to eat once a week. It's been a rough Monday. The cuts on Wall Street mean that the temp pool has been reduced by half, so Kit is doing the work of two people. No playwriting these days, only company business.

There's a letter from the Cherry Lane Theatre. How ironic, Kit thinks, theatres soliciting poor playwrights for donations. Can things get any worse? She opens the letter anyway, because it might contain good news for some lucky playwright, word of upcoming productions and workshops. But as Kit reads the letter, she sees that they don't want money and there's no mention of another playwright or another play. It's from the artistic director, Angelina Fiordellisi, and it's about Kit's play *Things Said While Dancing*. The artistic director loves the play and wants Kit to come and work on it at the Cherry Lane. She asks if Kit would be willing, and if she is, to please call her at her office at her earliest possible convenience!

Kit opens her door and tosses the rest of the mail onto her sofa. Without stopping even to take a sip of water she shoots straight up the stairs and raps on Lucia's door urgently, knowing this news will thrill her to bits.

'Lucia! It's me. Kit!'

'Coming,' she hears from inside the apartment.

'Hurry, I've got good news!'

Lucia opens the door. She looks fabulous, in a pink suit with a big brooch, an enamelled yellow rose.

Kit says, 'You look amazing! I have news. Finally somebody in the American theatre wants to work with me. The Cherry Lane wants to develop one of my plays!'

'That's fantastic!' Lucia beams.

'Sorry. Have you got company?'

'I do,' Lucia says, trying to communicate with her eyes.

'Oh. Who?' Kit whispers. 'A guy?' Lucia nods. 'Oh, wow!'

'No, no, come in,' Lucia says and opens the door wide.

A suave older gentleman in a classic navy sportcoat and charcoal slacks is sitting on one of her chintz chairs.

'Kit, this is Mr Dante DeMartino.'

'Oh my God! I've heard all about you.' As he rises to greet her, Kit notices he's holding the picture of Lucia on New Year's Eve. 'She was stunning, wasn't she?'

Dante looks directly at Lucia, and Kit can't help but compare this to the way John Talbot closed his eyes and seemed to prefer an image from memory. 'As beautiful as she is in this photograph, she was even more so on the inside,' Dante says. 'Still is.'

Kit decides to lighten the moment. 'And you *do* look like Don Ameche. I have the DVD of *Midnight* downstairs.'

'Besides my striking resemblance to Mr Ameche, what else did Lucia tell you about me?'

'Just wonderful stories about what life was like when you were my age. What the Village was like. How you lived. She told me you didn't have to carry a gun in your purse to the San Gennaro Festival and girls wore gloves and men worked in the family business and everybody was happy.'

'She told you the truth, then.' Dante smiles.

'At least for Italians, right? So, what are you two doing tonight?'

'I'm taking Lucia to dinner.'

'A date?' Kit grins.

'I hope so.' Dante winks at Lucia. The way he winks is sexy, Kit decides, and it's a small revelation to her. How could someone her grandfather's age be sexy?

'Well, I'll leave you two alone,' Kit says. 'Have a wonderful time.'

Lucia walks Kit to the door and steps out into the hallway with her. Kit gives her a silent thumbs-up.

'Congratulations on the play, Kit. I'm proud of you.' Then Lucia lowers her voice. 'And thank you. Dante has been widowed for three years, but I never had the guts to call him. The trip to Sing Sing put everything in the past, where it belongs. And I have you to thank for it.'

Kit goes back down to her apartment and grabs a Diet Coke. She takes the letter from Miss Fiordellisi and reads it over and over until she has committed it to memory. She leaves an identical message for every one of her friends on speed dial, giving them all the details. Then she sits in the window and looks at Commerce Street, leaning out to see the bright red barn doors of the Cherry Lane Theatre, a place she dreamed would produce one of her plays someday. Kit looks at her street with its stoops and window boxes and beat-up trash cans and remembers why she moved to New York. Passion brought her here, the desire to live the artist's life in a place that inspires it keeps her here. She takes a moment to be grateful and to remember that talent may be a gift, but persistence is its own reward.

She hears the downstairs door slam shut and leans out the window again to see who's leaving the building. Lately, she has a little bet with herself about Tony Sartori's bald spot, which from the fourth floor looks worse by the month. With his ego, she predicts a toupee by Christmas. But it isn't him.

Dante DeMartino and Lucia Sartori walk down Commerce Street hand in hand on their way to dinner. When the sidewalk narrows, he puts his hand on the small of her back to guide her. She turns to him and smiles. Another couple, about Kit's age, come around the corner. Once they have passed Dante and Lucia, the young woman nudges her boyfriend, as if to say, see, that could be us some day. Kit wants to shout out her window, 'Only if you're lucky! That's not just any single girl out on a date, that's the most beautiful girl in Greenwich Village. And some day I'm going to write a play about her.'

If you missed it the first time around . . .
discover the wonderful world of Big Stone Gap
in this exclusive extract from

Big Stone Gap

by

Adriana Trigiani

Also available from Pocket Books

CHAPTER ONE

This will be a good weekend for reading. I picked up a dozen of Vernie Crabtree's killer chocolate chip cookies at the French Club bake sale yesterday. (I don't know what she puts in them, but they're chewy and crispy at the same time.) Those, a pot of coffee, and a good book are all I will need for the rainy weekend rolling in. It's early September in our mountains, so it's warm during the day, but tonight will bring a cool mist to remind us that fall is right around the corner.

The Wise County Bookmobile is the one of the most beautiful sights in the world to me. When I see it lumbering down the mountain road like a tank, then turning wide and easing onto Shawnee Avenue, I flag it down like an old friend. I've waited on this corner every Friday since I can remember. The Bookmobile is just a government truck, but to me it's a glittering royal coach delivering stories and knowledge and life itself. I even love the smell of books. People have often told me that one of their strongest childhood memories is the scent of their grandmother's house. I never knew my grandmothers, but I could always count on the Bookmobile.

The most important thing I ever learned, I learned from books. Books have taught me how to size people up. The most useful book I ever read taught me how to read faces, an ancient Chinese art called *siang mien*, in which the size of the eyes, curve of the lip, and height of the forehead are important clues to a person's character. The placement of ears indicates intelligence. Chins that stick out reflect stubbornness. Deep-set eyes suggest a secretive nature. Eyebrows that grow together may answer the question *Could that man kill me with his bare hands*? (He could.) Even dimples have meaning. I have them, and according to face reading, something wonderful is supposed to happen to me when I turn thirty-five. (It's been four months since my birthday, and I'm still waiting.)

If you were to read my face, you would find me a comfortable person with brown eyes, good teeth, nice lips, and a nose that folks, when they are being kind, refer to as noble. It's a large nose, but at least it's straight. My eyebrows are thick, which indicates a practical nature. (I'm a pharmacist – how much more practical can you get?) I have a womanly shape, known around here as a mountain girl's body, strong legs, and a flat behind. Jackets cover it quite nicely.

This morning the idea of living in Big Stone Gap for the rest of my life gives me a nervous feeling. I stop breathing, as I do whenever I think too hard. Not breathing is very bad for you, so I inhale slowly and deeply. I taste coal dust. I don't mind; it assures me that we still have an economy. Our town was supposed to become the 'Pittsburgh of the South' and the 'Coal Mining Capital of Virginia.' That never happened, so we are forever at the whims of the big coal companies. When they tell us the coal is running out in these mountains, who are we to doubt them?

It's pretty here. Around six o'clock at night everything turns a rich Crayola midnight blue. You will never smell greenery so pungent. The Gap definitely has its romantic qualities. Even the train whistles are musical, sweet oboes in the dark. The place can fill you with longing.

The Bookmobile is at the stoplight. The librarian and driver is a good-time gal named Iva Lou Wade. She's in her forties, but she's yet to place the flag on her sexual peak. She's got being a woman down. If you painted her, she'd be sitting on a pink cloud with gold-leaf edges, showing a lot of leg. Her perfume is so loud that when I visit the Bookmobile, I wind up smelling like her for the bulk of the day. (It's a good thing I like Coty's Emeraude.) My father used to say that that's how a woman ought to be. 'A man should know when there's a woman in the room. When Iva Lou comes in, there ain't no doubt.' I'd just say nothing and roll my eyes.

Iva Lou's having a tough time parking. A mail truck has parked funny in front of the post office, taking up her usual spot, so she motions to me that she's pulling into the gas station. That's fine with the owner, Kent Vanhook. He likes Iva Lou a lot. What man doesn't? She pays real nice attention to each and every one. She examines men like eggs, perfect specimens created by God to nourish. And she hasn't met a man yet who doesn't appreciate it. Luring a man is a true talent, like playing the piano by ear. Not all of us are born prodigies, but women like Iva Lou have made it an art form.

The Bookmobile doors open with a whoosh. I can't believe what Iva Lou's wearing: Her ice-blue turtleneck is so tight it looks like she's wearing her bra on the outside. Her Mondrian-patterned pants, with squares of pale blue, yellow, and green, cling to her thighs like crisscross ribbons. Even sitting, Iva Lou has an unbelievable shape. But I wonder how much of it has to do with all the cinching. Could it be that her parts are so well-hoisted and suspended, she has transformed her real figure into a soft hourglass? Her face is childlike, with a small chin, big blue eyes, and a rosebud mouth. Her eyeteeth snaggle out over her front teeth, but on her they're demure. Her blond hair is like yellow Easter straw, arranged in an upsweep you can see through the set curls. She wears lots of Sarah Coventry jewelry, because she sells it on the side.

'I'll trade you. Shampoo for a best-seller.' I give Iva Lou a sack of shampoo samples from my pharmacy, Mulligan's Mutual.

'You got a deal.' Iva Lou grabs the sack and starts sorting through the samples. She indicates the shelf of new arrivals. 'Ave Maria, honey, you have got to read *The Captains and the Kings* that just came out. I know you don't like historicals, but this one's got sex.'

'How much more romance can you handle, Iva Lou? You've got half the men in Big Stone Gap tied up in knots.'

She snickers. 'Half? Oh well, I'm-a gonna take that as a compliment-o anyway.' I'm half Italian, so Iva Lou insists on ending her words with vowels. I taught her some key phrases in Italian in case international romance was to present itself. It wasn't very funny when Iva Lou tried them out on my mother one day. I sure got in some Big Trouble over that.

Iva Lou has a goal. She wants to make love to an Italian man, so she can decide if they are indeed the world's greatest lovers. 'Eyetalian men are my Matta-horn, honey,' she declares. Too bad there aren't any in these parts. The people around here are mainly Scotch-Irish, or Melungeon (folks who are a mix of Turkish, French, African, Indian, and who knows what; they live up in the mountain hollers and stick to themselves). Zackie Wakin, owner of the town department store, is Lebanese. My mother and I were the only Italians; and then about five years ago we acquired one Jew, Lewis Eisenberg, a lawyer from Woodbury, New York.

'You always sit in the third snap stool. How come?' Iva Lou asks, not looking up as she flips through a new coffee-table book about travel photography.

'I like threes.'

'Sweetie-o, let me tell you something.' Iva Lou gets a faraway, mystical twinkle in her eye. Then her voice lowers to a throaty, sexy register. 'When I get to blow this coal yard, and have my big adventure, I sure as hell won't waste my time taking pictures of the Circus Maximus. I am not interested in rocks 'n' ruins. I want to experience me some flesh and blood. Some magnificent, broad-shouldered hunk of a European man. Forget the points of interest, point me toward the men. Marble don't hug back, baby.' Then she breathes deeply, 'Whoo.'

Iva Lou fixes herself a cup of Sanka and laughs. She's one of those people who are forever cracking themselves up. She always offers me a cup, and I always decline. I know that her one spare clean Styrofoam cup could be her entrée to a romantic rendezvous. Why waste it on me?

'I found you that book on wills you wanted. And here's the only one I could find on grief.' Iva Lou holds up *As Grief Exits* as though she's modeling it. The pretty cover has rococo cherubs and clouds on it. The angels' smiles are instantly comforting. 'How you been getting along?' I look at Iva Lou's face. Her innocent expression is just like the cherub's. She really wants to know how I am.

My mother died on August 2, 1978, exactly one month ago today. It was the worst day of my life. She had breast cancer. I never thought cancer would get both of my parents, but it did. Mama was fifty-two years old, which suddenly seems awfully young to me. She was only seventeen when she came to America. My father taught her English, but she always spoke with a thick accent. One of the things I miss most about her is the sound of her voice. Sometimes when I close my eyes I can hear her.

Mama didn't want to die because she didn't want to leave me here alone. I have no brothers or sisters. The roots in the Mulligan family are strong, but at this point, the branches are mostly dead. My mother never spoke of her family over in Italy, so I assume they died in the war or something. The only relative I have left is my aunt, Alice Mulligan Lambert. She is a pill. Her husband, my Uncle Wayne, has spent his life trying not to make her angry, but he has failed. Aunt Alice has a small head and thin lips. (That's a terrible combination.)

'I'm gonna take a smoke, honey-o.' Iva Lou climbs down the steps juggling two coffees and her smokes. In under fifteen seconds, Kent Vanhook comes out from the garage, wiping his hands on a rag. Iva Lou gives Kent the Styrofoam cup, which looks tiny in his big hands. They smoke and sip. Kent Vanhook is a good-looking man of fifty, a tall, easygoing cowboy type. He looks like the great Walter Pidgeon with less hair. As he laughs with Iva Lou, twenty years seem to melt off of his face. Kent's wife is a diabetic who stays at home and complains a lot. I know this because I drop off her insulin once a month. But with Iva Lou, all Kent does is laugh.

I like to be alone on the Bookmobile. It gives me a chance to really examine the new arrivals. I make a stack and then look through the old selections. I pick up my old standby, *The Ancient Art of Chinese Face-Reading*, and think of my father, Fred Mulligan. When he died thirteen years ago, I thought I would grieve, but to this day I haven't. We weren't close, but it wasn't from my lack of trying. From the time I can remember, he just looked through me, the way you would look through the thick glass of a jelly jar to see if there's any jelly left. Many nights when I was young I cried about him, and then one day I stopped expecting him to love me and the pain went away. I stuck by him when he got sick, though. All of a sudden, my father, who had always separated himself from people, had everything in common with the world. He was in pain and would inevitably die. The suffering gave him some humility. It's sad that my best memories of him are when he was sick. It was then that I first checked out this book on Chinese face reading.

I thought that if I read my father's face, I would be able to understand why he was so mean. It took a lot of study. Dad's face was square and full of angles: rectangular forehead, sharp jaw, pointy chin. He had small eyes (sign of a deceptive nature), a bulbous nose (sign of money in midlife, which he had from owning the Pharmacy), and no lips. Okay, he had two lips, but the set of the mouth was one tight gray lead-pencil line. That is a sign of cruelty. When you watch the news on television, look at the anchor's mouth. I will guaran-damn-tee you that none of them have upper lips. You don't get on the TV by being nice to people.

On and off for about four years straight the face-reading book was checked out in my name, and my name only. When I went up to Charlottesville on a buying trip for the Pharmacy, I tried to hunt down a copy to buy. It was out of print. Iva Lou has tried to give me the book outright many times. She said she would report it as lost. But I can't do that. I like knowing it's here, riding around with old Iva Lou.

I guess I'm staring out the windshield at them, because they're both looking at me. Iva Lou stomps out her cigarette with her pink Papagallo flat and heads back toward the Bookmobile. Kent watches her return, drinking her in like that last sip of rich, black Sanka.

'I'm sorry. Me and Kent got to talking, and well, you know.'

'No problem.'

'Face reading again? Don't you have this memorized by now? Lordy.'

Iva stamps the books with her pinky up.

'See you next week.' I wave to Kent casually, just to make him feel that there is absolutely nothing wrong with talking to single, available, willing Iva Lou and sharing a smoke. He smiles at me, a little relieved. I think most folks in Big Stone Gap know their secrets are safe with me. (God knows I don't get any pleasure in knowing that the town manager performs self-colonics).

I have a delivery to make. I promised Mrs. Mac – MacChesney is the full surname – that I would bring her a new prescription to tame her high blood pressure. She is known around here as 'Apple Butter Nan' because nobody cans it better. Her house is way up in Cracker's Neck Holler. There are lots of twists and turns to get there, and I sort of fly around the curves like Mario Andretti (another great Eyetalian). There's an element of danger in mountain roads – there are no guardrails, so it's you and your rack-and-pinion steering. If you lose your concentration, you could go over the mountain. One foggy night the Brightwell brothers lost control of their truck and drove off the cliff. Luckily, the trees broke their fall. A state cop found the boys hanging in the branches like fresh laundry the following morning. They lost their truck, though. On impact, it fell off of them like pants. Now it rests at the bottom of Powell Valley Lake.

The Gap, or 'down in town' as the holler folks call it, is in the valley. The hollers are little communities nestled in the sides of the Blue Ridge Mountains. I couldn't give you directions to places up in the mountains, but I could take you there. There are no signs anywhere; you have to know your way. When you climb to the highest peak around here, you are standing on the borders of five states: Virginia, Kentucky, North Carolina, Tennessee, and West Virginia. You can't actually see the divider lines of course; you just know that you're standing in five states because there's a plaque that says so and because we were taught that in school. Tiny Miss Callahan, my fourth-grade teacher, would be very happy that I retained this information and shared it.

Each holler has its own name and singular history. Families found pockets that suited them in these hills and never left. Where people settle tells a lot about them. This is the only place I've ever lived, except for college. I went away to school, all the way up to South Bend, Indiana, to Saint Mary's, a small women's college. It was just big enough for me. When I got my B.S., I came home and took over management of the Pharmacy. I was needed here. My father had gotten sick and had to quit, and Mama couldn't handle it alone. It wasn't that she was a weak woman; she just couldn't handle change.

I've made it up to Cracker's Neck in record time. The MacChesney homestead sits in a clearing. It's a square stone house with four chimneys. Hearth fires smell better in stone houses, and Mrs. Mac always has one going. I park and wait for the dogs to circle. We have hundreds of wild dogs in the mountains, and they travel in packs. Most aren't rabid, and when they are, they get shot. I count six thin dogs sniffing my wheels. Buying time, I unzip my window and toss out the sign that identifies me to customers. It's a white plastic square that says: THE MEDICINE DROPPER. (I sprung for the extra artwork, a silhouette of a nurse in a rush.)

I usually find the guts to get out of the Jeep when I see Mrs. Mac peeking out of her window. The last thing I want to appear to customers is chicken. Truth is, I appreciate her watching out for me as I open the door and swing my legs out. Ever so casually I pull myself to a rigid standing position and walk confidently through the yard to the front door, like Maureen O'Hara in every movie she ever made with John Wayne. Maureen O'Hara is short-waisted like me. She is my inspiration in wardrobe and courage. I've even taken to wearing my hair like her – simple and long in a neat braid. I pack less punch though; my hair is brown, hers lustrous red.

The porch is freshly painted gray without a speck of dirt anywhere. The firewood is stacked neatly to the side of the house in a long row, in a lattice design. I try not to have favorites, but Mrs. Mac and her orderly home definitely top my list.

'Took you long enough!' Mrs. Mac exclaims as she snaps open the screen door.

'Iva Lou and I were chatting.'

'I done figured that.' Mrs. Mac points to the fire. 'Is that a good un, or is that a good un?' The flames lick the grid in hungry yellow bursts.

'That is the best fire I have ever seen.' And I mean it.

'Come on back. I made corn bread.'

I follow Mrs. Mac to the kitchen, a sunny, spacious room with exposed oak beams on the ceiling. I hear a noise behind me. Praying that it's not another dog, I slowly turn and look, first low, then eye level. It's not a dog. It's a man. Mrs. Mac's son, Jack MacChesney, in his underwear, a faded-to-pink union suit that sticks to him like a leotard. We look at each other, and both our faces turn the color of his underwear before it faded – blood red.

'Jesus Christmas, Jack. Put some clothes on,' Mrs. Mac demands.

'Yes, ma'am,' he says to his mother, as if on automatic. 'Good morning, Ave Maria,' he says to me, and goes. I can't help it, I watch the man go. He has a fine, high rear end. I wish I did. I pull my belted CPO jacket down over my flat behind and follow Mrs. Mac into the kitchen.

Mrs. Mac and I cross the kitchen to the big table by the windows, where she pours me a cup of hot black coffee that smells like heaven. She serves me fresh cream and snow-white sugar, which I dump into the mug. 'So what's happening in town?' Mrs. Mac asks. She has a mountain-girl face – a fine nose you could draw with a compass, shiny green button eyes, Cupid bow lips, smooth cheeks. You can tell that she was a great beauty in her youth, and she still is.

'Is 'Nan' short for anything?' I ask her.

'What? You mean my name?' Mrs. Mac cuts the corn bread in

the iron skillet into neat triangles. 'My mamaw's name was Nan. My middle name is Bluebell because that field was covered with 'em when I got born.' She points out the window with her spatula to indicate the field in the back.

'Nan Bluebell. Pretty. What was your maiden name?'

'God-a-mighty, you got a lot of questions this here morning. Gilliam. Nan Bluebell Gilliam.'

'I like it,' I say as I sip my coffee.

Jack stands in the doorway. He lingers there for a moment, as if to assess the situation. Or maybe he doesn't want to interrupt our conversation. In town he is known as Jack Mac. He's a little over six feet but seems shorter because he's all neck and torso. His face is round and soft, with a determined chin. He has thin, straight eyebrows and hazel eyes. He has even lips – the top and bottom one match (very rare) – and a nose that suits his face – it's a strong nose, one that doesn't break where it's connected between his eyes but shoots out like a clean wedge. He has a defined jawline, which means he goes after what he wants in life and gets it. Jack Mac is dressed now, in a flannel shirt and old blue jeans. His hair is slicked down wet; in the sunlight it is gray and going. Jack Mac and I are the same age, but he looks a lot older than me. I don't think he said two words in four years of high school; he's one of those quiet types.

Mrs. Mac pours her son coffee. 'Sit down youngun,' she says to him with great affection. 'I was just asking Miss Ave here about the goings-on in town.'

'Jack Mac ought to know more than me. After all, musicians get all the dirt.'

'We do, eh?' Jack Mac says and laughs. 'You're the big director, you're in charge of the flow of information.'

Jack Mac is referring to my 'job' (volunteer, of course) as director of our musical Outdoor Drama *The Trail of the Lonesome Pine*. A mountain love story, or so the poster says. The Drama was put together sixteen summers ago. There's a lot of dramatic and musical talent in the area, so local leaders decided to capitalize on it. We figure tourism will be a good business alternative if the coal mining dries up. The Outdoor Drama draws audiences from all over the mid-South.

'Well, I don't want to say anything,' I begin ominously, 'but a certain Sweet Sue Tinsley is quite smitten with a certain picker in the pit band.'

'Mercy, Jack, are you still seeing that little slip of a thing?' Mrs. Mac arches her eyebrow, annoyed.

'Mama, I'm proud to say I am,' Jack says and winks at me.

'That girl is not built for heavy lifting.' Mrs. Mac looks at me and sizes me up; obviously, I am a girl built for heavy lifting.

'Now, Mrs. Mac, you're just a little territorial about your only son. I'm sure you'll grow to love Sweet Sue,' I say, getting off this topic. Jack Mac looks at me, relieved.

Mrs. Mac goes on a long run about some sewage problem up in the hollers that she read about in the weekly paper, the *Post*. It's hard for me to read our local paper because there are so many misspelled words in it. Spelling happens to be one of the things I'm good at, so I take notice when it isn't perfect.

As Mrs. Mac loads up the table with eggs, grits (hers are homemade pale yellow, not the store-bought kind), bacon, honey, and

Lord knows what-all, Jack Mac eats. For a mountain man, he has fine manners. Delicate almost. And no matter how his mama drones on, he listens intently, like everything she says is of the utmost importance. What kind of life do the two of them have up here in Cracker's Neck? I wonder how he sneaks off to see Sweet Sue, how he maneuvers spending the night away from home, what he tells his mother. This is one of the obstacles the adult child faces while living at home with his parents. I went through it until a year ago, so I know it's hard. Maybe he goes down and stays with Sweet Sue when her kids are with their father on alternate weekends. Maybe they make love in the car on some road somewhere, like down at the Strawberry Patch, or up to Huff Rock, where the teenagers go. Or maybe they meet at a hotel over in Kingsport, Tennessee, where nobody would know them.

'Ave Maria, are we losing you?' Mrs. Mac says as she pours me coffee. I'm caught, I blush, and they both notice it.

'She's off in dreamland, Mama.'

'No, uh-uh. I was thinking about the Pharmacy. You know, Fleeta gets an attitude when I stay away too long.'

Jack Mac rises like a gentleman as I stand.

'No, sit down,' I tell Jack, a little embarrassed by his chivalry. 'Your food will get cold.'

Mrs. Mac nudges Jack. 'See her out, Jack.'

'Thanks for the coffee. And let me know how you like that new pill Doc Daugherty put you on.'

'I will, honey,' Mrs. Mac says as she waves me off with her spatula. 'Y'all scoot.'

Jack Mac is careful to let me precede him through the doorways.

At the screen door it's a little awkward because I reach for it first and so does he, and he brushes my hand. 'For a coal miner, you've got mighty soft hands,' I tell him. He smiles. What possessed me to blurt *that* out?

I'm on the porch now, and he stands in the doorway, his broad shoulders filling it from frame to frame. He reaches up and plucks the coil on the screen door like it's middle C.

'Not really. Touch the tips.' Jack Mac extends his right hand and with his left takes my fingers and touches his fingertips to mine.

'You've got calluses.'

'From the guitar.'

'You've been practicing.'

'Have to. Pee Wee Poteet and I have an unspoken competition. Guitar versus fiddle.'

'I think you'll win.'

'How do you know?'

'His wife smashed his fingers in the car door last night. I had to take him some painkillers.'

'Poor old Pee Wee.'

'It wasn't an accident. His wife was in a jealous rage and went after him—' I stop myself. I am telling this man confidential things. I never tell confidential things!

'I like your perfume.'

'It's just residual from Iva Lou,' I say, turning four shades of red gingham (the curse of pale-skinned girls).

'Well, it's mighty nice, wherever it came from.' I walk down the steps into the yard. The dogs circle.

'Are any of these your actual dogs?'

Jack Mac laughs. 'No. They're all wild. This time of year, when the rain stops and the leaves turn, they get scared 'cause they can't find water. They know I'm a soft touch.' I look down at the dogs, and for a moment I sort of like them, with their soft eyes and pink tongues.

'You ain't scared of 'em, are you?'

'Me? No. Heck no. I'm not scared of much.' I guess he doesn't see that I'm invincible, like Maureen O'Hara. As I make my way back to the Jeep, Jack Mac hollers at me.

'Hey, Ave Maria, what do you think of my new truck?'

Jack Mac points to a clearing by the shed. His 1978 Ford pickup gleams red-hot and shiny in the sun.

'It's a beauty,' I holler back.

'Fully loaded.'

'Can't beat that.' I wave good-bye and climb into my Jeep.

As I drive back to town I'm thinking about how everything at the MacChesney's is clean.

There's a traffic jam in the middle of town. Everybody's out doing their trading. Plus, it's due date in full on the electric and gas bills. I love town when it's busy; makes me feel like something exciting might happen. Zackie Wakin, a compact Lebanese peddler-turned-local entrepreneur, is rolling racks of clothes out onto the sidewalk in front of his store. He is small at about five feet, his complexion café au lait, his lips full (sign of generosity). I've always loved his storefront: ZACKIE'S BARGAIN STORE: CLOTHES & SUCH FOR THE ENTIRE FAMILY. And he's not kidding. He has everything from toasters to gold shoes. (I know because I needed a pair of gold shoes for a pharmaceutical-convention formal once, and he had them!)

'Miss Ave!' Zackie waves me over. (Zackie looks like a feriner, but his accent is pure mountain. It always sounds funny coming out of his mouth. He looks like a desert sheik from the movies, but he sounds like the rest of us.)

'Another sidewalk sale?'

'You betcha. Gotta clear out for the new fall merchandise. I got Frye boots coming in big next week. You keep that in mind, will ya?'

'I'll be over for my pair,' I promise. Zackie beams. The man was born to sell.

The lot at the Pharmacy is full, so I double-park in the alley and leave the keys in the Jeep in case I block anyone. I see that Iva Lou is still at the gas station, and Kent is now sitting inside the Bookmobile with her. (Progress.) I examine the exterior of my building as I enter. Paint is chipping off the window casings, the sign is fading, and half of the neon mortar and pestle is flashing pathetically. I let the place go when Mama was sick. Fortunately, my customers don't care about fancy trappings; I'm always busy.

Fleeta Mullins, my only employee and the thinnest woman in the Gap, chain-smokes behind the counter. I've never seen Fleeta without a cigarette in her hand, regardless of how many conversations we've had about smoking being bad for her. I hear the start of emphysema in her cough, but she refuses to give it up. She's only in her fifties, and her face is already wrinkled, a series of tiny pleats.

'Hi-dee, Ave Maria,' she barks.

'Nice do, Fleetsie,' and I mean it; she just had her hair put up.

'I copied Jeanne Pruett's upsweep.' Fleeta pats the spit curls gently. 'I wish I could sing like her, too.'

'Singing isn't the be-all. I bet she can't name all the wrestlers on the world-federation roster.'

'You got you a point there.'

'Busy morning.' I clear the register.

'I need to declare me some sort of moratorium on these damn fund-raising jars,' Fleeta complains. 'I can't hardly ring up a sale without flippin' one over.'

She's right. Our counter is overrun with homemade jars that have coin slots cut into their lids. Kids bring them by from school to raise money for all sorts of things. They glue their school pictures to the front of the jar with their names and a handwritten slogan to solicit funds. Right now the competition is heating up for Halloween prince and princess at the grade school, and I don't like to play favorites, so anybody who makes a jar can leave one. Teena Lee Ball, a cute second-grader, stands by the register. Teena Lee looks at Fleeta and thinks better of asking her for a favor, so she turns to me.

'Miss Mulligan, my mamaw said you'd put my jar on the counter 'cause we trade here.'

'Your mamaw is a smart woman, and she's got a point. It's called 'turnabout fair trade.' You put your jar on the counter. Maybe we'll raise a million dollars for your campaign!'

Teena Lee smiles and shows the space where her front teeth should be. She scoots the jar in front of the others and goes.

'You're too much of a soft touch. Let me handle them kids that come in here. If it wasn't for me, people'd run all over you all day long. I'll tell them damn kids to take their jars to the Piggly Wiggly. We ain't got the room; they do. They got three register lanes over there. We've only got the one.'

I lift a jar off the counter. 'Did that Coomer boy ever get his kidney?'

'I think it was in the paper that he did.'

I unscrew the Coomer boy's jar and pour the coins into the March of Dimes canister.

'Lew Eisenberg wants you to come see him over to his office. And I'm quitting.'

'You're kidding.'

'Ave, honey, I'm sick of people. I want to set home and watch me some TV. Portly has his Black Lung comin' through. It's time to enjoy life.'

Obviously, Fleeta hasn't let herself make the connection that in order to collect Black Lung benefits from the coal company, her husband has to be sick. This isn't exactly the time for celebration.

'I don't want you to go.' I sound pitiful, not like a boss at all.

'You'll get over it. I ain't met nobody yet who ain't replaceable.'

'It won't be the same.'

'It's time for a change is all,' Fleeta announces like a Greek philosopher. *Change*. Why does that word send a chill through me?

Lew Eisenberg's office is next door to the Pharmacy on Main Street. I sort of dread going in there, the place is so cluttered. Inez, Lew's wife, is also his secretary. They met when Lew came down to do some legal work for Westmoreland Coal Company. Inez had just graduated high school. They had a romance and she got pregnant. Lew did the right thing and married her. (Well, the right thing for Inez, that is).

'He's inside,' Inez says without looking up. Inez still has a pretty face, but she has gained about a hundred pounds since they married. It's been frustrating for her, since she was known for her gorgeous figure when she was a cheerleader. Now she's always on a diet. She's tried Metracal shakes, AYDS, the reducing-plan candy, and Figurine Wafers (I carry all flavors) – nothing has done the trick.

Lew sits behind his desk, smoking a cigarette. His round pumpkin head looks large atop his thin frame. He has small brown eyes behind thick glasses and a space between his front teeth (the Chinese call these lucky teeth). I haven't seen the space recently; Lew rarely smiles.

'Coffee or tea or something?' Lew asks. He always sounds agitated, but it doesn't make him unpleasant. You can see he's a sweetie underneath.

'No thanks.' Lew looks relieved that I don't want anything; the less contact with Inez, the better. He closes the door and sits in the chair next to me. He has never done that. 'We need to talk.' He is quiet for a few seconds, but it seems much longer. He stands and paces. 'I finished up your mother's paperwork. Her will. The house, the Pharmacy, the life insurance – all that goes to you. Essentially, my job is done. Except for one thing.' He stands at the window, flicking the blinds.

A floorboard creaks outside the office door, sounding like two hundred tiptoeing pounds. We look at each other. Lew turns on the radio for privacy – Inez has a reputation for snooping – and sits down next to me again. 'There's a letter.'

Lew gives me a large manila envelope. It is addressed to me in care of Lewis Eisenberg. In the upper left-hand corner it says, 'From Fiametta Vilminore Mulligan.' I'm one of those folks who opens her mail as she stands at the mailbox, so I rip into the envelope immediately and unfold the letter. I see my mother's handwriting. (The letter is written in English; I assume it's because Lew would have needed to read it, too.)

My dear Ave Maria,

When you read this letter, I will have left you. There are things I could never tell you about myself. Many times, I tried. But then, I would think better of unburdening myself and stay quiet. The first thing I want you to know is that you are the best thing that ever happened to me.

At this point, my heart is pounding so hard it's moving the buttons on my shirt. I look over at Lew, who is now lying down on the floor, smoking and staring up at the ceiling.

'Did you read this, Lew?'

'Yup. Don't mind me, my back's out.'

When I was seventeen, I was a very happy girl. I worked as a seamstress in my father's shop in Bergamo. My mother was beautiful, and my father a very respected man. A boy used to stop by the shop, his name was Mario Barbari. He came from a good family from Schilpario, a small town in the mountains. He was quite handsome and made me laugh. One time, my father had business in Schilpario. I begged him to let me ride along. I hoped I would see Mario, and as luck would have it, I did. Once he took care of business, Papa decided to stay in Schilpario and play cards. Mario offered to show me the town. He showed me the church, the waterwheel, the school. I felt like I had known him all of my life. I fell in love with him that day.

'May I have some water, please?' I swallow hard. Inez enters with water. Lew and I look at each other. Inez goes.

Mario came down to Bergamo to see me. My father found out about our friendship and forbade me to see him because I was too young to court. I did what no good daughter would do: I defied him and would sneak out to see Mario. I was so happy whenever I was with him. We shared such good, happy times. I knew I wanted to spend my life with him. We made a plan to run away together. He was to meet me at the Bergamo station and we would take the first train to Milan. I waited and waited but he never came. A courier arrived with a letter from him explaining that he could not meet me that day. I was going to tell Mario that I was expecting you so we could marry immediately. I am sure that he was not suspicious of my condition or he would have kept our appointment.

I knew that I must leave my home or the shame of what I had done would never be resolved. I remembered that we had a cousin in Lake Maggiore. I bought a ticket to go there, hopeful she would take me in. When I arrived in Lake Maggiore, I could not find my cousin. I had no place to go. My heart was broken. But I thought of you. I had to take care of you. Then, something very lucky happened to me. I returned to the train station. Everyone rushing around, having somewhere to go, comforted me. I sat alone on a bench. I fell asleep. When I woke up, a beautiful lady was sitting next to me. I will never forget what she looked like. She was tall, slim, and wore a blue coat. The buttons were blue jewels. And on her head was a hat, exquisite blue velvet with peacock feathers and tiny blue stars. Her face was creamy pink; she smelled like garden flowers. She offered me a sweet roll. I was so hungry, I took it. She said, 'Now, my dear, what shall we do?' 'I have no place to go,' I said to her. 'But of course you do. You're coming with me. I am going to America. You will stay with me. And when we get there, we will find you a position.' I was so afraid. But this woman smiled at me and I knew we would be all right.

I am crying. Lew stands and stretches. He comes over to me, puts a limp hand on one of my shoulders, and pats me like an old dog.

I asked the beautiful lady what her name was. She said, 'Ave Maria Albricci.' I told her that she had a beautiful name and she laughed. She thought it too ornate. I told her when I had my baby I would name her Ave Maria. She laughed again. She asked me how I knew I was going to have a girl. I told her I just knew. The ride on the ship was lovely. Ave Maria had a beautiful cabin. Servants laid our clothes out. The food was plentiful, even with the war on; I felt you healthy and happy inside of me. Four weeks passed and we arrived in New York City. Ave Maria's relatives greeted us at the port. We took the train to Hoboken, New Jersey. Ave Maria bought the *Italia Oggi*, the newspaper. We read the want ads. In those days, immigrants were cheap labor and would work in exchange for room and board. 'What is Virginia?' I asked the Albriccis. They laughed. I responded to the ad: 'SEAMSTRESS WANTED: MINING TOWN: BIG STONE GAP, VIRGINIA. GOOD PAY.'

Mama had taped the actual ad to the back of the letter to verify her story.

I knew this job was a good opportunity. I wrote a letter. The gentleman that placed the ad owned a dress shop in the town. He hired me immediately based upon my letter. By chance, his friend, a merchant from Big Stone Gap, was in New York City on a buying trip. His name was Fred Mulligan, of the Mutual Pharmacy. Would I like an escort on the trip to Virginia? I was so happy. Fred Mulligan took the train to meet me. I was surprised. He was young, like me. He understood Italian, having studied it at the University of Virginia. I liked him. He told me later that for him it was love at first sight. In truth, he suspected my condition and knew it would be easier on me if I was married. I agreed to marry him. It was an arranged marriage; I arranged it.

I never heard from Ave Maria Albricci again. I sent many letters to her family in Hoboken through the years; all were returned. I prayed for her every day of my life, though, never forgetting her kindness. Whenever I spoke your name, I thought of her and how she helped me. She was an angel.

I felt you should know the truth. I hope I made the right decision in telling you this. I asked Mr. Eisenberg to be present with you. I love you, my darling girl.

Mama

I turn the envelope upside down and shake it to make sure I haven't missed anything. A small, square lace-edged black-and-white photograph falls into my lap. In gold letters it says, 'Ti Amo, Mario.' On the back, in my mother's handwriting, 'Mario da Schilpario Italia 1942.' The picture fits in my palm. The man in the picture looks to be about seventeen. He has black hair and a trim physique. He is laughing. This is my father.

Inez stands in the doorway. 'Ave, they need you up to the school. There's been an incident.' The floorboards creak as Inez ambles toward me.

'Ave, you need to get up to the school. Principal called.' Lew's voice brings me back to earth. 'They need the Rescue Squad.'

Besides being a pharmacist, I am chief of the Rescue Squad. Doc Daugherty roped me into the job a couple of years back. We're a volunteer emergency-response team – the team is the fire chief, Spec Broadwater, and me. We handle everything from car wrecks to removing buttons from kids' noses, and once we even resuscitated Faith Cox's cat.

'Spec's outside waiting fer you,' Inez says, a touch too impatiently.

Spec is wedged into the driver's seat of Rescue Squad Unit One, a white station wagon with bright orange trim. I don't know why he's called Spec; he is the opposite of a speck, he's a giant, the tallest man in the Gap, at six feet seven. I climb into the car. Fleeta runs out of the Pharmacy and hands me my emergency kit through the window. Spec steps on the gas so fast, Fleeta practically loses her hand. I hear her curse at Spec in the distance as we pull away. Spec shoves a blue siren onto the roof of the car through the driver's-side window.

'Problem up to the school.' Spec offers me a cigarette. I must look like I need one. My face is puffy from crying.

'It's bad for you, Spec.'

'Self-medication. When they come up with a healthy way for me to calm my nerves, I'll quit.'

Powell Valley High School is a stylish, brand-new red brick structure that sits back off the main road, in a wide field. It is the jewel of this town, built with monies from the War on Poverty of the late 1960s. Spec ignores all traffic laws and careens up the circular driveway in the wrong direction.

'Problem's in the West Wing,' he explains.

The principal, Dale Herron, meets us in front of the school. The kids call him Lurch. I sort of see why – he's slope-shouldered and his head juts forward. Lurch leads us inside to a rest room marked BOYS. The building is dead quiet.

'Where are the students?' I ask.

'In the auditorium,' the principal says. 'Miss Mulligan, I think you ought to wait out here.'

'I'll handle it,' Spec says, patting me like a Pekinese.

The men disappear into the rest room. A few moments pass. I hear mumbling from the lavatory. Finally, the two men emerge.

'Let's go,' Lurch says, pointing toward the assembly down the hall.

We follow the angry principal into the auditorium. Every seat is filled. The teachers line the side aisles like guards. There are some whispers but not many. Onstage is a lectern and two students squirming in chairs: the student-body president, a young man with a long Renaissance curl, and the chaplain, a pudgy girl with thick glasses. Lurch takes the stage.

'Good afternoon, students. That greeting right there is for the ninety-eight percent of you who are law-abiding kids. I'll get to the remaining two percent here in a minute. I have called this emergency assembly to alert y'all that there is a sicko among us. There is a sign outside this door which reads, UNITED WE STAND, DIVIDED WE FALL. The hijinks and shenanigans of a small percentage of us will cause the whole to suffer. To fall. Mike. Brownie. Bring up the evidence.'

Two young men rise from their front-row seats and disappear backstage. They enter sheepishly from the wings. Mike is a small platinum blonde. I recognize him as the point guard on our championship basketball team. The other kid is mousy; his diminutive name suits him. They carry a large tarp between them.

'Dump it,' the principal barks.

The boys dump the contents of the tarp. White ceramic chunks hit the stage with a clatter, making a cloud of dust. An intact toilet seat tumbles out, confirming my suspicions.

'This is what someone setting right here in this auditorium has done. Destroyed school property. Committed a crime with evil intent. How? By rigging a sophisticated round of cherry bombs to a ter-let in the boys' rest room in the West Wing.'

A few nervous giggles escape the student body.

'This is no joke, people.' Lurch searches the audience for the gigglers. Then he pauses. He pounds the podium. 'Some unfortunate young man might have been sitting on that ter-let when it blew to high heaven. I ask you, what would have happened then?'

'Jesus,' Spec says under his breath.

'Anybody actually injured?' I whisper.

Spec ignores me.

'I'm scared,' a familiar deep voice says behind me.

'You should be,' I whisper back. 'The teacher's lounge is next.'

'Dinner tonight? After the show?'

'I'd love to.'

The deep voice, and now my date for the evening, is my best friend, the band and choral director of Powell Valley High School, Theodore Tipton, formerly of Scranton, Pennsylvania. Every once in a while the mines or the school will hire someone from the outside world. Inevitably, they move in and shake things up. Theodore brought our band back to life and simultaneously goosed the libidos of all the women in town. ('He's a humdinger,' Iva Lou says with relish every time she sees him. 'The man makes a pair of Levis sing.') Theodore also stars as Preacher Red Fox in the Outdoor Drama. We became friends when he auditioned nine years ago and I cast him on the first round. I had to. His face reading told me that he was loyal and true and fiercely protective. I knew if I cast him we would spend lots of time together, and we have. His face is square-shaped, with a defined jaw. He has a firm chin with a dimple in it. He can look strong, like an Irish pirate, or intellectual, like a preoccupied poet. He is tall, with blue eyes and a red beard. Even though all the available women in town chase him (and a few married ones, too), he spends all of his spare time with me. We're 'feriners' – even though I was born here, I'm considered a feriner because my mother was one – but that's just the start of what we have in common.

The principal wraps up the assembly with a couple more threats for the student body. If the guilty party doesn't fess up, he promises to suspend the smoking areas outside. This brings a groan from the students. The chaplain places a shoe box marked ANONYMOUS on the podium. Lurch tells the kids it will be placed in the gym so anyone with tips regarding the toilet incident can leave them in there. He dismisses the assembly. The student body rises. As the kids exit in an orderly fashion, most of them acknowledge Theodore. He is popular and respected, the perfect reputation for a teacher.

Only one student stops to speak to me: Pearl Grimes, fifteen years old, a sweet mountain girl with a weight problem. She often window-shops at the Mutual. I walk down the hall with my arm around her.

'My skin's done broke out agin.' Pearl hangs her head sadly.

'I got something for that. Come by the Mutual and see me.'

'All right.' She shrugs. She doesn't believe me.

'Don't you know the more pimples you got now, the less wrinkles you'll have later?'

Finally, Pearl smiles. Her face, heart-shaped, with a high forehead, tells me that she is emotional yet fair. Her nose is small and turns up slightly. Her cheeks are full and round – the cheeks of a monarch – which means she can handle power.

Pearl blends off into the sea of students. Theodore takes my arm.

'I'll walk you to your car.'

'Sure.'

'What's new?'

'I'm a bastard.'

Theodore laughs, which gets me laughing too. 'Did you bust a shoplifter or something?'

'No. I didn't behave like a bastard. I mean the literal definition.'

'What?'

'I settled Mama's will today. She left me a letter. Fred Mulligan wasn't my father.' Theodore is surprised but remains cool for my benefit. He knows everything about Fred Mulligan and me. When I shared all those stories, Theodore always got a look like he'd kill anyone who hurt me. This new information surprises him.

Theodore leads me out the front entrance to the car. Spec sits behind the wheel.

'Get in, Ave,' Spec grumbles, lighting a cigarette. 'That was a waste of my time.'

'See you tonight,' Theodore says as he closes the door. He touches my cheek. I look up to the second-floor science lab. Pearl Grimes stands in the window, watching us. From here, in the mellow afternoon light, she has a regal countenance, like a queen looking down on her subjects. I give her a quick wave good-bye. She smiles.

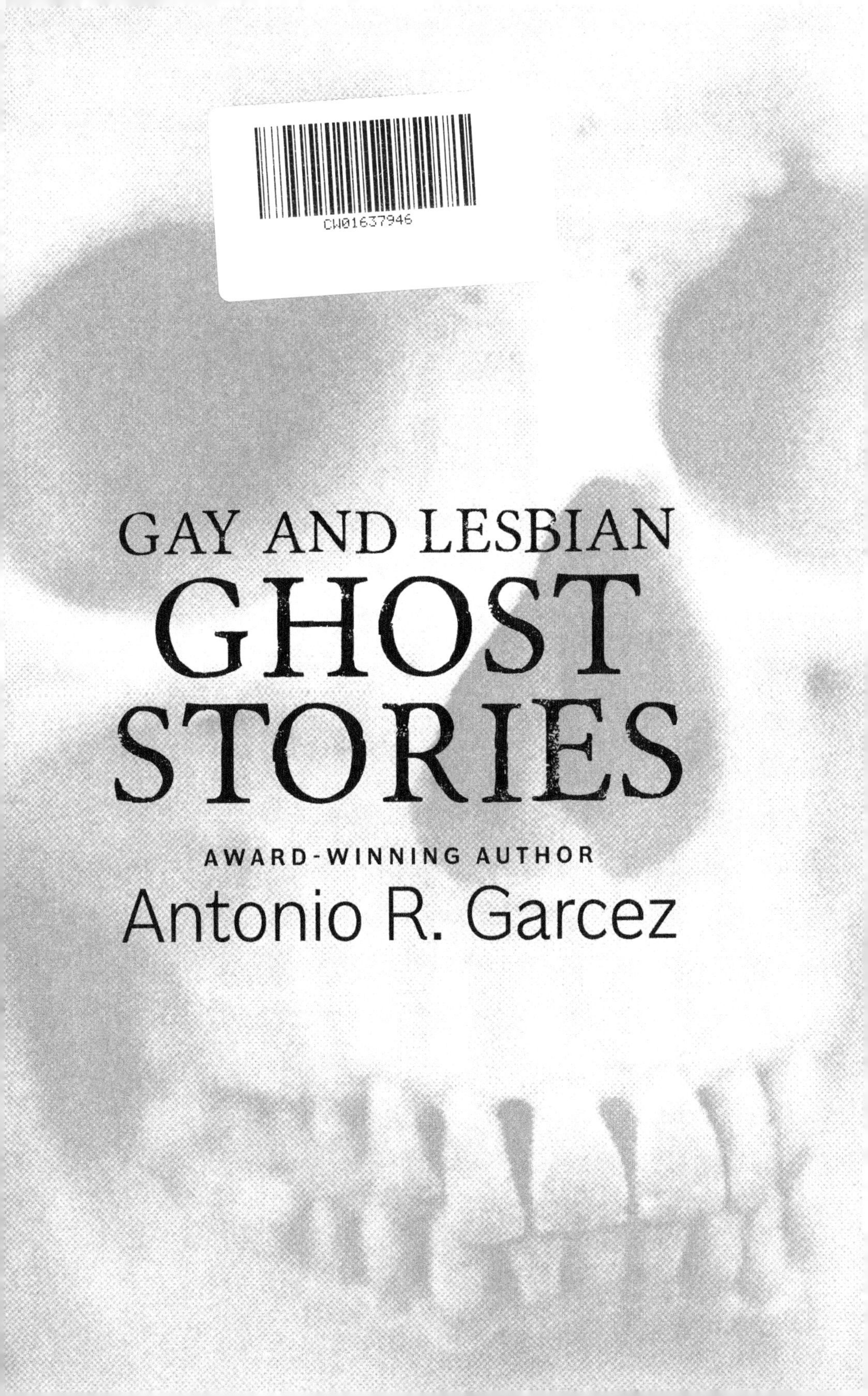

GAY AND LESBIAN GHOST STORIES

AWARD-WINNING AUTHOR

Antonio R. Garcez

Gay and Lesbian Ghost Stories

1st Print edition—2016
ISBN 978-0-9898985-3-9

1st Ebook edition—2013
ISBN 978-0-9898985-0-8

New Mexico, USA

Some of the places that appear in these stories may have changed ownership or names since the printing of this book. Also some of the individuals that appear in this book have, since its printing, moved on either within this world or into the next. Their stories appear here as they were directly bestowed to the author at the time they were interviewed.

The author may be contacted through:
GhostBooks.biz

Praises for the Author's Other Best-Selling Books

American Indian Ghost Stories of the West

"The accounts range from sweetly sentimental to truly terrifying, but all share the benefit of Antonio's sensitivity and attention to detail. He shows respect for the tales, and those who tell them, and understands that history and culture are inextricably bound to all folklore."

—*Jo-Anne Christensen,* Haunted Hotels

"These are not long-ago cowboy yarns, but very real, very current ghost stories from a rich and chilling mix of voices. Antonio has a rare talent for telling detail; he paints unforgettably creepy images that linger long after the book is done."

—*Chris Woodyard,* Haunted Ohio

New Mexico Ghost Stories

"This collection of personal encounters with the 'spiritual' or 'supernatural' certainly supported some of my own experiences. These stories are made more frightening by their very proximity."

—*Stephanie Gonzales, former New Mexico secretary of state*

"I highly recommend that both local citizens and visitors to Santa Fe read this book!"

—*Sam Pick, former mayor, Santa Fe, New Mexico*

"Fascinating to read ... offers the reader insight into our town's unique traditions, folklore, and history; don't miss it!"

—*Frederick A. Peralta, former mayor, Town of Taos*

Colorado Ghost Stories

"Mr. Garcez is an authority on the paranormal!"

—*Patrick Powell, producer, TAPS (The Atlantic Paranormal Society)*

"Good stuff. Some of the best books ever written!"

—Fortean Times Magazine, *London, UK*

"Get ready for some scary nights!"

—Every Day with Rachael Ray *magazine, October 2009*

Arizona Ghost Stories

"Gives a hauntingly accurate overview of the many reports of haunted sites all over the state. It not only lists the places from north to south, but also quotes the interviews of eyewitnesses, giving a remarkable feeling of being there with them as they encounter the unknown. Such sites as the Copper Queen Hotel in Bisbee and the Jerome Inn come to life in Mr. Garcez's investigations. His chapter on the reports of ghosts at Tombstone is perhaps one of the best accounts I have seen on this subject."

—*Richard Senate,* Hollywood's Ghosts

"Arizona could not have asked for a better chronicler of its supernatural landscape than Antonio R. Garcez. From Arivaca to Yuma, Arizona's most haunted places are all here! These stories will send shivers up your spine, and rightly so—they all really took place! If you have ever wanted to experience something paranormal, let this book be your guide."

—*Dennis William Hauck,* Haunted Places: The National Directory

Ghost Stories of California's Gold Rush Country and Yosemite National Park

"If you're a lover of the supernatural, get cozy in an easy chair and prepare yourself for the inevitable. Eyewitness accounts told in a straightforward manner!"

—*Tim Palmieri, Western Outlaw-Lawman History Association*

"As a subject where many of the books written simply regurgitate previously produced material, author Antonio R. Garcez does an excellent job of locating and interviewing primary resources to provide fresh stories of ghost folklore. Each chapter contains a brief introduction that supplies some of the background of the town and sites in question, followed by transcriptions of the witnesses' stories. Garcez's style is simple and easy to follow; the stories he has found are quickly engrossing. The fact that he put the time into his field research is impressive. Garcez can always be relied on to provide fresh stories of the supernatural, and this book is no exception. He does his field research to find firsthand accounts from the people who witnessed them. When so many other writers concentrate more on information other paranormal researchers produce, Garcez deserves a great deal of credit."

—*Adrienne Foster, book reviewer, Epinions.com*

Table of Contents

DEDICATION

To every LGBT person we've lost to crimes of hate, violence, and murder driven by intolerant, antigay discrimination campaigns, legislation, and sermons.

And to those LGBT souls driven to suicide.

My deepest appreciation to
each socially visible LGBT person
living a peaceful, productive, and fulfilling life.

Author's Note

Some of the names associated with the storytellers mentioned in this book have been changed. This was done for the sole purpose of not identifying those individuals because of their cultural beliefs or their personal requests to disguise their identities. Thus, any name used in the book that might be associated with anyone known to the reader is simply coincidental.

INTRODUCTION

Ghostly encounters are frequently described as mystical phenomena pertaining primarily to heterosexuals and rarely to gay, lesbian, bisexual, or transgender people; however, history proves otherwise. Anthropological research has referenced compelling scientific evidence that homosexuals have often been sources of counsel, wisdom, honor, intuitive power, guidance, social status, and spiritual strength throughout virtually all levels of human culture. Gays and lesbians have ruled prominently within Egyptian empires, Roman society, and Native American cultures.

Before Christianity became a major religion, both male and female psychics were regularly accepted and consulted in the ancient world. But as soon as Christianity gained prominence, spiritual mediums and psychics were condemned as "servants of the devil" and driven into hiding. Specifically, the Catholic Church perpetuated this persecution until the eighteenth century, with frequent tortures and executions. Gays and lesbians have even made their presence known from within the tepees of the great plains of North America to the grand royal stone temples of the Aztecs and Incas. Throughout this grand history, gays and lesbians have played prominent roles within their own cultures' religious and spiritual sects.

Gays and lesbians have been both honored with wealth and burned at the stake for the spiritual power they possessed and harnessed. In my experience recording and researching ghost stories over 45 years, gays and lesbians, both in the past and in the present, are intrinsically gifted in their psychic abilities. This begs the question: are there higher percentages of gay and lesbian psychics serving today? My belief is that we, gays and lesbians, have been given a very unique and precious gift—a gift that, if developed, allows us to see, communicate, and experience the paranormal from childhood.

The sad fact is the AIDS epidemic has brought the gay community to intimately experience innumerable deaths within our communities. The afterlife encounters with those who have passed have only added to our firsthand knowledge of the paranormal. We have become uniquely aware of ourselves as exceptional spiritual beings experiencing a corporeal moment on earth.

Given the personal self-searching, societal hurdles, family struggles, sensitivity to creativity, health-related challenges, and for many, a deep spirituality, it's no wonder that the universe is so easily accessed by such a "chosen" population. Within these pages, you'll read of individuals, from Alaska to Florida, who have experienced direct contact from spirits either at home or at work. My partner and I traveled to these particular states as I personally interviewed gay men and women and a few straights for the firsthand accounts of their encounters. We were not disappointed.

These interviews cover paranormal subjects such as extrasensory perception (ESP), near-death experiences (NDE), and, most definitely, ghosts! Our investigations continue to expose the potential for further validations that encompass all the elements of such experiences. I am therefore thrilled to share with you this new, intimate collection of ghost stories as experienced by members of LGBT communities throughout the United States.

— Antonio —

ALASKA

Francine C. Raisor's Story

Anchorage, AK

I'm originally from Santa Maria, California. I moved to Anchorage 12 years ago to live with my girlfriend, Rachel, in her family's home of three generations. Rachel was also in the medical field and worked as a pediatrician in a different hospital than I did. We used to do quite a lot of outdoor activities before her untimely death. Rachel died of complications from hepatitis C. She contracted this disease from a deceased patient while conducting the autopsy. So I am left to manage alone on our property since her death two years ago.

I graduated from Keck School of Medicine of USC in Southern California with a degree as a surgical technologist (OR tech). My job at Alaska Regional Hospital requires me to assist within the operating room during various invasive surgical procedures, especially open-heart operations. Because I've been at this job for so many years, I've become very friendly with my fellow associates. I know it might sound corny, but we genuinely regard each other as extended family members. We rely on each other for emotional support when a patient we're fond of dies while in our care.

My personal ghost story took place eight years ago in the hospital. We had an excellent female surgeon who worked at the hospital for just a few months. She died one Thanksgiving holiday in an auto accident while driving back home to Anchorage from the town of Dawson City. Somehow she drove her car off the road, first hitting a tree and then coming to a stop in a shallow water channel. She sustained fatal injuries to both her skull and spine and was pronounced dead at the scene.

It was not long after her funeral that a few staff began to talk among themselves about seeing the doctor's shadow image standing at doorways, and at one time it was even spotted by Arnold, our anesthesiologist, standing against a wall in the operating room!

Arnold himself once told me that during an operating procedure while he was adjusting the concentration of anesthetic vapor *isoflurane* for a patient, an unexpected movement caught his attention. He looked to see what moved and spotted the image of the dead doctor standing about four feet away from the patient on the operating table.

He told me that he happened to glance about the room and noticed two other staff also captivated by the same paranormal image. Arnold said, "We elbowed each other to look in the direction of the ghostly figure. One nurse, a Catholic, made the sign of the cross and said in the direction of the spirit, 'Thank you for your assistance, Doctor.' As this was said, the doctor's image suddenly disappeared. Because we had a patient to tend to, we got back to the business at hand and only freely spoke of seeing the doctor's apparition later after completing the operation. We all had to admit that the good doctor was continuing the work in death she loved so much in life."

Despite surgery room instruments being moved about, doors opening on their own, and footsteps being heard in empty halls, our job responsibilities continue as normal and as usual. I know the rational mind works to disprove, even deny, what I'm describing, but eventually, even the most hardened minds can change with enough evidence. I sincerely believe this to my core.

ARIZONA

Lisa and Geri's Story

Prescott, AZ

My interview with Lisa and her partner of 33 years, Geri, took place in their home 20 miles south of Chino Valley in the nearby town of Prescott. The women purchased the house and 15 acres in Chino Valley in 1962 from a woman who lived in the house for only three months. Lisa and Geri were attending a party in Phoenix and, by chance, happened to meet the seller of the property. As their conversation progressed, the seller informed Lisa and Geri about the home. That night, Lisa and Geri made arrangements to meet her at the property the next day. They drove 150 miles north to Chino Valley and immediately fell in love with the old two-story house and surrounding land.

What now follows are both women's stories of an incredible ghostly experience. I don't believe many people would choose to remain in such a negative house unless they had to. What happened to Lisa and Geri in their home is a testament to their strong will to conquer what evil existed in the house. Did they eventually overcome this evil presence?

Lisa's Account

After buying the property, Geri and I immediately went to work. With a hammer in each hand and the will to make a home out of a real fixer-upper, we set our goal to start with the most important rooms: the kitchen and bathroom. The bedrooms were next, followed by the living room and dining room. We decided to leave the outside of the house for last. The roof had been patched six years before with hot tar, so we felt it could withstand the elements for another year or two.

We spent the days in our new house hard at work. Our evenings were spent in a beat-up old trailer we bought and parked on the property.

It was nice to have the trailer to relax in after a day of dust and sweat. Eventually, the kitchen was completed, and in a few days, so was the bathroom. The two upstairs bedrooms were next. Strange things began to happen to both of us after we decided one day to tackle the bedrooms.

One morning after breakfast, I left Geri at the kitchen table reading the paper as I walked up the short flight of stairs to the second floor. As I reached the top floor, the door in one of the bedrooms slammed shut with a loud bang. The noise was loud enough to startle one of our small dogs. He ran right up the stairs to the door, where he excitedly barked and barked.

Geri, who was in the kitchen, called out to me, "Hey, what's going on up there?"

I answered, "Nothing. The wind just blew the door shut."

Geri called to our dog, who was still upstairs with me, and as he ran down the stairs, I approached the door and reached for the knob. I turned the knob and pushed on the door to open it. I heard the clicking sound that the knob made, but it would not open. I thought it might have gotten stuck from the force of the slam, so I played with it for a second or two. I managed to open it about an inch, and then it came flying right back to its closed position. I had the feeling that something was not right. I called to Geri, "Get up here right now!" I told her that I thought someone was in the bedroom. We readied ourselves for the possibility of encountering a prowler. Again, I turned the knob and pushed on the door. This time, it gave a little, and with Geri's help, it opened.

We entered the bedroom and immediately felt a chill. An overwhelming feeling of what I can only describe as heaviness or thickness hung in the atmosphere of the room. Geri said, "Let's get the hell out of here!" We both rushed down the stairs and into the kitchen. Noticing our excitement, our two little dogs barked like crazy animals. Needless to say, we decided to leave the cleaning of the bedrooms for another day. The memory of what happened to us that morning stayed with us throughout the day.

That evening, we were having our dinner, once again sitting at the kitchen table. Our only form of entertainment at the time was the radio, which was plugged into one of the few working electrical outlets in the house, in the living room. Suddenly, our dogs began to bark. Above our heads on the second floor, Geri and I heard the hurried footsteps of someone suddenly running from one end of the bedroom to the other. We looked at each other and froze. Between the footsteps, the barking dogs, and the music on the radio, our senses became overloaded. We were scared and again concerned that someone might be in the house. Geri stayed in the kitchen while I ran to the trailer. Ready to confront any burglar, I loaded our shotgun and returned to the kitchen.

With the dogs leading the way, Geri and I cautiously walked up the stairs. Geri reached for the light switch, and the single lightbulb hanging from wires at the top of the stairs turned on. Our dogs dashed into the same bedroom where we'd experienced the negative vibes earlier in the day, and then they ran out crying as if someone had hit them. I immediately thought, *No SOB is going to hit our dogs.* I yelled out, "Hey, we've got a gun! Get out of the room now!" The only sound we heard was our dogs barking behind us. Then I yelled out, "I said, I've got a gun! Get out now!" There was no answer. We decided to enter the room anyway.

We soon discovered there was no one in the bedroom. We checked the closet and opened the closed window and looked outside. No one. We then checked the adjacent bedroom, and again, the window was closed shut, and the room was empty. We were at a loss to explain what was going on.

We sat down at the top of the stairs, trying to make sense of something that made no sense. Geri cried, and I placed my arm around her. She was really frightened. Just then, we heard a hideous laugh, followed once again by the slamming sound of the bedroom door! I got up and pointed the gun at the door. "Get out of here, I say. Out of here now!" The laughter began again, and with a courage that even surprised me, I walked to the door and turned the knob and kicked the door open. The room was empty. That was enough for us. We took off out of the house and spent the most nervous night we've ever experienced locked in our trailer.

In the comforting light of the morning, we walked out of the trailer and whistled for our dogs. The dogs were nowhere to be seen. They were probably out among the desert brush, chasing a skunk or something. I grabbed my gun once again, and we cautiously reentered the house. It was strange to be walking softly, as though we were visitors in our own house, but we did not want to take any chances. Upstairs, nothing seemed strange or out of place. The feeling was totally different from the frightful night before; everything seemed calm and peaceful.

As the morning progressed into the afternoon, we returned to our normal working routine. When one of our dogs reappeared, Geri became concerned about the whereabouts of our other dog.

After searching for a few minutes, Geri came running to where I was mixing paint. Geri cried, "Come look. I found our other dog, and she's dead!" I followed her inside the house to the living room. There in the corner, where a water pipe was exposed next to the wall, was our little dog. Her head was at an angle, lodged tightly between the wall and the pipe! There was no rational reason for this to have taken place. None at all.

We had to forcefully pull the pipe away from the wall in order to dislodge our poor dog's head. We buried her in the yard and, of course, cried for days. Everything was so mysterious to us—the footsteps, the laughter, the slamming doors, the eerie feelings in the bedroom, and now the death of our dog.

The weeks passed, and we did not experience any additional strange happenings. The energy and time we put into the house was showing. It looked great! We then progressed to the second floor. We started with the farthest bedroom. After that one was completed, we entered the bedroom where weeks before we'd experienced the ghostly happenings.

The walls were covered in very old print wallpaper, which we wanted to immediately remove. There were faded square marks on the wallpaper that showed where picture frames had hung for many years. Geri was going to tackle the removal of the paper, while I scraped the old paint off the window and door. Geri can tell you what she discovered.

Geri's Account

As I was tearing away the old wallpaper, I reached a part of the wall about two feet above the floor. I pulled the paper away from this section of the wall, and underneath was what appeared to be bloodstains on the wallboard. I called Lisa to look at it and to give me her opinion. She also said it appeared to be old, dried blood. We got goose bumps. I quickly tore away the rest of the paper. And as soon as Lisa finished mixing the paint, I painted over the wall and the stains. The following day, we brought in a bed, a dresser, a small table, and a lamp. We were done at last!

We had a gathering of friends over one day, friends who'd traveled from Phoenix and who'd greeted us with housewarming gifts. They loved the house and the decorating we spent so much effort on. Five of our visitors chose not to make the long return drive home that evening, so they decided to spend the night. We stayed up late that night eating, drinking, and enjoying each other's company in the living room.

Suddenly, we heard a loud crash come from the upstairs bedroom. We ran up the stairs, and when I tried to open the door, I found that it was not opening. Now, with all our friends witnessing, I pushed and pushed. Just as before, I knew there was someone inside the bedroom pushing against my efforts. I could feel the power of the "person" playing tug-of-war with me. A friend came to my rescue, and with her help, we opened the door wide.

We were not ready for the scene of destruction the bedroom was in. The lamp lay broken on the floor, and blankets were strewn all about the room. Strangest of all was the wall by the bed. The bloodstains had reappeared! They had come through the newly painted wall!

The sight took us all aback. Our friend said, "Girls, you've got ghosts in this house!" Lisa and I kept quiet, but we knew she was right. With the help of our friends, we cleaned the mess in the bedroom and returned to the living room. Lisa and I informed our friends of the other happenings we'd experienced months before. Everyone was shocked to hear our story. As the discussion continued, suddenly from the upstairs came that horrible laugh once again. We all heard it.

Our friend Yolanda let out a scream. We pleaded with everyone to help us solve this thing once and for all. We decided to walk up the stairs and talk to the ghost and ask it to leave the house. There was strength in numbers, so up we went to the bedroom. The bedroom door was wide open. On the bed we had just remade lay clothes. The pieces of clothes were arranged on the bed in the form of a body. The only thing missing was the actual body. They were neatly placed in such a way as to give us the impression that a body was lying in a coffin. The arms of the shirt were folded at the elbows and crossed over the chest.

I grabbed the clothes and threw them back into the closet. We decided to immediately hold hands and form a circle and pray. We prayed to Jesus to remove this ghost, or ghosts, and to forever cleanse our house of any evil. We took turns asking for blessings and help. Suddenly, in the middle of our ceremony, we heard the quick footsteps of someone rushing down the stairs and out the kitchen door. We held on to each other's hands with such force. I cried and thanked Jesus for getting rid of the ghost. I knew that would be the end of our haunting. We all felt so wonderful after that. Thankfully, we have not had any more ghostly things happen to us since that night.

Yolanda Huerta's Story

Phoenix, AZ

I interviewed Yolanda at her home on the far north side of Phoenix. Yolanda has lived in Phoenix for 14 years. Born and raised in Phoenix, she moved to Los Angeles to attend college and eventually married a man. Her marriage was, in her own words, "a disaster." After her divorce, single and without children, this 42-year-old woman decided to return to the city of her birth. She bought a small lot of land on the north side of the city and purchased a two-bedroom mobile home.

Because of the extreme heat Phoenix is famous for, Yolanda built a ramada (arbor) directly outside her front door under which our interview was conducted. While we sat under its protective wood slats, the ramada offered us much-welcomed shade from the intense heat of the day. Looking out from the ramada to the north is a dramatic, panoramic view of the Tonto National Forest. This forest is composed of a blanket of desert flora, including saguaro cactus, paloverde (green thin-trunked trees), prickly pear, and other such drought-tolerant plants. The mountains rise in their unique and contorted splendor up to the blue sky. What a sight!

"I love it here," Yolanda said. "I have several coyotes come visit me each night. They sniff around and catch any mice that might want to make a dash inside my home."

Looking to the east, my eyes caught the sight of several large homes and, farther beyond, even more indications of human encroachment upon the desert landscape. "Things sure have changed here since I was a child," Yolanda said. "My whole family used to hike in the foothills each summer and gather saguaro tunas [fruit]. Mom would make a jam out of the tunas. It was delicious! Now with all the changes and rapid growth of this city, it's hard for me to even comprehend how things used to be back then."

I had a wonderful time listening to Yolanda's stories about the times she spent up in the mountains. I especially enjoyed the story she told me about the time she and a new girlfriend hiked into the Tontos one spring and experienced something unforgettable—something frighteningly unforgettable.

Last year my girlfriend, Erlinda, and I were sitting right out here one evening under this ramada. We were enjoying a few beers and talking about how frustrated we both were about how life was going for us. We decided the best thing for us to do would be to get away from the world and hike for a couple of days and nights into the mountains. We had done this before, so we were well prepared for the journey. Our sleeping bags and backpacks were dusted off, and within two days, we were off.

The first day of our journey was wonderful. We brought plenty of water and food, so we knew we would get along fine. On our second day, we decided to change our usual course, which was to follow the trail north, instead veering to the east, hoping to go around a large mountain and meet up with the trail up ahead. We hiked for hours, until the sun began to cast long shadows on the ground. Earlier in the day, we'd decided to make camp for the night while the sun was still out. We spotted a blue tent just off the trail about a mile ahead. As we got closer, we heard beautiful music. A small dog barked at us as we approached the tent, and a young guy who was playing a flute turned and waved hello to us. We stopped and talked to this interesting guy. He was from Taos, New Mexico. After a while, we were introduced to his wife, whom we'd awakened from her nap in the tent. They invited us to pitch our tent next to theirs for the night. Erlinda and I agreed that it would be a good idea, so we chose a patch of ground with the fewest rocks and set up our tent.

We had an interesting conversation with our new friends about city life versus living with just the basics as we passed around a bag of trail mix. Even though the sun was just setting in the west, there was still plenty of light. Suddenly, their dog began to growl at something in the distance. We stopped our conversation to look to see what the dog was barking at. We were surprised to see the figure of a woman running over the landscape about 200 feet from us. She was a short woman and had shoulder-length hair. Surprisingly, she was naked and holding on to her stomach. We were definitely caught off guard by the woman. I yelled at her, and she must have heard me, because she stopped running and turned to face us. We could see that she was not acting in a normal manner. Again, I yelled, and she just stood there, frozen in place. Erlinda said she was going to walk over to the woman. I decided to follow her as well.

As we came within about 40 or 50 feet from her, she turned away and ran into a small grove of paloverdes. We got close enough to her to see her facial features. The woman was an American Indian. What instantly alarmed us was the blood that covered her hands and stomach. I yelled at her not to run away as both Erlinda and I attempted to catch up to her. When we got to the paloverdes, there was no trace of her. She'd disappeared! There was no way anyone could have gotten away from us that quickly. The whole episode left us disturbed. The poor woman's face was filled with so much fear and panic. It was difficult to get that picture out of my mind. Just then, the couple we were camping with came up to us.

The wife asked us where the woman went. We had no answer. They must have seen the look of amazement on our faces because they lowered their voices and said, "Are you all right? What happened? What did you see?"

I began to shake with fear as I answered, "We've just seen a ghost!"

Erlinda said, "Let's get the hell out of here, now!" Once back at the camp, we told them the details of the woman and her bloody stomach.

The couple decided, while there was still enough light, to return to the grove of paloverdes and search for the woman. They looked everywhere in the general area. The couple's dog sniffed the ground but did not seem to pick up any scent. After a while searching, they decided to stop, since it was getting dark and they didn't want to risk the chance of being bitten by a rattlesnake.

That night, it took Erlinda and me a very long time before we felt comfortable enough to fall asleep. The couple that also saw the woman from a distance must have had more questions they wanted to ask us, but under the circumstances, they must have sensed it would be best to save their questions for the morning.

Morning finally did arrive—not soon enough for Erlinda and me. We discussed the details of the night before and returned to the site of the woman's disappearance. Once again, we did not find a clue or any indication of what transpired the evening before. Erlinda turned to me and said, "I think it would be best if we hiked back home today. What do you think?"

I didn't need any further prodding. I answered, "Let's get going!" We said our good-byes to the couple from Taos and headed on the trail back home.

As you can imagine, all Erlinda and I talked about was the woman. We tried to make sense of what we had seen, but it only caused us to have more questions about something that seemed impossible to explain.

Once at home, I bought and read our local newspapers for any report of a woman who had disappeared or had been reported missing. I didn't find a thing. The local television news didn't report any missing woman either. Erlinda and I decided to drop the subject and get on with our lives.

However, my curiosity prompted me to pick up the phone and give my uncle a call. My uncle is retired after working 25 years for the US Forest Service as a surveyor. I decided to give him a call simply to inquire about anything unusual that he may have experienced or heard during his employment. He found my questions to be rather odd but soon told me about several fellow workers who had encountered a woman's ghost that fit my description.

He told me that about ten years ago, two men were surveying a small tract of land farther north of the area where Erlinda and I had seen the ghost. He said the men saw this strange Indian woman running naked among some short desert brush. Aside from her nakedness, the men were interested in another odd occurrence. Getting a better view with binoculars, they could see her disappear and reappear. All this took place in broad daylight.

The woman appeared sporadically and watched the men at their work for the full four days they were in the area. She never got any closer than several hundred yards from where they were. It was obvious to them that she did not want anyone approaching her. Not wanting to arouse any jokes from their fellow workers back at the office, the two men kept the ghost woman a secret from the other employees. My uncle was the only friend they felt secure enough to trust with their information. Aside from what my uncle knew from rumors, he was unaware of anyone else experiencing any strange apparitions of this ghostly Native American woman.

Erlinda and I have not heard any more about this ghost. I would like to know what she is doing up there in the desert among the cactus and boulders. Does she have something to tell us about how she died? Who killed her, perhaps? Maybe she has appeared to someone else. Whatever the story, I won't be hiking in that part of the mountains ever again.

Catherine Two Bears's Story

Tonto National Forest, AZ

In 1992, I was attending the University of Arizona in Phoenix. I was in my senior year and majoring in biology. During the summer of that same year, five seniors (including myself), four graduate students, and a professor were conducting fieldwork at Theodore Roosevelt Lake. The lake is located in the Tonto National Forest, about a two-hour drive northeast of Phoenix. Our two-month study and research focused on native amphibians of the lake, specifically bullfrogs. Throughout the years, this particular species of frog had begun to change the ecology of Arizona's lake and streams. Although the bullfrogs had increased, smaller native populations of frogs were showing the beginning signs of extinction. Bullfrogs have a voracious appetite and will consume anything smaller than themselves, including snakes, other frogs, lizards, and mice. Our focus of study was to specifically record data and ultimately discover a link to the bullfrog population explosion.

Although I enjoyed the research fieldwork, it was wet, muddy, and smelly, and I had to wade in waist-deep cold water. In order to catch the frogs, I had to dress in watertight rubber overalls. Also part of my uniform was a net laundry bag that I tied to my belt, a pith helmet with a flashlight strapped on top, and of course a fishnet attached to a four-foot pole. My colleagues and I would get in the water at about eight in the evening and begin our hunt, which would last until around ten or so at night. We initiated a process of surprise by which we would catch these fast and alert bullfrogs by slowly wading toward a floating mass of leaves or plants. Using the light strapped to my helmet, I would scan the area until I spotted the bright telltale sign of a bullfrog's reflecting eyes. Once spotted, I would make my way toward the frog, careful not to make any ripples, and using my fishing net, quickly catch it and place it inside the net bag tied to my belt.

This system, although primitive, would bring in about ten to twenty frogs a night per student. Each pair of students had a section of lake in which to capture the frogs. After finishing our work for the night, we would drive back to the lab and place the frogs in a large stock-water tank for study the next day. Our evening captures took place three nights a week. Because of the many frogs in the area, we had enough specimens and paperwork to keep us very busy.

So what does capturing bullfrogs have to do with ghosts? Well, one evening during a night of bullfrog catching, something very, very strange happened to me. Another girl—who just happened to be my girlfriend—and I went off for the evening to do the night's frog gathering. We went into the water at about eight in the evening. The frogs were making their croaking sounds as usual, and we got right to work. But at about nine o'clock, I began to feel sick. My stomach was turning. I figured it was something I had eaten earlier at dinner. I decided to end the evening's hunt and get back to my warm bed. I informed my partner that I would be taking the truck and asked her to catch a return ride to the lab with the others. "No problem," she said. So off I drove.

The road was dark. I had to drive slowly due to javelinas (wild desert pigs) and other small animals that were out and about. It was summer, so to get fresh air, I had both the windows in the truck lowered. Suddenly, I felt something come in through the passenger-side window and hit the right side of my body. It gave me a terrible scare. I quickly put on the brakes and nervously turned on the interior truck light. Then I saw it—a small owl! Apparently, the owl had flown across my path on the road and mistakenly entered the truck through the open window.

Well, there it was on the floor of the truck, flapping its wings with its beak wide open. I can look back now and say that confused bird gave me a good scare. I opened my driver-side door and scrambled outside. I walked over to the passenger-side door and opened it to allow the owl a way out. But when I opened the door, the owl was gone. Where had it gone? I carefully looked under and behind the truck seat, but there was no owl. If it had exited the truck on its own, I would have heard it or even seen it because the light was still on inside the truck. This was definitely a strange thing that had just occurred. The owl in my truck simply disappeared. Knowing something about animal behavior, I knew this was unusual. Also, being an Apache gave me a cultural knowledge about such things. Traditional Apache people do not consider owls to be positive animals to be associated with. I knew this owl was not a good omen. To Apaches, owls are messengers of bad news and even death. My parents have told me that some medicine people do evil by using the owl's spirit in their witchcraft.

I hurriedly got back into the truck, rolled up both windows, and drove quickly to the cabin. I admit that at the time I was scared being all by myself. When I entered the cabin, I went straight to the bathroom and showered. I still had the stomachache, but now I was more concerned about my recent owl incident. After making sure all the doors in the cabin were locked and the outside light was on, I got into bed and waited for the return of the others.

After about twenty minutes, no one returned, and I began to get worried. I got out of bed and looked out the window and saw nothing but darkness. I thought it best to try to sleep even though my stomach was a ball of nerves. As soon as I got back into bed, I heard the sound of footsteps in the front room. I knew there was no way someone could have entered the cabin without opening the locked door and making a sound.

Something bad was definitely going on, and I was scared. As I gazed from my bed at the open doorway that led into the bedroom, the footsteps stopped. Then there was silence for a few seconds. Soon, I heard the voice of what sounded like a small child speak in my Apache language: "Can I go see Mama? I want to see Mama. Can I go see Mama?" I couldn't stop trembling. The words were very clear, and because they were spoken in Apache, that made them even more terrifying to me. I had had enough of this, so I jumped out of the bed and, in the darkness, scrambled for the light switch on the wall. Nervously, I tripped over my own shoes, fell to the floor, hit my left shoulder, and smashed my big toe against the dresser. I was in pain. I figured my toe was broken. I managed to crawl across the floor and then find the wall with the light switch, turn it on, and crawl to the bathroom.

No sooner had I entered the bathroom, I heard the sound of my fellow students' trucks returning to the lab. I was an emotional mess. I decided it would be best not to tell anyone about what had happened to me. After all, what could they say or offer me? One thing that I did need was to get some medical help for my toe. It was already swelling up when my girlfriend came in the door. I told her that I had fallen and that was all.

My girlfriend drove me that night to the student university clinic in Phoenix, where an X-ray was taken and I was given the good news that the toe was not broken. Still, it hurt quite a lot and was very bruised. Unable to do any more night wading for frogs in cold lake water, my research ended. I spent the remainder of the summer at home. Once I arrived home, I told my parents all about the experience with the owl and the child's ghostly voice. They told me to pray and to never again be out alone in that area. My parents could not offer an explanation regarding the owl that came into my truck or the ghostly voice of the child. All I was told was that sometimes these things are forces that foretell a future event. As of this date, I have not had anything happen to me that I can connect to that summer night in 1992, but that does not mean I won't. I'm hoping not to ever experience anything like that again. I'm not the type of person that goes looking for ghosts and things. Ghosts scare me.

CALIFORNIA

Gerald and Lee's Story

Sonora, CA

I moved to the town of Sonora about 15 years ago from San Francisco. Searching for a more peaceful and less stressful life, I contemplated making a move out of the city for several months. The daily grind of living in such a large city as San Francisco had become more and more of an effort. I wanted a stressless quality of life that a smaller community like Sonora could offer.

Prior to my move, I was employed as a juvenile probation officer. My caseload of kids was between 38 to 45, a ridiculous number and as much a stress-producing job as any could be.

In theory, I was supposed to make contact with each client once or twice a month and make contact with their parents, schools, and social workers; write reports that were submitted to the juvenile court; attend meetings; chart in the clients' files; be called into court by deposition; attend to numerous emergencies—the list went on and on. And all this was to be accomplished within a month's time. I became psychologically numb, or as is commonly termed within the department for a worker who has reached his limit, a burnout.

So 11 years ago, I made the decision to leave my job, move, and settle into the more relaxed community of Sonora. I purchased a small two-bedroom bungalow on the south side of town, a short walking distance to Main Street. I wasn't into making new friends immediately. I wasn't antisocial; I just wanted to take things easy for a time and do some fixing up and gardening around the house. One of the renovations to my home I accomplished was to turn a bedroom into a computer room. Soon after, I began my own designing and advertisement business out of this room.

Friends still living in San Francisco and new acquaintances in Sonora began to use my skills and services. Quickly, word got around about the new advertising guy in town, and within a week, I acquired four accounts! One of these new accounts was with a gentleman named Lee, who, like myself, moved away from a big city to seek the sanity of a smaller town. Again like myself, Lee also started a small, home-based business. Lee responded to the local newspaper ad I placed, and when he stopped in to describe his advertising needs, we really hit it off. Unknowingly, our business relationship became, in time, a great friendship and eventually developed into a romantic partnership.

At the time, Lee's business interest was raising locally grown organic herbs and flowers. He singularly handled the full duties of the business, including planting seeds, harvesting, and eventually distributing his organic produce to restaurants in the Sacramento area. Also, twice a week, he would load up his Nissan pickup and attend the popular farmers' market in San Francisco. The town of Sonora also has a wonderful farmers' market located at its fairgrounds that Lee occasionally attends to this day.

Well, one day during one of Lee's initial visits to my home, as we were seated in my living room discussing the direction that he wished to go with his advertisements, he happened to mention an experience he'd had just one week prior.

Lee began by first telling me, "I know we don't know each other very well, so I hope you don't think I'm crazy or some kind of a new-age loony as I share this with you, but I've had an encounter with a ghost."

I was, of course, taken aback by his announcement, but I assured him by stating, "I was a probation officer for several years; I can't imagine anything stranger than what I experienced on the job." After sensing my acceptance, Lee began the story of his encounter with a spirit. Little did I know at the time we would share this experience.

Lee told me that one early Friday morning, while on a produce run to Sacramento, he decided to visit Lillian, a 78-year-old friend of his. Lillian, who lived alone on Sonora's north end, had recently been released from the hospital. She suffered from diabetic complications and a long battle with congestive heart disease. Lillian and Lee had become good friends over the years, and because of her ill health, Lee was Lillian's transportation to and from her doctor, as well as for hospital visits.

The day before, prior to driving to Sacramento, Lee spoke to Lillian on the phone and told her he would be visiting her early the next morning. She sounded well and was in good spirits. The next morning, on Friday, Lee drove up to Lillian's house, walked up to her front door, and turned the knob. Finding that the door was locked, he gave a few loud knocks. There was no answer. Since Lillian did not respond to his knocks, Lee thought that she must have forgotten about his visit and had overslept. Normally, she would have left the door unlocked for him. Immediately he became concerned that something was not right. He called out her name and then heard Lillian softly answer, "Lee, oh, Lee, come inside, honey."

At this point in Lee's telling of the story, for an unknown reason, I was covered in goose bumps. I felt the hair on the back of my neck stand on end. Not wanting to interrupt his story, I kept these reactions to myself and allowed Lee to continue.

Lee responded to Lillian's voice, "Lillian, the door is locked. You need to unlock the door." When she did not respond, he took a peek through the window and saw a darkened living room. Lee called out once again, "Lillian, unlock the door." Not getting a response, he walked to her backyard and up the few stairs leading to the porch door. He found the door unlocked and quickly entered.

From her living room, he could see that her bedroom door was opened and the table light by her bed was on. Lee stood in the living room and, so as not to startle her, called out her name. When she did not answer, he cautiously walked into her bedroom, where he found her lifeless body in bed. He reached to touch her round face, and when he held it in his hands, it was cold as ice. Lillian had no doubt been dead for several hours! Unable to hold back his tears, he said a few private prayers and then used her phone to notify the authorities.

I asked Lee the obvious question: What did he think about Lillian's disembodied voice answering him from within the house? He said, "I got a little sacred—how could I not be?—but because I was so shaken by discovering my friend's dead body, somehow all my senses were not functioning normally."

Lee then looked at me and asked, "Gerald, are you all right? You look disturbed."

I nervously answered him, "You know, Lee, I also had something strange happen to me." I reached for one of my files and asked him, "Did Lillian live at this address, and was this her phone number?"

Lee gave me a look of amazement. "Yes, yes, Gerald, that's Lillian. Did you also know her?"

I told Lee that I had called and spoken to Lillian on the phone the previous Monday! She had asked me to design an inexpensive personal business card and letterhead logo for her just the month before. Because of personal issues, she assured me she was in no rush and asked me to take all the time I wished. I called her on Monday at 3:00 p.m. to inform her that the work was completed and she needed to give a final approval on the job before it could be printed. Lillian said, "I'll have to first take care of some loose ends. I'll be by your office sometime before the week is up." If Lillian had died on Friday morning, then I definitely spoke to her three days after Lee had found her dead in her home!

Lee and I were speechless. At the time, there was not anything either of us could say that would make sense other than to acknowledge that Lillian's spirit was conducting business as usual and was not ready to pass on to the other side.

At the time of Lee's visit to my home, Lillian's burial was scheduled in two days. I decided to attend the funeral with Lee.

After the funeral, when we arrived at my home, I told Lee that I was going to get rid of the work I had completed for Lillian. I needed to clear my mind. I gathered all the paperwork, walked to the backyard, and put everything into the Dumpster in the alley. I spoke softly, telling Lillian that I hope she was satisfied with the logo I had designed for her and that she did not need to pay me a home visit, because as far as I was concerned, her account was paid in full!

Thankfully, I've not had any ghost activity at my house or anything on a spooky level, but I have to admit that from time to time, when my office phone rings, a little hesitation comes over me. Will a living person be at the other end or a voice from beyond?

Leo Ott's Story

Grass Valley, CA

I was born and raised in Fresno, California. During my childhood years, my parents enjoyed taking the family on visits throughout the gold rush country. As I got older and able to drive a car, I found myself taking frequent trips on my own into this historic area of Northern California. I enjoyed the history and architecture of the area and knew that when the opportunity presented itself, I would one day make it my home. Nine years ago, after a major turn of events in my personal life, I decided to make the move from Fresno and settle in Grass Valley.

At the time of my move, I had a wonderful relationship with a man who unfortunately died in a motorcycle accident. I was devastated by the loss and was going through a bout of depression and needed to find a focus to my life. John and I were together for only two years, but I've never really gotten over the pain of losing him. I don't know if I'll ever fully recover from this loss. I imagine I sound as if I want pity or for people to feel sorry for me, but on the contrary, I just want to let you know what I was going through at the time. Surprisingly, I've grown to enjoy the privacy and ease of doing things on my own.

Before moving out of Fresno, I studied yoga for five years and became interested in following a healthy lifestyle, eating only vegetarian-based foods, and eliminating milk and egg products from my diet. This change also prompted me to look at the direction my life was headed. I decided to make the move out of a large city, and when the time came to begin my search for a property, my focus was to locate a house and land that would allow me the peace and quiet I needed. I searched around the area for weeks looking to purchase a home and small acreage to start a business growing organic vegetables and flowers.

In Fresno one morning, I was having coffee at a local bakery. As I read through a listing of available properties in a local paper, a description of a house in the gold rush town of Grass Valley caught my attention. Grass Valley was not my first choice, but after reading the property's description, I knew I had to take a look.

After driving the long highway and arriving at the property, I was not disappointed. The house was just what I was looking for, and the sloping four acres of land were perfect for growing plants. I moved in two months later and soon felt very comfortable in my new home. Living alone was at first difficult for me, but I soon got into the routine of doing the daily chores and such.

As for my ghost experiences, they began during my first winter at the house. At first, I rationalized it all as just my imagination, but it didn't take long for me to finally realize there was something more complex going on.

The first time I noticed something strange taking place was in the bedroom. It was in November. I was typing an e-mail to a friend one afternoon when I heard the sound of footsteps in the hallway. I had no doubt there was someone in the house with me because the footsteps were loud and distinct. I was startled out of my chair and took a few cautious steps as I made my way to the bedroom door. I wanted to call out and ask who was there, but I thought it would be best to surprise whoever it was who'd entered the house. Perhaps it was a visiting friend or the real estate agent who'd sold me the house.

I searched the whole house and didn't discover anyone or any evidence of anyone entering the house. The front and rear screen doors were still latched from the inside. At that moment, something in me, an inner voice, said things were not going to remain the same for me. I knew and was convinced that what I had heard was not my imagination.

As the rest of the day progressed, I kept an open ear for any further visits. Then a few hours later, the footsteps returned.

This time, I sat firmly in my chair, my hands frozen in position over the computer keyboard as I held my breath. With each step, the footsteps made the old wooden plank floor creak. Slowly the steps made their way to the room where I was seated. I heard them stop at my door. I turned apprehensively to face whoever or whatever would be standing at the door. I saw the smoky figure of a person. It was not a white form as most people might imagine a ghost to appear; this ghost was a hazy gray color. I quickly stood up out of the chair where I was seated, and I remember saying out loud, "Oh, God!"

I'm not ashamed to admit that I was terrified. I took a few steps back and let out a scream. The impression I got was that the ghost was not friendly or familiar. It was dark and ominous. Without thinking, I yelled, "Get out! Get out of my house!" Immediately, the ghost began to shrink into itself until it became a little sliver of black. It turned into a long strip of darkness that hung in the air for about 30 seconds until it simply ceased to be visible. It faded into nothingness. I stood there in shock.

Slowly, I got the courage to walk toward the door and into the hallway. I searched every area and room of my house. Nothing was out of place. I looked at my wall clock. The time was 4:00 p.m. The day was sunny. I do not drink or do drugs. The only medication I use is for seasonal allergies, and that's it. I swear I saw this thing come into my house and appear to me in broad daylight.

The next incident took place just a couple of days after this one. I was outside, hammering a garden hose holder to the side of the house. I was coiling the hose around the holder when I noticed movement in the yard. I glanced over to the porch and saw a man sitting on my porch chair. I was only about twenty feet away, and there was a leafless rose vine covering most of the porch, but I could see this man in his midforties sitting on the porch, staring straight ahead. I dropped the hose I was holding and, with command in my voice, said in his direction, "Can I help you?"

He turned his head toward me and then disappeared. This all happened within the span of about five seconds. I had had enough. I was convinced that my house was haunted. There were ghosts not only in the house but also existing on the property. I didn't know what to do about it. What was I supposed to do? I walked back into the house, grabbed a few clothes and my car keys, and drove to Fresno for the night. No way was I going to stay alone in the house. Imagine having to actually look at the face of the ghost of the old man just a few feet away. I was not going to go through that experience alone again.

Arriving in Fresno, I spent the night at my cousin Duke's apartment. The next day, I asked Duke, who was unemployed at the time, to come spend a week or a few days with me. Duke was intrigued with my ghost story, and he accepted my offer. His curiosity was definitely aroused, and he excitedly said, "I'd enjoy having an encounter with a real ghost. After all, how many times does such an opportunity come up—to spend a night at a haunted house?"

I spent one more day in Fresno, and then the next morning, Duke and I drove back to Grass Valley. Everything seemed normal and ordinary when we reached the house—no evidence of any ghost activity that I could see. The front door to the house was locked as I had left it. I started up the furnace, and we both soon found our own comfortable positions in front of the television. I thought to myself, *No more ghosts. Please, no more ghosts.*

We were watching the evening news, when suddenly from the kitchen, we heard the sound of a dish fall into the porcelain sink. The sound startled me so much that I jumped straight out of my chair. We stood still, looking at each other, waiting for something further to happen. But nothing did. I cautiously walked to the kitchen and saw that a small serving dish was lying in the sink. I picked it up and returned it to the dish rack. *Nothing unusual that couldn't be explained,* I thought. *Just a dish that slipped off the dish rack, that's all.*

I turned and walked back to the living room, saying to Duke, "No ghost; just a dish." Not more then a few seconds after I sat back down on my chair, once again, the sound of the dish being moved broke the silence. I knew this was not normal. You had to be there in the room with us to see the frightened look that came over both our faces.

Duke said, "Let me go take a look." As he walked to the sink, he reached inside and pulled out the same dish I had just placed on the rack!

"That's impossible," I said. "You know I placed it on the rack. That dish could not have jumped back in the sink again like that on its own."

Attempting to make light of the situation, Duke said, "We got a little Linda Blair thing going on here." He picked up the dish, gave it a quick look-over, and then placed it back in the sink, saying, "Well, Mr. Ghost, if you want to play house, go ahead and enjoy yourself."

Duke came back to the living room, and we continued to watch the television. I remained nervous, but Duke did not seem to be bothered at all by the kitchen incident. His lack of concern must have transferred over to me because I soon began to feel more at ease. I grew sleepy and said, "Duke, I'm going to call it a night. You know where the blankets are. See you in the morning."

That night, I slept very lightly. Twice I heard Duke walk down the hall and make his way to the bathroom. I thought it was odd that he didn't flush the toilet, but I thought he didn't want to wake me by making noise. Nothing I could call strange or paranormal took place during the night. However, the next morning changed my mind.

I was the first to wake, and leaving my bedroom, I walked into the bathroom. I could see that Duke had not used the toilet. When I went into the living room, I found him asleep on the couch. The television was turned on with the volume off, and he had also turned on the light on the desk by the front door. I said, "Duke, wake up. What are you doing asleep here in the living room?"

He explained that not long after I had gone to bed, he turned all the lights off except for the television. At about 11:30 p.m., he heard a noise in the kitchen. He turned to look and saw some guy leaning against the sink! He could tell it was a ghost because of the transparency of the figure. In a shaky voice, Duke spoke to the ghost, saying, "What do you want? Don't hurt me." Duke said the ghost then smiled at him and disappeared. Duke was shaken by the apparition but did not want to wake me. Instead, he decided to turn on the lights and sleep with the television on for the rest of the night.

I asked Duke why didn't he just come over to my bedroom and wake me. He could have told me about the ghost that appeared to him when he got up twice to use the bathroom during the night. Duke looked at me and said, "What do you mean? I didn't use the bathroom at all last night. To get to the bathroom, I would have had to walk through the kitchen. I wasn't going to get up and take a chance of meeting up with that ghost again! Your house is haunted, Leo. I believe you. This house is definitely haunted!"

We both were deciding what to do next. Duke described the ghost in detail, but neither he nor I could identify who it might be. Finally, I made the decision to remain strong, and I told Duke that I was not going to leave and give up my house to a ghost. I was planning on staying for good. I made sure to speak loudly, directing my words to the ghost. "One of us is going to have to leave the house, and it's not going to be me! So whoever you are, you'd better leave now!"

Duke spent another night with me, and neither of us experienced another disturbance. Although we were both a little unnerved, things seemed to be going all right. I drove Duke back to his home in Fresno. All the while, I was apprehensive about returning to my home. But I drew strength from my conviction of knowing it was my home, and after all, I did not want to let the ghost get the better of me. I had been through too much in my life to give it all up to some wayward ghost.

Returning home, I walked into the darkened living room, turned on the light, and said, "Look, I want to be at peace with my house; I hope you can understand this. I don't want to have to be on the lookout for you. I don't know what you want, but please, leave me alone to live my life. You've already lived yours, so you should go on and live your own life doing whatever you need to do. Do it somewhere else and leave me alone." I must have said something that the ghost understood, because as soon as I finished saying the last word, I heard a loud *crack* like that of a breaking board. It was sudden and loud. It startled the heck out of me, but I knew this must be the answer to my firm declaration. The ghost heard me and respected my stand. Immediately, I felt the heavy atmosphere in the room change. Difficult as it is to try to explain, I felt that the ghost had left my house.

I know I took a chance of angering the ghost, but it was, after all, my house. I couldn't keep spending further nights in other people's homes. It was my house, and I was willing to fight to keep it.

It's now been a few years since all those occurrences took place, and nothing ghostly has appeared to me at the house. I don't hear noises at night or see shadows or dishes flying in the air. I am finally living a normal life, the life I always wanted.

One reoccurring question people ask me when I tell them my story is, "Do you think the spirit you saw was your partner who died and wanted to make contact with you?" My answer is that this ghost was definitely not even closely related in any shape or form to John. I don't believe loved ones want to come back and scare us. The ghost I experienced was a dark and mischievous one.

As I said before, I was frightened and could feel the negative presence of this ghost. Love gives a very different presence, very different from what this ghost was presenting to me. I haven't had any more incidents, and I don't want any. So far it has stayed away.

Jay Cusker's Story

Sutter Creek, CA

My partner and I took the time to carefully choose this house as the best location for our gift shop, which we named Passages. The house had been empty for about 40 years before we occupied it. As of this day, we've operated the business for three years. Prior to this location, our gift shop was elsewhere in Sutter Creek. Before we occupied the house, we had been told that the house had ghosts. Even more surprising was the news that these ghosts were definitely not happy ones.

The primary caretaker who would regularly clean the house informed us of her own personal experiences with these ghosts. These ghosts caused her enough concern for our regard that she sat down with us and sincerely recounted her own experiences at the house. She told of one example when she was alone in the house, generally cleaning up the place. Both the mop and broom she placed against the wall were picked up into the air and thrown across the room. Immediately after this event, all the doors in the house opened and slammed shut all around her!

She also informed us that the house was used only occasionally by the owners as a weekend retreat. Eventually, the owners used the house less and less until they finally decided to lock it up.

Again, historically speaking, the house was built in the 1850s by a sea captain. When you study the house's design, it reflects the maritime owner's tastes because it was built using a ship's blueprint. The porch was built to simulate a ship's decking, and as such, each room of the house opens out to this "deck." Also, the main front door entrance leads to a flight of stairs that take a person to a galley-like lower level.

This sea captain was probably from the East Coast because there is a very old, large eastern sugar maple tree growing in the backyard. There are also two other large trees in the front yard, which the nurserymen informed us are either ash or elm and, just like the maple, are also native to the East Coast. They've also said there is a strong possibility that these trees probably don't even exist any longer in their native habitat, which is due to East Coast diseases such as Dutch elm.

After the captain died, an Italian family, the Brignolis, who had ten children, bought the house. The Brignoli family was one of the original families in the Sutter Creek area. I have some old photographs of this family that were taken at the house, on the porch, and in the yard. Gus Brignoli, the father, was the last man to have lived and died in the house. He was very well known in the area as a philanthropist of the community. The Brignolis still own the house by way of the female lineage. As far as I know, the men never married.

Now, as for spiritual activity, I definitely do feel a presence here at the house, and customers, from time to time, will describe being followed around the rooms by an unseen person. Customers have said they get the strong impression of a man who follows them. Customers also have reported catching the scent of a man's smoldering pipe tobacco. I have had my own personal experience with this. I was once talking to two women customers about the ghosts in the house when we were suddenly enveloped by the scent of tobacco smoke. I stared at them and asked, "Do you smell anything strange?" Without hesitation, they nodded and both responded that they smelled pipe tobacco.

I know there are two ghosts in the house—one a man and the other a woman. I've seen them both, but I see the woman's spirit more often. Interestingly enough, whenever we have sponsored an artist's reception or other small social gatherings at the house, inevitably, I'll catch a glimpse of the woman's ghost as she passes by a doorway or behind one of the party attendees. She's always dressed in a long white dress, and again, she only appears when lots of people are gathered in the house. She also likes the nursery room, where I've both seen and felt her presence.

I recall when, during our store's grand opening reception, I took a picture of a friend, Susan Ross, as she was walking down the stairs that led to the parlor. Before taking the picture, I began to feel and to sense the invisible presence of someone standing over me. Undeterred, I went ahead and took Susan's picture, and as you can see by the photo, a resulting photo image of a large light or spirit appeared on the stairs with Susan. I've been told that these balls of light are called **ghost orbs** by parapsychologists and are explained as being a spirit's energy that is sometimes captured on film.

I've also had other creepy experiences as I go around the house placing new gift items on various shelves. I'll get an impression that a ghost might not approve of where I placed an item. Suddenly, I'll feel a heaviness enveloping the room I'm in, and I know it will be best if I move the gift items elsewhere. When I do this, the energy in the room will change to a cheerful and happy one. These days, I'm very sensitive to this.

The house and its unique history is an amazing one. My sincere hope is the ghosts that dwell within it are now as content with it as we happen to be. I believe the old captain's spirit is also still here because he must have enjoyed and loved his house very much. He must have been very attached to it given all the personal touches he added. He must be happy with all the attention and positive comments visitors to the house make. A Native American friend of mine who visited the house told me she feels that the captain's spirit is content with the house in its present state.

I would enjoy the opportunity for the sea captain's spirit to appear to me. I hope I wouldn't be too scared. But who knows?

Savina Corballi's Story

Yosemite National Park, CA

I've worked and lived at the Yosemite National Park since 1994. What began as a housekeeping or maid position has since turned out to be my career. My girlfriend and I both began working at the park together after we completed two years of college. We were looking for summer jobs and were told by a friend that Yosemite was always hiring summer, seasonal workers. We applied and were soon hired at Curry Village as maids. Although my girlfriend returned to finish college, I decided to stay on at the park. It's now been over seven years since that summer.

Though I haven't made very much money throughout the years, I have managed to save a few dollars. My meals and rent for a one-bedroom cabin are both deducted from my salary, and I know I'll never get rich working here, but the location of working in such a beautiful environment like Yosemite more than makes up for my lack of money.

I've had several weird experiences at the park. A lot of these experiences have not given me much cause to fear ghosts, but one in particular sure made me change my mind. This special experience began in the spring of 1997 while I was hiking by myself in the backcountry of Tuolumne Meadows. I've hiked many of the back trails before, and I especially enjoy the John Muir Trail. This has undoubtedly got to be among the most beautiful hiking trails in the world!

The meadows are beautiful in the springtime, and the spring of '97 was no different. I decided to hike alone with only my backpack and adventurous spirit. It's not at all unusual for the employees at the park to do a solitary hike. Eventually, most of the employees get the urge for exploring the park, and because of the availability of good trails and time off of work, we definitely take advantage of our beautiful location. However, mutual friends' employment schedules don't always match, so hiking alone is not uncommon.

One spring evening, I got all my gear ready for the six-day-long hike I had planned. On day two of my hike, I reached my destination and set up my base camp. This is where I would be spending three wonderful days alone, swimming in the streams, hiking, and sleeping. What a life! I also brought two books with me. One was written about the history of Yosemite National Park, and the other was written about the American Indians of the gold rush country.

This second book was basically written about the sad history and ultimate extermination of the American Indians. I wanted to get a perspective of what most Americans don't learn in school. I know I certainly didn't get much of an education throughout my school years regarding the treatment of the native people of California. Like most visitors to Yosemite, I fell in love with the beauty of the area and equally was unaware of its terrible history regarding the white man's treatment toward the natives. I decided to take the opportunity on my hike to read and educate myself in this area. I also brought along a camera to take lots of pictures.

Coinciding with my hike, the park service was sponsoring a photography contest for nonprofessionals, and I decided to enter. The first prize of $500 was something I wanted to take a chance on winning, so I brought along about eight rolls of film. Everything went well on my hike, but on the second day, things turned out differently.

It was a warm afternoon, and I was lying on my sleeping bag inside my tent. As I was reading my book, I heard the footsteps of someone walking up to my camp. I glanced out of the tent and saw no one. This bothered me to the point that I got up and walked outside of my tent to take a look around. I saw nothing. I thought perhaps it might be a squirrel, a raccoon, or a bird. But the footsteps were very identifiable to me as the sound a walking human would make placing one foot in front of the other. Even though the day was clear and bright, I saw no one around my camp.

I disregarded this minor incident and decided to take a short walk to the nearby stream. As I splashed myself with the cool stream water, I thought about my earlier experience with the footsteps. Subconsciously, the incident was still bothering me. I decided to walk back to my tent and get a snack.

As I rose and turned in the direction of my camp, which was about a quarter of a mile away, I noticed that someone was standing by the tent. I could tell it was a young guy wearing blue shorts and a blue cap, and holding an orange backpack. I yelled out, "Can I help you?" The guy turned his head to look in my direction. I held up my arm and made a waving gesture to communicate that I had my eyes on him. He said nothing and made no movement other than to face my direction to indicate he knew I was yelling at him. I felt a bit alarmed and unsure about what he might be up to or what I should do next, so I yelled once more, "That's my tent! Can I help you?" Keep in mind I was alone in the woods, so I didn't want to necessarily get too close to this strange guy. I'm smart enough to know there are lots of kooks who would like to take advantage of a single woman in a situation like this.

When he failed to respond to my calls, I knew and felt something was definitely not right. I decided the best thing for me to do was to stay put. Then he slowly turned away and walked toward the open foot trail directly above my camp. I kept my eyes on this weird guy while at the same time wasted no time briskly making my way to my tent.

Arriving, I looked over everything inside and outside the tent. It soon became clear to me that everything was untouched, though strangely, there was an area of water soaking the ground directly below where this guy had been standing. Hoping to get a better glimpse of him, I looked in the direction of the footpath. I spotted him and then noticed something unusual in the way he was walking. He moved abruptly from side to side, kind of staggering with each step. I imagined this guy might be drunk or under the influence of drugs.

I sat down on the ground and observed as he slowly made his way a few more feet until he slowly disappeared. And when I say disappeared, I mean *disappeared*! The path was located in an open meadow without any trees or large rocks to hide behind. It was midday, without any shadows. The sun was bright and high up in the sky. This guy was there one second, and in the next, he just suddenly disappeared.

I quickly stood up, thinking he must have taken a fall, and I cautiously walked over to where he might have hit the ground. There was no evidence of the guy anywhere. No cap, no backpack, nothing! The meadow grasses and flowers were only about a foot or so high, so he couldn't have been hiding among the plants. I didn't want to contemplate the situation any longer. I knew the only explanation was that a ghost had visited me. And it had appeared to me in broad daylight no less! Admittedly, this shook me up, and as I returned to my tent, I decided to cut my stay short, pack up my things, and return home.

As I gathered up my belongings, I noticed drops of blood on the paper bags I had next to my camp stove and at the side of my tent. These were fresh drops, and there was only one way they could have gotten there—the ghost! In just a few minutes, I hightailed it out of there. Because of all the adrenaline that must have been coursing through my body, I got on the trail and walked at an accelerated speed that approached a run.

Soon I met up with two women hikers from Germany, who were headed down to the valley floor. Although I'm sure they must have noticed the tormented look on my face, they said nothing. I attempted to act as normal as possible. I told them where I had camped the previous night, and they said they had seen my tent pitched in the meadow. They were pleasant and soon invited me to accompany them back down the mountain. Not wanting to alarm them, I didn't dare tell them about the ghost I had seen.

The three of us made camp that night without any strange incidents, and then we all got up early the next morning, had our breakfast, and were soon back on the trail. After reaching Yosemite Valley at around 1:00 p.m., we went our separate ways. I was so grateful to be among familiar surroundings, though both mentally and physically exhausted.

As I crossed the last stone bridge that led to my residence, I noticed a gathering of people to the side of the bridge who were all wearing blue caps and shorts. They were holding candles and praying. An uneasiness came over me. I recognized the outfits as the same one the ghost had been wearing. I asked one gentleman what the gathering was for. He said that a friend in their group, named Russell, had died just two days before while swimming in the river. The gathering was to offer prayers to this person before they all got into their cars on their return trip home. After he finished his sentence, I turned to stone!

With emotion in my voice, I asked him where Russell had died and how old he was. He told me Russell was 17 years old and had gone with a group of four on an overnight hiking adventure to Tuolumne Meadows. Apparently, while swimming in one of the deeper streams, he had misjudged a rock's slipperiness, slipped, and fatally struck his head. I didn't ask any more questions. I walked a few feet away from the gathering, and I began to silently and privately sob. I couldn't bring myself to tell him that I had seen the ghost of his friend. I was shaking all over. I watched as the group got into their cars and drove off.

I was a basket case. I felt numb and unable to do much more other than think over and over about what I had experienced. My thinking took over the remainder of that day and the next. My thoughts were of life, death, and unanswered questions I had of the afterlife. I knew I had seen Russell's ghost. The water and blood drops, the cap and shorts, and the manner in which he disappeared on the trail were all the evidence and proof I would ever need. I had seen a ghost!

My experience with Russell's ghost took place only four years ago. Since then, I've told only a few trusted people. I've discovered that whenever I told my story to someone, it would motivate them to share a story of a ghost experience at the park of their own. Although my personal experience is a hard one to top, fellow Yosemite park employees have some stories that are real chillers.

These days, I won't go hiking in the woods without a partner. I'm not necessarily afraid of encountering bears or snakes. It's the other type of encounters I don't ever want to have again. I think you can understand why.

Father David M. Eggers's Story

Los Angeles, CA

I'm gay and happen to be a Catholic priest in the Jesuit order. My story took place in the winter of 1982. At the time, I had been one of four staff chaplains for the county hospital. Prior to this position, I had cared for the spiritual needs of patients at Good Samaritan Hospital in Central Los Angeles. I received my master of divinity from Loyola Marymount University, and 12 months before my acceptance to Good Samaritan, I immediately undertook pastoral ministry within the Los Angeles Archdiocese. I stayed at this hospital for two years until eventually ending up at USC Medical Center.

The hospital was founded in 1878, and the Los Angeles County + USC Healthcare Network (LAC+USC) is currently the nation's largest academic institution. It is one of the largest acute care hospitals in America and has been the primary teaching facility of the Keck School of Medicine of the University of Southern California since 1885. Originally established as a 100-bed hospital with 47 patients, it is currently licensed for 600 beds and budgeted to staff 745 beds.

The time period of my work at the county hospital coincided with the tragic beginning of the HIV/AIDS epidemic that was gripping the United States. The hospital was mobilizing its staff to be at the forefront of treatment and care giving to patients of this plague. As chaplain, I encountered many, many men and women, gay and straight, with various degrees of this condition. One man in particular, named

Gustavio, remains in my memory still.

Gustavio was a 22-year-old Hispanic man. When he arrived at the hospital, he stood five feet five inches tall, was very thin, and was prone to vomiting episodes. His initial arrival and the day he passed away were not more than two weeks apart, but during that short time, he and I bonded as spiritual brothers. When Gustavio's family back in Guatemala found out their son was gay, they gradually decreased regular phone correspondence with him, ultimately terminating all communication when he next disclosed his AIDS diagnosis. They simply abandoned their son to face his health struggle alone. I found this wrenching and so un-Christlike. Sadly, this outcome was to become more the norm for thousands of affected AIDS patients rather than the exception. I experienced this to be tragically true with the ones I came into contact with on a daily basis.

Even though Gustavio was weak and had lost so much weight that his facial features resembled a mask of death, he managed to hold on to what was encouraging about life, joking at times and remaining very positive.

One afternoon, as I sat by his bed, I noticed under his wisps of hair several shiny metal ballpoint-looking dots jutting out from his scalp. I asked him about them, and he said, "Oh, I thought you knew about the probes the doctors implanted into my skull. I was told it's some type of experimental therapy they're trying out."

I asked, "Do they hurt?"

He said, "Yes, at times they do, when I forget they are there and touch one." I was upset to hear him describe this as "experimental" and painful. Because of my rising outrage over this particular attempt at care, I chose to change the subject.

That following weekend, I was called away to assist with a religious retreat in Santa Barbara. A new class of young postulants was visiting from Oklahoma, and I was asked to conduct the afternoon discussions. All went well, but on my last night, I had an unusual dream. I dreamed of Gustavio, who was surrounded with thousands of electric-blue butterflies fluttering in unison. "Gustavio, they are so beautiful," I said. He looked at me and simply smiled. He did not speak a word to me, but the impression I received was that he was in paradise.

The following Monday morning, as I made my rounds through the hospital, I entered Gustavio's eighth-floor room and found him standing at the window, gazing out at the sky. I stood at the door and said, "Good morning. How are you today?"

He turned, faced me, and said, "Oh, Father, I'm so happy."

Just at that very moment, a loud commotion commenced behind me in the hallway. A nurse immediately approached me and screamed an order for me to follow her to the room where the commotion was happening. Upon arrival to that room, we encountered the aftermath of one patient's family member physically assaulting another patient's family member. It was clear that several people had already subdued the aggressor and were forcibly holding him down on the floor for hospital security personnel to arrive and take over.

Concerned with all that had just transpired in the hall and that it may have caused Gustavio undue alarm, I quickly walked back to his room. When I arrived at his room, I looked around and noticed he was gone. I checked the bathroom and found it empty. Then I noticed his bed and saw that it was completely made up and all his personal bedside table items were gone. Unusual as this appeared, it was common practice to move patients as vacancies or hospital population needs require.

Eventually, I visited three more patients before opening the door to my office. On my desk were several patient files that Martha, the hospital social worker, left for me to look over. Social workers and hospital chaplains tend to work closely, sharing notes when appropriate to patients' well-being.

I looked over the five files and pulled out Gustavio's familiar blue file. To say the least, I was shocked to spot the note stapled on the cover with the handwritten word *Deceased*! While reading the social worker's notes, I discovered that Gustavio had passed away on Sunday morning, the day before. I thought to myself, *How could that be? I was just in his room three hours ago and had spoken directly to him and he to me!*

I closed and locked my office door and then walked down to the hospital coroner's office. I was taken to the refrigerated holding area where Gustavio's thin and diseased body was placed. I offered my personal prayers, all the while anointing him with holy oil and water.

Speaking for myself, I've never been the same since that day. My experience with Gustavio's spirit has forever added to my convictions and has immensely strengthened my faith in God's universal divine plan for us all, in Christ's name.

Garth A. Massingill's Story

San Francisco, CA

I was born in the town of Rockford, Illinois, and graduated with a degree in physical therapy from North Park University in Chicago. I moved to San Francisco in 1996, where I was immediately hired at UCSF Medical Center as an adult acute care physical therapist, and have been employed there ever since. I'm responsible for administration of physical therapy treatment and patient programs, coordinating discharge plans, and so on. Lots of paperwork is involved as well. Overall, I view my work as a team effort between myself and other hospital staff members. Surprisingly, my ghost encounter experience took place only two months ago.

I started my day going through my regular routine at the hospital's physical therapy and rehabilitation clinic. I had a 10:00 a.m. appointment with a young 42-year-old man, Carl, who was in therapy for an ischemic stroke. This stroke affected the movement on the right side of his body, and at the point when I first met Carl, he had been a patient of the clinic for three months. He was required to continue lengthy ongoing therapy and to be evaluated every six weeks.

The clinic had several patients undergoing similar therapies, with high degrees of achievement and success. Carl's brother always accompanied him to his therapy sessions by pushing Carl's wheelchair and was helpful in accessing patient feedback as it pertained to his rehabilitation progress. As is the case with patients such as Carl that are enrolled in our long-term program, our staff grows emotionally attached to them, and a bond of sincere caring is established. This was particularly the case with my interactions with Carl.

Although I am a 100 percent heterosexual man, Carl disclosed early on to me that he was gay. He held no reservation in telling me this, and I respected him for his honesty and trust. This personal information allowed our future conversations from that point on to be free from any misunderstandings or assumptions. We became buddies.

Well, when Carl failed to appear at the appointed time, I phoned his home and spoke to his father. I was informed that Carl had taken his life the week before by overdosing on the prescription sleep aid Ambien. Carl's father apologized profusely for the family's lack of communication to our office and had only this emotionally traumatic, tragic family nightmare as an excuse. I offered my condolences and, after ending the conversation, remained in a state of shock from hearing this terrible news. From the information I was given, Carl had committed suicide from an ongoing state of depression brought about by his stroke.

Prior to his stroke, Carl had been an avid Bay Area cyclo-cross bicyclist, and given his intense love of the sport and his now limiting stroke, I can only guess at the internal depression he must have struggled with. Apparently, the hurdles of having to adjust to his new wheelchair-bound reality were far too much to bear for this active, vibrant athlete.

It was just four days after Carl's funeral, a Monday, and I was working late that evening. I took my dinner at the hospital's cafeteria, and due to a hard rain that was coming down outside, I stayed inside the dry building for close to an hour. That particular week, I was having transmission work done on my car; it had been in the service department at the dealership for two full days. I was depending on public transportation to get me to and from work, and I didn't want to wait outside on a wet bus bench, but I had no other choice. I remember taking a large plastic trash liner from the cafeteria kitchen and positioning it above my head as a makeshift umbrella. Using this as protection from the rain, I made a dash out the cafeteria side doors and found myself on the long walk to the nearest bus stop at the opposite end of the large hospital complex.

Strangely, I was the only person outside on the otherwise heavily traveled sidewalk. As the rain was coming down all around me, I spotted a tall man about fifteen yards ahead, walking with the help of the illuminated walkway lights, looking straight at me and coming toward me. Then he abruptly stopped in his place while I kept my pace and reached him. It was Carl!

Still holding the trash liner above my head, we stood in place with no more than ten feet between us, facing each other.

I said, "Carl, what's going on? What are you doing here? Your father told me . . ." Then it hit me like a lightning bolt. The person I was speaking to, Carl, was standing tall before me and out of his familiar wheelchair! I stared at him as the rain was coming down on both of us, but surprisingly, he showed no sign of being wet. In fact, his clothes and hair were bone dry.

Before I stopped to allow him to respond, our eyes locked as Carl smiled while raising his palm toward me in a gesture I understood to mean, "It's all right. I'm fine." Without saying another word, I stood frozen in place as Carl turned and walked away from me, took about five steps, and then faded away! I was speechless.

I got the urge to say something, so I spoke out, "God take care of you, my friend." I knew and was totally convinced that I had seen his spirit. I didn't feel any fear or apprehension at all. I was, on the contrary, filled with an all-consuming sense of elation and peace. Because his spirit was not threatening or unpleasant, I felt no danger and was remarkably at ease. I knew I had just experienced a wonderful gift.

I chose not to mention this experience to anyone, but when I feel the time is right, I'll speak to Carl's brother. He's the second person I'll describe my encounter to. This happened only two months ago, so I need a little more time to think things through.

COLORADO

Olivia Sagehorn's Story

Grand Junction, CO

Mrs. Sagehorn, who is 91 years old, and I had a wonderful discussion before our interview. She was very candid and direct about the experiences with spirits that both she and her family had. On a personal level, what impressed me most was her insight into how society, so many years ago, dealt with such an issue as a person's sexual orientation during Colorado's frontier era.

Clearly, not all communities handled such an issue in the same manner as Olivia's, but I no doubt believe there were many who tolerated, if not embraced, gays and lesbians of past generations. There is direct anthropological documentation that proves not only Native Americans but also many other preindustrial peoples throughout the world, prior to European contact, held gay individuals in high regard and with cherished respect.

Olivia Sagehorn was a delight to speak with. I conducted the interview with her at a convalescent hospital in Grand Junction within the facility's garden courtyard. Her recollections of past events and detailed memory were always on point.

I must tell you, first of all, I am one of a set of twin girls. My brother, Harold, died after contracting polio in the late 1940s. The disease quickly traveled from his legs to his lungs and spine. Immediately, the government quarantined our family, and thankfully, we were spared any more illness.

We buried my brother on a hillside just north of Gunnison, in the town of Almont. The twenty acres of land where he lies buried belonged to my family. My great-grandfather Walter McClain, along with his brother, William, homesteaded the land in 1877. Great-grandfather Walter married my great-grandmother Ophelia, who was from Orchard City, and together they had two boys and one daughter.

My grandmother Catherine was their only girl.

In 1913, Mother married and, two years later, gave birth to my eldest brother, Harold. A year later, Mother gave birth to my twin sister, Rosella, and me. So now that you have an idea of my family history, I'll get on with my story.

My older brother never married, but he did live with a man for most of his short life. His life partner's name was Clayton. Both of them lived in Orchard City for a few years and then moved to Grand Junction until Harold got sick. Clayton moved in with us, and he cared for my brother in a room Father had converted from a goat house into a bedroom. During Harold's convalescence, Clayton also contracted polio, but he managed to survive the illness.

Homosexuality was not looked upon as negatively then as it can be today. People knew about it and just accepted such things as two women or two men living together as God's plan. Back then, we had other more important things to concern ourselves with, like making a living from the land. It was unusual to see two men living together as a couple, but you know, I knew that there were other couples like my brother and Clayton who owned property in the area because Clayton would tell us about them.

Our family lived acres away from most of our neighbors, separated by hills and even mountains, so we didn't get to have much contact with each other. Our time was spent doing the usual chores that come with trying to make a living from the land. Most of us didn't have the time to spend gossiping about other families.

I remember when, before Harold got polio, he and Clayton visited Denver for a few months. Clayton was an architect by trade and helped design the Denver Club Building in downtown Denver. With the money from this project, they purchased a home in Grand Junction. After my brother's death, Clayton returned to Grand Junction and eventually sold their house and then moved to Denver.

During the time when my brother was ill in bed, I remember him telling us about the different people whom he had seen standing by his bed. These people, he told us, were relatives of ours who had passed away years before. He would point out to us where in the room they were standing, what they were wearing, and sometimes what they would be saying. My mother and father knew but didn't tell my sister and me until after my brother's death that seeing the dead was a sign that he himself was not going to survive for much longer.

During Harold's funeral and after the burial, Clayton was very sad. Right before Clayton moved away, he gave my mother all of my brother's belongings and presented my father with Harold's rifle. A year after Clayton moved away to Denver, we received a few letters from Clayton, but eventually, the letters stopped coming. I don't know whatever happened to him.

One day, while Rosella and I were outside washing clothes, Rosella came up to me and said, "Olivia, I heard Harold calling me last night."

I answered, "What do you mean?"

Then she told me that she had been seeing our brother's spirit walking about the bedroom and once even saw him staring at the front door. She was too upset to tell anyone, but she decided to confide in me because she felt it was time to do so.

I was caught by surprise by my sister's information, and I told her that I believed what she was saying, but I didn't think it was necessary for her to keep it to herself. She needed to tell our parents about this. That evening, while the two of us were seated with our parents at the dinner table, Rosella broke down and described to us what she had seen.

My father took this news the hardest. He cried a little and then told us that he believed my sister because he had also seen my brother's spirit standing a short distance away from where he was building a wall behind the house. Something caused my father to look in the direction of the yard, and there he spotted his son's spirit, standing and looking straight at my father.

"Harold didn't say anything; he just stood in place," Father told us. Father asked him, "Son, is that you? Is it you, son?" Then my brother's image slowly faded away. The only ones in our family who didn't get a visit from my brother were my mother and me. That would change a few years later when I was in my twenties and was about to give birth to my only child, a daughter.

It was a difficult birth, and as soon as my daughter was born, I passed out from all the stress and loss of blood. It took me a long time to recover, but after I did, a few days later, I again landed back in bed with a terrible series of headaches. These headaches were the worst you could ever imagine. Day after day, I'd suffer with migraines. They were terrible.

During one of these headaches, I was in so much pain that I remember crying out, "Lord, I can't take this any longer! Take me to you!" After having said this, I remember lying on my right side in bed, staring with tear-filled eyes at my infant daughter. Just then, I first sensed the presence, and then I heard the footsteps of someone walking in the room. I turned my eyes to look at the door, and I saw my brother slowly walking toward me! I was overcome not with fear but with joy. Even though I was unable to move, even a finger, I knew my brother was in the room with me.

Strangely, as soon as he reached my bed, he held out his hand and placed it on my forehead. At first, I felt coldness and then immediate warmth spread from my head to my shoulders. I closed my eyes and whispered, "Thank you, Harold, my dear brother. Thank you." The terrible headache pain disappeared. I remember falling asleep and waking up when my husband came into the room and sat on the bed and called my name. Since that day, I haven't ever had another headache episode. I really haven't. The headaches have never returned.

When my daughter was about six or seven, she began talking and playing with an imaginary playmate she named "Uncle Man." Because she was so young and precocious, I didn't think much of this, and I didn't question her regarding her playmate until she reached her teen years, when she brought up the subject of her imaginary playmate once again.

She mentioned to me if I remembered the playmate she had when she was younger, and I answered, "Yes, I do remember you telling me once or twice about him."

She answered, "Well, Mother, he told me he was your brother and that he was always going to be your brother."

I answered, "Do you mean to say that you were talking with your uncle Harold?"

"Yes, yes, Mother. That's who he was. It was Uncle Harold."

My immediate response was to not believe my daughter, but she was now old enough to know right from wrong, and she was very serious about this. I looked her straight in her eyes and said, "You are not lying to me, and you actually were talking with my brother?"

"Yes, yes, I was, but somehow I knew, even as a little girl, that I would have gotten into trouble if I were to keep bringing him up time after time. Anyway, he didn't visit me very often, just maybe two or three times total."

That conversation with my daughter took place many years ago, and in 1976, my daughter died of breast cancer. She was my only child. Before her death, during my prayers, I asked my brother's spirit to come and take my daughter, his niece's soul, with him to heaven. My daughter died a peaceful death, and I would tell you more about this, but what happened was very personal and beautiful. I will keep this as my own secret between my daughter and me. My husband died eight years later in 1984.

Because of all the examples of love and the connection that I've seen in my life with my parents, with my family, and on a personal level, I have no doubt that the spirits of our family members will continue to help us when we need them the most. My time will not last too much more than a few years; it might end earlier than that. I have a peace that has carried me throughout many years of hardship and even a few tragedies. My brother has made it known to me that life goes on after death. This is something wonderful to know. I know I have been blessed.

Paul R. Green's Story

Denver, CO

I interviewed Paul at his sister's home in Denver. She mentioned that her brother was on his way to her home from his home in Colorado Springs and that his story was a fascinating one. Paul and his partner's haunting experiences might be the best account of a ghost I'd ever heard. With an obvious smile on my face, I assured her that after we finished up with the interview, I would decide if his story would be one that I'd consider including in this book. As it so happened, Paul's story is one of those, in my estimation is quite fascinating, and gives a home buyer reason to think seriously about investing in any property that might cause one to feel the least bit uneasy.

Originally, I'm from Denver. I was born there and, after graduating from college, became a schoolteacher and worked at my profession for just four years. I retired from the school system for health reasons. One day, a student with whom I had a disagreement decided he would take revenge for my recommending his expulsion by throwing a chair at me as I was walking down a flight of stairs. Later, I was told that the chair could have easily killed me. The injuries I sustained were to my upper spine, and one neck bone was fractured when I fell and rolled down the stairs. Because the student was a minor, not much in the way of punishment was handed to him, at least not to my satisfaction. So today, I'm forcibly retired and making the best of a situation that could have been quite a lot worse.

Two years after the incident and after completing the mandatory rehabilitation program, my partner, Rodney, and I decided to move to Colorado Springs, purchase a house, and invest in our future by purchasing two other houses that needed upgrading. These two investment properties would need improvements to bring them up to a level where we could rent them, but with a little hard work and, of course, money, we were confident we could do this.

At the time, real estate was a good investment, and refurbishing properties that had been neglected and putting them back on the market was proving to be a very good way to go. Before I met Rodney, he had experience doing this to one house and then another until he amassed a nice little personal financial nest egg. When we became a couple, we decided to pool our resources together and jointly work toward some sense of financial freedom. Anyone who has ever been a teacher knows the time and emotional work involved in our profession is rarely reflected in our paychecks. The unexpected accident thrust upon me put a strain on us and delayed our future plans, but we got back on track nonetheless.

So, as for my story, I'll begin by telling you I was never so scared as when I experienced the spirits at one of our properties. I never, ever thought I would have such an encounter. I didn't even believe in such things as ghosts, but I certainly do now.

One of the properties where this took place was on the east side of town, on a street off Palmer Park Boulevard. Before Rodney and I purchased this house, I was very hesitant to even consider it because of the terrible state it was in. It needed so much work to bring it back to a somewhat livable condition that I thought no way was I going to be a part of this money pit. But Rodney convinced me in the end, and in a few days, I signed the real estate contract, and soon I was its hesitant and somewhat proud owner.

We decided to do most of the demolition work ourselves, which meant removing trash, a non-load-bearing wall, cabinets, doors, and a few windows. For all the major construction, we hired a licensed contractor. I remember the first morning I entered the house, I was by myself because Rodney was away at the time, working at his office.

As I entered the house, the first thing that struck me was how it smelled. The odor of what seemed to resemble rotting wood and moldy carpets hung heavily in the air. I also felt there was an overall eeriness to the house. It was a weightiness that pushed on me from all sides. I immediately had the unreasonable thought that a serious illness was about to come on. I knew this was absurd, but that was what I was feeling. It was an irrational and very weird, negative feeling.

I immediately opened wide the front door and went about the house opening all the windows. When I walked toward one of the bedroom windows, I noticed there was a person's shadowy outline on the curtain. I took hold of the window's frame and pulled the shear curtains aside, and the figure was gone. I opened the window and looked all around the small yard, but he was gone. Strangely, I never did actually see him even after searching the backyard and checking the door locks on the gates. He just—*poof*—disappeared!

I was concerned that perhaps this might have been a burglary in progress I had unknowingly stopped, so I cautiously went back into the house and reluctantly investigated every corner and room. That's when I noticed the pictures—crayon marks on the walls in one of the bedrooms. I did not expect to see them. It was as if a child had chosen a small section of the wall, a six-by-four area to draw a series of pictures. There were about eight of these faint pictures about four feet from the floor. As far as subject matter, they were what a child would draw—clouds, houses, animals, and the like. I didn't pay them any further attention and chose that bedroom to begin the cleaning.

I began by removing the carpet at one of the room's corners. As I was cutting it into sections before carrying them out to the front yard, I pulled up a three-by-three section of carpet by the wall where the child's drawings were.

Suddenly, I was hit on the back of my head with a flying roll of toilet paper! I dropped what I was doing and spotted the roll of paper rolling along the floor until it stopped against the wall. I didn't hear footsteps or any other sound.

I called out, "Rodney, what are you doing here?" I waited for his voice to answer, and when none came, I jumped up and walked to the living room, calling his name, but he was nowhere. I walked to the front yard and didn't see a car or sign of anyone else on the street. Instantly, my thoughts became so upsetting I didn't want to return inside the house. I was genuinely scared at that point.

I threw my carpet knife inside the living room, closed the front door, locked it, and got into my car and drove back home. You need to keep in mind the time of day was early morning, the sun was out, and people were already busy with their daily activities. Once I arrived home, I called Rodney and described my experience. He said he would return home at his lunch break so I could give him a more detailed explanation.

When he finished hearing my story, he said he would not return to his office and would accompany me to the house. He changed out of his office clothes, and when we got to the house, we entered the front door and were hit with the reeking stench of what resembled old urine. "What's that?" Rodney said. "What died in here?" Because the windows were still open, I surmised that whatever was causing the stench must have come in from the outside. Both of us walked all around the outside of the house and didn't see or smell anything close to what we smelled in the house.

Things were getting stranger and stranger. Rodney was first to speak about the possibility that maybe the house was haunted. I didn't want to even speak the words, but when he said that, I looked at him and said, "Yeah, well, what could have hit me with that paper roll, and how about that figure I saw outside the window?"

We simply could not explain why these odd and ghostly things were happening. I felt very reluctant to go back inside the house. As we were standing on the driveway discussing the predicament, Rodney turned to face the small kitchen window above the sink, raised his arm to point, and said, "Who's that?" I turned and spotted, just as it was disappearing, the same figure of the man I had seen earlier from inside the kitchen now looking out!

We both ran to the sidewalk and didn't need any further evidence to convince us that what we had both seen was a ghost. The house was as haunted as any house could be, and so we decided to put it back on the market.

We swore not to tell anyone of our experience, but we couldn't keep such a story to ourselves. That same Saturday, we had a preplanned dinner party with two other male couples, and we described to them our house and what we had seen. The response from our friends was predictable; they didn't believe us and had a good laugh at our expense. Rodney and I looked at each other, and without saying a word, we decided to go along with the fun and act as if we had just been caught spinning a long tale.

After the evening's get-together was over, we knew that they did not believe our personal story, so why would anyone else? So in an attempt to save ourselves any problems, we've not disclosed this to anyone else until my interview with you today.

We sold the house and have not had any further contact with the new owners after signing the closing papers. Personally, I don't venture out to that area of town if I can help it and definitely not to the street where the house stands. I'm not quite sure why we experienced the ghost at the house, what it wanted, or why it was hanging out at the property, but that's for someone else to discover. Rodney and I don't want to mess around with the spiritual. We believe it's best to let God handle those matters.

Blanca Fuller's Story

Cortez, CO

Blanca described her story to me at her home. We were sitting in her living room as her partner, Rebecca, listened in. After Blanca told me her story, Rebecca stated, "I think it would be important to tell him about the arrowheads and the pottery shards you collected. I think that might have had something to do with the man you saw."

I turned to Blanca and asked her about this. Blanca said, "Well, yeah, we found an area where there were several ancient fire pits. We knew these were fire pits because of the obvious black charcoal marks on the ground. All around there were pottery shards and arrowheads that my brothers and I gathered and placed in our pockets. I only kept one. I'll show it to you when we're done with the interview."

Blanca's story will give some readers cause to leave ancient artifacts alone. If you happen to be hiking in the wilderness and come across something in the order of pottery shards or other evidence of ancient human workmanship, it would be best to leave it where you found it. That is unless you don't mind the possibility of having the person who made it many centuries ago pay a little "friendly visit" to your home.

I've lived in Cortez all my life. I've only discussed my experiences with just two close friends and my immediate family. My strange experience took place within the national forest. I'll tell you what happened to me, but a few of the specific details I'll keep to myself. I have my reasons for doing this. Two of my brothers were also with me when we encountered the spirits. Of course, they've told their wives, and I've informed my partner, Rebecca. I'm not aware of anyone else knowing our story.

When I reached the age of 18, my two older brothers decided to surprise me by giving me a memorable birthday. They wanted to take me on a hike into the mountains and camp in the nearby canyons to the south of town. They both knew how much I loved the wilderness, so I was ecstatic. I had gone into the mountains before with my father as a teenager, but since his death two years before, I had longed for another opportunity to retrace our shared experience. My brothers both knew how much I would appreciate the opportunity, so when they told me what my birthday present was, I hugged each one and without hesitation said, "When do we leave?"

The following week, we gathered all the necessary equipment and set out on an early Friday morning for a full weekend of camping.

At the time, my mother drove the three of us several miles into the mountains. We entered the national forest, and eventually, she dropped us off at the beginning of an unpaved county road. We knew the direction we would be traveling and what the terrain would be like, so we were well prepared.

After walking for several hours, we came upon some landmarks that years before my father and I had made along the trail. For instance, we had gathered a few rocks and made a small pile to one side, indicating that the trail we were on was the correct one. My brothers and I hiked for a few more hours until we decided to take a lunch break. The weather could not have been better: blue skies and billowy white clouds. I was in heaven.

After lunch, we continued on our way up and around a large mesa. At home, we had decided to reach the top of this natural monument before nightfall and make camp for the night. We were making good progress until my brother Eric slipped and fell. His water bottle and glasses went flying. Because of the weight of his backpack, his balance was off center, and that caused him to have a pretty hard fall, but aside from scraping the side of his face on the ground, he was not hurt. He was just a bit bloody, but all in all still intact.

We reached the summit at around 6:00 p.m. that evening and located a good spot to make camp. Our mother had made us several burritos that she tightly wrapped in aluminum foil, so we had plenty to eat that night. We did manage to get a good fire going and cleared away some brush and rocks in order to have a comfortable area to lay our sleeping bags.

As I cleared my sleeping area of stones and twigs, I discovered what appeared to be a broken pot! At closer inspection, I picked up two, then three pottery shards and joined them together like a puzzle. Soon I had the makings of a small, half-formed Anasazi pot. I gathered all the shards in my pocket and thought about, once at my home, the fun I'd have gluing the shards together. My brothers were as excited as I was with my find.

As night approached, the darkness was both beautiful and somewhat spooky. The night sky was filled with stars, and we spotted several shooting stars among all the constellations visible. Before our fire died out, Eric placed a few more sticks on the glowing embers, and a rebirth of flames soon started up. I was glad to be there on that mountain and glad to have my two brothers, whom I loved, with me.

Soon our conversation turned to talking about my girlfriend, Rebecca, who I had recently started dating and was definitely falling in love with. My brothers both knew I was attracted to women at an early age and reminded me of the time when I chose to play cowboy with them. I wanted to be Roy Rogers and hated, simply hated being told to play the role of Dale Evans! We laughed and laughed. I loved my brothers, and I remember getting a little teary-eyed by telling them so that night. I guess I even cried a little. Thinking back, it must have been the isolation of being in the open and in the wilderness, which encourages honesty and the expression of human emotions. At least, for me it did that night. And I'm glad for it.

Anyway, a moment after that conversation, something, a movement in the nearby bushes, caught all of our attention. We turned in the direction of the noise and spotted the dark form of a mountain lion. We froze and didn't take our eyes off it. I'd seen lions before, usually quite a distance away, but never one so brazen as to come just about 20 feet from me. We had no time to react, but I do remember saying, "Stay still. Let's see what it does."

The lion took a couple of steps and then turned its head in our direction. Its eyes reflected brightly in the campfire, and I was about to reach for a nearby stone to pitch at it, but when I moved my arm, it must have noticed and quickly turned and ran off into the darkness. Wow, we were all startled by this. Eric quickly got out of his sleeping bag, gathered a handful of rocks, and with all the force he could muster, pitched each one at the direction of the cat.

My other brother and I also did the same and loudly tapped a few large pieces of firewood together for good measure. With all of us causing so much noise, I doubted that any animal within a mile would have chosen to come close to our camp after that. When I think back, that was a pretty brazen animal. It was also pretty large—the largest mountain lion I'd ever seen.

So you might imagine how difficult it was for us to sleep that night. Any small noise, coyote howl or owl hoot, would cause one of us to sit upright and say, "Did you hear that?" Luckily, the moon was semifull, so that offered us the comfort of having a bit more light. Everything around us seemed to glow a silvery blue. Eventually, we did get to sleep. But several hours later, before sunrise, something woke me.

I was awakened by the sound of cracking twigs. I opened my eyes, and standing directly above me, bent over, was the figure of a man! I was so scared, I tried to yell to my brothers, but I could not make a sound. I remember the man's hair was cut right below his ears in a straight line, and his eyes were the deepest and darkest black I'd ever seen. His features were definitely those of an American Indian. Although he was standing right next to me, I don't remember if he was wearing any clothes. All I remember seeing was the portion of his body above his waist; everything else below was a foggy blur.

He stood there, more or less, just checking me out, and he didn't make a sound. Because I was so startled and scared, I couldn't make a move. But I did manage to get a few words out. I softly said, "Who are you?" That was the extent of my conversation because he bent his body back and turned away from me. Without hesitation, I thought the pottery shards had something to do with this spirit. I reached into my pocket and threw all of them at him. No sooner had I flung them at him, he disappeared.

I thought to myself, *I've just seen a ghost, an Indian ghost!* I sat up and glanced over at my brothers, both of whom were in their sleeping bags with their eyes wide open. I asked them, "Did you see that?"

Jim said, "Yeah, yeah. What the hell was that? We've been watching him for a few minutes before he walked over to you."

Eric said, "I saw him first and woke up Jim. That was some strange shit!"

The sun was beginning to turn the dark sky a light blue, and morning would soon be coming. The three of us seemed to be, on some level, in shock. We lay deep inside our sleeping bags and shared our thoughts with each other.

"Was this an Indian from long ago, or just a guy who died recently?" Jim said.

I told them, "I think it was a ghost from a thousand years ago because look how he had that strange haircut. And his eyes, I'll never forget the look of his eyes. They were so dark and ancient."

Soon we fell back to sleep, and around an hour or two later, one by one, we woke up. After making breakfast, it took us no discussion at all to arrive at the conclusion we were not going to spend another night on that mesa. We rolled up our bags, packed everything up, and began our long descent back to the main road.

Eventually, we did come across someone who was driving along the road we were walking. In fact, it was my brother Jim's friend who was taking pictures for a photography class project. He asked us about our hike. We all looked at each other, and instinctively knowing better than to share any information about our experience, we simply told him how wonderful and beautiful everything was. He didn't ask any more questions other than discuss generalities as he gave us a ride back to our home.

So there you have it. That's what took place up on that mesa several years ago. It's interesting to know that all three of us witnessed the spirit. If it would have only appeared to me or one of my brothers, there might have been some doubt, but it appeared to the three of us at once. Pretty difficult to explain away, don't you think?

As I said in the beginning, only a few people know about what took place. We decided to keep it, more or less, a secret among ourselves. Now, of course with this book, a lot more people are going to know about our experience, but I hope some of the readers are not going to go into the hills looking for ghosts. That just wouldn't be the right thing to do in my mind. I believe the ancient ones need their privacy; they want to be left alone. I hope people understand that.

Trent V. Ostenburgs's Story

Pueblo, CO

I was informed of Trent's story by way of an interview I conducted in the city of Pueblo. After interviewing Steven Kakemoto for his personal story, he mentioned a friend of his who had gone through quite a rough time with a relationship and might be willing to discuss his ghost experience with me.

Steven asked if he might make a quick phone call and find out if his friend Trent might be interested in speaking with me. After explaining to Trent the purpose of my book and possible visit, Steven handed me the phone, and Trent and I scheduled a date for his interview.

What you are about to read is Trent's personal story of tragedy and loss. His story is touching and, in the end, an eye-opening example of a spirit's longing and need to make sense of a desperate situation. Never is such severe and extreme means to an end a real solution. My hope is that such psychologically torn individuals seek help before reaching the ultimate irrational choice from where there is no turning back. Ever.

First off, I won't go into too much detail about where my experience took place in town because I don't want the people who have remained on the property to relive the same tragic scenario I did. Having had a suicide in your family is bad enough; having to explain it over and over is terrible. If you can just imagine what a negative impact it would have on you to have someone commit suicide in your place of business, then you'd understand my reluctance to say more than I have to.

I'm a delivery truck driver for a major food supplier. My company supplies primarily restaurants with all their fresh and frozen foods. If you've ever eaten at any restaurants in Denver, well, you've most likely eaten food my company has delivered to that restaurant.

I guess I should begin by stating I'm also not ashamed to say I am a gay man. My story is about the very discreet relationship I had with the owner of a local restaurant where my experience took place. Today, I still live in Denver, and even though my experience took place several years ago and the years have gone by, my heart and spirit are still heavy from the experience.

Three years after I began my job, I got a new account delivering supplies to Jerry, the owner of a well-established restaurant. Jerry and I hit it off immediately. Jerry was a divorced man and, as such, had a young child of whom he had joint custody and visiting rights. Jerry loved his child and did not want to take the risk of jeopardizing their relationship, so we had to keep our romantic relationship to ourselves. We got together on many occasions, and when holidays came about, we even went for short vacations together. Of course, he spent the major holidays like Christmas and Thanksgiving with his boy.

All in all, we had a close but obviously awkward relationship. I loved him deeply, as he did me. But as time went on, our relationship became inconvenient for me. Not being able to be fully satisfied as a loving couple, having to keep our lives together a secret was psychologically a heavy burden and eventually took an emotional toll on me.

I finally decided to end what we had begun years before, and although we would keep our special friendship, it would not be much more than a friendship. I decided sex would not play a further role in our relationship on any level.

Less than a year later, I met a terrific man in Denver, and we began to see each other more and more until one day he moved in with me. I wanted to introduce Jerry to him with the hope we could all be friendly toward each other, but Jerry would have none of this. Jerry's emotional hurt became apparently clear to me one night when he and I got together after dinner, and he expressed how much he still loved me. I made it clear I was not able to reciprocate this and that I was now involved and deeply in love with another man and that was that. Jerry sadly relented, and although we both still kept in communication with each other from time to time, things were never really the same between us.

Seven years ago, as I was driving my truck one early morning in January, I made my usual stop at Jerry's locally owned restaurant. It was an early winter morning, and aside from the bitter cold, it was not an unusual morning for me. I had already made four delivery stops previous to this one.

As is usual in my work, I drove my truck to the rear of the business, where the restaurant's delivery door is located. I didn't notice anything unusual at first. I parked the truck to the side of the door, and with the purchase order forms in my hand, I got out of the truck and approached the back door. Walking through the cold and slushy snow, eager to press the doorbell, I knew Jerry would be inside getting things ready for the day's workload. This was just an ordinary delivery for me, and anyway, given all we had gone through, we were both still on speaking terms with each other. I always looked forward to seeing and talking with Jerry.

As I approached the rear door, I noticed the screen door was closed, but the inner solid door had been left wide open despite the cold weather. I opened the screen door and called out, "Hey, Jerry. It's Trent. You around?" Not hearing a response, I opened the screen door and walked inside.

The kitchen light was on, but no one was around. I called out again, "Hey, Jerry. Where are you? It's Trent."

Then I heard Jerry's voice call to me, "Over in the dining room!" I walked to the darkened dining room and found Jerry standing with his back to me, staring out the side window that looked into a side yard. "It sure is cold out there, isn't it?" Jerry said.

I responded, "Yeah, but life goes on in the food business. Hey, Jerry, did you know your back door is wide open?"

Without turning to look at me, he said, "Yeah, that's all right. I'm expecting a few more people to come running in any minute now, so just leave the cases and the purchase order in the kitchen. I'll get you a check by the end of the week."

Perplexed by Jerry's unusual behavior, I walked away, returned to my truck, unloaded the boxes, and then left the paperwork in the kitchen. At most, it took me all of about ten minutes. But something in Jerry's strange demeanor puzzled me and made me concerned, so I decided not to simply leave but instead to approach Jerry and ask him if everything was all right. I walked back to the dining room after I'd finish my delivery, but he was gone. I called out his name, but he did not answer. Immediately, I assumed he had gone out the front door or maybe to the bathroom. Pressed for time, I decided to get back into my truck and drive to my next appointment.

Less than one hour later, I received a call on my truck's radio. My dispatcher asked me where I was, and after responding to her, she informed me I was to return to the company warehouse as soon as I was able. I was to suspend all further deliveries and head back immediately. After I asked if everything was all right, the dispatcher said, "Well, you just need to get back here quick—that's all I'm supposed to tell you."

When I arrived at the warehouse, I was ushered into my supervisor's office, where one of two police officers asked me to take a seat. Bewildered by everything, I asked, "What's going on?" One of the officers asked me if I had been to Jerry's restaurant and if I knew anything about Jerry's death! The officer also asked me what I knew about a letter he handed to me. I immediately recognized Jerry's handwriting.

The letter read:

> Trent,
>
> I'm so sorry for being such a burden on you and for causing you so much trouble. I know my life has had its ups and downs, and even though we have shared so much, I know I've caused you much disappointment. I hope you can forgive me for that. My death will finally free you from this. It's all I've got to give you. I want you to take the best care of yourself and your new partner. Please forgive me and know that I will always love you.
>
> Signed,
>
> Jerry

I was an emotional mess. I wept and wept. It wasn't until a few seconds later that I was able to comprehend that Jerry had committed suicide. The officer informed me that Jerry's body had been found seated against a wall on a stack of wooden pallets in the yard to the side of his restaurant. He had wrapped a large bath towel around a handgun to silence the blast and then shot himself in the head.

In the weeks that followed, the forensic examiner determined Jerry killed himself at about 10:00 p.m. the night before. This was shocking news to hear because I had not only seen and spoken to Jerry the following morning, I had watched him standing at the window, gazing at something in the side yard. I did in fact inform the officers of what I had seen, but none of it was of any importance to them or the case. It was just another case of suicide to them.

So that was my experience with the spirit of my beloved Jerry. Make of this story what you will, but I know I witnessed his spirit, and I'll never, ever forget his passing.

Garden of the Gods

Located west of Interstate 25 and north of State Highway 24, this majestic area with its rugged windswept formations must be visited to be truly appreciated. Containing a naturally dramatic landscape of towering, eroded Redstone formations, some over 300 million years old, Garden of the Gods is without doubt extraordinary and awe inspiring.

Initially, Charles Perkins, who was the president of the Chicago, Burlington & Quincy Railroad, purchased the land in 1879. Following Charles's death in 1907, the Perkins family gifted the land to the city of Colorado Springs with specific stipulation that it is used as a free city park and that it be named Garden of the Gods. Today, entrance to this large 1,340-acre city park, now a registered natural landmark, is free of charge.

Before entering the park, be sure to spend time at the park's Garden of the Gods Visitor and Nature Center. The center provides visitors with a multimedia presentation, free maps, lectures, educational exhibits, three gift shops, a restaurant, and summer bus tours. A portion of the proceeds is directly applied toward the park's preservation. Also, the privately owned Garden of the Gods Trading Post, Colorado's oldest and largest, is located nearby.

David Zambrano's Story

Manitou Springs, CO

My interview with David was conducted at a local and popular Manitou Springs café on Dale Street. David's time was short, but I did manage to gather enough information that clearly described both his and his wife's paranormal experience.

Although not at first appearing to be a man of much emotional display, twice during the course of this interview, David's obvious affection for his friend did become apparent, at which time I had to stop my questioning.

Throughout the many interviews I've conducted for my research and books, there are some that I leave with mixed emotions. This particular one left such a mental image of genuine love and release between friends that even to this day I find it difficult to erase.

I was born in the small town of Sterling, Colorado. My wife, Sherrie, and I moved to Montrose 15 years ago. Not having children, Sherrie and I had the financial ability to travel and to do just about anything we wished. We also lived for a short time on what could be termed a hippie commune in Northern California. Soon after, we made a major move across the Atlantic and settled in London's central district.

In London, the two of us began a custom clothes business, something resembling a hippie line of tie-dyed bedspreads, shirts, and other linens. Our shop was located on Tottenham Court Road, at the time a very hip area with trendy shops. That turned out to be another short-lived venture for many reasons I'll not elaborate on.

We worked this business until we reached our physical limits. Being very successful, within four years, we were totally and mentally exhausted. We sold the business and decided to return to the United States, this time settling on the southern coast of California's Venice community.

Within the year, we restarted our tie-dye business, only this time, we enlarged our products to include a greater variety of T-shirts. That's when we hit the big money and focused all our attention on producing T-shirts exclusively. We sold this business within two years, and with our nest egg securely in the bank, we returned to Colorado and settled in Montrose.

During the second time we lived in California, we became acquainted with a wonderful woman named Cassandra. Cassandra was not your typical 55-year-old woman. In fact, Cassandra was a transgendered individual. By this, I mean Cassandra used to be a male until she had a total sex-change operation. Cassandra was very educated and spoke several languages, including English, Portuguese, German, Italian, Spanish, and French. She soon became one of Sherrie's best and dearest friends. I always enjoyed Cassandra's company because of her quick wit and worldly personality. The three of us made future plans to travel together and to eventually settle in Montrose.

As the moving day grew closer, Sherrie and I noticed that Cassandra was giving us mixed messages about the upcoming move. Eventually, Cassandra verbalized her true thoughts to us. She feared moving to a somewhat conservative state as Colorado would not provide her with the stimulating atmosphere she was accustomed to, and she also feared a little for her safety.

Sherrie and I assured her we knew Montrose was filled with positive, open, and caring people, but there were no guarantees things would be better for her in Colorado than in California.

Cassandra was a very beautiful woman, but the obvious distractions to her female beauty were her height of six feet three inches and her large hands. I must admit, each time Cassandra got dressed to go out in public, she was stunning. As Sherrie put it, "I wish I had the hips and legs of that woman. I'd look like royalty in heels!"

Eventually, Cassandra decided it would be best for her to stay put in Venice. Sherrie and I moved to Montrose, but we kept in touch with our good friend Cassandra throughout the following years.

Then three years after our move, we received a midday call from a mutual friend of ours. Cassandra had had a terrible allergic reaction to takeout food that she'd eaten for dinner. Unknown to Cassandra, she had eaten a Chinese dish that was prepared in a shrimp sauce. Cassandra was allergic to both shrimp and most seafood. As she lay on her couch, her allergic reaction became so severe that her esophagus constricted; she passed out and suffocated to death, alone in her apartment. Two afternoons later, a visiting friend contacted us by phone; he'd discovered her lifeless body in her apartment.

Sherrie and I were devastated by the terrible news. We suffered a deep and heartfelt depression. Even at this date, we find it difficult to speak her name without shedding a tear. She was one of a kind and had such a huge heart and a great love of life. We both loved her so much. So with this background, I'll tell you my ghost story.

Immediately after Cassandra's memorial and following her preplanned wishes to be cremated and have her ashes distributed to her many friends, Sherrie had the idea that spreading Cassandra's remains among the beautiful boulders and rock formations within the Garden of the Gods would be a wonderful and beautiful manner of honoring her. I agreed with this, so one Sunday in the early afternoon, carrying our small portion of Cassandra's ashes, we drove to the park and hiked about a mile before finding just the right spot to place her remains.

We located an area at the base of a very large, red stone formation. There, Sherrie and I lit a candle and burned sage. We chanted a few Reiki chants and Christian prayers before placing Cassandra's ashes on a small, flat stone. It was a very personal and touching tribute to our friend.

A few seconds after ending the small ceremony, we remained quiet in meditation. Suddenly, we were startled by the sound of a family of quail passing about ten feet in front of where we sat. Without moving, we watched as they walked about and then quickly scampered away into the brush. Sherrie and I glanced at each other, and smiles returned to our faces. I spoke to Sherrie, telling her this had to be a sign from Cassandra. As Sherrie was about to respond, there was a movement to our left. We both turned our heads, and there, at the edge of the area where we had placed Cassandra's ashes, a small whirlwind was forming.

The small, whirling little mass of wind grew bigger and bigger. Soon, it moved over to where the ashes of our friend were located and grew into a very elongated and tall wind tube! Right after the moment, the tube of wind lifted itself off the ground, up, up, and disappeared into the atmosphere high above, taking Cassandra's ashes up into the sky!

We both felt such an emotion of gratitude and joy. We were ecstatic with delight. Our tears simply poured out as we wept like children. We kept saying, "Good-bye, Cassandra. We love you, we love you!" Even now, I find it difficult to not be moved by the memory of that day. We knew our friend had given us a sign, and we were thankful and knew we had been very blessed to experience it all.

If anyone ever has any doubt about the existence of the soul or any doubt about the strength of love, they need to know that I have personally witnessed love's divine force. Both Sherrie and I know without a doubt love conquers death; it conquers death without thinking twice. We love you, Cassandra!

Josh Kahn's Story

Mancos, CO

I conducted the interview with Josh in the living room of his home. Josh's right leg was in a cast due to an accidental fall two weeks prior to my visit. Given the great weather, we soon decided the best area of his home in which to continue the interview would be in his backyard, where a nice set of patio chairs and a relaxing couch were located. I sat on one of the chairs while Josh lay on the couch, resting his leg on two pillows.

Josh presented me with his unusually intriguing personal story of love, loss, and eventual state of calm. As Josh stated, "I found a level of mental satisfaction where the monster of the unknown is vanquished and where my world was remade into one where I can now recognize the beauty that lies beyond death."

Josh's story can offer us all a great deal more than an ordinary ghost story. His story, as you will read, is thought provoking and one that will dwell in your heart. To communicate with those who have passed on to the afterlife can be a bit psychologically inhibiting, but in Josh's case, the experience was comforting.

I've lived in Mancos since November of 1989, having moved here together with my two-year-old cat, Buddy, from Seattle, Washington. Originally, I was going to relocate to Durango, but I was surprisingly unaware of Durango's expensive real estate market, and so I decided to choose the town of Mancos—I have not regretted it. I bought a two-bedroom house on the north side of town, which I still live in today.

I decided to move from the Seattle area after two people who were very close to me died of AIDS. The first was a friend, Edward, whom I knew from high school. At first, he and I were best friends, and after dating for a few months, he moved into my house, and we became partners. We lived together for six years. I was aware beforehand that he was infected with the HIV virus. He disclosed this to me when we began our early stage of romance, but we were in love, and AIDS was not going to prevent us from enjoying a full and loving relationship as long as we were careful and took the necessary precautions.

Sadly, I went through the whole ordeal of seeing Edward slowly succumb to the disease until he eventually and peacefully died. I was devastated beyond words. During this stressful time, I had a true friend who was my support and shoulder to lean on. Her name was Jennifer, a woman who also had the HIV virus. I met her one afternoon at a support meeting for partners and friends of persons living with the disease. As I said, Jennifer had the disease and suffered with it for several years before she herself succumbed from its complications and died in 1989.

Given all my recent past history of sadness and memories, I decided to leave Seattle for my own peace of mind and relocate to the southwest. I had visited the state of Colorado years ago and believed I would return as a permanent resident one day. This became a reality for me in the spring of 1989.

My story takes place in September of 1993. I had been living in Mancos for a few years when one day I took a drive to Durango, intending to spend most of the day shopping and have a meal at a favorite restaurant. I did the typical visit to Walmart and eventually purchased a vacuum cleaner. While strolling up and down the aisles, I noticed there was an older gentleman who I guessed to be about the age of 65 or so, who was obviously following me. My own age at the time was 51. In my estimation, he was not a bad-looking man, and given my need for companionship and loneliness, I eventually found the courage to approach and speak to him.

He told me that his name was Michael Elbaum. *A Jew like myself,* I thought. *If this works out between us, it would be wonderful to share our cultural similarities.* As you can tell by my thoughts and eagerness, I was already making plans for our future together. And all this after a simple chance meeting in Walmart of all places.

Michael turned out to be a very friendly and intellectually stimulating man. After talking briefly, he asked me if I wished to continue our conversation over coffee. I eagerly agreed, and we drove in separate cars to a Denny's restaurant.

We sat in the nonsmoking area located at the rear of the restaurant. Michael told me a little about himself. He was staying with fellow seminarians in Durango but was visiting from the state of Delaware and was Jewish by birth but raised Catholic. In fact, as it turned out, he was a missionary brother—not a priest—in a religious order of priests and nuns who devoted themselves to the service of the poor or, as he explained, pastoral work, particularly in the cities. Their work had an emphasis on the study of theology as well. He was not in the least attracted to me romantically, but instead wanted to inform me of something that was causing him to follow me around the aisles. I was thinking to myself, *What have I gotten myself into? This guy is not at all what I expected him to be and is now appearing to be some type of oddball.*

I asked him, "I'm not sure what you're getting at. Are you going to explain to me what's going on?"

Michael answered, "I hope you don't think I'm crazy, but because of what I have experienced in my work and studies, I've become sensitive to the spiritual world and have developed the ability to see things. In your case, I see a man who is very, very much devoted to you. His image or spirit stands close to you, and I can tell by his light he shared a close relationship with you. He's actually with you now, here as I am speaking to you. Before you ask me where he is, I'll tell you he is standing to your left and is extending his left arm, and in his open hand, he is holding two rings. I'm assuming he was your partner. Am I wrong?"

As you might imagine, I was totally amazed and somewhat taken aback by Michael's insight and, without thinking, just answered, "No, you're not wrong. His name is Edward, and we were indeed partners. He died after a long illness." Turning my head and taking a quick glance to my left, hoping to see an image or something, I returned my focus to Michael and asked, "How do you know this? I mean, are you a medium or what?"

Michael answered, "No, I'm not a medium, but I am able to see spirits, and before I go any further, he's now gesturing to me to tell you not to worry about him, and he's holding up a record album. I don't know what this means, but it's an older album, and on the cover is a picture of Donovan. He's singing a song you might remember. He's singing the song 'Jennifer Juniper.' Does this mean anything to you?"

I quickly got the connection between the song title and my friend Jennifer, who had passed away. I was so amazed at Michael's description and, at the same time, very uncomfortable with what he was telling me. I took a deep breath and said to him, "I don't know what you're up to, but with all due respect, I think you're setting me up for something. Who told you about me?" Michael apologized for upsetting me, and before he finished his explanation, I interrupted and said, "I can't believe what is happening. I'm so sorry for reacting like I just did!" After we spoke a bit more, I got up off my chair, gave Michael my phone number, and thanked him. I left the restaurant, got in my car, and then drove off.

I drove back to Mancos, crying and shaking most of the way. After arriving home and feeding my cat, I took off my shoes and then sat down in my living room and turned on the television, hoping to ease my thoughts. I watched only a few minutes of television before my emotions again surfaced, and I pressed the mute button. I began to cry, and after just a few seconds, I heard a loud *crack*! I was startled by the sound and immediately stopped weeping. Then, as I sat staring toward the door, I noticed a movement directly above. A small white feather came floating down from the ceiling fan, and I watched as it landed on top of my left shoe.

I was amazed. It did not take me long to realize what this meant. I felt Edward was giving me a sign and, with it, trying to show how he was still with me. As soon as I realized this, an unexplainable peace came over me. I was so happy and comforted by this. I said, "Thank you, Edward. I'll love you always."

I took the feather and placed it in front of Edward's picture that I had placed on a table in the second bedroom. I closed the bedroom door and returned to the living room, thinking about all that had taken place that day. I felt totally blessed that Michael and I had connected on a spiritual level. We've visited with each other only once, when I traveled to his home in Delaware, but we've kept in contact by phone ever since. I now know Edward steered our ongoing friendship together.

Royal Gorge

Fremont County is fortunate to have within its boundaries one of the most visited and scenically beautiful historical landmarks—the Royal Gorge Bridge and Park. Spanning the gorge is a well-known and frequently photographed landmark—the world's highest suspension bridge. The bridge, built in 1929, spans the gorge, a chasm 955 feet deep! Given its height and the unimaginable human labor involved in building this awe-inspiring bridge, it's amazing not one single loss of life occurred during the construction.

Directly below the bridge flows the historic Arkansas River. Its origin is in Colorado's Rocky Mountains. If you were to ride upon the surface of the river, beginning at its origin and then pass through the gorge on its 315-mile journey within the state, you would experience some of the most spectacular landscape ever to be seen—not to mention the Class V whitewater rapids.

Another great adventure is to get on board the Denver and Rio Grande Western Railroad and take the 24-mile ride named the Royal Gorge Route. This trip has been named one of the most scenic train rides in the world!

Note: The long drive to the gorge could be worthwhile, unless you have a family and funds are tight. The Cañon City government would be wise to reconsider the enactment of its excessive public entrance fees to the park. Furthermore, the tourist trap theme park atmosphere, created by the present, private concessionaire whom the Cañon City government contracted, adds little to the natural beauty and setting of the gorge. All that being said, the gorge remains an extraordinary wonder to behold.

Kristine Sargent's Story

Cañon City, CO

I met Kristine at a Cañon City Mexican restaurant, where the interview took place. Over a plate of tacos, I asked about her experiences at the park, and she responded by giving me an unusually personal description of meeting up with a ghost in broad daylight.

Kristine, as she explained, never had much of an interest in the subject of ghosts, but after her experience, she has become quite knowledgeable. She has attended meetings of paranormal investigators and even was an attendee at a séance or two.

Today, Kristine lives in Cañon City with her life partner, Chelsea, and works for the city's department of labor. Kristine said, "I've got a few other ghost stories I think you'd like to hear, but they have to do with the state of Oklahoma."

I answered, "When I write my book of Oklahoma, I'll look you up, Kristine."

I presently live in Cañon City and worked for the Royal Gorge Park in the summers of 1994 and 1995. My job at the park was to operate the incline railway car, which would take visitors down the natural gulch in the gorge to a total depth of 1,550 feet. It's a 100 percent grade drop at a 45-degree angle, so it's quite a ride down to the Arkansas River. It is considered to be the world's steepest incline railway.

I enjoyed my work and especially liked conversing with the tourists, who would visit from all over the world. I liked answering their questions and hearing their loud cries of excitement as they'd start the descent into the gorge. It's a very scary ride for someone who has never experienced anything like it. I recommend that everyone take the trip at least once in their lives. It's great!

When I spent the first summer at the gorge, I recall the day when I was having lunch with a fellow worker named Roger. Roger and I were discussing different things associated with the building of the bridge that spans the gorge, and for some reason, we started talking about suicides and other deaths that had occurred at the park. Surprisingly, there were not many that he was aware of, but for obvious reasons, if there were any, the park administrators would most likely want to keep these statistics quiet.

Anyway, as we were talking, another employee interrupted and said, "How about the spirits in the park? Have you heard the stories about the spirits?"

I answered, "No, I haven't."

Roger added, "Oh yeah. I've been told there are spirits of several people who wander about the area. One popular story is about a guy who hangs out at the bridge, and there's another one about another guy who's been seen at the bottom of the gorge. I've never seen anything like that, but maybe ghosts aren't attracted to me."

I was curious about the subject of ghosts at the park, but that's all the information I was told until a few nights later when I spent the night with my girlfriend, Chelsea.

Chelsea was renting a cabin in a nearby campground, and from time to time, we used to spend a few nights together. We met at the park, and our friendship soon developed into a romantic relationship. It was also convenient for me to stay over with her because it saved me from making the long return drive alone at night to Cañon City.

Chelsea had worked for the park twice before, so she was familiar with several of the employees. One afternoon, I asked her if she had heard talk among the staff about anything regarding ghosts in the park. "Oh yeah. There are a few that I know of. But why do you ask?" she said.

"Oh, just curious, that's all," I responded.

Then Chelsea began to tell me about a black dog that employees believe is an animal spirit who has appeared for years at the park and who won't allow anyone to approach him. She said, "He always makes his appearance at night. Sometimes he'll just follow a person for miles during a hike and then—he's gone! But like I said, he's been spotted around here for many years. I don't know if that could be considered a ghost, but he sure does act like one."

Another story Chelsea shared with me was about the white figure of a woman who is seen walking—or better yet, floating—against the gorge walls. Chelsea said, "She'll appear for just a few minutes some nights. She moves a short distance and seems to be in the act of walking, but she seems to float against the granite walls of the canyon! Of course, this is impossible for any living person to do, but being a ghost, she has no problem in maneuvering this way. She does not appear very often, but she is seen from time to time as a small figure at the west wall of the gorge."

I asked Chelsea, "Have you ever seen her?"

She responded, "I saw what I thought appeared to be her ghost one night. I was walking alone on one of the trails at the opposite side of the gorge. This was before anyone informed me of her, so I didn't know what that white, little moving object was at the opposite wall way over to the other side of the gorge. She looked like a lit match slowly bouncing around the walls. But that's all I've seen of her since I began working at the park. I've often heard footsteps along some of the trails I have been hiking on. I was sure someone was behind me following me, but when I'd turn around, there would be no one there. Now that's kind of weird and creepy. But other than that, that's about all I've seen and heard as far as ghosts are concerned."

I didn't mention to Chelsea or anyone else anything more about ghosts for a long time. But one day, my curiosity began to change. I personally had what I believed was a ghost experience that took place not at night but late in the day.

I was assisting Buddy, one of the park staff, by helping him move some boxes from one office to another. I needed to use the bathroom and told Buddy I'd be right back. On my way, I walked past one small building. As I turned the corner, I spotted an older man several yards away, who was alone and leaning against one of the buildings. Strangely, I didn't think of asking him if he needed anything, but I should have because the park was closed for the day. Something within me at that moment compelled me to keep on walking and to avoid this guy.

He was not threatening in his appearance, but he did have an overall appearance of darkness. Again, it's difficult to explain, but he gave me the impression that I was looking at a shadow. I would not usually react so flippantly as to disregard a stranger, even one with such a weird-looking appearance, but something came over me that I believe was protecting me by having me keep a distance from this guy. It's weird, but even I can't understand it myself.

Avoiding this guy, I walked past him and entered the bathroom and went into a stall. I thought a bit more about him and my reaction. Then it came to me; I must have been subconsciously afraid to confront him, so I chose to avoid a possibly negative situation. Sort of an intuition. As I was thinking about this, suddenly I heard the sound of footsteps walking around the outside of the bathroom. Without hearing the door open, I heard the faucet turn on. I said, "Is anyone there? I'll be out in just a second." No one answered me. Again, I said, "Is anyone there?" Nothing.

Not wanting to stay another second in the bathroom, I decided to get out of there quickly. But soon after I exited the stall, the bathroom stall door opened wide and then slammed shut with a huge bang! I stood as solid as stone with fear. The faucets were still running, and I shot out of there like a bullet.

As soon as I arrived back at the office, I told my coworker what happened, and surprisingly, he just stood looking at me. I was not crying, but was close to it. I yelled at him, "What's the hell's wrong with you? I'm serious! I just saw a ghost!"

He came over to me and gave me a hug. "I know, I know. Others have also seen him too. Don't let him scare you. He always keeps his distance. He never hurts anyone."

I was so surprised by his response and statement that I said, "You mean, you've known about this ghost, and not one of you guys ever bothered to tell me about him?"

He said, "Yeah, well, the dude hasn't appeared for a long time. The last I heard, he was spotted by a hiker on one of the trails last year." Then Buddy asked, "Was he wearing a uniform?"

I answered, "No, I don't think so. He was just a dark shadow."

"Well," he said, "he usually is seen wearing a military type of uniform, something from the Civil War era or, because of where we are, a uniform from the US Cavalry. He also staggers or walks with a limp. Probably from being shot in the ass by an Indian. Who knows?"

I didn't appreciate Buddy's devil-may-care attitude. I was in no mood for jokes, and I was still shaking. Fortunately for me, Buddy said he would finish moving the boxes and told me I could clock out for the day. I left in a rush, got into my car, and drove to the cabin, where Chelsea was making dinner. I told her about what I had experienced, and she said, "Oh, that's right—the soldier! I haven't heard about him for a while. You mean you actually saw him?"

I said, "Yes, yes, yes, I did, but everyone seems to think it's no big deal!"

Chelsea answered, "Did you really see him? I mean, Kris, did you really see the ghost of the soldier?"

I answered, "Hell yes, I did!"

Well, I spent most of the night describing to Chelsea in great detail all I had experienced, and soon I felt at ease enough to finally put it behind me.

I never again spoke about it to the other coworkers. Even though some asked me, I just gave them a few details, but nothing more. I knew I saw a ghost that day—a real ghost. Since that time, I've read all the magazines and books I could get my hands on that describe ghosts and hauntings. There must be others at the park who have seen one or two of the ghosts.

FLORIDA

Chet Benson's Story

Miami, FL

I've been employed at this facility going on five years this Christmas. Originally, I'm from the state of Montana, and after falling in love with a man from Sarasota, Florida, this is where we both ended up settling down and making a life for ourselves. My first partner of thirteen years, Daniel, was murdered during a hate crime in broad daylight at a supermarket parking lot in Missoula, Montana. His murder was extremely difficult to understand and ultimately accept. Adding to this horrific crime, Daniel was deaf since birth. We met while attending a deaf conference in Seattle. Like Daniel, my older brother was also born deaf, and because of this, my whole family and I are well versed in American Sign Language, or ASL. I knew I had to move away from Montana if I was going to ever attempt to find the necessary courage to move forward with my life.

I graduated with an AMA bachelor's degree in respiratory care seven years ago and am currently licensed to practice respiratory care in Florida. I am registered as a respiratory therapist with the National Board for Respiratory Care. Additionally, I am certified and currently registered with the Board of Registered Polysomnographic Technologists.

My current job involves my performing a variety of tests and studies related to the diagnosis and treatment of sleep-related breathing disorders. The facility has recently hired a new director who has been assigned to head the new sleep study research program. This particular program performs and evaluates the technical aspects of overnight sleep patterns and nocturnal pulse oximetry. Some of my responsibilities are to set up and apply polysomnographic-monitoring devices, ensure patient safety with accurate test results, and provide summary analysis and reports of all studies for physician review.

Because of my skill in sign language, I'm at times called upon to assist deaf and hearing-impaired patients communicate with staff in other areas of the hospital. This being the case, one early morning at around 3:00 a.m., we had a middle-aged African American deaf woman brought into the hospital by ambulance who was being prepped for emergency surgery due to having taken a terrible fall that resulted in internal bleeding. She was found semiconscious by a neighbor in her home's backyard hours after her fall. Her prognosis was not very positive. When I arrived at her side, I could see she was terrified from the pain and in shock. She definitely needed someone who could sign to offer reassurance and to walk her through the emergency room process she was about to experience. I introduced myself in sign language, and the tension in her face turned to relief.

Immediately, I could tell that her whole composure was beginning to change from one of dread to a more tranquil demeanor. Before long, she was sedated and taken into surgery. Before she closed her eyes, I assured her in sign language that all would be well, and I promised her I would be at her side in the recovery room. I held her hand until she fell into controlled unconsciousness.

Sadly, the poor woman never made it out of surgery and died in the operating room. Her death affected me deeply. Having a deaf partner and now this deaf patient die hit an extremely sensitive nerve with me, and I fell emotionally apart.

Looking to recover and compose myself from the tragic event that I had just witnessed, I walked over and entered the brightly lit break room located a few doors from surgery. I was exhausted. I reached for the light switch and turned off most of the overhead lights, leaving only one light on. I planned to sit quietly in the darkened room before heading back to my station.

As I was seated in our small break room, I bent over the table, resting my head on my arms, and fell deep asleep. Suddenly, the loud voice of a coworker shouting at me in the break room doorway woke me up. "Chet, Chet, quick, look!" He was pointing as I sprang up off my chair, turned, and faced the deaf patient who had just expired! My coworker said, "Do you see her, Chet? Tell me you see her too!" Yeah, there she was, clear as life.

I was dumfounded by the woman's apparition. I could see that a thin, blue, glowing light surrounded her and the expression on her face was of peace and calm. Nothing in the least displayed any sense of pain or fear.

Then in one smooth movement, she raised her right hand to her mouth, touched her fingertips to her lips, and extended back her hand toward me, giving me the universal deaf sign of "Thank you." I was so completely unprepared for this and couldn't think of the proper "You're welcome" sign to acknowledge her. Apparently not bothered by my oversight, she smiled, turned, and walked right through the wall behind her and vanished!

I remain confident that we all have opportunities to share our life spirits while we are living and when we transition over to the afterlife dimension.

NEW MEXICO

Owen D. Pettigrew's Story

Santa Fe, NM

I was born and raised in Gatlinburg, Tennessee, and relocated to Santa Fe in the winter of 1989. I attended college at the University of Tennessee at Knoxville, received my undergrad degree, and then transferred to graduate school at the University of New Mexico in Albuquerque for my master's in speech language pathology. Soon after, the NM Speech-Language Pathology, Audiology, and Hearing Aid Dispensing Practices Board licensed me. I waited one year before landing the job at St. Vincent Medical Center, renamed Christus St. Vincent Regional Medical Center.

As of today, it's been 11 years that I've been employed at the hospital where I engage with patients of all ages having various disorders, including Asperger's and autism. My goal is pragmatically instilling language and social communication skills.

My ghost story began when I lived in Tennessee. I was 14 years old at the time, and my family moved into a house that belonged to my aunt Rita. Aunt Rita was never one of my favorite relatives because as a child she once gave me a painfully hard spanking when she caught me throwing clumps of mud at her beehives. Aunt Rita produced her own honey and sold it at farmers' markets.

As I remember back now, I don't blame her much, but those hand swats were unforgettably painful at the time. On Aunt Rita's property was a large, very old two-story barn. For some unknown reason, after my aunt's death, I never felt good being at that barn and never went anywhere near it, and now I'll tell you why.

Aunt Rita died at age 90 and had battled cancer for three years before succumbing to the disease. My mother discovered Aunt Rita's body as it lay on the ground in the barn, she guessed, for about five days. Mother said, "The odor of her body lying there in the high Tennessee humidity is something I'll never forget!"

We moved onto my aunt's property in the spring of 1969, and wherever I walked on that property, I never felt totally comfortable. Strangely, I always felt her presence, even her now invisible eyes watching me. This uncomfortable feeling reached a high point when I began to experience disembodied footsteps at night coming down the short hall right outside my bedroom and into my room. I never saw a ghost or heard a voice, just the sound of footsteps approaching. I never found out what caused the footstep sounds and just accepted them when I heard them.

One strange occurrence people would report to us seemed to happen when we were not physically in the house. People told us when they would call the house, an elderly female voice would pick up the receiver and answer, "Hello." Then silence and nothing else was said again, just the word *hello*.

One time while I was in the living room, the phone rang, and when I lifted the receiver to my ear, I distinctly heard my aunt's voice speaking my name. I couldn't believe what I'd just heard, and the hairs on the back of my neck stood up. I threw the receiver down and shouted, "Don't call me anymore! I don't ever want to talk with you again!" This time, when I put the receiver back up to my ear, all I heard was the busy tone.

As soon as I reached the age to move out of that house, I entered college, and with my two roommates, we rented a house near campus, where I finally felt completely at ease.

As you can see, I have had my share of spiritual experiences as a young boy, but as an adult, I can also describe a significant level of spiritual experiences as well.

In June of 1999, I had been assigned a young 27-year-old man that had a problem speaking after undergoing surgery and radiation treatments on his throat. This young guy, named Thomas, was strikingly handsome, and each time he came into our clinic, the female employees went into a flurry of excitement.

Thomas and I worked well together, and with each of his clinic visits, his speech was progressing at the expected level. I began to look forward to our therapy sessions due to the fact that he and I were both gay men and could relate easily on our mutual orientation. Our association grew into a friendship—nothing romantic, simply a comfortable, friendly relationship. I was already in a committed five-year relationship, and Thomas and his partner had been together for nine years.

Well, one Friday afternoon on my day off, my partner, Armando, and I wandered into a local imported goods store. As we strolled down one aisle, I just happened to look up at the far end of the aisle and spotted Thomas unusually dressed, wearing all white—white shirt, white pants, and white shoes. It was without a doubt Thomas, but something about him wasn't quite right.

As he slowly moved past a large antique blue cabinet, I called out, "Thomas! Hey, wait up!" Overall, he appeared to be preoccupied and not listening to me in the least. As I tugged on Armando's arm to look ahead at Thomas, Thomas seemed to glance over at us and then instantly faded away into thin air. He dissolved into nothing right before both our eyes—he was gone!

I asked Armando if he also just saw Thomas disappear. Armando responded, saying, "What just happened? Are we seeing things?" I quickly maneuvered around a large display table of glass Moroccan lamps and took no more than five seconds to reach the area where we had spotted Thomas. He was not anywhere. We searched all around the medium-sized store but never saw him. We also thought, *Perhaps it wasn't even Thomas at all.*

The experience left us with a very odd feeling of unease. I assured Armando that I would be seeing Thomas on Monday when he came in for his therapy and I'd be sure to ask him about this.

At no time did either Armando or I bring up the issue of Thomas's ghostly disappearance in the store. I imagine that to do so would open up the uncomfortable topic of death, and we were just not ready to discuss this at that time.

Well, early Monday afternoon, I received a phone call from the clinic director that he had been notified that Thomas had been shot to death outside a liquor store the night before Armando and I had spotted Thomas in that store!

The details were that he had been innocently caught between the cross fire of an armed robbery attempt. I was devastated and depressed on hearing the sad news, but I knew there was so much more to his death. Thomas had appeared to both Armando and me the day after his death to acknowledge his passing and to leave us with a vision of him dressed in pure white, perfectly prepared for his afterlife journey.

Four nights later, Armando and I attended the funeral wake and were shocked upon viewing his body at it lay in the casket. Thomas was dressed in a white shirt, tie, jacket, slacks, belt, and shoes—just as we had seen him when he appeared to us! His partner had also placed a beautiful rosary of white beads.

If there is a lesson to be learned in all this, I take from it that each one of us is much too important to be taken for granted. We must honor the divine presence, the spiritual essence that makes us who we really are, and not dwell on lifestyle differences but on our shared humanity.

Valerie W. Tisdale's Story

Albuquerque, NM

I was born and raised in Los Angeles, California, and graduated with my medical degree in phlebotomy in 1998. I worked at Cedars-Sinai Medical Center for three years until moving to Albuquerque to live closer to my son and grandchildren. Today I work part-time between two hospitals, Presbyterian and University of New Mexico Hospital.

As a phlebotomist, I'm trained to draw patients' blood for laboratory tests. I collect blood from finger sticks or with a needle from veins or arteries. I work with doctors, nurses, and other medical professional team members, but mainly I work independently, visiting patients in their hospital rooms.

At the time of my experience with a ghost, I was living and working at Cedars-Sinai Medical Center in Los Angeles and also searching for an apartment. A coworker told me about a two-story, four-bedroom house that was for rent in the Elysian Park section of Los Angeles. He knew the owner and said he would be happy to give me a good recommendation if I were interested. I jumped at the offer and, after meeting with the owner, moved into the house within the same week.

The owner informed me that a retired 88-year-old doctor, Norma Ellers, who died the previous summer of lung cancer, once owned the old house. The house went into the legal process of estate administering of the deceased doctor, resolving all claims, and distributing her property under the directions of her will. Dr. Ellers was a heavy smoker and was known to suffer bouts of deep depression. She lived alone and never married. I was also shown two pictures of the doctor; one taken at her hospital office, wearing her white coat, and in the other, she is seated at the house's front porch, wearing an attractive striped-pattern skirt. In both pictures, Dr. Ellers is shown holding a lit cigarette. Ironically, in life, she was an oncologist, a cancer specialist.

Within one month of moving into the house, I found a small candy box sitting on top of one of the closet shelves on the second floor. Inside the box were fourteen love letters and envelopes addressed to Dr. Ellers from, it turns out, a married female doctor who lived and practiced in San Diego. Apparently, the two women had an ongoing love affair that they kept closely guarded for many years, ending with Dr. Ellers's death.

The letters described tender and sweet thoughts between the women and of a future plan to join together as a couple under one roof. I'm not lesbian, but I was brought to tears reading the honest sentimentality that these two women shared and their unrealized plans for a future life together. I placed the letters back inside the box and put the box back on the shelf, closed the closet door, and left the empty room with an overwhelming sense of sadness.

Well, in the days to come, I took in a new roommate named Rosie. Rosie worked at a nearby gift shop in LA's Chinatown. She also had an obvious limp in her walk, having lost her left leg to childhood cancer, and had worn a prosthetic leg since the age of nine. Rosie and I soon decorated the house using a subtle Chinese color palette of reds and gold. Rosie was also an excellent cook and always kept the pantry well stocked. We got along very well together.

The unusual or ghostly things that I'll now speak to you about started up around a week after Rosie moved into the house. To this day, I get goose bumps traveling up and down both my arms just thinking about what we experienced.

I first began to hear a female voice that would whisper my name at all hours of the day or night. It did not matter if I was in the kitchen or bedroom, or even in the front yard or backyard, the spirit woman's voice would even wake me from a deep sleep. One evening at about 6:00 p.m., after having heard the now-familiar voice in my kitchen, I quickly turned around and caught the sight of a long skirt suddenly moving away from a doorway, headed down the hall! I immediately recognized the patterns on the skirt as the one Dr. Ellers was wearing in the photo. I had a suspicion that it might be the doctor's spirit, but now here was possible confirmation. A chill following this recognition overcame my body. *So she didn't leave her house after all*, I thought.

A few hours later, Rosie arrived from work, and I mentioned what I had seen. I was surprised to hear her tell me, "Oh no, Val. I knew there was a ghost in this house; there had to be. I've been experiencing knocks on my bedroom walls, knocking all around, closet doors opening and closing on their own, and I was even pushed down into my bed once! I didn't think about mentioning any of it to you, assuming you might think I was crazy."

As we stood in the kitchen discussing the matter, suddenly there was a significant drop in temperature that overtook the room to such an extreme we both felt our skin tingle. "That's enough talking about ghosts. I want us both to be able to sleep tonight and through the night," I said. Rosie agreed. But that would not be the case, as later that night, I was awakened by a dream where the spirit of Dr. Ellers approached and yelled at me to never, ever go into her bedroom closet and read her letters again! In the dream, I responded to her anger by yelling back at her, "This is my house now! I'm here, and you have to leave me alone!"

I woke up just then, and standing at the side of my bed was Dr. Ellers! Her spirit was a light, whitish-blue color, but no doubt it was Dr. Ellers. I lay in bed with my eyes wide open and said, "What are you doing here? I told you to leave, didn't I?" I don't know where I found the courage to confront the ghost like that, but as soon as I finished speaking, she vanished. I scrambled out of bed, switched on the wall light, and called for Rosie. I had forgotten at that moment about Rosie's prosthetic leg. After I realized my oversight, I rushed to her side and, with tears in my eyes, described every last detail.

When I returned to my own bedroom, I immediately noticed a rank, sour odor of cigarette smoke hanging in the air. I thought, *Damn if she's not a persistent spirit!* That night, I slept with the light on, but never again did Rosie or I have any further disturbances of the ghostly kind at the house. But just to make sure, Rosie contacted a Buddhist priest, and he and two other priests arrived at the house and performed a house blessing. Since then, everything at the house had a very peaceful atmosphere without further ghostly whispering or visits from the doctor.

The only other weird thing that happened was the fact that I never discovered a reason for the disappearance of the candy box containing the love letters. The day before I moved out of the house, I entered the empty bedroom and looked in every inch of that closet and did not locate the box. My belief is that Dr. Ellers thought it best to retrieve her most personal property, and I couldn't agree any stronger with that thought.

Steven O. Goody's Story

Grants, NM

There are times during my research when I encounter examples of how hesitant and even stubborn people can be when the evidence for spirits stands literally in front of them. Is it denial or fear that causes such a disregard for the facts presented? Steven's story offers much evidence for the existence of ghosts and, in this case, witchcraft. Both Steven and his partner, Patrick, a physician, encountered something unfamiliar to a Western, college-educated, and thinking mind-set. But when has the spiritual world ever cared about education or social standing? If spirits want to communicate, they will. The choice is theirs, and all we can do is sit back and admit to ourselves the truth—or simply remain in a world of denial. My readers already know my position on this topic.

My partner, Patrick, and I moved to Grants, New Mexico, on May 10, 1988. Originally, I'm from Gallup. My parents owned and managed a small hotel in Gallup, and after I graduated with a degree in English literature from the University of Southern California, Patrick and I moved to Grants. Patrick is a physician, and at the time of my story, he was practicing medicine on the Navajo reservation in the Crownpoint area.

Our strange ghost experience with unexplained phenomena began at the time when Patrick was treating an 85-year-old Navajo man named Tom-John. His younger sister's family stated that the man was suffering from an illness that was brought about, of all things, by a witch. Perhaps I should state at this point in my story that on the reservation, there are numerous common illnesses attributed by the locals as being a direct result of witchcraft. Your readers also need to understand that culturally, on the reservation, many Navajos view most illness in this manner. Also, practitioners of Western medicine who conduct their practice on the reservation are required to complete an in-service training program. These training sessions are actually provided to all medical staff by the Navajo tribe in order to educate non-American Indians about the Navajo culture's views. This service is a cultural sensitivity training that medical staff undergo prior to beginning their employment on the reservation, and it's very informative.

Patrick told me that when Tom-John was brought into the clinic for medical evaluation, the poor man's eyelids were swollen shut, and his legs were equally swollen from edema—a medical term to describe one of the body's reactions to illness by retaining water. Tom-John's family stated that he had been suffering with these symptoms for a week, and they believed the cause of his illness was due to a witch, a woman in the Crownpoint area who was known locally to the Navajos as Mexican Crow.

Mexican Crow was given this name due to the fact that as a young woman, she learned to do witchcraft from a Mexican woman. Mexican Crow, who was Navajo but fluent in Spanish, lived in Sonora, Mexico, for many years. The name *Crow* was attached to her because she liked having crow feathers on her person whenever out in public. Crow feathers are definitely taboo for Navajos, since the bird and its feathers are a symbol of dark forces. Apparently, Tom-John's eldest grandson, Shelby, did something to cross Mexican Crow that she did not appreciate, and Mexican Crow decided to revenge his family by witching the patriarch, Tom-John.

By the time Tom-John's family brought him to the clinic, he had already been given a "sing"—a Navajo healing ceremony attended by two medicine men—without success. The sing was conducted within a traditional Navajo hogan, or adobe and log house. When Patrick asked Tom-John's family to help undress him for the routine physical exam, Patrick was amazed to see how Tom-John's skin was covered in a yellow hue, so he examined Tom-John's eyes for jaundice, which would be an indication of liver problems. His eyes were clear, and after examining his abdomen, nothing to indicate a liver problem was evident. Patrick ordered the usual blood tests and X-rays appropriate for his diagnosis. But the most unusual part about Tom-John's exam was when Patrick lifted Tom-John's left arm and a dark crow feather fell out from his armpit! It was not a long feather, but more of a black, short plume.

Immediately, the two family members who were in the room gasped as one family member said, "See? There's another one! We've been finding these feathers in his bed! It's the witch; she still wants to hurt him. We don't know what to do."

Patrick reached down to pick up the feather and, examining it, said, "Well, I'll have to put this aside, and I'll look it over later." Not wanting to alarm the family any further, Patrick placed the feather on the nearby table, covered it with a paper towel, and finished Tom-John's examination. After the exam, the family assisted Tom-John out of the clinic, and Patrick let them know he would give them the results of the tests within a day.

Now comes the part of the story that involves me.

That evening when Patrick returned home, he informed me of his first documented witched patient, and then he showed me the feather. Personally having grown up in the area, knowing a little bit of the Navajos and their traditions, I felt a bit nervous sitting in our home and listening to Patrick's story. Viewing the actual feather on the table before me, I got a bit unnerved and asked Patrick what he was going to do with the feather.

"I'm not going to do anything with it. The family doesn't want it, and I'm sure the clinic doesn't want an object with an attachment of witchcraft on the property, so I don't know. I guess I'll just leave it on my desk as an artifact."

I didn't want to think any more about the feather, so I walked over to Patrick's home office and placed it on his desk, on a small dish where he kept a few red beads, a pencil, and two pens. We didn't mention the feather any further and went about our usual routine.

Later that night while we were asleep in bed, I was awakened by a noise. The noise resembled an object that carried some weight hitting the wall, but not so heavy that it would make a loud bang—more of a loud thud. I opened my eyes, and in the darkness of the bedroom, I spotted a quick flash of light. The light darted through the room. It appeared as though a person holding a flashlight was quickly moving about the bedroom! I sat up in bed, and sensing this, Patrick immediately woke up.

"Patrick, there is something in the room with us," I said.

He said, "What do you mean? Where?"

"In here, right in this room!" I answered.

Suddenly, we heard a noise coming down the hall from Patrick's office. It sounded like his file cabinets were being moved about. We both jumped out of bed. Switching on the lights in the bedroom, we made our way down the hall to his office, making sure to switch on all the lights.

Reaching his office, Patrick turned on the wall light switch, and we noticed that, strangely, nothing was out of place. Realizing our imaginations were working overtime, or so we thought, we decided to return to the bedroom. Right before Patrick reached for the light switch, we both heard the faint voice. It was a murmuring sound, which we could not understand but without mistake we clearly heard. As we stood in place, trying our best to hear what was being said, we were suddenly shaken to our core. All the items that were on top of Patrick's desk came crashing off! It was as if an invisible, angry person had taken his or her arm and, with one motion, pushed everything aside! Boy, talk about being scared. We both jumped back. Then an unnerving silence overcame the room. We stood in place attempting to make sense of things, then cautiously walked over to where everything lay scattered on the floor. Patrick said, "Well, Steve, this is one for the books. I don't have an explanation, do you?"

I responded, "Patrick, do you notice something strange? What's missing? Look on the floor. See all your things? Everything that was on your desk is on the floor, right? Everything but the feather—it's gone!"

At that moment, I could tell by the look on Patrick's face that fear was taking over. This university-educated physician was actually scared.

"Let's get back to bed. I've had enough of this crap for the night," he said.

We returned to bed but decided to leave the lights on for our own peace of mind. Nothing else of an unusual nature took place that night, but we sure did find it difficult to fall back to sleep. Eventually, after talking it all through, we fell asleep.

In the morning, Patrick drove off to work, and I was left to clean up his office.

As I was busy picking up all that lay on the floor and returning it to the desk, I again was reminded that the feather was nowhere to be found. Later in the day, I walked into the office to use the stapler, and I happened to glance at a picture of Patrick's father and mother hanging on the wall. It was a picture of them taken while on a cruise to Alaska. What caught my eye was that placed on top of the picture, between the frame and the wall, was the feather! How it could have gotten there was a mystery. I didn't want to touch it, so I left it alone, and I decided to give Patrick a call at his clinic. After reaching him, but before I got a chance to get a single word across, he interrupted me by saying, "Oh, Steve, I've got to tell you that I just got a call from Tom-John's family informing me that Tom-John died during the night!"

Not wanting to upset Patrick, I decided to keep my story about finding the feather on Patrick's parents' picture to myself. After finishing the phone call, I walked to our kitchen and then returned to Patrick's office, and with a pair of kitchen tongs in hand, I grasped the feather, walked to the garage, and then, locating a small can of cigarette lighter fluid, I doused the feather with the liquid, walked out to the backyard, and set the feather on fire. I didn't want to take any chances that something evil might be attached to the feather, so in my mind, I chose to burn it back to hell. Perhaps it might have been a little too late, but at least I could rest assured I had destroyed it.

When Patrick returned home that evening, I mentioned to him about finding the feather and what I had done with it. Although he stated what we witnessed the night before was very unusual, I found his words difficult to accept. Because of Patrick's education and training, I knew that his background didn't allow him to believe witchcraft might have played a role in what had happened.

"I know you think it was a ghost, Steve. I know you do," Patrick said. "But there is a rational explanation for it. There has to be."

Well, a sad ending to this story is that just a couple of weeks later, we received a phone call that Patrick's 73-year-old father was found dead of a heart attack. The man was as healthy as they came, so his death caught us both off guard. To this day, Patrick refuses to believe the witch and feather had anything to do with his father's death. But given my personal knowledge of Navajo beliefs, I don't believe it was a coincidence. It's all too strange and unusually weird. What I can say is that as of this day, Patrick's understanding of the Navajo culture has been greatly enhanced by our experience. There is so much to learn and understand, and the spiritual aspect of this is also very important. Perhaps the most important of all is that such things as ghosts are real.

Joseph Nightwalker's Story

Antonio & Hank's Adobe Guesthouse

I conducted Joseph's interview one day during a two-hour drive from Santa Fe to Taos. With the tape recorder placed between us on the seat, he freely recounted an experience he and his wife, Ruby, had at a bed-and-breakfast my partner, Hank, and I own called Antonio & Hank's Adobe Guesthouse in Santa Fe. Take from this story what you will, but remember that sometimes attachment to what used to be our home can prove to be so strong that even after death, we find it difficult to move on.

My experience with a ghost took place in Santa Fe six years ago. My wife, Ruby, and I wanted to get away for a couple of days and wanted to stay in an upscale hotel. Because of our last-minute plans, we found out that all the hotels in Santa Fe that evening were booked up. Our second choice was to look into staying at a bed-and-breakfast. Santa Fe, among other things, is a city known for its excellent accommodations. An employee at the Hotel St. Francis recommended that we contact Antonio & Hank's Adobe Guesthouse on the south end of town. Ruby called, spoke to Hank, and booked the room.

The bed-and-breakfast was very nice. The large house had four rooms. Our room was located down a long hallway at the front of the house. During our check-in, Antonio handed us a sheet of paper describing the history of the house. Then he showed us to our room. As Ruby unpacked the suitcase, I started a fire in the corner kiva fireplace. We got comfortable, and I read the sheet of paper that was given to Ruby. A family named Martinez built the house in the early 1920s, and it was the first adobe house built in that part of Santa Fe. I read that the house was bought from the Martinez family by the first archeologist of New Mexico, Dr. Bertha Dutton. Life partners Antonio and Hank bought the property directly from Dr. Dutton. I remember these details because, being an artist myself, I knew about Dr. Dutton and the stories about her association with the well-known artist Georgia O'Keeffe. So these two names certainly are not easy for me to forget. I put the sheet of paper back on the nightstand, and my wife and I took a short nap.

About 45 minutes later, Ruby and I woke up and drove into town for our dinner reservation. After dinner, it started to snow, slowly at first and then harder and harder. We walked around Santa Fe Plaza, window-shopping, but when we saw how heavily the snow was falling, we decided to call it a night and drive back to the B&B.

When we got back to the room, I looked out the window and saw about a foot of snow covering the ground. I also noticed there were four other cars parked in the lot. There was a full house at the B&B. Ruby and I got into bed and quickly fell asleep at about 10:00 p.m.

I was awakened suddenly from my sleep when I heard the sound of breaking glass coming from down the hallway. I looked at my watch and saw that it was 3:00 a.m. I turned to see if the sound had also awakened Ruby. She was sound asleep. When I didn't hear any more noise, I thought I had imagined it. I closed my eyes to fall back asleep, but soon I heard the sound of footsteps walking down the hallway toward our room. I kept quiet. As the footsteps got closer, I heard them stop at the other side of our door. Then I heard the doorknob slowly turn.

By this time, I was wide awake and was fully aware of what was going on. I kept my eyes focused on the doorknob, but because of the darkness, I only heard the knob turning; I couldn't see it actually turn. Then the strangest thing happened. I saw a white, misty figure come right through the door!

It didn't have any particular shape; it was just like drifting smoke. I decided to wake Ruby, so I hit her side with my right elbow. As she woke up, I whispered to her to look in the direction of the door. The smoke then started to change into the outline of a small woman. Ruby saw the same thing and said, "It's a ghost, Joseph!" Then she pulled the covers over her head.

I guess I found my courage, because I yelled out to the image, "Get away! Get out of here!"

The ghostly figure took two steps toward our bed. I grabbed my pillow and threw it at the ghost, and then I reached over and turned on the light. As soon as I turned on the light, the ghost disappeared.

Both Ruby and I slept with the light on for the rest of that night. In the morning at breakfast, I asked the owners, Antonio and Hank, if the house was haunted. They looked at each other and then at me, and Hank answered, "Not that we're aware of. No one has ever mentioned anything about ghosts in the house. Why do you ask?" As Ruby and I described our experience the night before, the other guests seated around the table began to tell their own similar experiences.

Although the others didn't mention seeing any ghosts, they all said they heard the sound of breaking glass, and a few even mentioned hearing footsteps in the hallway. Ruby got nervous talking about the ghost and asked us to change the subject. We finished our breakfast and went back to our room. Some of the guests returned to their rooms, while others drove off to explore the sights of Santa Fe.

After a few minutes passed, there was a knock on our door. I opened it, and Hank was standing there asking if he could talk to us. I invited him in. He started to tell us a little bit more about the house. He had a nervous smile on his face and then apologized for not being totally honest with us at breakfast. As he put it, "I didn't want to upset the other guests who might be a bit sensitive about such a subject." But now he wanted to set the record straight and admit that the guesthouse was haunted, and yes, there had been several other guests who had seen ghosts in the house, including him. He said the previous owner, archeologist Dr. Dutton, kept a collection of American Indian artifacts in one room of the house.

During her many archeological digs throughout the Southwest, she would return to her house in Santa Fe with stone axes, pottery, and various other samples of Pueblo culture. In fact, in one room of the house, she kept several medium-sized cardboard boxes with actual American Indian skeletons stacked one on top of another!

He added that our room was not the room where the skeletons were kept, so we could feel safe about that, but our room used to be Dr. Dutton's bedroom. He also mentioned that Dr. Dutton was still very much alive and living in a local convalescent home, which shocked Ruby and me. He said that throughout the seven years of owning the property, both he and his partner had witnessed many ghosts in the house.

Hank also said there were many times when he would be in the kitchen and notice a shadow of a person walk from the hallway into the living room. He'd investigate only to discover there would be no one there. Other times he'd hear his name being called from an adjoining empty room. When he walked to the room, he'd see the fleeing image of a shadow.

Hank mentioned that guests of the B&B had the common experience of hearing ghostly footsteps and the sound of breaking glass.

Ruby asked, "What have you done to rid the house of these ghosts?"

He said that Antonio and his 75-year-old father had conducted a cleansing ritual in the entire house, and since that time, the appearances of ghosts had stopped. He was unsure of why the ghosts decided to return. We talked a little more about several things before he left to make the beds in the other guests' rooms.

My wife and I felt a little better after having this conversation. We left to do a little shopping in town, and when we returned to the house, we noticed the faint scent of burned sweetgrass incense. Antonio knocked on our door this time to inform us he and his father had once again blessed the whole house. That night was spent without any further visits from a ghost. The prayers and incense chased whatever was still in the house.

A few days after Ruby and I returned home to our pueblo, we got a phone call from Hank. He mentioned that we should read the local newspaper because on the front page was an article about the recent death of Dr. Bertha Dutton.

Apparently, Dr. Dutton died at a local convalescent home less than a mile from her old home, now the B&B. But what we should take notice of, Hank said, was the date of her death. She died the same night the ghost of the white woman visited my wife and me!

Was the ghostly woman who visited us that night in Santa Fe the ghost of Dr. Bertha Dutton? I don't know how this could be proven, but we were in her bedroom, in her beloved home on the night she expired. It just makes sense to us.

NORTH CAROLINA

David R. Scroggins's Story

Raleigh, NC

I'm from North Carolina and received my nursing degree from East Carolina University. After graduating, I enrolled at Fayetteville State University, where I graduated with a master's degree in public health. I currently am a state employee for Colorado Environmental Public Health Tracking, and although I live in Colorado, my experience with ghosts took place in 1987 when I was still living in North Carolina and was working at my first job at Central Prison.

The prison was completed in December 1884 and is historically the first prison built in North Carolina. The authorities at the time used a workforce of inmates to build it, and it took them a total of 14 years to construct it. It's located west of downtown Raleigh. The prison serves many functions. It houses the state's execution chamber, deathwatch area, and men's death row. The infirmary and mental health facility serve the needs of male inmates from around the state. It also serves as a diagnostic center; the point of entry into the prison system for male felons is age 22 years or older with sentences greater than 20 years.

My job description was as an infection control nurse. I was hired to investigate and monitor potential sources of suspected HIV infections in order to determine and ensure control. I counseled prisoners and staff on HIV infection control issues. I collaborated with other members of the team to follow up on exposure incidents, participated in multidisciplinary team treatment plans, and trained new staff regarding standard personal protective precautions using required equipment.

Personally, being an openly gay man, I was not always viewed positively by fellow employees, especially in a conservative, born-again Christian state like this one. Given my level of education and connections within the medical community, I was respectfully treated and even honored, having been presented with two service awards. Surprisingly, I was asked to "secretly" assist in the HIV treatment of three separate, "closeted gay" family members of prominent conservative politicians—one woman and two men. Now if that is not the height of hypocrisy, then I don't know what is!

My ghostly experiences at the prison began late one Friday autumn morning as I was walking down a hallway within the prison's infirmary unit. I was on way to the kitchen to make myself a hot cup of herbal tea before entering my office. I had overslept and missed our usual staff meeting that morning.

I walked past the closed door of one of our administrator's offices when I heard the retching sound of someone vomiting coming from within, even though I knew that the administrator was away on vacation in Europe. Immediately, I stopped and then walked into the office, hoping to assist whoever the ill person might be. As I entered, I was suddenly overwhelmed by the strong, vile odor of fresh vomit, but when I looked around, I saw no one. With the two fingers of my right hand, I pinched my nostrils, attempting to prevent inhaling the putrid odor any further and quickly looked about the office. The darkened office was empty of any living soul. Perplexed, I walked out and continued walking toward the kitchen.

Once inside the kitchen, I met a fellow employee. We spoke briefly until I felt the overwhelming need to tell him about my experience in the office. He responded, "Oh, David, if you had attended the staff meeting earlier, you would have known that one of the HIV patients died in Italy. He was discovered three days ago in his hotel room in the town of Siena, dead from an apparent heart attack. He passed during the night in his sleep. It was reported his bed was covered in vomit and blood."

This was my first encounter with an unusual incident at the prison, and things progressed from that point—and not for the better.

About two weeks later, I was approached by Jake, an inmate who served as our unit's janitor, regarding something strange he not only experienced but also visually witnessed while working in the women's restroom. "I saw the ghost of a prisoner who died here years ago," he said. "It was Artie 'M&M.' I knew him; we were good buds. We all called him 'M&M' because it was his favorite candy. I was on my knees, wiping the back of the sink, when I turned my head and saw M&M walking—no, floating—right past me, and he disappeared right into the door! I'm not afraid of his ghost, Mr. Scroggins. M&M was my friend, my buddy."

Five days later, approximately two hours after I returned from a lunch meeting in town, I was seated at my office desk, going over my calendar, when I caught someone standing at my open door—a prisoner wearing a dirty T-shirt, his right arm completely covered in tattoos. I asked the strange prisoner, "Can I help you?" He looked at me, smiled, and then moved away from the door and, I assumed, walked down the hall. I jumped out of my chair and ran to the door. Walking toward me were two women about twenty feet away. I asked them about having seen the prisoner and where he went. They answered, "We've not seen anyone." I was dumbfounded! I contacted security, and after an intense search of the facility, followed by a head count, absolutely every prisoner and facility visitor was accounted for.

Of course, I approached Jake, the janitor, for some further information. I asked him to give me a few more details about M&M's physical appearance. Jake took a good look at my face and said, "Mr. Scroggins, you saw M&M, didn't you? He paid you a visit, didn't he? I can see it in your eyes."

I was caught off guard by Jake's question but responded truthfully by describing my encounter in full detail. Jake responded, "Well, his spirit must have a reason for returning back here. God knows once I'm released, I'm never setting foot in this place again, living or not!"

Jake also informed me of the manner of M&M's death. A few weeks after his release, he was crossing a street one night and was struck and killed by an 88-year-old man who was driving drunk.

Initially, Jake never mentioned to me about M&M's tattoos on his right arm, but when I brought it up, sure enough, he confirmed to me that M&M indeed had his entire right arm covered in ink art. My suspicions were now confirmed—I actually had a spirit visit me, no doubt, and in the middle of the afternoon!

I must confess I was not scared by this realization. I felt a sort of privilege to have been given the opportunity to experience a fleeting glimpse of the afterlife. For the last months that I worked at the prison, I kept a small candy dish filled with M&Ms on my desk, and I used to refer to it as "Artie's dish."

TEXAS

Dr. Armand M. Faulker's Story

Abilene, TX

I've been in private practice now in Abilene, Texas, for over 15 years and prefer it rather than working in a large corporate-sponsored hospital environment. My husband and I met while we were both doing our respective residency work in San Antonio, and we've been together for 33 years.

My patient call is not heavy, and I've found the community to be very well suited for my family's needs. Speaking fluent Spanish is a plus in Abilene, and through the years, I've taken Spanish language courses for my work and Italian for the simple pleasure of it. My medical profession has prepared me for a lot of unusual situations but never for what I experienced over eight years ago on the paranormal level.

I remember the afternoon I had an older female patient come into my office complaining of a severe neck ache accompanied with earaches. After examining her and taking blood vials for comprehensive metabolic panel work, I noticed three large red marks on both her upper right arm and abdomen. When I asked her about how she acquired these obvious marks, she stated, "Doctor, I'm afraid to say, but sometimes a bad spirit comes to me and attacks me." As you might imagine, her explanation left me puzzled. My facial reaction must have appeared obvious because her next response was, "Oh, I can see you don't believe me." I told her I'd never heard this before and concluded the appointment by writing her a prescription for pain and scheduling a follow-up exam in two weeks.

At her two-week follow-up exam, we discussed the results of her blood work that came back from the lab free of any pathological abnormalities. I mentioned that I was at a loss regarding the issues with her neck and ears that were still of concern to her, but I referred her to a specialist and assured her that it was most likely a bad sprain and not something more to be concerned about.

Then I asked her if the red marks had disappeared from her body, and she responded, "Well, see for yourself." When I examined her, I could see that the marks had obviously increased, and more had spread onto her abdomen. Concerned for her well-being, I was about to ask her once again about the marks when she stated, "I can't tell you how much I want the evil spirit to go away from my house. He comes up and yells vicious things at me. It also knew I was coming to see you, and it screamed at me not to talk to you or it will hurt me in front of you." I attempted to reassure her that nothing like that was going to happen. I immediately knew this was a game changer, and that I was dealing with a woman displaying a psychological pathology I was not familiar with.

I mentioned to her that I was going to refer her to a therapist. She responded that she was okay with that. Before ending my examination, I asked her to open her mouth wide, and with a tongue depressor, I was about to look inside her throat when she unexpectedly pushed my arm away and cried out, "Doctor, it's here. It's here in the room with us!"

Before I could respond, I felt instantly wrapped within a sudden, unexplained, bone-chilling cold. Even more disturbing was witnessing skin on her neck depress down and forming red finger marks from some invisible hands!

What I'm about to tell you next is equally more difficult to believe, but she appeared to be slapped violently from her right side and was knocked against the wall. She jumped up, stumbled to stand before me, and spit out two front teeth! She was struck violently by something invisible and right before my own eyes.

I yelled for my assistant to come help, and she quickly entered the room. Both the patient and I stood shaking with terror, staring at each other as blood slowly drooled out of my patient's mouth. Using a paper towel, my assistant picked up the two teeth and then helped me sit the patient on a chair. My assistant couldn't believe what she was seeing, and I told her I would tell her what happened later. I could see that the woman was in shock, and my first concern was to call for an ambulance to take her to the nearby hospital, which we did.

The last time I saw this patient, she told me that she would never see me again and was visibly terrified as she told me. She reminded me that the spirit warned her in her home not to see me or something bad would happen. I never forgot this patient's words, symptoms, and experience in my examination room. I don't know what happened to her or even if she is still alive. I think about her and regret that this was one area of my professional career that I had absolutely no knowledge of what to do or how to help.

To this day, I still cannot believe the description of these events coming out of me as I speak them. This one extreme paranormal experience—bizarre, terrifying, and unbelievable as it was—compels me to explore and investigate further claims of paranormal encounters.

THE END
FINIS CORONAT

ABOUT THE AUTHOR

Antonio R. Garcez is an award-winning author and publisher of multiple books about firsthand interviews of actual paranormal encounters. Since 1982, Antonio has researched and interviewed hundreds of people about ghosts. His sensitivity, respect, and professionalism regarding life-after-death subjects are key to his acclaimed writing style and popular ghost books.

Antonio and life partner, Hank, will celebrate 34 years together in 2017.

Other titles by Antonio R. Garcez:
New Mexico Ghost Stories, Volumes 1 & 2
American Indian Ghost Stories of the Southwest
Arizona Ghost Stories
Colorado Ghost Stories
Ghost Stories of California's Gold Rush Country & Yosemite National Park
Ghost Stories of the Medical Profession

Antonio may be contacted through GhostBooks.biz.

Printed in Dunstable, United Kingdom

75456532R00067